Praise for the Freak Scene Dream Trilogy, including "Untitled"

"Oral prose. School of Twain and Salinger. It's improvised, and its immediate and delayed echoes, its ellipses, its obsessions, make music."

> LARRY BECKETT, author of "Morning Glory" and "Paul Bunyan"

"Michael Goldberg's sharply drawn characters, vivid musical nods, and keen eye for detail transport us back to the post-countercultural mid-1970s when sex and drugs and rock & roll were a way of life. In this third installment of the Freak Scene Dream Trilogy, antihero Writerman takes us along for the rollercoaster ride – angel dust, anyone? – while he tries to make sense of a life littered with broken hearts. A page-turner."

> HOLLY GEORGE-WARREN, author of "A Man Called Destruction: The Life and Music of Alex Chilton"

"Relive the 1970s – the music, the dope, the clothes, the books, the confused and restless sexual politics – in all their filthy glory."

> MARIA BUSTILLOS, author of "Dorkismo: the Macho of the Dork" and "Act Like a Gentleman, Think Like a Woman."

"Michael Goldberg is comparable to Kerouac in a 21st century way, someone trying to use that language and energy and find a new way of doing it."

> MARK MORDUE, author of "Dastgah: Diary of a Head Trip"

"If Lester Bangs had ever published a novel it might have read something like this frothing debut by longtime music journalist Michael Goldberg... Readers from any musical era will come away with a deeper appreciation of how nostalgia can shape our lives, for better and for worse."
COLIN FLEMING, Rolling Stone

"Penned in a staccato amphetamine grammar, its narrative is fractured and deranged, often unsettling but frequently compelling, an unsparing portrait of the teen condition: assured then despairing, would-be sex god then impotent has-been, from erection to dejection, an only child battling the wills of his domineering father and interfering mom in the anonymous, suburban fringes of Marin County."
SIMON WARNER, author of "Text and Drugs and Rock'n'Roll: The Beats and Rock Culture"

"Just call it a portrait of the rock critic as a young freakster bro, coming of age in the glorious peace-and-love innocence of the '60s dream, only to crash precipitously, post-Altamont into the drug-ridden paranoia of the '70s, characterized by the doom and gloom of the Stones' sinister 'Sister Morphine' and the apocalyptic *caw-caw-caw* of a pair of ubiquitous crows."
ROY TRAKIN, Trakin Care Of Business column

"There was a time when (rock) music was the living pulse of a generation, when wanting to be a rock critic was a credible dream. That is the era of the Freak Scene Dream Trilogy, an ambitious and ultimately successful attempt at recasting the coming-of-age-in-the-wake-of-the-sixties-experience in innovative but authentic language, Kerouac in the 21st century."
DENNIS MCNALLY, author of "A Long Strange Trip: The Inside History of the Grateful Dead" and "Desolate Angel: Jack Kerouac, The Beat Generation & America"

"Aspiring rock journalist Michael Stein (aka Writerman) returns in the second installment of Goldberg's Freak Scene Dream Trilogy, picking up the narrative where he left off and fumbling his way across the countercultural landscape of the early '70s like some less jaded, wannabe-hippie version of Holden Caulfield. This slightly-older-but-not-necessarily-wiser Stein, along with his inner circle of equally confused post-adolescents, is more fleshed-out as a character than in the previous (though superb) 'True Love Scars.' As a result the scenarios he finds himself thrust into, not to mention the occasional disaster of his own making, ring with an additional authenticity that will leave anyone who lived through the same era nodding with recognition. Some will even fidget uncomfortably in their seats, as I did—credit to Goldberg's keen ability to channel his/our own misspent youth while sketching a series of remarkably believable portraits.

"Among the more memorable scenes: a hamfisted attempt to get his rock journalism published in the college newspaper, even more awkward attempts to get laid (that include at least one success, with his best friend's girlfriend, no less, in a gondola at the top of a Ferris wheel), getting thrown out of a Neil Young concert by one of Bill Graham's goons, navigating a surreal Halloween party while peaking on LSD, and kibitzing with a popular Lester Bangs-esque roccrit. Along the way we get cameos from Bob Dylan, the Rolling Stones, Captain Beefheart, the New York Dolls, Slim Harpo, James Brown, John Fowles, Sartre, Dostoyevsky and Godard. Settle in, crack open a bottle and/or spark a doob, and get ready for an emotional rollercoaster ride. Oh, and don't touch the Thorens."

FRED MILLS, editor, *Blurt* magazine

"So who is this protagonist anyway? Holden Caulfield meets Lord Buckley? Speaking in a crazy-assed, hell-fucked jargon, yet choosing his words so carefully it seems like his words are choosing him? And exactly what's happening here? Coming of age in the era between the Beats and the Punks? Licking the combination plate of sex, drugs and rock 'n' roll? Balancing on the tightrope between horniness and empathy? Carrying a torch along the route of Teenage Heartbreak Olympics? Revealing a threesome among guilt, blame and accountability? Tripping on the power of shared musical obsession? Naïveté serving as a gradual learning experience morphing into sophistication, layer by layer. Caught between Dylan's suggestion, 'Take what you have gathered from coincidence,' and Freud's observation, 'Being entirely honest with oneself is a good exercise.' Excuse me, what was the question again?"

    PAUL KRASSNER, author of "Confessions of a Raving, Unconfined Nut: Misadventures in the Counterculture"

"'True Love Scars' reads like a fever dream from the dying days of the Summer of Love. Keyed to a soundtrack of love and apocalypse, Writerman pitches headlong into a haze of drugs, sex and confusion in search of what no high can bring: his own redemption. Read it and be transformed."

    ALINA SIMONE, musician, author of "Note to Self" and "You Must Go and Win"

"A gonzo look back at misspent youth in the 1960s… It's a crackling good read, filled with humor, pathos, drug use and Dylan references (seriously, I think there's one on every page). Goldberg's freewheelin' style captures a certain late 60s/early 70s vibe (think the autobiographical writings of Lester Bangs) that makes 'True Love Scars' a pleasure through and through."

    TYLER WILCOX, Doom & Gloom From The Tomb

"There never was a Seventies. They never existed. You could, however, construct a reasonably functional Seventies love-doll, inflating it (you guessed right) with canned or frozen Sixties sexual effluvium. Fill it fat, saggy or shapeless—your call. CAREFUL: there will be some broken glass and flammable scum. Shards of chthonic Romance—whew—as radioactive as Godzilla. Only the BOLD need apply. Whoops—beware!—Mr. Goldberg has been there first, and 'had' her first. Reader-side litrachoor is often a matter of 2nd in line. Bon appétit!"

RICHARD MELTZER, author of "The Aesthetics Of Rock" and "Tropic of Nipples"

"[His] passion for the counterculture and the music that informed it shines bright in Goldberg's semi-autobiographical novel, 'True Love Scars'... the novel is a whirlwind tale of a young music fanatic's [Writerman] quest for true love, high times and "the authentic real" (not necessarily in that order). ... [Goldberg] narrates most of the tale with a retrospective viewpoint, which enables the reader to empathize more with Writerman's youthful mistakes and sometimes naïve viewpoints. Writerman is wiser now, but he wants us to see how it all went down, because there's meaning in the journey. ... Goldberg develops a unique voice as he flashes back and forth, mostly between 1965 and 1972. The literary gold is in the details. The novel is filled with colorful references about the bands and songs that bring out the halcyon days of that influential era. ... True Love Scars is deeply dialed in to rock's dichotomy of enlightening powers versus stoned party time."

GREG M. SCHWARTZ, PopMatters

"Goldberg's virginal sex scenes unwind at the same racing-heart-awkward-self-conscious-anxious pace one can almost remember from those good old, bad old days when the forbidden fruit was all one ever wanted..."

M. SELDOF, Ragazine.CC

"Michael's written quite a series of novels about the early Seventies and the death of the Sixties and the rock 'n' roll dream. I think they're very good. I've never seen a novel talk about Feminism and the Seventies like his Freak Scene Dream Trilogy does. Plus he's a total rock 'n' roll geek. He knows everything about everybody. Believe me, every detail from Captain Beefheart to the New York Dolls. Bob Dylan is God. And a straight guy with a raging sexual agenda searching for his 'Visions of Johanna chick.' It's a terrific read."

TOM SPANBAUER, author of "Faraway Places," "Now Is the Hour" and "I Loved You More"

"Michael Goldberg reminds us of the difficulties of remaining true to our own visions amidst the powerful exigencies of young adulthood. He paints crazy intimate portraits of the excesses and eccentricities of the sexual revolution. And he speaks to us in the voice and language of the brave microculture of his youth. In this, he opens a door to the rough adolescence of our own 'grown up' disillusioned macroculture. All the dreams and wishes and bright energy buried therein is still brawling for a release. Our inner teenager still wonders what the fuck we think we are doing. To hear a voice from this realm is a blessing. Goldberg makes of himself a channel from that forbidden country. Through his recounting, we remember how we learned to love, how we learned to listen, and how we learned to do whatever it is we do best."

JOLIE HOLLAND, recording artist, whose albums include *Catalpa, Escondida* and *The Living and the Dead*

"Everyone knows the dizzying Sixties gave way to the sobering Seventies, but few writers have captured that wild ride and its consequences—the road from folk Dylan to 'Sister Morphine'—the way Michael Goldberg does in his debut novel. His prose is hallucinogenic in all the best ways."

DAVID BROWNE, author of "Dream Brother: The Lives and Music of Jeff and Tim Buckley," "Fire and Rain: The Beatles, Simon & Garfunkel, James Taylor, CSNY and the Lost Story of 1970" and "Goodbye 20th Century: A Biography of Sonic Youth"

UNTITLED

The Third of the
Freak Scene Dream Trilogy

a novel by
Michael Goldberg

Neumu Press
P.O. Box 6740
Albany, CA 94706
insider1@neumu.net
www.untitled-anovel.com

ISBN: 978-0-9903983-6-3

To my beautiful wife Leslie,
the love of my life. You make every
day the "authentic real."

UNTITLED

"Make love, take a bath, make love
again."
   —FRIDA KAHLO

"Look at this tangle of thorns."
   —VLADIMIR NABOKOV

ONE

1. SUSAN SIMONE

I HEAR SIMONE'S DARK soprano, she's singing along to
Joni on the 8-track. They could be sisters those two, the way
their wild women voices blend over the jazzy groove. Simone's
name is really Susan, that's the name she uses, you remember,
Ms. Braveheart. She's the teacher chick I met at the Halloween
party last year. But all summer long I thought of her as Simone
'cause of that feminist writer. Simone de Beauvoir. Sometimes I
thought of her as Susan Simone. Sometimes Susan, I guess
when she left behind her studied libber persona, let the dogma
fall off her and we lay together naked on her mattress. When I
thought she needed me, when I thought she was my Visions of
Johanna.

Joni's voice has that hint of tremolo, floating up toward the
stars. Simone's is tougher, and those shadows, and she always
left herself a way out.

We love our lovin', But not like we love our freedom.

It's the last day of August, 1973, and I, Michael Stein, AKA
Writerman, stand there watching Simone's white Chevy van
drive away from me on Morning Glory Way. I can't see the
God's eye hanging from the rear view mirror but I know it's
there, swinging gently, and over the engine noise all I hear is
Joni coming out the open window on the driver's side, Simone's
side, and that bumper sticker, such a gut punch:
A woman needs a man like a fish needs a bicycle.
OK, I get it. Women under the thumb of guys going back

to the Stone Age, Simone taught me all about that, and how the New Trip chicks need to feel free, feel they don't gotta lean on a guy, or be under his thumb. Still, the bumper sticker bugs me 'cause if Simone doesn't need a freakster bro, well you tell me how come all summer long when *she's* in the mood, she had me down there sticking my tongue in her? And how come there's a list of guys going all the way back to when she's in the sixth grade? Don't tell me she doesn't need a guy around 'cause there's never been a time she didn't have one.

Dust rising up behind her dirty white van, the hard light of the late morning sun burning up everything out there, and her van smaller and smaller and I don't hear Joni any more.

For four and a half months, from the night in April I first went home with her until right now, Morning Glory Way been the golden road that led to Simone's Freak Scene Dream junkyard box of a house. When I'd turn onto Morning Glory off Poppy Lane I'd look out past the cliffs, see the ocean, sunlight reflecting crazy beautiful, the Forever Infinite Pacific stretching out to the horizon, the fields on either side of the road dusty green with strawberry plants, and feel the glorious high.

I was goddamn goddamn alive.

Tim Buckley. I thought about him too when I turned onto that road, and his "Morning Glory" song. Imagined him naming it after the road. Or maybe after dropping acid out there, same as me and Simone did, the Saturday afternoon after she first brought me home, tripping down on the beach, running naked, fucking in the hot sand, getting my ass burned by the sun. That was a Days of the Crazy-Wild day for sure, a day when something extraordinary happens, when you feel the rush of being alive in every cell.

Fuck yeah.

Morning Glory. Groovy name for a tab of acid, a song, a road, the flowers in Simone's front yard. Those morning glories. I didn't know anything about them before I came home with her, but that first Saturday, in the morning before we dropped, those flowers blooming beautiful, she told me.

"Ephemeral beauty," she said. "They'll be *dead* flowers by the late afternoon."

That's how me and her lived our life together at first, or tried to anyway, sparklers shooting into the sky, high as we could go, flaming out. I didn't get it as I stood there watching the back end of her van. She tried to clue me in it was over. It was all there, but I wouldn't see it.

Man, what was with me and chicks? First I blew it with Sarah, right at the climax of my senior year, high school days. Three years we were together. She was the first chick I loved, first chick I fucked. 'Course we had problems in that department. She couldn't come. At least she never came when I was inside her. I mean that wasn't why it ended. That was me fucking her over, betraying her, losing track of what I had. What *we* had. Yeah that was all my fault.

And then Elise, traumatized, anxiety-ridden artist Elise, spring of my sophomore year, college days. And finally Susan Simone. Yeah, third time's the charm alright. Or maybe it was the Keith Richards snakeskin boots I always wore back then that were cursed. Or The Dylan, this cigarette lighter I stole from Jerry Garcia. He bragged *he* stole it from Bobby Dylan, and how I got to hang out with Garcia, well that's a story for another day.

Or then again, maybe it was Doom and Gloom, those two black-billed magpies that seemed to show up whenever trouble was on the way—or had arrived. I saw them all summer long, perched atop Simone's roof.

Me, under a bad sign.

Simone never called me Writerman.

To her I was always Michael. To everyone else, my friends, I was Writerman. Except when I was Michael, which was when they had something serious to tell me. Or something same as that. I guess.

Simone didn't give a fuck about the future, everything in the moment, everything based on how she feels *right now*, and on her female intuition, her *chick* intuition. Like the time these two friends of her neighbor Saul show up in an old black Mercedes

—The Wizard and his old lady, Serena—and Simone decides we're all going to the lesbian bar, the Lavender Club. Soon as we each do a square of *The Wizard's righteous blotter.* And when I said *no fucking way,* 'cause who knows what Simone's gonna do on acid around all those dykes, when I said I don't wanna go, and certainly not on blotter spiked with meth, she said *fine, stay home, but we're going. And don't wait up for me, Michael, maybe I won't be home 'til the morning.*

Yeah, that turned out to be the night Simone met Harper at the Lavender Club. Well, fuck. *Met* doesn't begin to tell what happened.

Fucking Morning Glory Way. Now it's the road Simone took to get on with her life. She left me behind. For good. Only I don't know that part. Yet. That day as I stand there sun burning up my bare forearms I think it's temporary. My neck sweating under all that hair, total freak-out Zappa hair way past my shoulders, and sweat at my armpits and across my chest under my black Alice Cooper t-shirt.

That day I still think she loves me. That teaching gig in Boston, she'd got it before me and her got it on. Well someone gotta take care of her house, and all those cats, and Lucky the dog. She can't load 'em up in the van and take 'em with her. In Boston she's got one room in a big 100-and-something-year-old Craftsman where a bunch of people live—students and another teacher. The animals gotta stay back in California. That's where I come in.

But she'll be back, and when the school year is over, and she gets back, it's gonna be all groovy. What I think that day. What I concentrate on so goddamn goddamn hard I feel the lines in my sunburned forehead, the ache above my nose, and I close my eyes so tight it hurts, so hard and tight I see sun flashes. What *has* to fucking happen. 'Course if there'd been time to change things around, teach up at The University again, not drive by her lonesome across this huge, weird, solitary country, still she'd have done it.

Her new big adventure.

I know it now. She knew it then.

The spooky choir I heard in the trees up at The University, it's in the ocean sound, a thousand murmurs foretelling my fate. *Love's made a fool of you,* they sing, *bye bye love,* they sing, *when blue turns to grey,* they sing, *I asked for water, she gave me gasoline,* they sing. And the birds. Doom and Gloom. Don't see 'em but they're there, perched on the rotting wood shingle roof of Simone's one-story shack of a house. Laughing at me.
Caw caw caw.
Lucky the dog. Simone rescued her at the animal shelter, and you'd swear that sweet mutt was the offspring of Rin Tin Tin and a black Lab, barking and jumping up on the gate behind me. That dog knows something's up. Dogs are psychic empaths. Psychic. I try to voodoo the van back onto Morning Glory Way, Simone getting to the end of Poppy Lane where it dead-ends into San Andreas, and hurting inside so Joni Mitchell heartbreak bad. *Oh you are in my blood like holy wine, Oh and you taste so bitter but you taste so sweet.* That would be something, if I were in her blood like holy wine. Her needing me so crazy bad, turn the van around and drive home.
Yeah, no way she can go through with this.
I stand there, my mouth dry, I need to get inside, get something to drink, but I don't move. The doubt in the spooky voices, in the murmurs, in the caw caw caw. I was her summer fling. Funny how perfect that describes it. When you fling something you toss it, don't pay any attention, it lands where it lands. I'm not in Simone's blood, not same as holy wine, not same as the merlot she loves, not same as Coca-Cola or even shit-ass Tab.
And summer is over.

I thought she was finally the one, my Visions of Johanna chick. I mean *woman.* My Visions of Johanna *woman.* That was rich. But no, I thought of Simone as my Visions of Johanna *chick.* I don't mean that in any kind of sexist way. I mean it's hip, calling a chick a *chick.* Woman or chick, doesn't matter now. She's gone.

On her way to Boston without me, and I hear Tim Buckley scream at the Hobo, damn the Hobo, weep to the Hobo.

I fucking hurt. If you love somebody of course it hurts. The pain is the proof your love is real. Razorblade teeth rip my heart. A summer fling. Yeah, rip it out and fling it God-who-don't-exist-only-knows-where.

I stand there and I'm alone, and I look down at my hands. Got a pack of Pall Malls, grip it so hard I've crushed some of 'em. Get one out and light it with The Dylan. A number would be better to take me away from this mindfuck, but no way I'm going back inside to roll a fat one with Simone's homegrown. Can't give up my vigil. Long as I stand here, long as my eyes stay focused on that dusty road I can believe Simone's gonna come to her senses, turn around and come home.

In a few days Harper's gonna move in. Oh man oh man oh man. Harper, now there's a story. Fuck, 'cause I don't know where I stand with that chick. Harper gets the bedroom on the right side of the house with the queen mattress on the orange shag carpet, no box spring, where me and Simone fucked. Where the three of us—me and Simone and Harper—ended up the night those two came home from the Lavender Club. Yeah, there's probably a whole lot to tell regards that night, but we don't have time for most of it.

Ghost of 'lectricity. That's from a Dylan song. I've appropriated it, turned it into a symbol, a way to clue you in that what I'll tell you next is a memory, or maybe a vision. From the past, or the future, or no future.

Ghost of 'lectricity. Mid-July of 1973. I wait in Simone's living room, smoke a Pall Mall, smoke a number, drink merlot, another Pall Mall, another number, another drink 'til I pass out on the couch. It's after 3 a.m. when I hear Simone and she's with someone, they're in the bedroom. Oh man, she has some guy in there she's fucking. Goddamn goddamn. There's part of me wants to beat the shit out of him, and part of me that's dying. Simone's stoned laughter, and what is she laughing about? Well I gotta deal with this prick, get him out of the house and have it out with Simone.

I walk into the bedroom that's got the queen mattress and the orange shag carpet. The room is grainy shades of gray to black. Simone cross-legged on the mattress, and when she sees me she laughs harder, fucked up as I ever seen her. She's naked, only there's paint on her, and in the darkness it's hard to see the colors, finger paint, a childish sun around one tit, and a moon on the other one.

Oh man, 'cause the guy isn't a guy. It's a chick and she's naked too.

I don't know why but all the rage and pain melts away soon as I see it's a chick. Instead of a betrayal it's a turn-on. Why the fuck does my chick getting it on with some stranger chick turn me on? Hellfuck if I know. But for sure I'm not the only one. The editors of *Penthouse* can attest to that. The chick is lying on her back across the mattress and there's paint smeared all over her, as if she been rolling in mud, and paint around her on the sheet, and Simone is leaning over the chick, her index finger got a glob of dark paint and she's painting a spiral from one of the chick's nipples, so it spirals out around her tit, a dark spiral spiraling over the mess of paint already on her, and there's a dark arrow on her stomach pointing to the Holy Grail, you know, her pussy.

Simone isn't painting any more, her hand squeezing the chick's tit, the dark paint, the nipple between Simone's thumb and index thick with paint, her other hand on the chick's pussy, and there's paint on those fingers too, and Simone gets her index and middle fingers in the chick, she's moving those fingers fast, and the chick isn't laughing she's moaning, a weird high moan, and I know that moan. All the while Simone finger-fucks the chick she's looking up at me, *this is what can happen if you don't do what I tell you. Next time it'll be a guy.*

"Michael's here," Simone says.

The other chick turns her head my direction, and she's all dreamy, and she's got a stoned smile going too. And that's when I see it's Harper.

Oh man oh man oh man.

"It's about time," Harper says.

When Harper moves in I'll have the other bedroom, the one with the antique brass bed frame, the single bed Simone slept in by herself those nights when she needed "space." You know, the way my former college buddy Jim Costello's chick Jaded needed "alone time." That's the new lingo. *Space. Alone time.* Now chicks *always* need their *space,* "a room of their own." I guess guys always had the neighborhood bar, or the weekly poker game, so it makes sense chicks want the same. Course now I've got a room of *my* own.

I'm worried about Harper moving in. Every time I've been with her it's a life-on-the-line sex deal. First time we met, it was a few days into my sophomore year, her freshman year, first time she'd been away from home and she was looking to live every taboo, ready to go trouble girl crazy. Seeking out a darkness that soon enough she found. She picked me up that day in the Arts College cafeteria and we ended up doing it on my dorm room bed.

Last time I saw Harper was that morning at Simone's place, after our threesome. She was into her tomboy look, not only the short blonde hair, but the men's clothes: a plaid flannel shirt over black jeans and black engineer boots. She probably had one of those awakenings, and maybe she let me fuck her 'cause sex with me while Simone watched, and then Simone going down on her while I watched, made it more of a kinky turn-on. I've been through so much with Harper, but in plenty of ways I don't know her at all.

The thing about Simone, she's into all the feminist stuff, but still she's sexy. She dresses the way a chick dresses, not a dyke. And she likes to fuck. Guys. That's what she told me. Until that night. When it wasn't only guys. Anyway, I hoped it would be OK sharing the house with Harper. Even if Simone was wrong about Harper having a thing for me. If she ever did, it's over.

The neighbors are OK. There's that nebbish Saul, he's a screenwriter. Simone said he had something to do with "Easy

Rider" and "The Graduate" and a couple dozen others. Yeah he's a real celebrity around here, Saul is, to hear Simone talk about him. He lives further down the road, got an old place he rents on the cliff. Saul's cool, I mean a screenwriter, man. And Leonard the Lech and Julie on this side of Saul, with their big-ass three-story Richie Rich house right at the edge of the cliff, and how ignorant was that, man. Leonard's a retired lawyer; Julie's his wife.

Ooo. A fucking *faux pas*.

I guess this as a good a time as any to tell you. Back then I thought I was pretty mature regards chicks. I never thought of Sarah, my first Visions of Johanna, yeah I never thought of her as a piece of ass, you know that about me. But the major turnaround was Elise. With her I learned what it is to love a chick. I mean sure I loved Sarah, but we were so young. Too young.

Elise made me work for her love, and it was as if we were partners in crime, her and me. A lot of guys woulda bailed—all that trauma. She'd been raped by her high-school boyfriend, and she was still fucked up from it, when me and her hung out. It was tough, dealing with her trip. But it made me love her more, made me understand the kinda shit some chicks come up against. Even with all that gone down between us, still I love her. If she needed my help, I'd help. Simone never saw that side of me. To Simone I was another in a long line of sexist pigs she took to bed, and it was her job to make a feminist outta me.

Which brings me back to Julie, you know, and her being Leonard the Lech's *wife*. Simone made such a big deal about it. Just because a chick marries a guy doesn't make her his property, Simone said. She wasn't *his* anything, she said. Leonard doesn't own Julie, she said. I mean Simone's right, but still. Chicks, I mean women, want it both ways. They want to have their space and be paid same as a guy and not be seen as a piece of ass, but they want a guy to take care of them, buy them shit, protect them, all of that. Maybe not every woman. Maybe it's only the women I've known.

Simone been married once, back before she found herself. A journey of self-empowerment, that's what she'd been on since 1968. That's what she told me. She dropped outta the whole straight Fifties-style wifey deal. Told her sexist pig ad-exec hubby—her *unconscious* sexist pig ad-exec hubby, though all she knew at the time was he's an uptight straight motherfucker who didn't turn her on any more—to go fuck himself, got on a plane for L.A. and became a Freak Scene Dream love child. A 29-year-old Freak Scene Dream love child.

She didn't change her name right off, not until 1970. First she had to join the Topanga Canyon commune and do the free love deal with all the freaky longhaired, unwashed, doped-out free love guys who thought it was so groovy to have a new chick to ball. But then Lucy Free—well she was Lucy Leftowitz before she changed her name—hipped Simone to the feminist deal. Loaned her "The Feminine Mystique" and "Sexual Politics." Now *that* was an awakening. Simone got it, you know, figured out the stinky unwashed free love guys were unconscious sexist pigs too, same as her ad-exec hubby. After she read those books she knew that's what he'd been and they were, and boy did that make her mad. There is nothing to compare to the anger of a chick who wakes up to the feminist deal and understands she's been royally screwed.

Yeah, Simone got her consciousness raised. That's what she told me, and trust me, she did.

Changed her last name to Braveheart, and I do get it. No way she'd want the name of her ex, or go back to a name that came from her unconscious sexist pig dad. She wanted a name of her own, a new name to represent the new Susan. The New Trip.

It wasn't easy living with Ms. Doctrinaire Feminist all summer long. A feminist matriarchal trip can be as abusive to a guy as the patriarchal trip is to a chick. There was an upside. I really did learn to give good cunnilingus.

Just ask Harper.

Despite the mind-body split of contradictions that is Susan Simone, I learned plenty from her about men and women, about how men treat women, and about how women want to be treated. Learned plenty about humans, and beyond humans, animals too. We're all hell of a lot more complex than it might seem. Surface of the surface and all that. And every damn thing is political, even if you think it's total personal deal. Susan taught me that. You know "Animal Farm," where the pigs take control of the farm and soon as they're in power they start acting same as men? Yeah well that's what can happen, even if the pigs are chicks.

Susan's never getting married again, she said. Doesn't want any strings. That was practically the first thing she told me. That was before we fucked. About an hour before we fucked. *You better not be possessive, Michael,* she said. *If I start feeling guilty,* she said. *If you start pouting, doing that jealous trip all guys do,* she said. *You do any of that, you're gone,* she said. *I can't feel tied down,* she said. *No strings,* she said. That was rich. As if being married or not has anything to do with it. There were a whole lot of strings. There are always strings. Ropes really. Tight around my ankles. Tying my arms to my body. Pulling on my fucking heart. Needles too. Right through my skull. *No strings,* Simone said. Maybe what she meant was she wasn't gonna have any kinda emotional attachment. *No strings* tying her to me. That's how she wanted it.

And everything was how Simone wanted it.

Simone was wrong. That chick Julie *is* Leonard's wife. Julie does all the cooking except when Leonard barbecues out on the deck. All the housework. Probably keeps silent when he fucks around. Me and Simone, we call him Leonard the Lech. I've seen his roving-eye deal, the way he'd look at Simone. The way he looked at that Lizzie chick Saul brought to dinner. Yeah I mean if Simone wanted to single out an unconscious sexist pig, Leonard's her man. Leonard always supported the two of them, him and Julie, on his fat lawyer's salary. I'm not saying he owns her, and this isn't a matter of opinion, but simply a stating of the facts. That's who Julie is. Leonard's wife.

First time me and Simone went over there, to see if

Leonard and Julie wanted some of the zucchini Simone grew in
Saul's huge-ass front yard, that's how Julie introduced herself.
That big custom-made oak door swung open and skinny-ass
Julie, looking same as Joan Didion's mom, standing there
looking at us. Julie in some kind of la-de-da beige pantsuit and
we're the freaks, Simone wearing those cut-off jeans and her
bright red 1972 Women's Liberation Festival t-shirt too tight,
you could see her nipples if you were looking, and if you're a
guy I guarantee you woulda been looking, those oversize crazy
shades and the psychedelic purple and red and yellow and blue
earrings and her hair all crazy-wild from the wind. And me
looking how I looked in those days, frizzed-out hair, my other
pair of Lennon specs, the ones with the dark green lenses,
black, blue and purple plaid cowboy shirt, flared jeans and the
snakeskin boots.

Simone said we're the neighbors down the road, said how
she'd talked to Leonard a few times out at the row of rusty mail
boxes on Poppy Lane, and Julie starts to shake, and that was
freaky, her skin-and-bones hands shaking a little, but I saw it,
Simone saw it. Cucquean shake. That was a shake that got
everything to do with Leonard the Lech's roving eye. And
Simone's talking too fast, saying too much about the zucchini
and growing them and Saul's vegetable garden and all that, and
Julie got her cucquean shake going, and she said, *Well I'm
Leonard's wife Julie.*

So there's the proof. Provided by a 100 percent reliable
source. Julie *is* Leonard's wife. That's how Julie thinks of herself.
Ooo. Na na ne na na, Simone. Yeah well that didn't stop Simone,
not at all. She said just because Julie identifies herself that way,
it doesn't matter. Plenty of women are *unknowing victims of the
oppressive sexist patriarchal system.* Same as Simone when she was
married to that guy she was married to before she woke up. All
the housewives simply don't know any better, Simone said.
They're not *conscious* yet, she said. Same as the actress chicks in
the porn flicks, she said. Same as the hookers, she said. Even
the Margo St. James-sex-worker-rights hookers, she said. They
all need their *consciousness* raised. And you know what, Simone's

right. Isn't only the guys who don't get it. Plenty chicks need some feminist theory. Need to get free of the bullshit, get out from under the thumbs of the *unconscious sexist pig guys* they're with, and all that. But it sure doesn't mean guys gotta get neutered. Nothing wrong with a guy being strong, taking care of business, getting the job done. Nothing wrong about that at all, Simone said.

Ignorant. That's what those two were. Leonard the Lech and Julie. You don't build a house right on the bluff like that, not if it's a sandstone bluff, a slowly eroding sandstone bluff, not if you don't want your mansion sliding down onto the beach. Only a matter of time. That was the deal with nature. Everything erodes. The sides of cliffs. Friendships. Relationships. We're all whores, Meltzer said. I still think about that, how convenient it was for Simone to have me living there when she headed off to Boston for her brand new life.

There was one night when Leonard the Lech and Julie had the bunch of us over. Simone and me, and that nebbish Saul, and Lizzie who's down from San Francisco fucking Saul all weekend. Hey, I'm relaying the facts. Saul for sure didn't have that red-hot 22-year-old babe shacking up with him for intellectual stimulus.

Just to clue you in.

And furthermore, let me digress briefly to tell you about this huge framed art Saul had hanging over the fireplace in his living room. It's a black and grey drawing on watercolor paper done in this sorta fantasy style—not a cartoon but not realist either. When you first look you think you're seeing the cosmos, this swirl of little drops of liquid, same as the Milky Way, taking up most of the drawing, but in the middle there's this little naked chick and she has the tits—for sure a guy done the drawing, and that chick is his idea of a hot chick—and she's riding this gigantic engorged cock, the way she'd ride a horse, straddling that thing same as the guy in "Dr. Strangelove" straddling the bomb, her head back, this ecstatic grin on her face, you know, *that* kinda grin, and spurting out of the cock, all those drops, a Milky Way of sperm.

There's something about Saul's personality, chicks always want to take care of him, serve him up a big-ass dinner including a big bowl of chicken noodle soup and a humungous piece of cheese cake, get him in bed and fuck him. Saul was nothing to look at. He was short, his face all wrinkled and pockmarked, kind of look you'd have if you fell asleep on a gravel path, your face pressed hard against the little rocks and those indentations never went away. And he was flabby, never got any exercise. But boy did the chicks dig him. Of course he's funny and super smart and the chicks that went for him were usually into the whole *revolution now* deal, you know, 'cause of him being associated with the Weather Underground.

Oops, forget I told you. How Saul was associated with the Weathermen. That's supposed to be a secret. Even now, if the Feds got hip, they could cause him plenty of trouble. So yeah, a screenwriter, that's Saul, a chick magnet screenwriter.

Anyway.

So we all go over to Leonard the Lech and Julie's place that night. Saul, he's 41 but looks older, and he's got that Lizzie chick, says she's 22 but looks 17, and Simone who's 35 has me and I'm still 19, and then Leonard the Lech and Julie, who gotta be a million years old, at least in their 60s. God-who-don't-exist-only-knows what those two thought.

I mean the whole age trip between me and Simone weirded *me* out.

Leonard the Lech and Julie had us all drinking their expensive Napa wines and eating the fancy food Julie spent all day cooking up and afterwards me and Simone and Saul and Lizzie and Leonard the Lech end up naked in the big round redwood hot tub out on that deck, right on the edge, that black ocean crashing below us, drinking champagne out of those fine-crystal champagne flutes while Julie's inside washing dishes. It was fucking weird, no way I could not have a hard-on with Simone right next to me, her left arm around my back, holding me against her, her other hand on my thigh, rubbing it, and then

Lizzie over there next to Saul. Lizzie was one of those uninhibited Jewish Freak Scene Dream chicks with the long black hair braided so it hung behind her, and her tits right at the water line and she's moving around, she'd get too hot and then she'd climb up so she's sitting on the edge of the wood tub, legs spread, really didn't give a fuck, and I can see her snatch and everything. Her and Saul fooling around, kissing, hands on each other, she was slapping him, telling him he was a dirty old man. Stoned and drunk and that going on. I didn't look but I'm sure Saul and Leonard the Lech were in the same state as me and none of us want to get out of that tub with our dicks sticking out. You're not supposed to have a hard-on when you're in the hot tub with a bunch of other people and it's not some kind of orgy deal—and this wasn't that.

It's not cool.

Well it was a fucking disaster that night. Simone saw me looking at Lizzie, how could I help it, that chick right *there*, sitting so her pussy and her tits are in front of me. I'm a freakster bro, man. I'm supposed to look away? What really bugged me was the double standard. Simone with her whole deal about non-attachment and no strings and how you weren't ever supposed to be jealous. She said she was monogamous, but if she wanted to be with another guy, she needed to be able to just walk away. Not have to explain herself. I don't know where she got some of that shit from. But me with that hot tub hard-on, that made her so fucking mad. I told her it was her hand on my thigh that got me going, but she didn't buy it. Simone slept by herself in the single bed for the next week.

The last night me and Simone slept together, the night before she split, she wouldn't let me fuck her. I was so sad and broken, and I want her to tell me she felt it too. I wanted her falling to pieces same as me. We lay on her queen mattress, me in her arms, and she was running her hand through my hair. She was almost buoyant. I mean if she felt any sadness or longing or anything painful she didn't let me in on it.

Simone said she hoped things clicked with me and Harper.

That shoulda been a clue. She said nine months was a long time to be alone, especially for a 20-year-old guy, and yeah, by then I'd turned 20. She said a freakster bro horny as me needed a chick he could fuck all the time, even if it wasn't my perfect Visions of Johanna chick. Simone didn't say "Visions of Johanna chick," but that's what she meant. She said she watched me fuck Harper the night Harper came home with her and she could tell we both got off. And Harper's nearly my age. Simone says maybe it's better for the guy to be a little older, or at least the same age. None of what she said sounded same as something you'd read in "Sexual Politics." Still, it's what Simone said.

The way Simone said Harper was into me made wonder about the two of them. Simone also said that feminist chick friend of hers, Loraine, always asked about me and when she, Simone, was away I really should catch a movie with Loraine. Man, with Simone saying all that, I should have figured. But I had this idea how I was going to hold out for Simone. After a while we stopped talking, and Simone's fingers around my cock and she told me to not to say a word, not to move, and she jerked me off. A sympathy jerk-off.

As I stand there staring at that desolate excuse for a road, my cigarette burning up between my fingers, head aching from too much sun, my life is Camus' *Le Mythe de Sisyphe*. Again and again I try to connect with a chick and find a way to escape the lonesome. Well our consciousness is big as the fucking universe, and we are alone in that universe and I can try and try to make these chicks love me, but it's futile. Alone, man.

Simone in her white Chevy van driving away, not waving or a look back. She's not gonna turn that van around, not coming back 'til next summer. I don't know it as I stand there, but already I'm one of her ex-lovers, and if she had a silver cigarette lighter, I'd be one of the checks scratched into it, the check right between that nebbish Saul, and Simon.

Oh but you don't know about Simon. Yet. Well soon enough you will.

Yeah, that day she drove off, Lucky leaping at the fence, barking for me to do something, bring Simone back, she's not hardly been gone, and already I feel different. Already our four and a half months is slipping away. Nothing gonna be bounced off Simone's feminist ideology any more. Not how it's been since that night she first took me home. The night back in April when me and her met downtown, after she walked into the Truffaut Theater.

2. ALONE TOGETHER

THE TRUFFAUT IS A red velvet cave. Tiny-ass dim lights
along the aisles so you can see when you walk down the tired
red carpet looking for a seat, and a few more dim lights on the
side walls. There's a red curtain so thick and plush and regal it
coulda been from the Royal Albert Hall hanging in front of the
screen, footlights aimed up at it super dramatic, makes what's
behind the curtain seem such a big deal. That's the joke of
movie theaters. Everyone gathered there waiting for the curtain
to part on a big-ass blank screen. Blank as our empty lives. And
then the Great Escape, light shooting through little celluloid
frames, and some whole other world unreeling that's not empty,
where shit happens as we sit in the darkness trying to forget.

That day I don't know I'll run into Ms. Braveheart, and I
don't know she's feeling the same as me. Lonesome. I don't
know that's the day she'll decide its time for a new teenage
boyfriend. Me. For her fucking amusement. Maybe that's not
fair. Maybe that makes it seem more calculated than it was,
maybe she thought it might lead to something. Who can ever
know with that chick.

So much mixed-up confusion, man.

I'm there alone.

Don't have Jim or Elise or Sappho to hang with any more,
and if the best I can do is sit in a movie theater with strangers
for company and pretend I'm not floating in the void, in the
universe of my mind, well that's what I'm gonna do.

I settle into one of the red velvet seats, middle of the row, about three quarters back. At least here there's no pretense. Things are clear. Crystal fucking clear. A person's either with someone they know, or same as me, a person's there with people they don't know. Alone together.

A few handfuls of people sit among the empty seats. Some couples, guys and chicks my age, but also some guys alone. Lonesome chicks too. One geezer needs to lose about 1,000 pounds. He's working hard on his popcorn, hustling to get it eaten before the film starts. Popcorn Man is competing with a guy who's chomping away on an ice cream bar. They're in a race. Popcorn Man in the lead, but it's too soon to count Ice Cream Man out. The winner gonna head out to the lobby before the film starts for more rations. The loser too. I'm certain of it.

I know those chicks are lonesome 'cause they do the quick glance every time someone walks down the aisle, and if it's a guy they give him the twice-over once. Pretty much every time a chick gives a guy the twice-over, he doesn't rate. Maybe that's why those chicks are lonesome. Set the bar so high no guy can reach it. Or it could be they have the same problem as Elise, traumatized by some jerk's abuse. That'd be sad, man.

Anyway, who am I to judge every other human.

I'm here 'cause they're showing "Cries and Whispers." I'm early but the semi-darkness of that red cave is better than my dorm room, or any place on campus, where every damn thing reminds me of Elise.

"Cries and Whispers."

Wrong film to see when I'm so bummed. It's Bergman so it'll be heavy traffic heavy and end in a hellfuck bad way. You can pretty much always count on Bergman to deliver an unhappy ending.

The red velvet curtain opens, and there we are, staring at the blank screen. Waiting for life to begin. That's the future, strapped into a chair, an intravenous bottle feeding chemical sustenance into a vein, getting fatter by the day. Watching. A human's entire life gonna be strapped into a chair watching shit on a screen.

Alone. Alone together.

I watch trailers for a pair of Godard films. "Weekend" and "One Plus One" are being re-released. "One Plus One," man, that's the one Godard shot with the Stones in the studio cutting "Sympathy for the Devil." Keith bashing out the chords, a cigarette hanging from his mouth. If I only was Keith Richards I wouldn't have any chick problems. I'd get to play rock 'n' roll and hang with the freakiest people in the world. And all the groupies. I could fuck a different chick every night. Or I could live with one chick for the rest of my life and that chick would be total devotion 'cause I'm Keith Richards, I'M THE MAN. Of course I'd also be a heroin addict and carry around a fifth of Johnny Walker Black 24/7.

Maybe it wouldn't be so groovy.

Well that's when she shows up. Can you dig it, man? On the screen The Stones jam out an arrangement of "Sympathy for the Devil" inside London's Olympic Sound Studios, June of '68 with the revolution burning up the world outside. Godard intuiting that the Stones rock 'n' roll revision of Mikhail Bulgakov's "The Master and Margarita" is a kind of splatter-art take on all the horror unfolding that year, the year of the Baader-Meinhof, and the assassinations of Martin Luther King Jr. and Robert F. Kennedy, and radical feminist Valerie Solanas' assassination attempt on Andy Warhol, and the SDS's "Ten Days of Resistance," and Nixon elected President and the My Lai massacre, and there in that red cave of a movie theater, the chaos of the Stones in the air, there's my Visions of Johanna chick. I don't know it yet but it's her. This chick with wavy hair that comes down past her shoulders takes a seat two rows in front of me.

Wait, *I know* the chick. She's that feminist teacher chick. The teacher chick I watched at King Editor's Halloween party make out with the freshman, the chick I met in the upstairs hallway that same night, the chick who's teaching the "Women in Film" class.

Yeah, that chick.

She's already 10 minutes late first day of class. I lean back in my chair, smoking a Pall Mall, my hair really fucking long, frizzing out all crazy-wild and the ends still black, my shades on 'cause I been up all night and my eyes bleeding, got on a black cowboy shirt, frayed-at-the-knee jeans and my Keith Richards snakeskin boots.

Man, I was a burned-out basement.

I'm at a table in the back as far away from Sappho and Elise and Jim as I could get, reading about Mott the Hoople in the latest *Creem*, trying to feel fuck-ass superior to all of them.

Oh man, those three, the troubles—*what a drag it is...*

Jim was once my good buddy, *Thee* Freakster Bro, the one and only, from when we met, first day of sophomore year, 'til our final blowout in the spring. Sure I fucked his chick, Jaded, the trouble girl of all trouble girls.

That night. In one of those China-style gondolas, high atop the Ferris wheel, looking out on the "Paint It Black" darkness, the Forever Infinite Pacific, waves crashing.

I wanted it to be her fault. The pint of Johnny Walker Black, undoing my belt, shoving her tit into my mouth.

Don't fuck me like a gentleman, Michael. Make me feel your teeth.

It wasn't her fault. I wanted it same as she did. Only later it turns out what she really wanted was to fuck up my friendship with *Thee* Freakster Bro.

So how does it feel Mr. Eagle Scout? Cheat on your best friend. You and Jim never will be the same.

Yeah, all the mess with Jaded and Jim went down after Elise, Elise with the long slender artist hands, Elise who couldn't shake the trauma of what her first boyfriend did, her 15, him climbing onto her when she was too blitzed to fight him off. The trauma that meant we couldn't fuck.

I thought sure Elise was my Visions of Johanna. I tried so hard to make it work. Too hard.

The torment of you wanting too much.

And Sappho, evil Sappho. Elise's best friend, only she was no real friend. Turned out she wanted Elise as much as I did.

Sappho and Elise share a table at the front of class, busy yucking it up. Sappho's name is really Kate, but I think of her as

Sappho 'cause she's a serious feminist and she looks same as some of those dykes at the Lavender Club. I try not to look at Elise but finally can't help it, and she's *different*. She's cut her hair, you know, the hair that grew out so crazy-wild beautiful when me and her hung out. Has her Audrey Hepburn deal again, and I know what this is about. If she can change who she is, who she sees in the mirror, she can erase the past. She's trying to be the chick she was before we met. That was sad-ass sad, man. Her trying to erase the past of me and her.

And Jim, man, Jim is the fuck different. And not just 'cause he won't look at me, won't say a word if we happen to be in the vacinity of one another. Of course he has the Stevie Winwood hair, but his clothes are lame too. A light pink button-down long-sleeve cotton shirt and beige slacks and brown-shoes-don't-make-it brown penny loafers. Total loser look. All the fucking coolness drained right out of him. I woulda blamed it on Jaded, but it always takes two. Me and him are the only guys in the class, everyone else is chicks. Brand new feminist chicks who want ammo to use against all the sexist pig guys.

She walks right in first day of class and soon as I see her I hear the Professor Longhair song, as if Longhair shadowed her into the room, working that boogie-woogie groove, lazy-ass New Orleans voice singing about a chick named Susan Brown and how she's the "walkinest girl in town," how she walks right in and then she walks right out, and I should've known right then Simone would do damage to my heart. Well she wasn't Simone yet, that didn't come 'til after I moved out to Morning Glory Way. She was Susan that day. Susan Braveheart. *Ms.* Braveheart to you Mr. Macho Man.

Yeah, walk right out as easy as she walk right in.

Ms. Braveheart had the brainiac Liv Ullmann face, only Liv Ullmann as a spinning-psychedelic-mandalas-in-her-eyes chick. You shoulda seen her entrance. She has on one of those newsboy caps, only hers is black velvet, her hair the long and thick and curly auburn deal. Dressed pretty much same as for King Editor's Halloween party. The white blouse with a ruffled collar and ruffles down the front, the black velvet skirt, the black velvet cloak with the red lining trailing behind her, strands of purple and green and gold Mardi Gras beads around her neck and those nearly knee-high black suede boots. Renaissance Pleasure Faire Freak Scene Dream chick is how she looked that day.

There's an urgency to how she walks into the classroom, no time to waste, and no way we're gonna fuck around in her class and I knew that was the way she lived, she has things to do, important shit, and we better get with the program. She hasn't even put her leather briefcase down. It's overflowing with books and papers and magazines, *Take One* and *The Second Wave* and *Women and Film*. She's out of breath, says her name is Susan Braveheart but call her Susan, gets out a Kool and I get to watch Sappho and Elise compete for who gets to light teacher's cigarette. Elise wins. Ms. Braveheart gives Elise a smile and Sappho hates it.

Next Ms. Braveheart asks for a volunteer. Her merlot voice earthy but the total self-confidence deal.

"Give me an example," she says, and takes off the shades and cape, digs in her purse for her tortoise-shell glasses. "Of how women are portrayed in the movies. Anyone?"

Sappho raises her hand, her hair braided down her back, got on denim overalls and no t-shirt and for sure no bra, and even from the back of the class I see the hair under Sappho's left arm when she raises it, her big feminist statement, not shaving under her arms, and her libber pack set in front of her with the women's lib patch aimed towards the front so Ms. Braveheart can't miss it. Sappho gets the nod from Simone.

"Well Susan," Kate says.

Sappho bugs the hell out of me.

"In 'Five Easy Pieces,'" she says, "there's a woman who plays a waitress."

Ms. Braveheart has her glasses on, which gives her more of that smart chick look. I know she's a Ms., 'cause that's what all the chicks who are feminists want to be called, not Miss or Mrs.

That's the whole point of that Ms. deal. Make it hard for a guy to get a preconception regards the chick being married or single. "Ms." doesn't give anything away.

"So why, Kate," Ms. Braveheart says, "is that important?"

Ms. Braveheart gets her Kool between her lips, stands there pulls her hair, all that long tripped-out groovy hair, back out of her face with both hands, those hands behind her head, getting some kind of hair-tie around it and there's no way a chick can do that without thrusting her chest forward, and that teacher chick so natural, yeah that's a foxy move, and watching her, I wonder about it, this feminist teacher chick doing a foxy move. What's that about?

Sappho doesn't know the answer, I see her desperate look to Elise but Elise doesn't pull a Lone Ranger, and I figure neither of 'em know what's important about the chick being a waitress in "Five Easy Pieces."

"Is it because Jack Nicholson's character hassles her?" Sappho says.

"Nice try, Kate," Ms. Braveheart says. "Anyone else have an idea about the waitress role in 'Five Easy Pieces'? What it says about women in our culture?"

I know, but I'm not sure I'm gonna speak up about it.

Elise sits there smoking, hating my guts, looking for a reason to laugh her cynical Leopard-Skin Pill-Box Hat laugh. And Sappho, Ms. Sarcasm, yeah she'd love to put me down. Get the spotlight off her know-nothing. Fuck them, lean back in my chair again, and from the back of the class, cool as I can be, I say, "Yeah."

"Yeah *what*?" Ms. Braveheart says, and walks slow between the tables towards the back of the class, and I hear Sappho snicker and right quick Elise laughs her Leopard-Skin Pill-Box Hat laugh. Mick and Keith got a song about chicks same as those two.

I don't think Ms. Braveheart likes me leaning back in that chair same as I'm not really paying attention. Which isn't true at all, I pay close attention, especially to that foxy move, you remember, thrusting out her chest, and the way her cigarette hangs from her lips. And her lips.

"You're Michael?" she says.

"Stein," I say.

And she's looking at me, and she's trying to remember, you know, me and her in the hallway at the Halloween party, checking each other out.

"You take photographs?" she says.

"Sometimes. Haven't had time lately."

She gives me a look, and if a libber has a look that means you-are-a-fucking-sexist-pig-asshole, that's it. Right then I didn't have a clue as to what that look was about. Turned out she'd seen the fuck-me photos of chicks that were up in this group show freshman year at X Marks the Spot, the Arts College gallery. That was what *she* called them. The "fuck-me photos." I'd taken them right when school started, my way of getting to know some groovy chicks. You know, *hey, I'm a photographer and I'd dig to shoot you. It's for a project I'm doing.* Often enough, if a chick knows she's a looker, she'll dig to have her photo taken. Weird how Ms. Braveheart knew I'd taken them. The fuck-me photos. Weird how she *remembered.*

"I have an idea," I say. "You know, why it's important."

Sappho, talking too loud to Elise. "Wow," she says. "Maybe he wants to make another creepy stalker film."

Ms. Braveheart whirls around so fast her skirt kinda twirls. "Speak up, Kate," she says. "We all want to hear what you have to say."

Fucking Sappho, she has so much chutzpah, lays on her supercilious smile and prissy-ass voice, pretends she's some kind of feminist good girl.

"I was just saying," she says. "Maybe *Mike* could use the obsessive stalker film he made that stars a friend of mine, as an example of the sexist roles men foist on women in the movie business."

Fucking bitch. So then I have Ms. Braveheart standing front of my table, looking down at me, asking 20 questions. Yeah that was when she knew for sure I was the guy who took the fuck-me photos.

"Is that right? A sexist stalker film?"

Sounds same as every chick in the room is laughing, but not Jim. He's keeping a low profile. A month previous and he'd be coming to my defense, but not today. Well I have more to deal with than whatever's goin' down inside Jim's brain. I got Ms. Braveheart and all these chicks giving me the twice-over once, and my face getting hot. Yeah man, guilty until proven innocent. Might not be that way in the courtroom, but in real life, well get a clue.

Guilty of being a fucking sexist pig.

"Was this for one of Andrew Fine's classes?" she says, and her face tightens, she's pissed, and this has to do with two things. Something between her and this other film teacher, Andrew Fine, the guy who teaches the French New Wave class, and her getting the wrong idea 'cause of those fuck-me photos.

"Tell us about it, Michael," she says. "I'm sure there's something we can all learn from a student film that exploits women."

Sappho looks at Ms. Braveheart and me, she has a Liquor Store kinda smirk, Liquor Store being the name I use for this jerk who clerks at Liquor King, the booze emporium just down the road from The University. But Elise, all I see is the back of her head as if she's staring down at the top of that table where she sits. She doesn't want anyone knowing she's in that film, or that once I was her boyfriend.

"It was a very unusual project, Susan," Sappho says. "Now I didn't get to see it. But my friend told me he had her play a sexy French beauty, and the camera zoomed in on her face, and stayed there, like he was watching her. My friend said it made her feel like she wasn't even a person."

Jim trying to keep his mouth from forming into a huge-ass grin, and the other chicks in the class whispering to each other.

"Kate's *wrong*," I say. "I didn't make any stalker film."

There's nothing same as the anger self-righteous 18-year-old chicks who've seen the feminist light can spew at a guy they think's a sexist pig asshole. Whole room giving me the libber death vibe.

"It was a personal statement," I say, and sit up, look right at Ms. Braveheart, her face four, maybe five feet away, and right then I notice all the freckles. Her face dense with freckles, and dark from the sun too. She got more freckles than Elise, and it's beautiful all those freckles.

Sex dust, how I think of freckles.

Elise gotta be freaking, thinks I'll say something about me and her and "Le Genou d'Elise," the film me and her made this past spring for Fine's class. Well no way I'll do that to Elise. Even bad as she hurt me, even her laughing her Leopard-Skin Pill-Box Hat laugh. I'm a stand-up guy. Everything gone down between me and Elise, that shit is personal.

"We, I mean *I*," I say. "It was a satire of 'Claire's Knee,'" and Elise isn't looking down at the table any more, she's turned around, looking at me and she sighs, sigh of relief kinda sigh, yeah she's appreciative I'm taking the heat, and how she's looking, there's a little of the way she used to look at me back when she was my chick.

"So your film makes fun of Rohmer's exploitation of women?" Ms. Braveheart says. "I'd like you to screen it for the class."

Another glance at Elise; she's back to staring down at the table.

"I didn't finish it."

"Why not?" Ms. Braveheart says.

"That's personal."

How Ms. Braveheart looks at me, she knows this is about more than a class film. And something more in her look reminds me of how she was looking at that freshman, night of King Editor's Halloween party.

"Now about the waitress," she says. "In 'Five Easy Pieces'," and the tone in her voice, lips closed, cheeks puffed out a little, that impatience deal, probably figures I don't have a clue about this stuff.

"It's kind of a one-down role," I say, and imagine myself some kinda philosopher of cinematic studies—Andrew Sarris

Untitled   29

maybe or Manny Farber. "That waitress deal. It's a subservient role that Lorna Thayer has in relation to Jack Nicholson. The roles of guys and chicks in the movies or on TV influence our ideas about guys and chicks. You know, in real life. A chick sees Joni Mitchell or Aretha on the TV and maybe it gives her hope that she could be a singer too. A guy sees Fonda and Hopper in 'Easy Rider' or Newman and Redford in 'Butch Cassidy and the Sundance Kid' and it reinforces that independent free spirit deal. The macho trip. If all chicks see in the flicks are chicks as waitresses or housewives or whores, they think that's all there is for them."

Ms. Braveheart tries to keep her face serious, but a you're-not-who-I thought-you-were smile breaking through, yeah she's impressed, and remember when I stood up to Sausalito Cowboy, and I wasn't Pizza Boy no more—same kinda trip.

"You're right, Michael," she says. "What we see up on the big screen has great influence. A waitress is a stereotype."

She scans the room, makin' sure all of us listen up.

"As Michael said, those stereotypes color our lives. We need to see women in power positions, in real life and in the movies, if our country is going to become more egalitarian."

I'm writing down what she said, and wonder if Elise is letting herself think different regards me.

"Hey Michael," Ms. Braveheart says.

I look up at her, see her brainiac Liv Ullmann face, and what's this about?

"Yeah," I say.

Liv Ullmann as Freak Scene Dream Summer of Love kinda chick.

"When you're in this class. we're not going to use any of the sexist language that demeans women," she says. "Like the derogatory term 'chick.' It's offensive. Understand?"

Sappho snickers, but I don't hear nothing from Elise.

"Yeah, sure, whatever," I say. "I hear you."

That was stupid though, I mean a chick is a chick. Same way if a guy and a chick are together, well he's her old man. What the fuck you gonna call a chick anyway, *a woman*? That's lame. I don't wanna have to start talking like a square.

Ms. Braveheart is back up front of the class. And those freckles
—I bet they're not only on her face.

"Over and over again," she says. "What we see in the
movies are women in stereotypical roles."

I bet the chick sunbathes in the nude. For sure she has
heavy traffic freckles all over her tits. I never seen that, the
intense freckle deal on a chick's tits.

"The waitress, the good girl," Ms. Braveheart says.

A hippie intellectual chick into film how she is, strong-willed
and feisty, heavy traffic freckles all over her tits. Yeah, man,
Holy Grail of chicks.

"The angel, the whore."

Better than Elise 'cause Ms. Braveheart is older, she knows
shit.

"The maid, the girlfriend. "

Not same as the college chicks, I mean they're chicks in
training bras. Ms. Braveheart been around, I could actually use
the term *woman* regards her. And there was something else, I
mean the concept of fucking a foxy older chick.

"The housewife, the hooker."

She gotta be crazy-wild in bed.

"The adulteress, the nympho."

If I could somehow get her into bed.

"It makes us think that's all a women can be," she says.

A chick same as her, independent, knowing all the shit she
knows.

"A sex object."

 So at ease with her body.

"Or just there to serve. Subservient to men."

And those *freckles.*

"The star of that film," she says.

I bet she really knows how to fuck.

"Was a man, Jack Nicholson."

So smart, and so sexed out. Yeah an older chick who knows
all kinds of shit I don't know, that's a turn on.

"The actors in 90 percent of the lead roles in American movies are men."

Ms. Braveheart's face is longish, narrowing to a prominent chin, and that chin of hers is more defined than Liv Ullmann's, got more angles and narrower and a little longer and more freckles. *Definitely* more freckles.

"And when a woman is the star or co-star, she's always cast as a sex symbol."

She's so serious about her feminist film theory, and those lips don't have any lipstick. Of course they don't. Some chicks don't understand—chicks look way more groovy when it's their bare lips.

"Garbo, Dietrich, Monroe."

She says something more about women as sex symbols but I don't hear it, I hear the curve of her lips, and how they'll feel against mine. Lips against lips.

"Audrey Hepburn, Jeanne Moreau."

She's got a pretty face but not in the way you think of when you hear the word "pretty," only it is pretty, pretty how Joni's face is pretty, you know, Joni on the cover of *Blue*, and I don't mean she looks same as Joni 'cause she doesn't, Ms. Braveheart's face isn't pretty same as a model or an American movie star. Sunburned and all those freckles and a beauty mark maybe an inch to the right of her nose.

"Grace Kelly. Even Jane Fonda."

You ever seen the inside cover of *For the Roses?* It's a photo taken from a distance of Joni naked, back to the camera looking out at the Forever Infinite Pacific. It took guts for Joni to do that, her naked ass there for every horny freakster bro to see. That's the kinda thing this feminist teacher chick would do if she felt like it. I can tell.

"It's always about sex," she says.

3. AT THE MOVIES

FUCK.

IT IS MS. Braveheart and she sits two rows in front of me, there in the lights-out of the Truffaut Theater, the back of her dark blue pea coat black in the grainy darkness, wavy auburn hair crazy wild. "Cries and Whispers" is minutes away from starting. Soon as they finish with the trailers for the Godard re-releases and his new one, "Tout va bien."

I lean forward, the metal back of the empty seat in front of me cold and hard against my chest, and real quiet, "Ms. Braveheart."

She doesn't hear me, so I try again only louder.

She turns, and I flash on her giving me the cold eye, you know, 'cause of the fuck-me photos and my "stalker" film. But soon as she sees me I get a smile—and I know her smile. It's the smile of being total loaded deal on killer weed. The smile that goes along with making all those weird-ass weird connections, of looking-over-your-shoulder paranoia trip, and the stream of non-sequiturs that make sense only to the stoner who says them and the stoner who hears them. Don't know the why of it, but beyond all that, something else in her smile.

Yeah, she's glad it's me.

She's twisted in her seat, and that's when I see her eyes for the first time, although it's only later when there's decent light I for real see 'em. Still. Might as well give you the scene now as later. Great white shark eyes—brown, with a thin circle of blue. Humans don't have eyes same as that, far as I know. Those eyes are reserved for sharks.

Well for Ms. Braveheart, those are the eyes she's got.

"He's so wise," she says.

Beautiful wild hair, hasn't brushed it, falling around her face, down past her shoulders. "Did I tell you," she says. Strands of hair on her face. "I'm doing a film series." Brushes a hand across her lips, gets a hair out of her mouth. "In the summer."

And there's something so sexed-out about it, a strand stuck against her lips.

Maybe being so stoned she forgot about "Le Genou d'Elise." Oh man, I gotta relax, and yeah, I could use a number.

"Bergman?" I say.

"The only one," she says.

She's dressed as if she's not trying to impress anyone, a low-cut kinda loose lavender V-neck sweater over jeans. And the pea coat. And no lipstick. And her lips.

And her *lips.*

"His films are *deep,*" I say.

Duh. Such a lame-ass lame thing to say.

"'Persona,'" I say.

Double-ass lame, bringing up "Persona," the one Bergman film where an older chick talks about having sex with a teenage boy. Fuck.

"'Wild Strawberries,'" she says.

"What I mean," I say. "Is 'Persona' is my —."

"'The Seventh Seal,'" she says.

"Well it's my favorite," I say.

"Mine's 'Persona,'" she says.

"That's what I said."

"Copycat," she says.

"No, really," I say. "'Persona' really is my very favorite."

"Really?"

Ms. Braveheart pulls that thick hair of hers back out of her face, and leans further over the back of her seat, those great white shark eyes zero in on mine and we both know, man, we're both seeing that scene in "Persona." Bibi Andersson's face, and she's talking about her and Katarina, the chick she met on the beach, the two of them sunbathing naked, the two of them making that teenage boy. And Katarina taking the other boy's cock in her mouth.

"That's what you like?" Ms. Braveheart says.

All I can do is nod, my head moving up down up down too too fast.

"I've seen it 20 times," she says.

"'Persona'?" I say.

"'Persona,'" she says.

"It's heavy," Ms. Braveheart says. "I haven't unraveled it all."

Popcorn man is making noise, got the look of a guy who wants us to shut up.

"If we're going to talk," I say.

"Sure," she says.

I had one of those epiphanies as I walked up to her row and sat next to her, the seat on the left. I'd been thinking about how sexed-out she was since the first day of class, freckles on her face, freckles on her tits, and how smart she was, some kinda wildness, but right in the moment of that moment I got the vibe Ms. Braveheart dug me as much as I dug her, and what all that coalesced into was one heavy traffic serious question.

Was Ms. Braveheart my Visions of Johanna chick?

Her perfume has that Freak Scene Dream scent, patchouli oil maybe, although authentic real of it, I'm not sure what patchouli smells same as, and I smell weed too, in her clothes, in her skin, in her breath. She did this giggle, a stoned laugh, the kind a human does when something strikes 'em hilarious that wouldn't seem funny if they were straight. It's too warm to be wearing a wool coat so she gets her arms out of it, turns and arranges it over the back of her seat. She faces the screen, pulls at the bottom of her sweater, and in the darkness I see her nipples push against that sweater. She turns toward me, her shoulder into mine, her face so close, too close, as if her skin touches my face, that close, and super quiet, "Are you high, Michael?"

"I wish."

Her stoned smile gets bigger, her eyes wider. "I smoked,"

she says, "a whole *big joint* in my van," and her giggly stoned laugh again. "Right before I came in here," and that's when her face gets that this-is-important deal that soon I'd learn was a prelude to her announcing something she'd swear was life or death serious.

"It's a ritual," she says. "Getting high before Bergman."

She could have been talking about finding religion, how life or death serious she sounds. "You understand *so much* more."

Tripped-out wavy hair falling all 'round her head, and the smell of weed so strong.

"You *have* to see 'Persona' stoned, Michael!"

And her lips. "This summer," she says, "when I get the reels for my series we can blast a stick. Watch it at my house."

What I say to her next, well I didn't think before I said it. It's one of those things that pop out because I gotta say something or else she'll start to think something's wrong with me, you know, sitting there not saying shit.

"The University is cool?" I say. "With you getting high with your students?"

The fingers of her right hand come up to her lips, a this-is-on-the-Q.T. deal. "We better get this straight, Mr. Straight," and she's stoned-ass laughing, laughing even as she's trying to be serious.

"You and me," she says. "Here and now. In this movie theater. I'm *not* your teacher. I'm me, Susan, talking to you, Michael. Personal. *None* of The University's business."

"OK," I say. "But that film I made, that came up in your class."

"We need to talk about *that*," she says.

"That's personal too, Ms. Braveheart," I say. "None of The University's business either."

She moves her head closer, those Great Whites probing the depths of mine. "You're right," she says. "Personal. We understand each other? You dig?"

"Yeah," I say. "Oh, yeah."

Too fucking eager I say something I wish a flash of a second later I didn't say. "I'd dig it the most, seeing 'Persona' stoned at your place," but once the words are out in the universe you can't take 'em back. Well it doesn't matter, she doesn't care if I said the wrong thing. I guess 'cause she's so stoned, probably smoked *two joints* in her van before she came into the Truffaut. I've got a contact high sitting next to her. Anyway, what I'm trying to get to is right in the moment of this moment I notice something funny about the way she's looking at me. Not only looking, but getting off on looking, how a guy does when he sees a foxy chick he wants to fuck, and all a sudden, well, the words come out of her mouth almost without her even knowing what she's saying.

"I've smoked doobies with students," she says.

Man, her arm on the armrest between us, and it presses against my side, she leans over the armrest, her shoulder into mine, and her mouth hot touching my ear.

"I've *fucked* students, Michael."

Oh man oh man oh man.

I should say something, but I mean what the fuck kinda comeback can I make.

Uncharted waters, man.

"One time," she says.

She scopes out whether that's gonna fly.

"Maybe two," she says.

She's not sure she should have told me so soon.

"Not so often," she says.

On her face I see the vulnerability, her wondering if this teenage guy, me, thinks she's old. Worst thing a guy can do to a chick, think she's old. Chicks hate that. If a chick thinks a guy she digs thinks she's old, right away she doesn't feel sexy, and if a chick doesn't feel sexy, no way anything gonna happen.

Just trying to clue you in.

"Almost never," she says.

"There was a young guy," she says. "In a summer class I was teaching."

Her kissing that freshman at the Halloween party.

"I guess two, maybe three years ago," she says.

Yeah, that was a lie.

I read that guys are at their sexual peak between 18 and 22. Chicks aren't totally there 'til they turn 30. So maybe the age thing isn't so fucked up. I was almost 20, and she was 34. It was cool, you know, to have a real *woman* dig on me. Rocked my ego. She didn't look *old*. She looked like an authentic real woman chick. I remember, before the movie started I saw the wildness in her eyes and sitting there next to her, her leaning into me, all I thought about were freckles. All over her tits.

The movie starts and she gets her tortoise shell glasses from her purse. She looks so smart with those glasses on. All the chicks I really dug were smart. A lot of guys want a dumb chick, or one that isn't smart as them, but that shows you the dumbness of those guys. I have a list of reasons regards what's groovy about a smart chick, but it's after-the-fact rationalization. Authentic real, it's a mystery as to why I only go for super smart brainiac-kinda chicks.

We watch "Cries and Whispers" and it's hard to concentrate, her leanin' into me. The film is about three sisters. Two of the sisters, Karin and Maria, try to comfort the third, Agnes, who's dying of cancer. That's the thing about Bergman, who else makes a film about a chick going psycho, or one who has cancer. Great way to get something going with a chick, watch a film about a woman in tremendous emotional and physical pain who's dying.

A whole film about death.

And the parts that aren't about death are so wrong. How about that Karin chick cutting her pussy with a piece of broken glass? When that happened Ms. Braveheart grabbed my arm. Man, she got her fingers tight around it. Freaks her. Chicks are chicks, you know what I mean? Feminist or no feminist, there's times when they need a guy, regardless of whether a fish needs a bicycle.

She held my arm for the rest of the film.

When it's over we go out to the lobby and she's total shaken up deal. Being stoned how she is, I figure she's gone off on some reefer madness paranoia regards those three women.

"I'm glad you were with me," she says.

We stand there, me getting on my burgundy velveteen jacket, her getting on her dark blue pea coat, humans walking by us. Popcorn Man's at the snack bar getting a bag for the road. Me and her, it's the awkward deal for sure 'cause it's not clear what's going on. Are we splittin' the theater together or sayin' goodbye?

"Sometimes I forget," she says. "How heavy. We're *so* fucked up."

Un moment decisif.

Am I in, or out? On the inside I got the shakes. Yeah well I've learned something about timing, and I gotta act quick.

"Let me walk you to your van," I say. "Or is that all wrong?"

How her thick brown eyebrows move, the is-he-serious-or-is-he-putting-me-on deal, wondering if I mock her whole libber trip.

"Guess I fucked up," I say. "Guys aren't supposed to open doors for chicks anymore. Right?" Only I go ahead pull the door open, and hold it. "Isn't that the New Trip? A guy isn't supposed to let a chick get into the elevator first any more. Or carry her books. All those Cary Grant moves are history, right?"

Gives me her stoner grin, and walks through the doorway. I hurry after her, out into the cold. Ms. Braveheart holds her pea coat closed with one hand, and we're side-by-side and she got a hold of my arm all over again same as it's the most natural thing, her holding my arm, us walking along the sidewalk on this spring night.

"There's nothing wrong with a guy doing things for a woman he likes," she says, "and vice-versa," and gives me that look from when we sat in the theater, you know, the look a guy gives a chick he wants to fuck.

We walk, and we're in darkness, her face a shadow, the moon hidden by a huge oak, and out from under the oak, moonlight on us, her face a wash of freckles, her pale lips the total no lipstick trip. So close. Those lips, man, not larger-than-life Mick Jagger lips, but almost. Her voice the stoned laughter of her grin.

"Michael, I have an absolutely *wonderful* idea. Let's smoke a joint in my van."

There's eagerness in her voice, in her face, how her hand grips my arm too tight.

"You want to?"

Her van is an old white Chevy from the early Sixties. Someone hit the back of it on the left side a long time ago and she hasn't done shit about it. I see rust where the paint's flaked. It's parked a couple blocks from the theater, on Elm, right out front of a rundown Victorian. They're all over Santa Cruz, those down-at-the-mouth turn-of-the century houses. They have some kind of half-life, probably still be around in another hundred years.

Ms. Braveheart gets in the driver's seat, leans way over to unlock the passenger side and her pea coat comes open and I see the top part of her tits, you know, where her sweater doesn't cover, the light from a streetlamp bright on them, and there's freckles, her hand pulling the lock button up, and she sees me looking. If that funny look she gave me before was a smile, yeah that's the smile, and her head shaking back and forth a little, *you guys, you can't help yourselves can you?*

The van's fixed up Freak Scene Dream style, a beaded curtain behind the front seats and the small God's eye hangs from the mirror, there to watch out for her, keep an eye on where she's headed.

Sitting in the passenger seat I say, "I don't have any weed on me."

The seats have knitted orange and brown seat covers. Through the holes in the knitting I see cracks in the vinyl. She has the ashtray pulled out, and in the little metal deal that's there to get ash off the end of your cigarette she's stuck a long incense stick.

"My stash is up at The University," I say. "Wanna drive up

there?"

She digs a motherfucker of a number from her purse, sits up straight and fucking *wow!* Ms. Braveheart's got that ragamuffin princess look, her wavy hair all crazy-wild and her face pale in the darkness, yeah it's that ragamuffin princess look Sarah had the day of her first abortion, only Ms. Braveheart is a ragamuffin *queen*. She's Sarah if Sarah were 14 years older, how Sarah might be when she grows up into a beautiful woman chick. She's Sarah if the self-confidence my gaze brought to Sarah that day at the meditation place had truly become her own, and she'd grown and blossomed and lived and loved. Only this isn't some grown up version of Sarah, this is a whole other chick, this is Ms. Braveheart, ready to share a number with me.

"Homegrown," she says, and holds that joint up to her nose and inhales, and her face beatific in the darkness of the van. "The best."

There's a small black and white photo of Gandhi taped to the dashboard, and next to it a photo of a woman. Gotta be one of those feminist chicks. Gloria Steinem maybe, or Kate Millett, a feminist rock star kinda chick.

"It's a spiritual trip," she says.

I figure that bald skin-and-bones saint of non-violence is her guru.

"Holy sacrament," she says. "Getting high isn't the point. It's one of the tools."

She's looking at me to make sure I understand. "To enlightenment."

"Where do you get it?" I say.

"It's a long journey," she says. "Most never get there."

"I mean the homegrown."

"Oh, in my back yard," she says. "I've found enlightenment there too."

"You grow pot?"

"The female spirit grows it," she says. "It's her earth. Her sun. Her seeds. We're her humble servants."

"There are pot plants in your back yard?"

She looks at me strange, her face tightens, as if for a flash of a moment she's got on a mask of suspicion.

"You a narc?"

"Me? You're kidding. Right?"

"Well are you?" she says, the mask gone, and she's laughing again, that crazy stoner laugh.

"I get paranoid," she says. "When I smoke a lot," and she holds the number out. I spark The Dylan, the blue-orange flame rising and she leans into it and I smell her sweaty chick smell, and the patchouli or whatever it is, and the weed and I see her freckles, man, top of her tits, and I got the wet end in my mouth, the end been in her mouth.

"Don't bogart," she says, and she's giggling and it's funny, she's giggling a high silly giggle. "I'm the one who gets to do that," and she sings, and that was the first time I heard her dark soprano.

Don't bogart that joint, my friend, pass it over to me.

After a couple tokes I remember why this is a mistake. The pigs cruise the downtown scene looking for dopers and burnouts and dealers. Pretty much anyone who even vaguely has some Freak Scene Dream vibe, they stop for questioning. Sometimes, if it's a guy, the questioning gets rough. The pigs cruising downtown are motherfuckers.

"This is a bad idea," I say, only I say it as if I don't care about the bad idea 'cause already I'm slipping into that mellow groove. Every stoner knows it. Everything rigid and tense and uptight begins to melt. That's how you know you're stoned, 'cause the normal reaction—coming to the realization that smoking a joint in front of the whole world makes us sitting ducks for a bust—would be total freak-out city.

"If a cop sees us we're toast," I say. "You'd lose your job," and I'm laughing the same stoner laugh she laughed when I first met her in the Truffaut, and she's laughing too, and I don't know why we're laughing and I bet she doesn't either.

"You're so right. We gotta split," she says, and we're both laughing the stoner laugh. The idea of us getting busted for dope is the most hilarious thing either of us have thought about for same as forever. She leans towards me, puts the index and middle fingers of her right hand to her lips.

"I have an absolutely *wonderful* idea," she says, stubbing out the joint.

"I hope it's better than your last one," I say, my voice quiet as hers.

"I've got to drive in to the University tomorrow," she says. "My class. Come back to my place. We can smoke the homegrown there, I'll cook us something good and we can have a groovy talk."

It's a damn good pickup line. Especially coming from a chick. Especially coming from a feminist teacher chick I wanna fuck.

4. LIKE A FISH NEEDS A BICYCLE

SOON AS WE GET tearing down Highway 1 she's ready to fly Mexican Airlines.

"Light my fire," she says.

And I can tell, nothing I say is gonna convince her otherwise.

That joint in her hand, the silent drum beat of impatience, waiting for my flame.

We pass the industrial park to the left, shoot past that squat rectangular Lavender Club building, no sign to hype it, you gotta know the Lavender Club's there, and it's gone. Her headlights on the highway following the endless white line, and the blur of the shadow trees bordering the road. What an adrenalin rush, man, the thrill of riding with her knowing it's gonna be us two totally stoner trip at her place.

It's grainy black and white, her sitting there in the splattered flashes of moonlight. Her face pale white when the light hits, all in shadow when it doesn't. Her hair covers most of her face, and when she looks forward the way she is, what I see: a little of her mouth, the tip of her tongue between her lips, nose angling out, an eye, a brow, a lash.

Reefer smoke fills the van, and the contact high tingle as she smokes it, before I get a taste. When it's between my lips, my mouth full of the reefer madness, inside me the Flying Burrito Brothers play Merle Haggard's "White Line Fever," and the line about the years goin' by like a *high line pole*, and I'll be 20 in three months and when is all this searching for my Visions of Johanna chick gonna end?

How many more times? How many more years?

In place of "White Line Fever" I hear "How Many More Years," Howlin' Wolf's 1951 recording for Sam Phillips at Sun Studios. Wolf's first single and his first hit. Yeah I've learned plenty about Howlin' Wolf since that day at Odyssey Records, you know, the day Odyssey's owner Lucky Larry hipped me to Wolf and his guitarist, Hubert Sumlin. Know pretty much everything there is to know about him. That 78-RPM gasoline-soaked voice sounds as if he sang through a megaphone above the whorehouse boogie-woogie and the barbwire guitar—Willie Johnson playing, *not* Hubert Sumlin 'cause Sumlin wasn't hooked up with Wolf when that record was cut. Rips a gash in my heart, that song.

How many more years, have I got to let you dog me around?

Ms. Braveheart's driving 65, all lit up from the reefer, one hand on the wheel, the number in the other, her hand turned so the end you suck on is towards me, and in the dark the other end glows hot bright, smoke drifting up hazy lit by the moonlight. Her hand, the hand holding out the joint, it's an older chick hand, not a perfect Freak Scene Dream chick hand, not perfect how Sarah's 15-, 16-, 17-year-old hands were, how Elise's 18-year-old artist hands were.

Yeah I see the veins in the back of her hand, her nails chewed off, her fingers rough from too much time in her garden under that hot California sun, and the van's shaking 'cause she's driving too fast.

"I've never known anyone," I say, "who did the grow-your-own."

I stretch my legs out as much as I can under the dash, and on the glove compartment door she has a purple bumper sticker, *WOMAN POWER* spelled out in white letters, and that women's lib symbol same as the one on Sappho's pack—the fist, the circle and the cross descending—and God-who-pretty-much-for-sure-don't-exist only knows what that feminist teacher chick has in her glove compartment.

What I imagine's in there: A baggie and papers and matches. A mother-of-pearl-handled pistol. Probably keeps her birth control pills in her purse, this huge carpetbagger bag. An extra lipstick. No, she doesn't wear lipstick. Maybe for special occasions. One of those feminist texts in case she needs to brush up on some libber theory. Extra pair of shades. Tampax —one of those six-tampon boxes. First-aid kit. Suntan lotion. Pair of panties—just in case.

Fuck, I wanna open it and take a look.

"This truck is riding my ass," she says, and I angle my head, try to see it in the side mirror but can't get in the right position and in the moment of that moment a black pickup pulls up on her left, honking and one of the guys in the cab gives her the finger and screams something, and the truck shoots ahead.

"What the fuck," I say.

"There are plenty of sexist pigs out here," she says. "They don't care for my bumper sticker."

You know, the one that says *a woman needs a man like a fish needs a bicycle.*

"A lot of guys might take that the wrong way," I say.

"I don't think there is a wrong way to take it," she says.

Fuck, she doesn't need a man, *any* man, that's what she's telling me, and Howlin' Wolf still sings inside me about how he'd rather be dead, *sleeping six feet in the ground,* than put up with any more years of his chick dogging him around. Amazing a freakster bro and a chick can even have a conversation.

Weird, her picking me up. Weird how she's the third chick. Harper, Jaded, and now Ms. Braveheart. Wasn't that way with Sarah or Elise, but maybe some chicks let you *think* you're taking charge. They've made the decision but want you to think it's your idea. One of those flash deals in my brain right in the moment of that moment. *This* is the New Trip, *this* is what the feminist trip is authentic real about. Chicks taking what they want and being public about it, instead of keeping it a secret. *Her mouth almost touching my ear. "I've fucked students."*

In the van, she has a hand in her purse but she's not finding what she wants.

"Michael, do me a favor," she says. "I've got another pack of Kools in here somewhere."

Her carpetbagger bag. She has all kinds of shit in there. A fat wallet. Hairbrush. Unopened Hershey's with almonds. Red wool knit cap. Well-read copy of Marge Piercy's "Small Changes." Two packs of Kools. One has one smoke left, the other isn't open.

And the knife. A big-ass bowie knife. I figure it's for protection, in case some creep attacks her or some such. Still, freaked me, man.

At least it wasn't a pearl-handled pistol.

Well what happened next was she starts talking about some feminist chick friend of hers named Loraine. All her friends were either feminist chicks or guys she'd fucked. Pretty weird how she couldn't ever only be friends with a guy, as if she had a compulsion to leave her mark.

"Her last name's Weinman," she says. "And yours is Stein. Funny."

I'm trying to figure out what's funny.

Weinman. Stein.

Stein. Weinman.

Nothing about the names is funny. Everything is fucking funny-ass funny with my head sponging from the weed, but those two names, nada.

"We both have Jewish names," I say. "Is that what's funny? You think Jew names are a big joke?"

Ms. Braveheart might be a Hindu now, but she probably grew up Catholic. Those nuns teaching her Jews were the scum of the earth. Neurotic money-grubbing horny-ass wolves desperate to get their dicks into a young, virgin Catholic school chick. That's why she wants to fuck me. I'm the dirtiest fuck she can get. Catholic chick fucking a dirty circumcised Jewboy.

Probably she could come just thinking about it.

"No, it's that you both have 'ein,'" she says. "Oh forget it," and she's embarrassed, first time she blushes. "Sorry."

I start the White Wall Zen Meditation deal to unwind my anger. I see it same as the scales on a snake, and as I count to ten those scales drift up through the van's roof.

"I hate the Jewish religion," I say. "All organized religion. They all suck."

There's a road sign she's coming up on fast, and she says, "It always makes me worry about the big one."

"The Holocaust?" I say.

"The earthquake," she says. "California sliding into the Pacific."

That road sign says we're a mile and a half from San Andreas Road, three miles from Mar Monte Avenue and four from Rancho Road.

"My exit," she says. "The earthquake exit. San Andreas."

My eyes still on her, and I'm still pissed.

"That 'joke,'" I say, and I stub out my cigarette hard in the ashtray. "Jews are sensitive to that shit."

The moonlight on her neck, lighting her chest and that V-neck sweater grey in the semi-darkness, her nipples hard against the sweater.

"And feminists are sensitive to other kinds of shit, Michael," she says. "Words like 'chick' and 'babe' and 'cunt.'"

"What do feminists want a guy to say?" I say. "'Vagina'? Make me sound like a white-haired librarian. Nothing sexy about 'vagina.'"

"You boys," she says. "All you think about is sex."

Ms. Braveheart drives maybe three miles along San Andreas, this two-laner that parallels Highway 1, and it's darker on San Andreas, we're the only car on that road, corn fields whizzing by and artichoke fields and strawberry fields, lettuce fields, spinach fields. At Poppy Lane she takes a hard right and we're on a bump-ass dirt road and she drives maybe another half mile and way out in front of us a sea of black, moonlight glittering off the Forever Infinite Pacific and I feel the hugeness of it.

She turns and we're bumping along Morning Glory Way, a half mile and the road veers to the left but straight ahead her gate and her yard and in the yard, to the right, a house, a one-story deal and that's her house. First time I see the house, can't see much of it in the dark, only the front door, a single French door, eight small panes of glass, the wood around them painted bright yellow and a little of the front porch lit by the porch light.

Lucky barking and Ms. Braveheart stops the van in front of the gate, motor running. She walks to where the gate's latched. "Hi Lucky," she says. "Hi sweetie," unlatches the wood gate, swings it into her yard, tells Lucky to sit, pats her head, *good girl,* and she turns around, stands there in the moonlight. Oh man, she was a crazy-wild ragamuffin Freak Scene Dream queen standing at the entrance to her yard, all of her bright from the sun that was off hidden somewhere, its light reflecting off the moon right down on her, the black-velvet-and-diamonds-a-glitter ocean out there, star dusted sky above her, the wind throwing her crazy-wild hair across her face and her hands pulling it back, nipples hard against the sweater, the dark pea coat hanging around her. Yeah she was something else.

My Visions of Johanna chick standing in the moonlight.

Yeah, she was the one.

We walk the dirt path to the wood stairs, four steps, the paint about gone, the faded grey of exposed redwood beat to shit by rain and sun, rising up to the porch and that needs some deck paint for sure. That was one thing about Freak Scene Dream freaks, even crazy-wild beautiful ragamuffin Freak Scene Dream chicks, they never got around to taking care of the nuts-and-bolts basics, too much heady intellectual shit to ponder. You know, whether or not to smoke another doobie.

Lucky jumps up and Ms. Braveheart stops, rubs her head. Top of the stairs, and she stops at the front door, all that glass, the porch light making the yellow paint glow, and a mat that says "¡Bienvenidas, Camaradas!" I don't speak Spanish so I don't know what the fuck that means. There oughta be subtitles in real life. So if a chick said *je veux sucer votre bite*, there'd be a subtitle so you'd know she was saying she wants to blow you. Or that mat, there'd be a subtitle, "Welcome, Comrades!"

While she finds her key I walk onto the porch. The roof comes out over it and there's a maybe four-foot-high railing so you can't fall off into the yard. There's an old couch over there facing the Forever Infinite Pacific. I called it the Sugar Mountain couch. Later. When the time is right I'll fill you in on that scene. On a groovy day you could sit out there, smoke a number, contemplate the cosmos.

I stand facing west, wet air on my skin, a half moon hovering and the light on the water eerie and beautiful. I see the ripples, and the reflected light moving with the waves and hear the silence of humans and loudness of the ocean, and that's the first time I hear the spooky choir and the thousand murmurs in that ocean sound, and the crickets and the frogs and this overwhelming silence of all-things-made-by-humans, of all that is human, and I never heard it same as that before, not even camping with Sarah.

Ms. Braveheart's voice is soft. "My house," she says. "It's a shoe-free zone."

One of her rules.

"It's a Zen trip," she says.

"I thought you were a Hindu," I say. "That picture of Gandhi —."

"I'm a pacifist," she says. "I'm conscious of everything I do."

Another rule. Or a hint. Bringing me home wasn't as spontaneous as maybe I thought. Her wanting to fire it up, right in her van, parked on that Santa Cruz street where any cop could have seen us. Maybe she means she *tries* to be conscious. Always a gap between what you think you're doing and what you're really doing.

I join her in front of the door. Her cats are crying, making the sounds that cats make when they want something. She takes my arm to keep her balance and with her free hand gets her boots off. It's my turn, get my Keith Richards snakeskin boots off, stand 'em to the right of the door. She places hers next to mine so they touch—those two pairs of boots, side by side, my rock star boots and her soft brown suede Freak Scene Dream chick boots, and it's sexy, those boots right together the way they are. Touching.

She's having trouble unlocking the front door. Maybe it's the weed. *Elise too blitzed to get the key in the lock.* What is it with these chicks who can't open their doors?

"Let me have a go at it."

The key on her palm, and my palm against her palm. Warm skin, cold metal. I take the key. It's silver colored. I don't have trouble unlocking the door. First time I open Ms. Braveheart's door, and oh man, I'm floating sky high and it's not only the weed, it's the anticipation, about to enter a chick's house, a chick who's brought me home, a chick who's told me she's fucked some of her freakster bro students.

Inside she drops her carpetbagger bag, six, seven cats rubbing up against her legs, meowing, making it known they need something, and they need it *now.* She takes off the pea coat, lets it fall on the rug, moving fast, turns on some lights, turns up the thermostat and she's in the kitchen, her tortoise frame glasses clicking on the counter, and she spins around, her arms out, taking in the whole place.

"It's all mine," she says. "Paid in full. A place of my own."

It's kinda same as a cabin, Ms. Braveheart's house. The front door opens right into the living room. Really, it's a living room/ kitchen, and not that big. The small kitchen is against the back wall, and there's a partition separating it from the rest of the room. On top of the partition—a cabinet made of polished light brown Swedish wood—are a ceramic bowl, an African carved zebra, and a 3-D collage of naked chicks doing each other on a zebra skin bed. If a guy had that thing, it'd be sexist, right? Does it make a difference 'cause the owner of it is a chick? But that doesn't make sense. I mean if a chick is objectifying other chicks, that oughta be as sexist as if a guy does it?

I was gonna have to ask her. But this wasn't the time.

I join her in the kitchen, check out the scene, all these cats rubbing up against her legs, her legs in those faded denim jeans.

"Hi Victoria," she says. "Hi Emma, hi Betty, hi Kate, hi Marge, hi Gloria, hi Gertrude, hi Alice."

Ms. Braveheart really did have eight cats. I like cats. But *eight* fucking cats? She'd gone directly to the movie from The University so the cats think they're starving to death, that's why they're rubbing up against her legs, and my legs too, meowing. Sounds same as a cat doo-wop vocal group gone crazy, only none of them in tune with the others. They've all studied with Cecil Taylor.

I'm no fool. No way I'm gonna let her think I'm a sexist pig asshole who expects the chick to serve me. Tonight I'm Mr. Feminist, man.

"What can I do?" I say.

"There's a bag of cat food in that cabinet," she says. "Below the counter, left of the sink. Their bowls are in The Lab."

The Lab. It's the back room of the house. I step through a doorway at the rear left of the kitchen, flip the light switch.

What I don't see at first:

Two immense handmade cat trees. Four empty bowls for cat food. Three big bowls partially filled with water. The wall to the right as you step into the room, parallel with the right edge of the doorway from the kitchen, has a door with a cat door that opens on the backyard garden.

What I do see:

The homegrown. Ten huge-ass marijuana plants, each six feet tall, maybe seven, hanging upside down. Drying. Right the fuck there in Ms. Braveheart's house. Cats are rubbing against me, and that's when everything else starts to come into focus and I pour the dry food into the bowls, and they're eating before I finish pouring, crowding each other. Only I don't care about the cat food. *Ten fucking huge-ass marijuana plants.* Gotta be a year's worth of weed.

I walk into her kitchen and inside me I'm hearing that Skippy James song, only it's The Charlatans' version, the one Lynn Hughes sang back in the mid-Sixties, sang it the way an old-timey blues singer woulda sung it, you know, Blue Lu Barker or Memphis Minnie or the great Geeshie Wiley.

I'd have to be the Devil, to satisfy my man.

And maybe that's the problem, maybe there's a part of us guys that need a chick who can free us from all our inhibitions, bring us to an ecstasy of freedom from guilt and shame, from regretting the past and worrying the future. Yeah that's what I need, a chick who's a doorway to the ecstatic.

That "Devil Got My Woman" song reminds me of the kitchen songs. Robert Johnson's "Come On in My Kitchen," which was actually Johnson's rewrite of "Devil Got My Woman," and The Doors' "Soul Kitchen." Those songs aren't really about any kitchen. They're about fucking. The kitchen a metaphor for the chick's bedroom. Or maybe her pussy. Her *vagina.*

Just tryin' to clue you in.

"The Lab is fucking happening," I say.

Ms. Braveheart's frying a tortilla, first one side, then the other, gets it real crispy, gets it onto a paper towel, gets another tortilla, does the whole deal again.

"Gonna have to turn you in," I say.

Her eyes go wide and her mouth opens for a flash before she knows I'm fucking with her. A *what-can-you-do-with these-kids* shake of her head. She's breaking those fried tortillas into pieces in a bowl.

"The *best* munchie food," she says, and yeah, I've got the munchies.

She crushes an avocado in a bowl, stirring in sour cream and salsa and lime juice and we stand in her kitchen, dip pieces of tortilla into the guacamole. Normally, I wouldn't touch sour cream, not after what Sappho said about it, Sappho the health nut, Sappho who cares about animals the way most people care

about people, but there with Ms. Braveheart I'm not rocking
any boats, not on this night. So we stand there eating and
looking at each other. None of the formality of having to make
conversation when all we wanna do in this moment is eat.

She puts a bottle of spaghetti sauce on the counter, fills a
pot with water and her stoned giggle.

"Spaghetti," she says. "You like?"

She's standing there, flyin' high, big isn't-life-the-best smile,
digs being in her own house, munching on chips she cooked up
herself, all her cats eating, and having me there. Right then I'm
not thinking about how much I wanna fuck her 'cause her
asking if I dig spaghetti takes me on a whole new mind-trek. I
dig it so much, her caring if I dig what she's gonna make for us
to eat, and in that moment I imagine me and her married, and
that's weird 'cause other than when Sarah brought it up, I never
thought about marriage. Why not just live with a chick? Seems
silly, but her asking if I like spaghetti makes me feel all lovey-
dovey and sentimental nostalgic for some Fifties trip where
everything is prescribed: the guy does this and the chick does
that, you don't have to figure out if the chick is straight or bi or
a dyke, and if you're married to them, of course you can fuck
them, and they cook your meals, you know, the whole deal.

Lasts about a second, and I don't believe it, and actually I
hate it 'cause it's bullshit. But still. Where the fuck did that come
from, and there are levels of me I don't have a clue about.

Yeah, that's for sure.

She flips on the backyard light and through the kitchen window
we can see her vegetable garden. She tells me she's got three
types of lettuce—butter and red leaf and endive—and Little
Finger carrots and rainbow chard and red radishes and hot red
cherry peppers and red and yellow onions and Blue Lake green
beans and heirloom tomatoes and a bunch of spices and there's
a Gravenstein apple tree. To the left of the vegetables, there's an
old plastic orange chaise lounge and she tells me that's where
she sunbathes *in the nude*.

Oh man oh man oh man.

She picks up a basket off the counter and she's singing, *"Come dance with me in the moonlight,"* sings those words to some jazzy tune—Van Morrison by way of Joni. Her left hand against my back, moves her palm onto my shoulder blades and her fingers on the back of my neck, her hand so warm, and her fingers up through my hair, and I've never been touched how this teacher chick touches me.

"Your hair is soft," she says, and she's got some in her hand, rubs it against her face. She steps past me, brushing her arm against me and I follow her through the doorway into The Lab, and through the side door out to the garden, the air cold and damp from the ocean. I wish I had my coat but she's in her purple V-neck sweater and jeans and no way I wanna be a pussy about it.

Pointing to the far side of the garden, to the second of two large raised beds, she says, "Tomatoes," and I can see a tangle of green vines and support wire, some of the plants bent from the weight. She leans over the first raised bed and I see the curve of her ass and I wish right then she wasn't wearing baggy jeans. I want to see her bare ass and her bare legs, and I know they're strong and lean, and her bare back, the pale skin of her back, I want to see all that, and her freckled tits and her pussy and the soft brown curly hair around her pussy and her smooth belly and all the rest. I flash all of that in my mind and more, us two on the ground doin' it.

Her basket is on the hard dirt. She's pulling out carrots, brushing dirt off, her hands dirty, putting the small plump carrots in the basket. I find two righteous tomatoes, perfect, put them in the basket. Right side-by-side, both bent over, we pull leaves off the lettuce plants until we get enough.

She leaps up and she's between me and the door back into the house, facing me, her hair backlit by the outside light, hands on her hips, black sky freckled with stars above us.

"I love it out here," she says. "It's so alive. *I* feel so alive."

And her arms around me and we're spinning 'round and there's nothing tentative in the way she holds me. Yeah, a real grown up woman chick who knows her way around a guy, how a guy and a chick fit together, so much she knows, between her teenage boyfriends and her ex-husband and all the other guys she's had, all the guys she kissed and fucked and sucked, every way a guy and a chick can do it, she's done it. Her lips against mine, her tongue darting against the inside of my lips, her hair falling crazy-wild in my eyes, against my face, on my shoulders and somehow we're still spinning. I'm faint, my eyes shut tight, can't breathe, can breathe, force my eyes open, her skin blurry close, one hand on her ass through her jeans, the other against her lower back, feeling each other, holding tight in the spinning and we fall apart and she says, "So alive out here," and looks up at that half moon. "Like I never felt anywhere else I lived. This is heaven."

We were back in the kitchen, her making the spaghetti, me making a salad when her mood shifted, and I can hear the spooky choir, the thousand murmurs, and she started talking about the fuck-me photos she'd seen at X Marks the Spot over a year previous.

"Photographs of beautiful girls," she says, and I know where this is going. Trouble, man. She's got a brush for getting the dirt off carrots, and she doesn't want me to peel them, says it's healthy eating them skin and all.

"I want to shoot musicians again," I say. "But photography takes so much time. 'Course so does writing," and it was weird, her talking about seeing my photos a year ago, and here we're hanging out together, as if in some strange way those photos drew her to me.

"What about the *chicks*?" she says.

I'm silent, 'cause I mean what the hell does she want from me?

She's stirring the sauce but now she sets the wood spoon on the counter, well "sets" doesn't convey it at all. It was as if she'd hit the counter—one of those old pink Formica counter tops with strange little sci-fi lines in it—hard, real hard, and she's giving me a hard look.

"The way you photographed them," she says. "As if they were objects of desire, not flesh and blood humans with brains and feelings. I made a point of checking out who took them, and I wrote the name down. *Michael Stein.*"

"You could get the wrong idea I guess," I say. "But yeah, I dig photographing chicks."

"*Women*, Michael."

"OK, sure," I say. *"Women."*

After all that stoned laughter, and her kissing me out in her garden, man, can't never figure out a chick.

"Why do you use a word that means little baby birds," she says, "when you talk about adult women? Is that what you think we are? Little baby birds for you to take care of? To get off on? For you to fuck?"

I get this humongous red onion from the fridge, slice a section off, separate the strips, cut them into little pieces, add them to the bowl.

"It's just a word," I say. "No big deal. Chicks, freakster bros, you know. No disrespect. Just the slang deal."

"So you don't have a problem calling a Black man 'nigger'? Just a word, right? Is that the *slang deal* too?"

Her Great Whites watch me dig the hole deeper.

"That's racist," I say. "Of course I have a problem with racist shit."

Yeah she's pissed. "You have a problem calling a Black man 'nigger,'" she says. "But not calling a woman 'chick.' How about 'cunt'? You have a problem calling a woman 'cunt'?"

"The pasta," I say.

"Damn," and she pulls the pot off the burner, gets a strand of spaghetti on a fork and tastes it.

"A little overcooked, but it'll do."

She's not looking at me, gets herself busy rinsing the spaghetti, pouring the sauce on it, mixing it all up. A fog of libber chill fills the kitchen.

"Ms. Braveheart," I say. "I'm sorry. I didn't mean to offend you."

Her face the serious deal, but at least she's looking my way.

"It's the words I'm used to," I say. "It's no big statement. I love chicks, I mean *women*. Got great respect. I don't mean it as a putdown."

And the vibe lightens, doesn't seem she wants to fuck things up between us before anything much has happened.

"The language we use has consequences, Michael," she says. "You use a word that means a baby chicken to describe a woman, it infantilizes her," and she laughs her stoned grin of a laugh. "I've got a lot to teach you."

One beat, and another.

"And it's Susan, please call me Susan."

We smoked another number, I guess to mellow out from the argument, only she was back at it, you know, regards the photos.

"So about these young women," she says. "How do you decide which *chick* to photograph."

"It's an aesthetic decision," I say. "When I was really into it, I photographed chicks, oops, I mean women, women who appealed to me."

Man, she's bogarting that doobie for sure, smoking it same as a cigarette.

"Susan, this was over a year ago," I say. "When I was a freshman. It was a way to meet some girls, I mean women."

"You mean chicks you want to fuck," she says.

"Yeah, sometimes."

"That's the criteria for your art?"

"I'm no different than Picasso," I say. "Only he always scored and mostly I didn't. Fernande Olivier, Olga Khokhlova, Marie-Thérèse Walter, Dora Maar. He fucked them all."

"Picasso!" she says. "He's your model? You emulate Frank Sinatra too?"

Fucking bummerosity, man. "That's so *straight*," she says. "And *sexist*. Can't you see how your approach to art supports the patriarchal society? Women as sex objects. It doesn't get any more literal than fuck-me photos of women you want to fuck. Wow."

"I wanted to make photographs," I say. "It's not about

patriarchal anything."

"Of course it is, that's *exactly* what it is," she says. "Being unconscious doesn't change what's really happening, *Mr. Jones.* Have you read any feminist theory?"

Yeah I've got that deer-in-the-headlights look going.

"Of course you haven't," she says. "You *must* read Kate Millet. Photographers have done terrible damage. All the images objectifying women that we see every day, and you want to be one of the gang. The sexist pig photographer gang."

"I'm no different than Bergman," I say. "In every film of his the women are total foxes. Bibi Andersson, Harriet Andersson, Ingrid Thulin, Liv Ullmann. And he fucked at least three of those chicks. *Women*, I mean."

"Bergman's an exception," she says, "to every rule. He's a genius."

"But he's a sexist pig too?" I say. "Right?"

We moved into the living room, brought in plates of spaghetti and a bottle of merlot and two glasses, sat cross-legged at this low wood wire spool table same as the one at The Pad, where these rock critics I used to be friends with lived, only this spool been stained and varnished and it has a thick round piece of glass on top. I poured us some wine, hoping she'd move on, leave the feminist rap for another day. We were across from each other and I was in trouble again, the vibe cold, and I figured I'd blown it, and she wasn't gonna wanna fuck.

Well I wanna fuck her, and I'm in beggar mode, and isn't that how it always is. Even the first time with Harper. Oh to be one of those guys who are in control. Who get the chicks to do what *they* want. Me being in beggar mode is how I come to say what I say next.

"I don't want to be sexist," I say. "Talking to you about this is opening my eyes to how *unconscious* I've been."

She gets that stoned look again, I'm feelin' it too— everything soft focus from the weed and the merlot we're drinking.

"So which chicks did you fuck?" she says, and when she said

it, first I don't get it, but then I know. She's still on about the chicks in my photos.

"Come on," she says. "You can tell me."

Already my glass near empty.

"I bet it was the one with the big tits," she says. "*I'd* fuck her."

 "I wanted them all," I say. "I had a crush on each one. Not at the same time, but when I took the photo I was totally wanting the chick."

Fuck.

"I mean woman."

"I think you mean chick," she says, and her stoner grin of a laugh. "Probably mean cunt."

"You don't get it," I say. "I wanted a girlfriend, not a one-night stand."

"Funny," she says. "Usually what I want is a one-night stand."

I guess I must have had some kinda disappointment goin' on my face, 'cause real quick-like she says, "But sometimes it turns into something more."

She didn't ask me any more about the chicks. We finished eating, drained our glasses and she refilled them, the wine softening everything. She lights a red candle there on the wood spool table, turns out the kitchen light, back with another bottle and the corkscrew, and it feels as if we're in some opium den, me and her sitting on this worn-to-shit Indian rug, the candle flickering shadows on the turquoise ceiling.

She said she wanted to dance upside down on the ceiling, and more, said she wanted to rise right up through the roof, up, up, up into the stratosphere and feel the stars beneath her feet.

"You're the rock critic," she says, "I want to hear moonbeams and blood red comets and all the glittery sounds."

Yeah, me, the *rock critic*.

She had a component stereo system, something one of her ex-boyfriends helped her buy. Set it up there in the living room. I remember a Garrard turntable and a tuner/amp combo and some kinda speakers. It was a pretty good system, I mean you could turn it up fucking loud and it sounded great.

She had all of Joni's albums and Bonnie Raitt's *Give It Up*, and Carole King's *Tapestry*, and probably 30 more. But what I put on was the Stones. Of course I did.

I mean is there any music sexy as the Stones? In 1973? I mean is there?

Sticky Fingers.

Those first harsh chords of "Brown Sugar," man, a shot of adrenalin and a snort of coke and before I can close the turntable's clear plastic cover Ms. Braveheart is on her feet twisting and turning, loose and wild and free.

I mean she was doing her version of the hippy hippy shake, total uninhibited scene.

Oh man oh man oh man.

I got the music so loud, shake the windows loud, and she says something but I can't hear her.

"What?" I yell.

Yeah we gotta shout to be heard.

"I can't help myself," she says. "I'm *addicted.*"

"To the homegrown?"

She floats towards me, feet, legs, ass, tits, arms, hands, neck, mouth, head and those Great Whites—all of her slipping and sliding through the air, slipping and sliding in sync to that Stones groove, slipping and sliding right up to me gets her mouth on my ear.

Her lips hot, and her breath, the heat.

"No, silly, to this sexist pig rock band. But I swear I'm getting rid of all my Stones records. I'll do it tomorrow. Gotta bite the bullet. Can't have this sexist shit in my house."

Un moment decisif of a different sort. A moment of clarity and revelation.

'Cause here I been digging on the Stones since "Satisfaction," since grade school, and I never thought anything about sexism. I mean until I started hanging with Sappho I'd never heard of sexism.

Only soon as she says it I get it. I mean *of course*. And how blind we are, walking around with blinders on, seeing what we want to see, and denying everything. All those songs. "Stupid Girl" and "Stray Cat Blues" and "Factory Girl" and "Midnight Rambler" and all the rest.

And this very song! Mick singing about a slave owner whipping his black women at midnight, singing about how she tastes so good. *Brown Sugar!* And yet you gotta listen, and more than listen, you gotta dance, and more than dance, makes you wanna to get naked and fuck.

And what kinda song is this?

She floats away, so loose and free, and despite the rug she's dancing serious, I mean Ms. Braveheart knows how to do the Freak Scene Dream dance, she coulda been one of those chicks I used to watch at the free concerts in Speedway Meadows and the Polo Field, back in 1968 when I was 15.

Blitzed from weed and wine and we dance and dance, and when "Wild Horses" starts up she's in my arms, and we slow dance, and this is a whole other deal than when me and Elise slow danced, I mean through her jeans she's pushing her pussy right up against my dick, moving her chest against my chest, her head on my shoulder, her hair falling around me, a hand on my ass, pulling me against her.

We dance through the whole first side and then she's had enough, back sitting at the wire spool table and another glass of merlot, and why not?

"Come sit next to me, Michael."

Don't mind if I do.

We sit with our knees touching and she raises a toast to our first night together.

Oh fuck, 'cause this is it. Gotta be.

Well that's when she starts talking about the rules. *Her* rules. Her rule regards not dating her students. Her rule about not doing dope with her students. Her rule about not fucking her students. Only she already told me about how she fucked students. And we've been smoking dope for hours. And I mean if this isn't a date, what the fuck is it? The disconnect is so weird-ass weird, her saying that and her looking at me, stoner-ass stoned.

I guess she meant rules were meant to be broken.

Next she talked about the jealousy deal and no strings and not being possessive—all of it. She wants me to understand that *if* we fuck there's no commitment, might be a wham-bam-thank-you-man deal. I try to play it cool, not make it obvious how much I'm in beggar mode, Ms. Braveheart talking the theoretical regards me and her fucking, and how am I supposed to deal with that? How could any freakster bro deal with that?

"I want hear about your stalker movie," she says.

"It wasn't a 'stalker' flick," I say, and she has another drink of merlot and some of it drips from her glass down her chin and onto her sweater. She looks down at the stain but she's too fucked-up to do something about it. She got a Kool out and I got The Dylan, yeah this is becoming a regular deal, me lighting joints and cigarettes for this feminist teacher chick. And how would that fly down at Libber Central.

Her stoner eyes zero in on me.

"Tell me everything, Michael."

You know how some people have the knack. Look at you in a way makes you trust them, and more, makes you feel if only you confide in them, all the heavy shit that's weighing down on you will lift. That's how it was with Ms. Braveheart that night.

"There was this chick," I say. "I mean she's a college girl. Oh fuck, a young woman, oh that's not right. She's 18, a *freshman*, you understand? Fuck, I was in love with her."

I told Ms. Braveheart how I wanted the film to express my feelings about Elise, and how when she saw the film I hoped she'd understand, and it would help me and her resolve problems we were having. Only before I could finish the film, I say, everything went wrong. I didn't say Elise's name, no reason for Ms. Braveheart to know.

Oh man, *Elise's face, flickering on my dorm room wall, the beautiful sadness, the projector whirring and clicking.*

And as I sit there, my knee against hers, well that's when *I* broke open, 'cause the beautiful sadness was too much. Absolute total hopeless. The blackness everywhere, and the crushed souls. I'd lost Elise, my Visions of Johanna chick. And gone with her the promise of escaping the insufferable claustrophobic of my obsessive ego. A chick, man, the doorway through which I could free myself from me, at least for an orgasmic moment, and experience the Forever Infinite Ecstatic.

Yeah well the doorway been walled over, and I been sentenced to a life of no escape. Knowing I'd lost Elise forever, and flashing on what that truly meant, well it was too much. There, in front of Ms. Braveheart, I was crying, and I mean I never cry. Got no control, and I'm so fucked-up.

Ms. Braveheart's face softens, and seeing me so vulnerable before her Great Whites, I guess all that touches her, but it's not only compassion. No man, there's an erotic tension. I'm pure of heart, and I still believe in true love, and my innocence and my tears are turning Ms. Braveheart on. You know how some guys get horny at the idea of fucking a virgin, yeah well this is kinda same as that. I mean even though she's not a guy, and I'm no virgin.

"It's alright, Michael," she says. "I'm so sorry for what you've been through. Come lie on the couch. You're safe here with me."

5. THE ENLIGHTENED BOY

I TELL HER I gotta take a piss, and it's true but it's also an excuse. I need to pull myself together, get the tears off my face, clear my head of Elise. As I stand she gets all spread out on the couch, gets her head on one of those big couch pillows, smoking her Kool. The waves crash, the deck rocks, almost lose my balance, wipe my eyes, but still I manage to keep upright.

Her bathroom, man, which was in this real short hallway to the right of the kitchen area, such a trip. The floor and walls and ceiling are mosaic tiles, abstract patterns of small oddly cut tiles. She has all different colors, and pieces of mirror tile too. If Jackson Pollock had worked with tile, this would have been the result. The walls of the shower are mosaic too, only with big fragments of mirror so body parts are reflected back at whoever takes a shower. Man, the crazy art of the bathroom rearranges my mind, reminds me that the world is bigger than my bullshit. And in the moment of that moment I pull myself together. Gotta focus on Susan. I got a chance to make it with *this* chick, and maybe she's the one. My Visions of Johanna.

I take a piss and when I'm done pump my dick to get the last of the pee out, and wipe the end with TP. It freaks me when I'm gonna have sex and gotta pee. Worry a little bit of pee gonna come out of my dick when I lay down with the chick and it'll total turn her off. Never happens, and logically, what's the big deal, not as if chicks never had to deal with piss. Get my jeans zipped back up, wash my hands, take a look in the mirror and I'm so wasted, hair a mess, spaghetti sauce on my t-shirt.

Splash cold water on my face. Yeah, get it together, man.

Ms. Braveheart's still lying on the couch, still smoking her Kool, but there's something different. Big fucking deal different. She doesn't have that lavender sweater on. She lies there topless, her tits right *there*. All those freckles. And when she sees me coming toward her she puts a hand on one tit, touching herself, rubbing the areola with her fingertips and it's too fucking much. I don't know if it's to get herself off, turn me on, or maybe both. She's looking at me, and right in the moment of that moment I knew. She was digging the concept too, you know, older teacher chick seduces teenage boy. How much of getting turned on is the fantasy, and how much is what's going on in real time between two humans?

I put my glasses on the table and right quick I'm in her arms and she gets the side of my head so it's against her tit and she's got the other one against my mouth, and with her hand she presses the nipple against my lips, and I feel it with my tongue. We lie there in the stillness of not talking, not moving, feeling how it feels to lie there together. Total stillness except for me sucking her nipple.

She strokes my hair, runs her hands though my curls. Her fingers gentle on my face, gets my head in both her hands and she wants to kiss me. I get myself up so my face is where hers is and she kisses my lips, a quick kiss, kisses my chin, my cheek. Her wet tongue sliding from my cheek up to my lower lip.. Yeah she knows how to get a freakster bro going.

"Don't say anything," she says.

She knows. She pulls at my t-shirt, pulls it up around my neck, pulls it over my head and it's on the rug. She looks at my chest, the brown hair curling up off it, and my bare arms, and my flat stomach.

"What a beautiful body," she says.

"Isn't the word supposed to be 'handsome,' you know, for a guy?" I say. "Chicks, I mean women, they're beautiful."

She pulls me against her, her fingers in my chest hair, and she touches my right nipple, touches my stomach. Kisses me again, and this time she keeps her lips against mine longer, her tongue between my lips and pushes into my mouth. She stops to take a breath and I start to say something and she covers my mouth.

"Quiet," she says, and yeah, that was one of her rules, although she never called it a rule. I wasn't supposed to say anything when we fucked. For a while, I don't know how long, she kissed me, her tongue rough and demanding, pushing harder into my mouth, and at some point she pulled away and told me to stand. I get up off the couch and she sits up, shakes out her hair. I'm right front of her, no shirt, my long Zappa hair soft against my shoulders. She goes at it, gets my belt undone, unzips my fly. Peels my jeans down below my knees. I still have on my striped boxers, my cock pushing them away from my body. She takes hold of it, feels it through the cotton shorts, feels the hardness, and in the moment of that moment I think she's gonna blow me.

Well she doesn't, and I wonder, man, I mean is feeling my cock the kinda turn-on for a chick that touching a chick's tits or pussy is for a guy? But maybe she's different than most chicks. You know, what turns *her* on. She pulls my boxers down and they fall to my ankles, where my jeans are bunched up, and she leans back in the couch. She's looking at my naked-ass self, and this jolt of embarrassment, her checking *me* out, and do I measure up, am I sexy enough or handsome enough or however a freakster bro gotta be to rate with her. I look down and see the dark blue vein that runs up my cock, and the engorged head. I look at her and it's even weirder than it was for me in the movie theater, how she's looking at me.

"Go in the bedroom," she says, and points in the direction of the short hallway that leads past the bathroom to the room with the queen mattress on the rug. The room that's gonna be Harper's room, but of course I haven't seen that room yet, and Ms. Braveheart hasn't met Harper yet, she's in my past, and she's in our future, but she's not in the moment of that moment. And is that the room where she fucked the guys she brought here before she knew me?

It's so dark in the bedroom can't tell if the walls are light grey or blue or some shade of light green. The mattress is covered by a comforter—dark blue or maybe black. And is that the mattress she lay on when the guys she brought home fucked her? Don't know if I should lie on the mattress or keep standing or sit on the wood chair that's between the end of the mattress and the wall. It's weird, me being naked waiting for her. Can't make a decision, so I stand there. To the left of the mattress there's a small low nightstand with a white candle and a glass that has incense, unlit, sticking up from it, and a jar of Vaseline.

Ms. Braveheart's a dark shadow in the doorway, she still has her jeans on, and again she's looking at me. Looking at me standing in the darkness. *The whiteness of me.* She keeps looking, doesn't say a word. Seems to me minutes go by, her in the doorway, she's a silhouette, a topless silhouette. Looking. Her eyes fuck me, and I feel what I felt that afternoon with Harper, and with Jaded too. The turn-on of being lusted after. Only this is so much more intense. Most times when I been with a chick before, you know, all those times with Sarah, and the couple times with Harper, I'm the one doing the looking, getting turned on seeing *her* naked. I'm the one with the wanting, and then I gotta say something romantic and kiss her and touch her to try and get her going.

This is a different trip. Ms. Braveheart—and though I try to think of her as Susan, this night she's Ms. Braveheart—looking at me and getting the way a chick gets when she really wants to fuck. I feel her lust, and it makes me dirty. I'm some kinda sex thing. Not a human. Something she's using to get herself off. She keeps looking, and my face is hot, and my cock hurts how it does when it's been hard for a while with no relief.

"Lie on the mattress, Michael," she says, and lit the candle, and that flickering light's the only light, and the room is some gypsy room, flickering light lighting it up so the room's dim instead of dark, and some kinda cool exotic rugs hanging on the walls, and the floor is thick orange shag, and the windows have dark Indian print curtains drawn closed. She lit the incense, and there's a sweet smell reminds me of the basement at City Lights Books where they have all the poetry books.

I get down on the comforter. Squat naked same as the African natives I saw in some old documentary film. She's standing, and I don't know how I should lie on the mattress. Should I get so I'm on my side, my lower arm and hand supporting my head, try for a casual I'm-just-lying-here-waiting kinda deal, or lie on my back and raise my knees, spread 'em apart so she can fit between 'em, you know, that come-on-let's-fuck-with-you-on-top posture, or maybe I should sit cross-legged the way you always see humans sitting on the covers of tantric sex books. So self-conscious, man, her standing and looking. Is this how chicks feel when they're getting photographed for a *Penthouse* centerfold? Is this how chicks feel all the thousands of times guys are staring at 'em?

Ms. Braveheart undoes her jeans, gets 'em off, kicks 'em aside, and she's naked except for her black panties, the flickering candle light on her, her skin brown from the sun. Her stomach brown, and her tits. She's darker on her shoulders and right below her neck. That was the first time I got a good look at her. You know, practically naked. She's waiting for me to get laid out there on the mattress, so what-the-hell, I get on my back, flat, looking up at her, checking all of her out.

Well there's nothing perfect about Ms. Braveheart. She's got a little bulge of stomach and her tits sag some and her thighs are a little on the heavy side. An older chick, you see the imperfections. But it's funny, 'cause all of Ms. Braveheart that isn't perfect makes me want her all the more, seeing how real she is, 'cause a sweaty, funky real chick who wants me as much as I want her, that's the best.

She looks at me lying on the mattress, and after Saul, you know, the neighbor I told you about, he's the last one she fucked, I gotta look so goddamn young. Those freckled tits, her looking at me, that horny current runs up my cock, and it's unbearable, the need to fuck her. Her skin so covered with freckles, not a few same as Sarah, no, she's practically all freckles and her tits may be sagging but they're bigger than any naked chick I ever seen who wasn't in a magazine. Her skin is weathered, but real sensual, the skin of a for-real adult woman. Yeah Ms. Braveheart has lived, she's known pain and she's known joy, she's fucked a lot of guys and been fucked over by a lot of 'em too. There's wisdom in her eyes, wisdom in her body.

I always thought what would get a chick interested in me was what I've done. They'd dig me 'cause I'm a good photographer, a good writer, and 'cause I know everything about rock and dig the French New Wave, and then here comes Ms. Braveheart, doesn't care about any of it. All she wants is my body. You shoulda seen her looking. It seemed as if her tits got firmer, and her brown nipples got harder, and her fingers under the waistband of her black panties and she peels them down to her thighs, and brings her index finger up to her mouth, licks it and sticks it into her pussy, rubbing herself, staring at me, and I'm a 3-D centerfold, her looking at me and rubbing herself some more, and then she stops, pulls her black panties all the way off and she's total naked too. She got down on the mattress and she showed me what she liked and we did it her way and we didn't stop until *she* was satisfied. And all the time we were fucking I kept seeing Sarah, all the times I got off and she didn't.

6. TEARDROPS WILL FALL

SIMONE HAD A T-shirt, "Women Belong on Top," it said. Morning after our first night together she put it on. I didn't like that shirt. I didn't like it because it was a lie. Chicks didn't belong on top, not all the time, not any more than guys did, not in bed and not in the world of running shit.

Well that t-shirt slogan was how it was at Simone's pad. And not just in a metaphorical way. If we were gonna fuck, Simone had to come on to me, that was the turn-on. Her turn-on. And we always did it her way, which was me eating her out 'cause she couldn't come with a cock in her, at least that's what she told me. I wish me and Sarah could have dealt with our sex problems that way. After Simone got off—always she had to come first—then I could get on her or once in awhile she let me do her from the rear. It was so weird though. I didn't have a clue if she dug *me*. As a human. As a companion. As her old man. All I for sure knew, she dug us getting stoned and getting it on.

Her way.

You know that "Jack Straw" song? I never played it for Simone. She woulda had a libber freak-out 'cause of the opening words.

We can share the women, we can share the wine.

That song reminded me of a photo from '67 of Garcia and Kesey and Mountain Girl. You remember Mountain Girl, right, I sorta met her at Garcia's pad the time I stole The Dylan. Her born name is Carolyn Adams. In 1964, when she was 18, Neal Cassady came up to her. Kerouac's Neal Cassady. The Neal

Cassady who inspired Kerouac to write how he wrote. The Neal Cassady that Dean Moriarty and Cody Pomeray were based on. The Neal Cassady who became one of Kesey's Merry Pranksters and drove the Furthur bus for the Acid Test journey across America. Cassady brought Adams to the La Honda commune, someone renamed her Mountain Girl and soon she was Kesey's old lady. By the time the photo got took, she was Garcia's chick.

Mountain Girl, man, when I was 15 and saw that photo I thought she was the grooviest Freak Scene Dream chick *ever*.

Of course that was before I met Sarah.

I'd hear those words, *we can share the women,* and think of Kesey and Garcia fucking Mountain Girl. Is that sexist? I mean it happened. She fucked Kesey and she fucked Garcia. And they were all still friends. But maybe I was looking at it cockeyed, 'cause Mountain Girl, she's such a free spirit. I mean *really* free. The one in control, smart and stubborn, fucking who she wants to fuck. Maybe that's why I was shacking up with Simone, an independent chick same as Mountain Girl, so unpredictable, does what she wants.

Yeah, maybe that was the turn-on. For me.

I have to tell someone about me and Simone, just have to. That's one secret I can't keep. Well the person I tell is *Thee* Freakster Bro, and how that comes to happen, well that's a story and now's the time for you to hear it.

The day I end up telling him, I drive in to The University with her. Simone. It's six days since I started living out at her place. It's late morning when we get to campus. Simone teaches "Women in Film" every Thursday, but first she has a department meeting, and another meeting to discuss her Ph.D. thesis.

Me, I'm dropping her class. Actually I'm dropping all my classes. I'm dropping out. Gonna live out at Simone's and take photographs and write. Well, I'm gonna smoke the homegrown and drink merlot and fuck Simone. And write. And take photographs. That was the plan.

So I have the whole day to kill. I can't be taking Simone's class and living with her. Smoking the homegrown with her. Fucking her. She could lose her job.

I don't know why she thought I came along. I sure didn't tell her the real reason. The real reason is I can't stand being a house-husband, feeling one-down, always waiting, all day doing a bunch of crap while Simone is off doing *important* shit that gives her life meaning. Already it's freaking me, even after a few days of her dealing with business up at The University and seeing friends in town while I'm left behind doing chores out at Morning Glory Way, hoping she'll be in the mood to fuck after she gets home. Lamest thing a guy can be, goddamn goddamn house-husband. Might as well let the chick get a giant tree-limb cutter with two three-foot thicker-than-broom handle poles coming out of a gnarly jumbo clipper-head and have at your balls.

Already there's The House-Husband List.

At first it was a couple of things. Later, after I been living there a while, it got longer.

The House-Husband List:

One. Wash dishes. That wasn't so bad. Except that already I was making most of the dinner, so why the fuck was *I* cleaning up?

Two. Vacuum rugs, living room, bedroom—vacuum is in The Lab. I could get into vacuuming sometimes, it was a meditation deal, going over every inch of the rug.

Three. Wash living room window—Windex under sink. I hate washing windows.

Four. Water vegetable garden—one hour. Put me right back to when I was 14, 15, having to do that watering around our house. Major bummerosity.

Five. Take Lucky for walk on beach—afternoon, one hour. That was fun. The beach in the afternoon, total groovy trip.

Six. Bake oatmeal raisin cookies—recipe on counter. Bake fucking cookies? Me? You gotta be kidding.

Seven. Make salad. No sweat.

Eight. Start brown rice cooking. Easy.

Nine. Clean cat boxes—all four. If a chick is gonna have eight fucking cats, she really oughta clean the goddamn cat boxes herself.

Anything but another day of house-husband hell.

I'm sitting on a bench in the Arts College quad smoking a Pall Mall, trying to shake that hung-over downerosity. I been drinking too much merlot, smoking too much of Simone's homegrown. I'm seeing everything through a lens of gray and tired. *Come on nicotine, do your thing.* That's when Jim, who I haven't spoken to since our falling out this past spring, comes slow-shuffle walking back into the frame.

There's two things wrong with the picture. So fucking wrong I almost don't recognize the freakster bro in my peripheral. First, the Jim I know doesn't walk across the quad, he bops along, river of life flowing through his veins, his walk a Coltrane improv, but this day he's not doing any bopping. It's a slow sad-sack shuffle, river of life replaced by heavy-ass cement, dragging his ass along the cobblestones. And he looks same as a straight-man loser. Has the Stevie Winwood hair, and the straight-man clothes. A pale yellow button-down shirt and the gray slacks and the brown penny loafers. *Brown.* And he's shaved off the 'stache and beard. He's trying to look professorial, a professor reluctantly heading for a funeral. Got that cane, the lucky cane, and he stops, leans on it. Something's knocked the fuck out of him.

Second thing wrong. After all that shit about Verdi and Brahms and Bartok, here's Jim singing Howlin' Wolf's "Evil." He's serious into it, it's his whole world, trying to mimic that sandpaper voice, only he doesn't sound same as Wolf when Wolf recorded that song, Chess Studios, Chicago, 1954. Still, in his own way Jim's got the spirit, lonesome sound of being two-timed or left behind or taken for all your dough. The trouble-girl misery blues of singers from Robert Johnson to J. B. Lenoir to Junior Wells. The hurt-so-bad hurt in Jim's voice, *if you're a long way from home, can't sleep at night, grab your telephone, something just ain't right.*

He's walking so slow, and that fucking cane, but where it once been an affectation of entitlement, William Zanzinger twirling it 'round his diamond ring finger, today it's a crutch. Pudge stomach pushing out against the button-down, head angled so it seems his eyes are on those new old cobblestones, the button-down having a hard time staying tucked into those straight-man slacks. He's got as nowhere to go as me, and he stops, gets his legs apart, and him standing there, well it isn't only the stomach but his face too, thickness of the flesh at his neck, the bulge of his cheeks.

For sure he doesn't see me sitting across the way, and he lifts up his damn cane, takes himself an air guitar solo, throws his head back, eyes pinched tight. I know that solo, and as his fingers flay at the air in front of the cane, I hear it, not from the studio recording, which has Wolf blowing harp. Nope, the solo I'm hearing is from a bootleg Jim played for me one time when we were hanging out, a Hubert Sumlin teardrops-will-fall solo. Then it's over, the air guitar deal, Jim leaning on his cane again, head angled down, doing that slow sad-sack shuffle.

That's evil, evil is goin' on wrong.

And I can't help it. He's hurting so bad.

"Hey man, Jim?"

He stops, and stands looking at me from the middle of the quad through his shitty mirror shades, same shades he wore the day I met him. What the fuck happened to the Ray-Bans Jaded got him? I walk over to where he stands and put my all into being upbeat.

"Great song, man," I say. "One of Willie Dixon's best."

He laughs that deep guttural laugh, his the-world-is-an-extraordinary-place-and-aren't-we-lucky-we-get-to-experience-it laugh, the laugh he used to laugh when we'd hang out and everything was groovy. Only it's more the world-is-OK-and-I'm-getting'-by-tryin'-to-make-the-best-of-things laugh. It's torn and frayed, but it's still his laugh.

"No one else at this shameful excuse for an institution of higher learning," he says, "has even heard 'Evil.' But Writerman knows who wrote it."

"May 25, 1954 it was released," I say. "Well, the studio version. 'Little Red Rooster' on the B-side. Al Benson probably had it on the air, on WGES, before midnight."

Jim smiles, but that smile of his, well he's trying, I give him that, but it's torn and frayed too.

"You heard that live version of Beefheart's?" I say.

"Oh man!" Jim says, and how he looks, for a moment he's playing hooky from all his troubles.

"Beefheart doing 'Evil'!"

My voice quiet, the enthusiasm I forced into it gone lost.

"I'd ask you if you wanted to check it out," I say, "but you don't listen to that teenage music anymore."

Silence and a struggle going on.

"I'm through with classical music."

"But Jade?"

I swear, man, a thunderbolt strikes his heart, and I get it, how come he's talking to me again.

"She's through with me."

The thunderbolt awakens the pain, a disease eating at the tree trunk that's his heart from the inside. Jim does something next I never seen him do, something I never witnessed any man do in real life, but only in the movies or some book or on the tube. Jim starts to cry. Grabs off his mirror shades and brings his other arm up, wrist in front of his eyes, as if there's any way he can hide those tears, or quiet the moan.

Oh that moan is the saddest sound. Sadder than "Alone and Forsaken" and "Oh, Lonesome Me." Sad as that saddest of sad songs, Love's "A Message to Pretty," and in Jim's moan I hear the choked howl harmonica, the death march tempo, the teary rust-metal guitar and the tragic damned utterances of Arthur Lee, the tremble in that singer's low bloodied voice, hard lessons only the scorn and loathing and rancor of a chick who's lost all respect for a freakster bro can teach.

I can make it if I just don't see your face.

All of that in Jim's moan and in the tears he tries to hide and I know something so terrible happened. Jim a goddamn

goddamn ruin.

I take that back about Jim being the first guy I seen cry 'cause he's not the first. There's one before him. Happened after Mom told Dad *get out,* when I was 17. Yeah I haven't told you about this. I saw it once, though it might've happened twice, day I visit him at that shitty one-bedroom apartment he rented for the two months they were separated.

That apartment was sad as Jim Costello's moan. Popcorn ceilings, nothing on the off-white walls, beige carpet has a smell and a faint stain no amount of carpet cleaner gonna get out, and a view of asphalt out the aluminum frame front window.

I have a Pyrex of lasagna Mom baked for him on the seat beside me as I pull in, right front of the apartment, first time I go there. He rented this boxy place right on the other side of Highway 101, less than five minutes from our driveway. It's in this boxy 12-unit apartment building. A box inside a box, that was his new digs.

It was crazy, Mom making him food when she was thinking about a divorce. Who can ever figure a chick out, even a mom chick.

It's a drizzly Saturday, and when I get in the door of the apartment, might as well be no one lives there. Soon as I see the place I get the message same as someones's shouting it through a bullhorn. This scene is transitory. He's killing time 'til Mom lets him come back. Doesn't want anything about it to seem like home.

The only furniture in the kitchen/living room combo is a cheap-ass folding card table and two metal folding chairs. Smells as if he just sprayed some kinda pine stink aerosol. I don't look in the bedroom but I'm sure all's in there is the folding guest bed we kept in the garage. His beat-to-shit transistor radio on the kitchen counter tuned to KSFO, some game on but he turns it off. Fucking miracle, that is. He's wearing one of the white polyester short-sleeve shirts he wears to the office, has a pocket protector in the pocket, and those ugly-ass plaid pants. That's a combo.

He asks if I want a Coke but when he opens the refrigerator aren't any Cokes 'cause he drank the last one. Sorry about that, he says. All he can give me is a glass of lukewarm water, which is fine 'cause I'm not thirsty. We sit in those metal chairs at the card table, the *San Francisco Chronicle* lying there, business section on top, probably checked his stocks before I got there. He's big on checking his stocks, keeping a close watch on Pfizer and Dow Chemical and Columbia Gas & Electric and some others. He's gonna get rich off those stocks, he's sure of it.

Guess everyone gotta have a dream.

Normal deal my dad has that rock solid iron man face, a life-is-hard-and-then-you-die face when it's not a fuck-you face. Today his face is different, and he's working at being nice. I don't remember any smile, I mean I don't think his face is capable of a sincere smile. I'd say he's trying for his idea of an I'm-your-dad-and-I-care face. His forearms and hands on the card table, nervous horse-gallop taps of his fingers. *Baby finger, ring finger, middle finger, index finger.* Galloping in place, over and over and over. He asks how school is going and what kinda grades I'm gonna get. *Baby finger, ring finger, middle finger, index finger.* Asks if I've started on my college applications. I swear the Lone Ranger and Tonto are riding across that card table.

Asks something about Rock 'n' Roll Frankie, which is a big surprise. Sometimes I wondered if he knew the names of my friends. He doesn't ask about Bobby or Polanski and I'm sure he never liked those two. He musta known they were no good from the start. And he sure doesn't ask about Sarah. Maybe he's still sore about me getting her pregnant twice. And the awkward phone call from Sarah's dad. The mess of that.

"Dad. You're bugging me."

Puts his other hand on those horse gallop fingers, reins 'em in.

All the other stuff, that's him straining to be social.

"Mike," he says.

"Now you're really bugging me, Dad. *Michael,* not Mike."

"You'll always be Mike."

He embarrasses me living in this dump.

"How's your mother doing?"

How she's doing is just fine. More than just fine. Hyped up. We didn't know she was bipolar, that didn't kick in serious 'til later, but she's for sure in a manic phase. Calling relatives on the East Coast at 5 a.m. Spending too much on stupid shit such as cheesy ceramic animals. Living in her world-is-flat world of isn't-this-wonderful, finally-I-don't-have-to-answer-to-no-one.

"She's OK," I say. "Really, you should ask her yourself."

"I'm not supposed to call."

That's when I remember the lasagna so I go out to the car and get it. The rain's takin' a brief vacation and some sun coming through a break in the clouds, which only makes the scene—12-unit aluminum windows dirty beige apartment building, paved parking spaces right in front and the whole thing too close to East Blithedale, the road cars coming off 101 take to get into Mill Valley—even sadder than when it was raining.

"Mom wanted me to give you this," I say, and put it on the card table.

"What is it?"

I don't know why he says that, you can see through the sides it's food. He's a big lasagna fan. He likes lasagna the way I like *Exile on Main Street*.

"She said she didn't want you to starve to death."

That's when it happens. He kinda collapses so his head is face down resting on his arms on the table top. I think he's had a heart attack.

"Dad!" I say. "What's wrong?"

He's making this sound and I think it's his breathing. Gasping for air. His asthma acting up. That's not it. He's sobbing. My whole body hot. My father sobbing. Invisible walls pressing in on me. The sweat, it's on my chest. Oh man. It lasts maybe a minute, but while it's going on it's one of those moments that open up in a way that seems eternal. Until it's over. Close your eyes and count to 1,000 and you'll get an idea of what it was like, you know, time slowing to a near stop. He's lost it, but I guess he realizes how pathetic it is, and what kinda example is he being, letting Mom do that to him. He sits up, gets a Kleenex from a pocket of those brown and yellow plaid pants.

"Sorry," he says.

I give him the sage nod deal, you know, same as I understand completely and it's no big deal and we can pretend it didn't happen.

We sit there, don't say anything, and time passes and dies, time gone forever and after what coulda been five minutes but maybe was one minute, he takes a look at his watch, this Timex deal he's had since forever.

"You better go," he says. "I gotta go to the store."

 Pulls it together enough to get me out of there.

"We should see a movie next time," he says. "'Waterloo' is playing at the Sequoia. Next Saturday."

Says it after I step outside onto the damp asphalt.

"Maybe something else," I say. I don't wanna see some war film.

I'm getting to the car when he calls out, "Mike," and I turn, him silhouetted in the doorway.

"It's *Michael,* Dad."

"Don't forget to tell your mom thanks," he says. "For the lasagna."

I got my mouth shut so tight I think it's gonna self-seal, move my head up and down a few times. I'm backing out when I put my foot on the brake and look towards the apartment and through the window he's at the card table. All I see is the top of his head, his greased black hair, him all collapsed.

Fucking disappointment, my dad. Such an asshole, but at least he was always a stand-up guy kinda asshole. Take-no-prisoners hard-as-a-rock guy kinda asshole. Get-the-job-done-and-no-excuses guy kinda asshole. I hate all that, but I guess I respect it too. So him crying, pathetic as shit. But there's something else I feel, only I don't know what it is that day. Try to pretend it's not there. I only let myself be angry at him, and hold onto my anger for years. I can't understand and I won't understand until the day with Jim. That's when the other thing I feel makes sense. Jim falling apart changes everything regards what I think about a man crying.

And there's more. There's another thing that makes me finally understand, and when it does I regret holding that crying against my dad. But it isn't until much later—when that other thing happens.

Jim is my bro. My freakster bro. Sometimes something is so much bigger than me it takes over and that's what happens that day in the quad. The truth of it, no matter what went down before, freakster bros-in-arms, me and Jim. He has spirit and soul and a stubborn-ass point-of-view, even if he's wrong sometimes. So Jim crying, a pain in my heart. I feel so bad. Our friendship in pieces. Fucking Jaded. Fucking New York Dolls. I goddamn want to fix it all.

Jim shaking, his arms and head and shoulders. His belly. I never seen anyone cry and shake how he is and I do something I never done before. I put my arm around his shoulder, my hand on his back and feel the soft flab of how fat he is.

"Jim, man, you're better than whatever gone down."

What Jim does, he turns to me and I do the right thing, get my other arm around the other side of him and his head against my shoulder, his unshaven face scratchy against mine. Freaks me, a guy so close. I hold him and he cries. Total freaks me. Jim in my arms crying and inside me Roy Orbison, his Grand Canyon-size opera voice, huge fucking orchestra behind him, singing that song of his, "Crying," the one where he's singing to this chick about how she couldn't tell he'd been crying over her, and how she left him alone and in tears. Yeah, that one.

Jim cries and cries. More than my dad. We're so close. Never been so close to a guy, I mean other than my dad when I was a kid and he gave me one of his abbreviated hugs. Too close. Holding Jim freaks me. Too the fuck close.

"What am I going to do, Writerman?" he says. "I'm dying."

Oh man, this pudged-out freakster bro shaking in my arms, don't know how exactly to untangle myself from him. That's when I realize this is the first time he's faced the truth. Alone, he could tell himself the lie that Jaded did love him. But he knows, that I know, that he knows. That's why he's crying. For the first time he feels the loss of *his* Visions of Johanna.

"She said, 'I don't love you,'" he says. "She said, 'I lied.' She said, 'Love you? Never! Not even for a second.'"

Where his stomach is touching my stomach, the shaking so intense.

"That's not true, Jim," I say, but what I say is a lie, a lie we both know is a lie. I lie 'cause I can't stand for him to feel the betrayal of Jaded's words, to let it harden into the cynicism that burns innocence and trust to a cold hard bitterness. "She said those hurtful words to hurt you."

"But she said them," he says. "The truth doesn't even matter. She said them."

There's nothing to say right then that means shit, so I say nothing, and we stand there, and I hug him one more time, final hurrah kinda hug, and it doesn't feel icky any more, and instead I feel I'm older, not a teenager. This is serious shit, what you do when you're a man and your best freakster bro needs help, but there's something else going on too. In the moment of that moment Jim is me, and I'm Jim.

I let go, step back, get some distance. He has that look of wanting to say something but what can he say that isn't one of those sappy-ass clichés, one of those warm-your-pathetic-heart homilies every square uses to express their plastic simulacra emotions. I flash on the whole planet covered with simulacra humans, and apart from them is me and Jim and a few others trying to live the authentic real—willing to bleed to feel something.

Anything.

"Freakster bros, man," I say, "and nothing we can fucking do about it."

I slap him on the back, one of them man-to-man, we're-in-this-together-against-them-trouble-girl-chicks back slaps. Freakster-bros-in-arms.

"Freakster bros?" he says. "We are, aren't we?" and that's when I know he's ready for a number. Clear his head. Rise above the black stain.

"Mexican Airlines, man," I say, and fuck, it's me jonesing for reefer.

7. MY CONFESSION

UP IN JIM'S ROOM I'm high just from hanging with my freakster bro again. He's in the orange Eames front of his desk, got the cane on the rug near him. Got the blinds all the way down to keep the sunlight away but still it seeps in, shards of light on that striped button-down and the wall behind him. A Mozart record plays low on the KLH, "Piano Sonata No. 8 in A minor."

Yeah he hasn't total turned his back on the highbrow deal. The highbrow deal.

In case you've forgotten, right before spring break, when Jim and Jaded were still lovers, she showed up at his dorm room one day with a pile of classical records and announced that rock was kid's stuff, and it was time to grow up. I mean she fucking insisted Jim stop listening to rock. Yeah and that probably was what fucked up our friendship, right along with me fucking Jaded, which he likely suspected, although the final blow was me showing up with that New York Dolls record. Boy did he make fun of me diggin' the Dolls. But anyway.

Jim doesn't know it, but that piece of music he was playin', it was one of Hitler's Top Ten. After a day of gassing Jews, Hitler in his bunker or wherever the fuck he had a record player, he'd listen to it. The piano player was Arthur Schnabel, a Jew.

Why the fuck Jim playing *that* shit.

I get a joint of Simone's homegrown lit, hoover a solid blast. I see Jim through the dark-ass dark filter of my shades in that dark-ass room, and it's almost the groovy old days of the fall quarter even though Jim doesn't look anything same as the groovedelic freakster bro of back then.

I think I already told you Jaded got the orange Eames for him. But anyway, she did. If it been me she'd got it for I'd throw it right through the blinds and the fucking window down onto the quad, and watch the chair bust apart and die on those cobblestones. Throw the shit Hitler record after it. How can he sit in that thing and listen to that music? It's same as having *Jade Kaufman Was Here!* written in blood across his wall.

Kicked back on the bed, and I'm one-up on my freakster bro, me reaching out, him leaning on me, and especially him crying. Since the last time I been here he's replaced the highbrow books on his desk with Miller's "Tropic of Cancer," Algren's "The Man With the Golden Arm" and Blake's "The Marriage of Heaven and Hell." And a copy of *Women and Film* magazine. A loaner from Simone, first day of class. Man, from reading that magazine you'd think every film has a subtext of female subjugation and patriarchy and sexism, as if those Hollywood moguls have nothing on their minds but layering subliminal anti-chick propaganda into their movies. Piece of work, *Women and Film.*

"She was my first," Jim says.

It's hot in the room so he's got his door open maybe a hand's width to get a crosscurrent going from his open windows. Occasionally the breeze causes the blinds to bang against the windows, a reminder the outside world won't leave us alone.

"There'll be others, man," I say, and the weed mutes everything.

The struggle inside showing up as the beginnings of lines at the outer corners of Jim's eyes, and a heaviness, a weight bearing down, man he needs yoga or something spiritual 'cause otherwise the hard shit gonna wear him out, turn him into one of those sadder-than-sad work-a-day drones lost their way in a maze that doesn't have an exit.

"Thousand hooks in my heart," he says. "All attached to a rope she's yanking."

"She's not yanking it," I say. "She's nowhere near that rope."

Sometimes a thing has to happen to your freakster bro before you see it. And dig it. Dig it deep in your soul to where you know it. All that misery after it was over with Sarah, over with Elise. I let that go on, felt it again and again. That pain was my drug of choice.

I look over at Jim and that's when I notice that while he's still mostly Mr. Straight, he's beginning to fray at the edges. Same as his room. His hair shorter than it used to be, but not so short, scraggly hair, curling over his ears, frizzing off his head and while he has no beard, there's fuzz on those chubbed-out cheeks and muted chin, and under that bulbous wide nose too.

The old Jim making a comeback. The freakster bro I used to know is gonna howl at the crazy-ass moon again, and how many more numbers will we smoke over how many more days 'til he's back in the groove? And in the moment of that moment I have a revelation. A number could be a measure of time. If I knew how many joints I smoked each day, I could measure the passing of a week or a month or even a year by the number of joints I smoked. Say I smoke three a day. Say I haven't seen Jim in a week. So when I see him I could say, "Hey, man, been 21 doobies since I seen you."

Anyway, what I do say to Jim is this:

"That chick is fucked up, man. She's Saraghina, she's Hella, maybe even Woland himself," and I quote from that Fellini flick, "8 1/2."

"That which is outside the City of God belongs to the City of the Devil."

Jim sitting in the orange Eames staring, those bloodshot eyes, at me, doobie between his lips burning up and he inhales, holds it, one beat, two, and another, exhales, one beat, two.

"Maybe you need to dial back the weed quotient," he says.

"You're one to talk, Mr. Blitzedkrieg," I say. "You're the fiend."

Those hard eyes on me gone loco, the smoke escaping his nostrils.

"I've had chick trouble," I say. "Sarah. Elise."

His voice, is it ironic or seething, is it me he's nailing or

Jaded?

"Aren't you leaving one out, old sport?" he says, and that "old sport" thing, that was an affectaion of Jim's, a phrase he'd borrowed from Fitzgerald.

This is when things change. Maybe the weed pushing me. I don't know but I'm overwhelmed with guilt regards me and Jaded and our deceit, and I can't keep it secret any longer. 'Til I come clean me and Jim can never be *true* freakster bros.

He picks the silver frame up off his desk, and holds it in both hands.

"Remember?" he says.

I look at the photo, and it's strange how I didn't see the stain when I took it, or when I made the print, 'cause it's all over her face, dripping onto his rug, and it's all over me *and* Jim. *Je devrais vous corrompre.* When Harper told me what it meant that afternoon in my dorm room, *I will corrupt you,* I thought she meant the sex—the things we were going to do. Later I looked it up. *Corrupt: To degrade with unsound principles or moral values; to become morally debased; to cause disintegration or ruin.*

Dead-on bull's-eye.

Me, corrupted into betraying my best freakster bro. Man, the power chicks have over a guy. No fucking limit what a guy will do. Once she's within reach. So close you can taste it. And the chance to taste it. You think you have some integrity, moral as Jesus fucking Christ. Then you're up in a Ferris wheel gondola with your best freakster bro's chick and she's unzipping your fly. Yeah, see how much integrity you've got.

Jim sets the photo on the desk.

"I remember," I say.

In the slowmo of my words, the both of us admitting, how our eyes meet, something that shouldn't have happened did happen.

Un moment decisif.

I have to tell him. I have to wipe the stain away, and before my stoned reverie gives way to a stoned freak-out, I speak. The door to his room still open, you know, that cross-draft deal.

"So Jim," I say, and first I tell about what gone down in the chicks' bathroom, the night of our glam makeover, when she dyed my hair, *If you had stepped up, said the right thing, coulda had me.* Jim in the Eames, watching, listening, me tripping philosophical on the nature of good and evil, and the hypnosis, the way Jaded reeled a guy in.

He reaches down, picks up the cane, holds it vertical between his legs, the ferrule set on the rug, a hand on the smashed-in brass lion's head.

"How could I resist?" I say.

Jim understands that one. He knows her Svengali ways. *Pretty please Jim. Really, as a favor to me.* I keep talking, go on and on, and I haven't told him yet. I slide forward, sit on the edge of the bed, Keith Richards snakeskin boots on the rug, and pray telepathy is real.

It was her, Jim, not me.

Aloud I say, "*Chicks,* man," and I start talking about Elise, and her mixed-up confusion, and the final freeze-out. Jim sitting in the Eames, the mystery of that stoner face, what the hell is he thinking, my freakster bro bogarting the roach. My nerves flash red alert, thin snakes beneath my skin, slithering the fear, my hands tight against the black bedspread. Damn I could use a toke. Look to the door. I tell him about Jaded flirting. All those times. What could a freakster bro do, man, her coming onto me *so* many times. Time after time I put her off. But a freakster bro got a limit, you understand. I'm not perfect. None of us are.

Jim's big. Same height as me, but he's got 50, could be 60 pounds on me, and when a big guy is mad and the adrenaline's going.

"You lining up the excuses, old sport?"

I read about a guy lifting up a fucking car. So all bets are off if he flips his lid.

"If only you hadn't been doing the sick grandmother routine."

It's easy to underestimate a pudgy guy.

"Got something to tell me?"

Passes the cane to his left hand, back to his right, back to his left.

"That I might not want to hear?"

Those judo moves, I remember a few. Nothing's for certain.

"Look, man," I say.

He's finished my joint, drops the roach and with the heel of his shoe grinds it into the rug, you know, fuck the rug, fuck the room, fuck the fucking planet. If Jim comes at me I've got a good shot at getting out the door.

Maybe.

If he didn't have the damn cane I'd take a chance, go one-on-one.

Maybe.

"You two were cheating on me?" he says. "You still balling her?"

He's trying to keep his cool, and he's leaning forward in the orange Eames. That would make it harder for him to go for me.

Maybe.

"No man," I say. "That's not it at all, man. I don't want any kind of misunderstandings regards what I'm saying, man."

I stand and he wants to know if I'm gonna split, 'cause he's certain I've got more to tell him. I'm off balance, he's off balance.

"You're exactly right," I say. "On all counts regarding what you just said, man."

I'm near the door, my back to it, and still I'm talking.

"The complexity of the situation is indeed complex and multilayered in a way that there could be misunderstandings," I say. "And I really wouldn't want that to happen, between bros, you know. Us being freakster bros and all."

Oh yeah he knows, for sure he knows, now that me and him are relating on a high plane kinda deal, freakster bros and all, and before we go any further he's in total agreement that another number is in order, that homegrown really is a fine fine fine-ass fine thing. One more number and we'll get this all sorted out, you know, *between freakster bros and all.*

I toss the baggie to him, tell him keep the rest, my treat. That's supposed to win me points but instead I'm one-down. He has the cane between his legs, and he gets busy, rolls a fat-ass paper blunt, gets it lit.

I walk between the bed and the door, the door and the bed, occasionally a side trip to pass him the number or him pass it to me, and I tell him about seeing Elise at The University theater, her giving me the cold eye, and Sappho, such a cunt-ass bitch, insulting Jaded, insulting me. Throwing a fucking Trojan at us. I have my eyes focused on Jim's face, reading every twitch of his left eye, watching as he wrinkles his nose, and forces his lips together. I tell him how Jaded wanted to split. Walking between the door and the bed, the bed and the door. He's shaking, not a whole lot, but I can tell. Out of the theater. Down to the boardwalk. Up in the Ferris wheel.

"I, I didn't have a clue where it was leading," I say.

I stop walking, and I'm about halfway between Jim and the door. *Jaded straddling me in the gondola, the Forever Infinite Pacific out in the darkness, the lights from the boardwalk below, her tit in my mouth, her salty blood.* The heat in the room, the air so heavy, the sweat on my face.

"She was talking," I say, "as if you two were over."

Is my stoned paranoia kicking in or does his face have that demonic look I seen the afternoon our friendship came unraveled?

"But she was still my chick," Jim says.

"Which wasn't exactly true, man," I say. "She just hadn't let you know. Yet."

"Yeah, that would be right," he says. "An oversight I'm sure, slipped her cute little mind. Preoccupied as it would seem, with *you,* old sport."

Those hard eyes scanning, and if there been a lie detector hooked up to me it wouldn't reveal more.

"It really was her idea, Jim," I say.

He's up outta that chair.

"You fucked Jade that night?"

He's got the cane, man, both hands around the shaft, gripping it tight. Fuck, I mean if he lands the lion's head he'll crack my skull open. I back towards the doorway. The room fills with a thick fog, and Jim's face struggling, his left eye twitching.

One false move.

"You trying to tell me it *just happened?*"

He's gonna hit me, this is it.

"Just an accident that you fucked my chick."

The cane in his hand, gripping the shaft.

"Jim, you *gotta* understand."

He falls to his knees, sad-dog moan of a sound, "bitch," and hits the rug with the lion's head.

"Fucking *bitch.*"

And again, hits the rug, and again and again, and throws the cane, it hits the frame, the frame on his desk with the photo I took of Jaded, and glass breaks, the frame and the cane falling, falling to the rug. Oh man is Jim a mess. He's yanking that rope so hard. The one with all the hooks. I walk over, my hand on his shoulder and fuck it, whatever happens gonna happen.

"You're playing me straight, old sport?" he says.

"I'm not gonna say I didn't want it, man."

Takes a while for Jim to pull himself together. When he does he puts the frame and the pieces of glass into the metal trash can under his desk. He takes the Mozart album off the KLH, drops it onto his desk, and he's going through all those albums 'til he finds his mono copy of *Blonde on Blonde*, places it on the turntable and Dylan sings that crazy blues about the straights stoning him.

"Motherfuckin' *bitch,*" he says.

He gets the Mozart album in his hands, got an iron man grip. If that record were a throat, his grip would be a death grip. Jim starts to bend the record.

"Jade gave me this," he says.

He keeps bending it and a loud pop kinda sound, the vinyl cracked, and he holds it up, wants me to see the big crack running across it, lightning bolt of a crack, and he tosses it in the trash can where it joins the photo of Jaded, and a serene calm comes over him, a kind of *satori.*

"Chicks come and go, old sport," he says.

Un moment decisif.

The lines in his forehead smooth out. I don't know how he manages, and it's gonna haunt him, but for right now he's decided Jaded wasn't worth it, not after what she did.

"You and me—you're my freakster bro," he says. "I let Jade come between me and my freakster bro. I'm not letting that happen again."

Dylan howling at the crazy-ass moon, you know, *everybody must get stoned.*

"We got something," he says. "Howlin' Wolf. Dylan. Zeppelin."

Right then I don't feel so lonesome.

"*Fucking* chicks," Jim says. "Don't have a clue."

"Fucking *chicks*," I say. "Clueless, man. Totally."

"You got another doobie?" he says. "Of that homegrown shit."

I point to the baggy on his desk.

"I don't blame you, old sport," he says. "Doesn't matter anyway. Not anymore."

Man, that was one of those moments. Beautiful. All the guilt and worry that's been same as a second skin since the night in the Ferris wheel, well I've shed it. Oh I'm so the fuck high and this is when I can't contain it, I gotta tell Jim about me and Simone.

Fucking *chicks.*

I didn't know it, but as me and Jim grooved with Dylan, as I was about to tell him the brand new big deal in my life, Sappho came down the hall and stopped outside Jim's room. The door partial open the way it was, cross-draft deal, me and Jim so fucked-up loaded and loud, no conscious trip between us around the way our voices floated out the door. Bitch Sappho. Thought she was the KGB. Or MI6. Or CIA. Probably humming "Secret Agent Man" to herself.

"Been living out at Susan's place, man."

"What'd you say?" and Jim reaches over, his fingers on the volume knob, and quiets down that Dylan scene.

"Susan, man," I say. "All week long."

And Sappho steps into our scene, goddamn bitch.

"Susan?" she says. "Susan who?"

The air turns red and Sahara hot. Weird-ass weird the trips the mind plays, the doped-up raging mind, the bloodthirsty paranoid mind. She's got no fucking right. She's trespassing, her presence a betrayal of what's right and decent in the world. Her standing there in the doorway means nothing's sacred, nothing's private. Even our secrets, the secrets one freakster bro shares with another, can be taken away. The way the Party imposed itself on Winston Smith and Julia in "1984," denying them everything, even their own thoughts and feelings. If Sappho thinks she has the right why doesn't Nixon think he has the right? Democracy transformed into a police state quick as Sappho blows apart the groovy stoned tranquility of our freakster-bro-to-freakster bro trip—and she doesn't even have to use rats to do it.

Bitch Sappho wearing blue denim overalls, braids hanging down, sick smile on her face, looking the Fascist libber version of the Swiss Miss chick only what I see is the Wicked Dyke of the West.

"Get the fuck out, Kate," I say.

The pounding blood loud.

"Sure I'll split," Sappho says. "Just tell me who's the Susie girl you're fucking?"

And I'm in Sappho's face. I never been this close, and that's when I see the ugly-ass mole, hairs coming out of it. Above her mouth, left of her nose. Across a table it looks kinda cute, but up close I see the cancer of her soul in that dark brown lump.

"Let's see," Sappho says. "Do we know anyone named Susan?"

Her eyes scan the room. The Mozart poster on the wall, the Stones poster on the floor, the lucky cane. The KLH, the black bedspread, the mess of records. The Pall Malls, the metal trash can with the photo of Jaded and Hitler's Mozart sonata, the groovy books—Miller, Algren, Blake—on the desk. The issue of *Women and Film* next to the books. Fuck. Simone's issue of *Women and Film*.

Sappho's eyes stop on the magazine. Simone's issue of *Women and Film*. She looks back at me, looks over to Jim, and one more time the magazine. Sappho's face has that alert deal, sensors out, eyes sending data to the brain. Magazine. Brain processing. *Women and Film*. Lips pinched. Ms. Braveheart. Nose scrunched. Thinking, thinking. Ms. Susan Braveheart.

"Oh, wow, *really?*" she says.

Modigliani-chick-possessed-by-the-Devil smile, and the thrill of knowing trumps her guilt at eavesdropping.

"So grandma got her wrinkled hands on you."

I look dead-on bull's-eye into her eyes, see the terror. 'Cause Sappho knows something else. She's way crossed over the line. And I'm at her. She's trembling and her eyes get wide, her mouth opens. Only as my hand touches her arm something changes, a shift in her body, she's still afraid, but she's self-righteous too, and it dwarfs her fear. My hand closes in on her forearm and as my grip tightens I feel bone through skin. *I've* crossed a line too. The libber line. The violence-against-women libber line.

"Michael! You're hurting me!"

"Goddamn peeping Thomasina," I say.

That's when Jim steps in, his hand on my arm, keeping me from doing something I'll regret.

"Let her go, old sport. She's a chick. You don't want to do this."

Un moment decisif.

"You're a sick puppy," she says, and closes her mouth, sticks out her lower lip, and she's superimposed every guy ever done her wrong on me.

Oh fuck, in or out, and this is a one-way trip to nowhere I wanna go.

"Violence against a *woman!*" she says.

Out!

My hand goes limp, and Sappho's through the door, out into the hall.

"First Elise," she says. "Now me."

Jim reaches past me, pushes his door shut. He takes a few

steps back, and I turn, my back to the door. He lifts his shoulders, and he sits back down in the Eames.

And from down the hall, "Elise! Elise!" and it's fucking too much, goddamn goddamn bitch.

I spin 'round, my hand on the door handle but I don't have a decent grip. The handle's not turning or the door's stuck, or maybe I'm too shaken by the whole scene—some goddamn thing.

Jim up from the Eames. "Relax, old sport. What's done is done."

Fuck that, and I twist the handle goddamn hard and yank it open and I'm in the doorway, and she's down the hall, got her little-miss-priss walk going.

Oh man, I'm out of control shouting so loud.

"Fucking feminism doesn't give you license to snoop, Kate."

Still walking, but her head jerks, those ponytails move, right after I said "snoop," and maybe that jerk is a moment of clarity and I hope, oh, I don't know what I hope.

8. SIEG HEIL, MS. MUSSOLINI

"YOU LOOK LIKE YOU need a drink, old sport," he says, and tells me to sit in the orange Eames. His prized chair. That was a big deal, I mean with Jaded getting it for him. He never let anyone sit in it.

"Got anything?" I say.

"Bottom drawer."

There's a fifth of Jack Daniel's, about a third full, more than enough.

Jim raises his hand to his face, as if he's holding a microphone, *That's evil, evil is goin' on wrong.* He gets a couple plastic cups out and splits to rinse 'em in the john down the hall.

I was safe right then, sitting in the orange Eames. All our troubles outside that room. To care about another person, gotta feel some of their troubles. I'd felt Jim's troubles. Troubles with Jaded, his Visions of Johanna, at least he thought she was, and maybe for a moment she really was, maybe she let her heart beat for Jim. Long enough for her to feel, for him to feel. Jim's troubles were different from mine, but troubles is troubles. My troubles, his troubles.

He sets the wet glasses on his desk and I pour some booze in one, hand over the bottle. He's drunk two thirds of the bottle in that room by himself. Man, life shouldn't be so lonesome. Maybe this time it'll be different. No betrayal. Freakster Bros, man, if they're loyal, well they watch each other's backs, and have an ease with each other. Total different scene than a freakster bro and a chick. A freakster bro and a chick, it's always about sex. I can't relax around Simone. Well maybe for a minute, right after we're done fucking. We lie there side-by-side on our backs, dreamy in the aftermath, the both of us smoking. Right then there's nothing else in the world I want. Not from Simone, not from anyone. Sitting in the Eames about to drink some of that booze, there's nothing else I want. Jim understands and I understand, we both know what it is going up against a chick. If we can keep the trust, it doesn't have to be so lonesome.

Dylan's never split the KLH, playin' so quiet it's almost subliminal, but Jim ups the volume 'til *Blonde on Blonde* is full-on blasting. Crazy-weird Dylan. Frizzed out freak hair Dylan. Gone electric, meth-amped Leopard-Skin Pill-Box Hat Dylan. That album never gets old. Tripped-out Cubist blues sound, and no one but Dylan ever got that kinda sound outta those Nashville cats. Ragged-ass harp noise blowing through the room. If a breeze been blowing with the force of that harp noise we'd be cool instead of sweating it out.

Blonde on Blonde, man. A whole album about fucked-up chicks.

The one who's got some other kinda lover. And the one he wants so bad. Louise with that handful of rain. And the one who forgot to close the garage door. The one he treated so bad. Who clawed out his eyes. Ruthie, who knows what he wants. And the one who screamed till her face got so red. The chick he wants to please come home. And the one whose heart is made out of either stone, or lime or just solid rock. Sweet Marie, who he waited for when she hated him. And the one with eyes like smoke and prayers like rhymes. The chick who breaks just like a little girl. And Johanna, gone, those visions of her, now all that remain.

Were all those songs about the same crazy-ass chick? Hard to imagine Dylan having so much chick trouble. And it wasn't only that album, went all the way back to his first one. Before his first one. Those Minnesota Hotel room tapes from '61, he was singing about chick troubles since soon as he started singing. Dylan's an expert on the subject. Got a Ph.D. in crazy-ass chicks. If Dylan had a streak of bad luck with his music career he could get into counseling guys on dealing with crazy-ass chicks.

Dr. Zimmerman, I presume.

I'm not going to Simone's class, and Jim's not going either. He starts talking about Sappho, and soon we're discussing the libber trip.

"Chicks gone weightless," I say. "No center of gravity. Don't know up from down."

I'm in the Eames and he's on the bed lying on his back, his cup resting on his chest, a lit Pall Mall in his other hand, reaches so the end of that cigarette extends past the side of the bed, shakes the ash onto the rug, and fuck if he cares if the room burns up.

"They don't know the difference between equal rights and a fascist state," he says, and carefully sips from his cup.

"If Mussolini had been a chick," he says, and he's done with that cigarette, lets the lit butt fall on the rug, and do *I* fucking care? "The feminists would all be going *Sieg Heil, Ms. Mussolini.*"

Guess I do 'cause I grind out the smoking butt.

"That chick Kate," Jim says. "Couldn't you see her in one of those SS uniforms sticking burning cigarettes into some poor fuck to get answers," and he mimics one of those German idiots in "Hogan's Heroes," Klink or Schultz. "Suzie who, Jew dog?"

"I didn't want to hurt her," I say.

"She was asking for it, old sport."

"One good thing I can say about my dad," I say. "Never hit my mom. Never did."

Jim tips his cup slow so the booze goes into his mouth but he tips it too much and booze dribbles down his chin, onto the collar of his button-down. He sits up, wipes his wet chin with the shirtsleeve.

"Dad broke my mom's jaw," he says, and it's me dials down

the volume to zero, and the whole spinning crazy-ass room comes to a stop.

"What the fuck, Jim?"

He brings his lips together, and the lines and shadows of his face, the disease eating at the tree trunk that's his heart been doing its work a long fucking time.

"She made some crack about the stink of booze. 'Makes me sick, a man stinking like that.' He slugged her. 'Now you got something to be sick about.'"

"Tragic, man," I say.

"Got her jaw wired, got a restraining order, got a divorce," he says. "That was it, Mom and I from then on."

Hellfuck of a thing growing up without a dad. Bad as my scene with my dad, still. I mean I didn't know who the fuck I was those months Dad was living in the shit-ass boxy apartment. A mom's a chick. There's shit a mom can't ever understand. I turn up the volume, let Dylan blow some harp through the room, let him sneer about that chick with the leopard-skin pill-box hat. The Warhol super-star chick. Edie. Dead of an overdose.

"There were times I should have hit Jade."

"What are you talking about, man?"

Jim rolls onto his side and tells me I'd never let a guy get away with what Sappho said, and I should have slapped her.

My hand feels the smooth orange Fiberglass surface of the Eames.

"Chicks are different," I say. "You can't hit a chick. They're off limits."

If Bergman made a modern up-to-the-minute film showing the emotions a freakster bro felt after he lost the fucking war, let his chick walk all over him after she fucked his best friend up in a Ferris wheel gondola, after she laughed at him, talked trash about him, a movie that showed all that, well that movie was in his bloodshot eyes and his sad-dog voice.

"Maybe if I'd knocked Jade around a few times, she wouldn't have gone up in that Ferris wheel."

I tell him it's bullshit what he's saying but he doesn't want to hear it. We let Dylan serenade us for a while, and then we argue some more.

"I can understand these chicks and the sexism deal," I say. "Pigs whistling at 'em when they walk down the street. A chick is more than her tits, you know."

"The feminists want you to act like they don't have tits," Jim says. "Like they don't have an ass that wiggles when they walk."

"We're wired to get hard," I say. "Survival of the species."

Soon enough we circle back to Simone.

"I'm not gonna pretend looks don't have plenty to do with it," I say. "But I dig who she is, it's not only about her ass."

"You really fucked Ms. Braveheart?" Jim says.

"She lives in this cool house off the beach," I say. "Twenty minutes south of here."

"Isn't she a lesbian?"

"Yeah, I'm sleeping with a dyke."

"She's bi?" Jim says. "You and her girlfriend do a threesome?"

That was funny, him saying that, especially 'cause of what happened later. I tell him he's gotta keep the whole deal about me and Simone hush-hush. Bad enough bitch Sappho knows.

"Just don't tell *anyone*," I say.

That's when he asks if it's weird, you know, sex with an old woman. I'm gonna say no, I'm gonna lie, pretend it's no big deal, only I can't. I need to talk about this and I want him to tell me the scene with Simone is groovy, that I'm not a freak.

"It's kinda weird," I say.

Jim still sitting up. "What's the rub? She has a lesbo girlfriend after all?"

"She's not that old, man," I say. "It's more that I'm young. If I were 32 or 33 you wouldn't think it weird. I'm mature for my age. Older chicks dig me."

"Don't they have a word for that?" Jim says. "An old person fucking a person seriously younger. Pedophilia?"

I pick up "The Marriage of Heaven and Hell," throw it at him, hit his foot.

"Seriously, Jim," I say. "Is it weird for a chick to want a freakster bro for his body, the way guys want chicks?"

"Let me get this straight," he says. "She sees your engorged instrument of pleasure and it excites her, as Henry Miller so eloquently put it, 'like a bitch in heat'?"

"Don't talk that way about Simone," I say. "That's fucking vulgar."

"Just quoting the master."

"You know when you see a foxy chick," I say. "And you don't even have to think about it, you're all about fucking her? That's the deal, only in reverse."

"So if you were walking down the street," he says. "And she's on a construction crew, she'd whistle at you?"

"She's *not* a lesbo!" I say. "But yeah."

"Chicks normally need to think you love them," Jim says. "They don't jump you 'cause you got a big dick. I'd be careful. Maybe a screw's loose."

"I want a chick to dig me 'cause of who I am," I say.

"What's it like?" he says.

"It reminds me of when me and Elise were in her room and I'd stare at her. Of course this is different. Elise had clothes on. Simone stares at me. She's into my body. I'm worried I'm just her latest free fuck."

That's what Henry Miller called it. A fuck with no strings attached, unhindered by the burden of commitment. Miller knocking on some chick's door, her half-asleep, lets him in and him not saying a word takes her on the bed, any way he wants, and he's out of there. Such a burden a guy shoulders having a chick in the real world, as opposed to the Henry Miller novel world.

In real life no one gets a free fuck. Not really. That's what free love guys and chicks don't understand. A free fuck is living your whole life at a shit house on Lowland Drive—a never-left stuck in a no-name and thinking that's all there is to the world. Not knowing about Paris. Or London. Or wild nature Big Sur. Not understanding the depths of history and beauty and art, oblivious to the richness of a world that began long long ago.

A free fuck is no commitment, but it's the commitment that gives a fuck meaning. Love really is the answer. Without love, without putting it all on the line, a fuck is worthless. And the more worthless free fucks you get, the more meaningless your existence, until no meaning. Absolute zero.

Jim gets this funny expression. "That's odd," he says. "A chick acting like that. Frankly, I'd say it's extremely odd."

"Thanks for the reassurance, man."

Jim shaking his head, "Still can't believe it, you fucking teacher!"

9. PARTY ON MORNING GLORY WAY

YESTERDAY FADE AWAY, FORGET about today, and there's no tomorrow.

Only the stoner moment.

Slow stoned grooving, and I'm in the TR4, key in the ignition, oh man.

You know when they say, *he was high as a kite*, about me that day they could have said, *he was high as the top of those Mount Rushmore heads*. So high he could have kicked dirt off the top of Washington. Could have said of me, if you figure how *lowdown hell is and go in the opposite direction, that's how high he was that day*. Could have said of me, *he was high as one of those SR-71 spy planes the U.S. Air Force flew over North Vietnam*. Those planes, flew them at an altitude no kite ever reached.

Me and Jim, both grooving the way me and my freakster bro groove when we been hanging out smoking reefer and philosophizing, philosophizing and smoking reefer. Concepts and the smoke, the smoke and the concepts, floating away.

Stoner sync.

We started in on the homegrown the night before, and picked it right up when we came to in the late mid-morning light that somehow worked its way into that room of his even with the blinds drawn.

I'm exhausted and sore from crashing on Jim's dorm room floor in my clothes. First night I didn't sleep at Simone's since me and her met at the Truffaut. She doesn't want me out at her place when the guests start showing up for the party.

Me living out there with her, and it's been over two months, still supposed to be a secret.

Don't know if it's the buzz of no sleep or the homegrown or antsy from being away from Simone, probably all three plus I have my suspicions about the acid. Whatever, I've got that bad, bad crave. A jones to buy something. My hands gripping the black plastic steering wheel, and I feel the toxins leaching into my fingers and palms.

Plastic people, oh baby, now you're such a drag.

Driving the Triumph, and the ill of the black plastic steering wheel reminds me, and I know what that bad crave is all about, it's a craving for a real wood steering wheel. Cool polished sunlight glinting, Triumph logo in the middle. I can get one salvaged from a wreck. Hardly cost me anything. Fernando's auto body shop, south of here maybe 20 miles. Danger, danger. Oh man, some bad luck scenario across those tracks. Dead car steering wheel, you're such a drag.

Turn the key, oh man, listen to the engine roar. Yeah that's a trip, the engine makes the whole car run, and what if there's an engine at the center of the earth keeping the earth going, only instead of gas it's wild nature keeps things running smooth, only nature's getting choked, man been royally fucking with nature same as forever, but it's catching up, getting close to payback time.

A fine, fine polished sunlight gleaming wood steering wheel. I want it.

What if I got James Dean's steering wheel outta his silver dead-end Porsche. Plastic and death, death and plastic. I guess it would be death and wood. If it was out of James Dean's Porsche. I'd never end up with that James Dean dead-end steering wheel. I need mine to say *Triumph*. Oh to hell with it. The toxins gonna get us anyway. No escape.

"So the guy's intrigued, man," I say.

Foot on the gas, steering the Triumph out of the Arts College lot onto Heller Drive, hell of a name for that road, heading for Route 1, destination Morning Glory Way.

Destination the party.

End of class, end of school, end of the world party.

Jim dialing in George Harrison's "Give Me Love" on the radio, and damn it makes me miss The Beatles, all those years, you know, when they were the world.

"And what guy would that be, old sport?" he says.

Tweaking. Nervous buzz. Shit cut with speed. That or the toxins. Bummerosity factor.

"The editor, man," I say.

We dropped. The Orange Sunshine. Dropped it right before we split the campus. Takes 45 minutes, or three doobies if you smoked them one right after another, 'til it kicks. You remember, if how long it takes to smoke a number is a measure of time. Two thirds of a doobie's worth of time already gone.

"The editor?"

The deep deep blue of the ocean way out there out past all the houses and streets and the downtown, out past the Skid Row pawn shops, pay-by-the-hour motels and Lost Weekend bars. In the distance, end of the earth, the Boardwalk and you could see the Tilt-a-Whirl and the Giant Dipper, and rising, rising, still rising, the Golden Dragon. The past forever daring you to forget the present.

If we fired up we'd be at Simone's in a joint and a half. Two thirds of a joint to spare.

Ready, set, go.

One hand on the wheel, digging for The Dylan. Got it in my hand. Spark The Dylan, Jim leaning into it, end of that number in the orange-blue flame, smoke filling his mouth, leaking out his nostrils. Snap the cover of The Dylan closed. Dylan's hand held it the way I hold it. Same hand that wrote those songs. Same hand that strummed those guitars. The Gibson. The Martin. The Telecaster. The Strat. Holding a lighter, even Dylan's lighter, doesn't make me Dylan. I ought to know that by now.

Everyone wants The Dylan. But it's only a fucking silver lighter. What if Garcia made it up, big fucking joke, a Harper story, saying Dylan gave it to him when really he bought it at a smoke shop. Or someone else gave it to him. Not Dylan. Funny the shit that impresses people. How does it change that lighter, whether Dylan used it, or not?

Still. I dug possessing The Dylan. It was the cool scene.

"Yeah, man," I say. "The editor, man."

Three months Jim been letting his hair go wild again, curling crazy-ass off his head, bird's nest out of control.

"That's what you said, old sport," Jim says. "You're repeating yourself. What editor?"

Looking more the old Jim, but he's not the old Jim. The old Jim, unselfconscious, didn't give a fuck what anyone thought about his crazy dancing air-guitar screaming Zeppelin rock 'n' roll 'scuse me while I kiss the sky.

Or some such.

"No man, you're the one repeating himself," I say.

Jaded. It was a class in how to be self-conscious he'd taken, those eight or nine months she'd been his old lady.

"The guy at *Dazed*," I say. "You know, the editor."

There's a sadness too, I guess some of it had been there before but this is different, and I know what it is, life beater deal. Beat the *vive la vie* out of you. Hadn't known the damage a chick could do, *l'érosion de l'individu*. Now he knew.

"Hippie rag," Jim says.

Yesterday fading away, forget about tomorrow, there's *only* today. In the fine, fine, fine stoned beauty, only *this* moment, and yeah Jim has to forget. In that purple haze he can almost, almost touch it, getting close, closer, closer still, nearly almost the old Jim who really really really didn't give a fuck. Too much reefer never too much. Break on through, baby. Flying that Sunshine trip. Gone, baby, gone, baby, gone, baby, gone.

"Don't you think?" Jim says.

My freakster bro bogarts that doobie, could be spacing on the chasm between who he is and who he thinks he's been, which isn't who he's really been at all probably, so easy to get it all mixed-up confusion.

"Think what, man?" I say. "Why don't you …"

The sweat forming on my forehead, wipe my right hand across it, doesn't do shit, my head still wet and now my hand wet with my sweat too. There's so many deals same as that, you try to fix something and not only does it stay broken, but you mess up something else too.

"... pass it over my way?"

"*Dazed*," Jim says. "It's a rag."

Sun on high, bright bright and blinding, burning into my skull through the frizzed-out wild freak of my hair and my fingers, thumb and index, receiving that doobie from my freakster bro.

"Well since neither the *New Yorker*, *Creem* or *Rolling Stone* have requested my services," I say.

And the deep inhale, bright bright sun burning my outside, reefer smoke burning up my inside. Hold it, hold it, oh man, and I hold it. Let the desire for air build and build and build some more, then the big exhale, and if how stoned a freakster bro is were to be measured by rings the way you can figure out the age of those huge coast redwoods, there'd be plenty of rings around me, and another one just added from that intense mindblower of a toke.

"Fucking grateful," I say. "*Someone* has the interest."

Top down, windows down, shoot onto High Street. I always crack up when I see the sign.

"And fuck you very much," I say.

Us two laughing that some jokester named the road up to the college High Street, the wind pushing back my hair. And my freakster bro looking freakier and freakier, a beached-bum down-weather Roger Daltrey kinda deal if Daltrey had the early stages of a crazy-ass beard and mustache, and the wind going wild with the bird's nest.

"Record reviews?" he says.

My Zappa-kinked hair down serious past my shoulders, no mistaking me for some nine-to-fiver drone.

"No, man," I say. "Done with the fucking record reviews."

Bright bright sun, feel it melting the cerebral cortex, one hand on the wheel, phony fake plastic people wheel, reach back behind the seats, grab at air, and where's my hat, damn it's somewhere.

"Well what is it, old sport?" Jim says.

Reaching, reaching, and still reaching, my hand's entered some black hole and I can reach through the whole fucking universe and still no hat. Where's the fucking hat?

"Not sure," I say.

Battle of wills, me and the TR4, man versus machine, and now it's a matter of principle. Not gonna look, gotta keep my eyes on the road, and I damn sure *am* gonna get my fingers on that fedora.

"Maybe a column," I say.

Fingers touching felt, oh man, fuck yeah!

"He wants *you* to write a column?" Jim says.

And we're the chosen ones, hip high freakster bros gonna fucking touch Nirvana, same as I've got my hat, it's out there waiting for us.

Total tripped-out Buddha state. *Dharmakaya.*

Oh man, Zen deal for sure.

We've been reading this book on Zen Buddhism, me and Simone, her idea of course. The whole trip's about getting centered, reaching a higher plane, controlling your breath, well, to stop acting like an impulsive freak of a nervous wreck. Nothing easy about any of it, not at all, 'cause it's so easy to feel all righteous about how above the fray I am, but it's an illusion.

I pull the black fedora down hard over my hair, over my head, down tight, right hand on top, hanging on so the hat doesn't take flight.

"You ever written a column?" he says.

Yeah Jim's a hairy freakster bro again, but he's a *chubbed-out* hairy freakster bro, his face has that bloated heft as if air been pumped into each cheek, as if he's a giant chipmunk with a stash of food on each side, as if he been serious about eating his way out of that trouble girl pain, but it's not working, I've seen it in his eyes. His eyes tired, and not from the five hours sleep and too much homegrown. Tired from the wrongness of life, and it's right then, glancing over, seeing those sad eyes, that's when I understand how a human, an old fart, how it is they look as if the life been sucked right out of them, and them cursing the world for the unfairness of it, and the grim fatality

face that means they've given up. Jim's sad tired eyes, so tired
from the wrongness, and why is so much so wrong?

Buddhist amnesiac.

Me on my get-on-your-mustang-Sally-and-ride high horse,
my rip-their-fucking-blind-eyes-and-deaf-ears-out-of-their-heads
rage, my revolution-is-now voice angry, so angry, more angry
even then when *I'm* cursing the damned world that God-who-
almost-for-certain-don't-exist has forsaken.

The acid hasn't kicked in yet, but it's gotta be cut with meth
'cause I'm feeling that crinkle buzz, yeah we're flying on weed
and speed. Trans Love Airways get you there on time. And I'm
not gonna be beaten down, not I, not Writerman. Let all the
trouble girls try to tear me down. I'm gonna be same as Dylan.
He never got the losing end. Always had the last word.

Always.

Wipe the sweat from my forehead, index finger feeling felt,
the bottom of my brim, and even in his stoner spaceout, even
with the tweak of that speed he must be feeling too, Jim's got
that *the revelation of it all* mouth open daze, yeah he's waking to
where I'm coming from, course my freakster bro can dig the
New Trip. *My* New Trip.

"Got to tell you, man, I'm tired of weighing in on records,"
I say. "Done with that cheap thrill. From here on out, building
my own sand castle."

I guess Jim isn't quite grokking the depth of my new vision.
And how can I explain? It's too much, the smoke rings of my
mind, to try and unravel the big, big, big-ass picture for my
stoned freakster bro. Oh man, it's so big, bigger than a town,
bigger than a state, bigger than the whole country, this novel
I'm gonna write, soon as I can catch my breath, soon as I can
settle down, soon as I can be alone, get me one of those Royal
typewriters same as Hemingway used, same as Jim's got,
probably the kind Salinger used. Maybe I'll set up out on
Simone's front porch, glass of sour mash and a Pall Mall
burning.

Fuck no.

And what am I thinking, the whole vice trip is gonna be

out the window. I'll have a clean, clear head, that Forever Infinite Pacific breeze coming up off the ocean, damp and cool, slapping my face, slapping me awake so I can get it all down, the story of the world, the story of my life, the story of the trouble chicks, oh man, the book I'll write soon as my head clears and that space appears and that Royal typewriter, oh yeah, baby. Gonna rip the façade right off of everything and the words gonna drip blood off the page, you'll see beneath the skin, see the scary-ass bones the skin conceals, and the smiles hide. See the reality of the authentic real. And that's only a hint of it and no way I can get into that heavy-deep-and-deeper-still scene in this moment, not at all. There's a time for revealing the heavy deep stuff. Another time.

"Ever written a weekly column?" Jim says. "Nothing easy about it, old sport."

Where the fedora sweatband meets my forehead, I feel the sweat soaking in, sweatband warm and wet, pull the hat off, toss it onto the seat behind me, dig for a handkerchief in my jeans pocket, wipe the sweat off. Already I know I'm not gonna write any column.

Too many wrong trips but I've got to take them on, use the right approach, figure the angles, gauge the odds. I don't want that sweat on my hand. Don't want blood on my hands either. Or the stain. Got to keep my wits about me, step to the side, fast, so the knife hits the wall, and not me.

"No worries," I say.

Liquor King looming up ahead, and actually it's not looming, that lame-ass excuse for a building, but we're almost there and I'm gonna stop.

"The wine, man," I say.

Pull into the parking lot, thick hot heat rising off the pavement, rising, rising, waves of it, sheets of clear light white heat. Desert mirage heat, rising, rising and still rising, the ghosts of all those dead and gone drunkards who came before us. And I stop the car and Jim stands up in the Triumph, and steps up so he's standing on the fucked-up leather seat.

"Tally-ho, old sport."

Jumps over the door, arms stretched out, his arms are
wings, lands himself on the pavement, staggers and for sure he's
gonna fall on his face, but he gets his balance, spins to face me,
straightens his shades, runs his right hand through the bird's
nest.

"The name's Bond," Jim says. "*James* Bond."

At least he's trying for the old Jim, can't quite get there.
What comes of knowing too much. And that's another irony,
you want the experience, the knowledge, the first sin, but it
destroys the innocence, you only get once for it to be brand
new, and the first time my lips against Sarah's lips.

Oh man oh man oh man.

We'd gone for a walk, me and Sarah, got those ice cream cones
at the sweet shop, she got the butterscotch, I got the cherry.
Black cherry. Van Morrison's "Beside You" drifting out the
upstairs window, someone living up there, above the sweet shop,
the jazz trip of that scene, of that music, that was music no one
had ever made before he made it, that was the music of the
dream world, music of the blood rushing in the underground
rivers, music I'd have risked death to hear. And it's playing just
for us, for me and Sarah, that's how I felt that day.

The sugar high of that black cherry ice cream, and I
smelled the butterscotch, she's close, her arm brushing against
me as we walked to the pond. That was the first time we went
there together. Later when we went we had that conversation
about being crazy same as Zelda. But this day, we don't talk
about that, this day, after we finish those ice creams she kisses
me. I had planned it all out, how I'd put my arm around her,
pull her to me, and kiss her, only she beat me to it. There was a
fragile deal to her, but she usually got what she wanted. But not
always. I was Dylan, that's what I thought, 'cause Dylan never
got the fucking losing end, always had the last word. And she
did get the losing end, worse even than me.

First time, she tasted of butterscotch and sugar cone and
girl, that's the first time I got an idea about the merging, about

the body and the spirit and the soul, how a freakster bro and a chick could blend into each other, and the ecstasy of that first kiss, the groovy high, the blossoms of flowers melting around us, the honey and raspberry and strawberry and black cherry, the late afternoon sun, the rays filtering through the trees, onto the pond, onto us, and it was never same as that again.

I open my door to get out, that's why they've got doors in car walls. Doors and walls. Walls and doors. Walls to separate one space from another. The interior of the TR4 from the exterior world. The interior of the TR4 is its own reality, obeys laws unique to itself, that's why Jim jumped over that door, jumping between the two worlds.

"A real *pissant* works here," Jim says.

"You're talking 'bout Kierkegaard of the Liquor King, man," I say. "Have some *fucking* respect."

Out of the car I stand there, sun glinting off bits of broken glass on the potholed blacktop and if you squint you see those poor man's diamonds shining against black velvet. Calming the tweaked-up stoner buzz, taking in that onetime 7-Eleven, still a square, squat, shit-ass goddamn excuse for a building. Those beige outer walls have acquired a patina of grime in the nine or 10 months since I first walked through those Liquor King doors in search of peach brandy. I mean the place looked the shits from the beginning, today it looks worse.

"Calls me Gatsby," Jim says. "Always smirking. I tell him, 'That's not my name, old sport.' But he persists."

Cross to bear, Liquor Store is, and guys same as him they're everywhere, getting in the way of where I'm going, where Jim's going.

"You know 'The Odyssey,' man," I say.

Jim nods, the slow solemn nod, head up and slightly back so his chin's sticking out, then lowering his forehead, and back up —the slow stoned nod of in-sync with his freakster bro.

"How Odysseus had all these trials?"

Oh baby oh man, for sure Jim knows that score.

"The philosopher dick who works this piss hole," I say.

"Yeah, one of mine."

And another trial, remaining conscious in the face of chaos, and I can do it, this time Liquor Store isn't gonna best me. I'll rise above, float on a sea of groovy vibes, let him be his small-minded self down there in the gutter. Nothing he can do gonna faze me.

There's a moat around Liquor King, but I can walk on water. Breathe deep, tweaking, taste-of-speed buzz, yeah I'm ready, man. There's walls around Liquor King too, separating the exterior world of bright bright sun and electric blue sky from the interior world of booze. Nothing but booze. You could fill a swimming pool with all that booze. Get naked with a naked-ass chick, go for a swim, yeah that would be some blissed-out swim, licking rum off her chin and neck and her thin fingers. There's temptations in this world no freakster bro can resist.

Susan Simone, man. She got me.

Liquor King has a pair of glass doors to get from the exterior world to the other one. Push one of those doors so it swings in, step inside, and there he is, Liquor Store goddamn him, skinny-ass surfer dude wearing a white captain's hat, can you fucking believe it, *a white captain's hat*. Long stringy dirty blond hair hanging down out of that idiot cap, face pimpled, his goddamn goddamn smirk, his nose in Jung's "Archetypes and the Collective Unconscious."

Calm.

As if I believe it for even a second.

Calm, calm, there's nothing of consequence to let your heart be eclipsed by anger.

No way that phony is into Jung as much he's making out to be. Or maybe the book is a front, him reading "Penthouse Letters." Or some such.

It matters not, keep focused on the breathing, always the breathing.

I know where they've got the half gallon bottles of Almaden red, get two, put them on the counter.

"How much, Captain Hegel?"

His pimpled nose in the book, eyes not tracking the words anymore, if they ever were, and for sure he's gaming me, as if he can't be bothered to look me in the eye while we speak.

"Where's your girlfriend, Writerman?" Liquor Store says.

Damn.

And quicklike, *bam*, slap my palms together, foot from his face, and oh yeah he isn't doing the fake-ass Mr. Philosopher deal any more.

"Can't look at much, can you man?" I say.

"She dump you already?" Liquor Store says.

Jim's got a fifth of Jack Daniel's, and he's staring at the label, tripped-out white lines with the curly-cues. The old-style lettering says "Old No. 7 BRAND," says "Jack Daniel's OLD TIME," says "QUALITY Tennessee S O U R M A S H WHISKEY."

That was rich. As if it'll be same as old times if you drink some. What old times? The ones when you blacked out. Or woke in the bed of some strange chick you've got absolutely nothing in common with other than you both drink too much. Or got in a fist fight 'cause you didn't like Merle Haggard's "Okie From Muskogee" the asshole spun on the juke box.

Jim looks up, turns in my direction and the mixed-up confusion on his stoned mug.

"How's he know about Ms. Braveheart?"

And me right there at the counter, still looking at Liquor Store, still waiting for him to ring up the wine and I'm not watching my fucking breath no more.

"He doesn't."

"Ms. Braveheart?" Liquor Store says. "You've got a third chick getting ready to dump you?"

That asshole isn't the only one who ever picked up one of Jung's books. I look hard at that fucker, burn holes in his eyes, quote Jung. "Everything that irritates us about others," I say. "Can lead us to a better understanding of ourselves."

Said it sinister, a threat, "Take note."

Freaks him, crazy-ass way my face gotta look, sinister voice trip and those words, and he cocks his head to the side, ignores me, talking to Jim.

"He's high, huh?" Liquor Store says. "Crazy and high, not a good combo."

"I spell p-h-o-n-y. Phony," I say. "You to a fucking T, man."

"I bet the looker you were with last time dumped you soon as you told her you were a writer," he says. "No future for a looker babe in making it with a starving writer."

"If not Simone, who?" Jim says. "Elise?"

"Damn, I forgot the brick," I say. "But you could put your numbskull head down and run real fast towards the window. Same result."

Oh, fuck, to remain in a *conscious state* at all times, impossible. Out at Simone's, when we're walking on the beach or sitting crosslegged in her living room, not so so hard to do some of that, but in the war zone of Liquor King, no fucking way. Take a deep breath and to myself, quiet-like, I say, "*Ksanti.*"

"Sandy?" Jim says. "You have a chick named Sandy? You got two chicks now? Simone and another one on the side?"

"No, man," I say. "Buddhist trip. I'm into it. Hard to translate and it doesn't exactly mean this, but the easiest explanation is patience in the face of idiocy or lame-ass bullshit. You know, our man Captain Hegel here."

Jim put the Jack Daniel's bottle on the counter.

"That was a pricey babe," Liquor Store says. "You could tell, just to look at her. Dumping the both of you. Smart girl."

Are there any examples of retribution or revenge or fucking over an asshole in the Buddhist tradition? I don't think so. Not the vibe. Practicing *ksanti* in the face of an unenlightened one such as Liquor Store is near impossible. He rings up the booze and we pay him, me covering the wine, Jim springing for the Jack Daniel's.

"The both of us?" Jim says.

"Your old babe, Gatsby," Liquor Store says. "Smoked Sherman's, expensive clothes, black Mercedes."

Jim facing me and his face—"Through a Glass Darkly" playing across it.

"How come he knows so much about you and Jade?"

"It's nothing, man," I say. "I'll explain in the car."

Liquor Store mocking me.

"It's really *nothing*, man," he says. "He'll explain everything in the car."

That's when I lost it, to hell with *ksanti*. Me screaming, push my face into his space, fright mask anger trip staring him down.

"You bend over, motherfucker," I say. "Aim the top of your head at the window over there, and run toward it fast as you fucking can."

Jim's surprise at Liquor Store knowing about me and Jaded, old news by the time we're back in the Triumph.

"Forget it," Jim says. "Lost my bearings. Ancient history, old sport."

Jim's right hand on the dial, searching for some groovy trip on the radio, and we've lost 10 minutes in Liquor King, two-thirds of a doobie, so the acid gonna kick right as we get to Simone's place.

Groovy. That old Coasters song, "Searchin'."

Nostalgia, man, you can drift away in it. The fuck with nostalgia. Nostalgia for old fart losers trying to get back to a feeling they convinced themselves they felt when they were 15, first crush, or being the star quarterback or class president, some past that isn't even how they remember it. New coat of paint or gilded or even a total remodel, the way the mind turns shit to gold.

Searching, always searching, still we're searching.

The acid kick that I wait for, and this is the second time I drop, and I'm flashing a scrapbook of non-sequitur visions from my past: Huxley's "Doors of Perception," the first freaky light show I saw when I turned 14 and for my birthday me and three friends go to the Avalon Ballroom, July '67, kaleidoscope light show moving collage trip on the walls, reefer in the air, Big Brother and the Holding Company crazy-wild guitars, Janis screaming those modern-day blues, and "Siddhartha." The "Siddhartha" part is probably most important. That's the part about the revelations. The part about the veil parting, a locked door into hidden recesses of my mind opening, oh man, break on through to the other side, and I want new perceptions, I want to know the world in ways I can't fathom, yeah that's what I want from the Orange Sunshine.

That's when Jim starts in with his don't-I-seem-totally-normal not-like-some-guy-tripping-on-acid routine. Jim doesn't really look his normal self at all. His eyes bug out the way they'd be if a grizzly bear's heading toward him. His right foot tapping out a double time rhythm to that "Searchin'" song and he's wiggling the fingers of his left hand in this frenetic way. For sure the acid's cut with speed.

"But can you tell, old sport?" Jim says.

I'm still shaking from that liquor store deal. Flying down Route 1, 75 mph, the speed limit 60, past that industrial deal off on the left, and the Lavender Club. You remember, where Simone hooked up with Harper and there's more, more to tell. About Harper. But not yet.

Patience, man, got to have patience.

"Almost the perfect fucking normal deal, man," I say.

"Almost?" Jim says. "What do you mean 'almost'?"

"I mean nothing," I say.

I feel the grin on my face so wide it oughta hurt.

"Other than the extreme twitching," I say. "And I mean anyone seeing that, they'll figure you're freaking on meth, man. No big deal. No one's gonna associate that spastic twitch trip with acid."

Jim's got his left hand up in front of his face, trying to catch the twitching.

"Man, it's only been maybe two doobies," I say. "Another doobie before shit happens."

"But we've only smoked one doobie," Jim says.

"I know, man," I say. "It's a figure of speech. Point being, it's not time for the shit to kick."

"So why am I twitching?"

"That's a joke, motherfucker."

"Oh?" he says.

But the way he said "Oh," slow and that question mark, he isn't sure which is the put on.

Jim had enough "Searchin'," searches the dial and finds Arlo singing "Alice's Restaurant Massacree," maybe seven minutes in. That song is 18 minutes, 34 seconds long. Another 11 minutes, give or take, take or give, you know, to go. Over two thirds of a doobie. When that song ends, we'll have a third of a doobie before the acid kicks.

First time I hear "Alice's Restaurant Massacree," that whole story-song about how the narrator got himself out of the draft, it's on the radio, that underground FM deal, KMPX, summer of '67 and I'm 14. Already against the war, even then. 'Cause of Rock 'n' Roll Frankie who was gonna be a conscientious objector, 'cause of Joan Baez writing about being a pacifist in that "Daybreak" book, and 'cause of *Ramparts* magazine.

But I'm sure that song played its part. Helped me understand the steady decay of hypocrisy at the core of the fucking country. Three branches of government. That was rich. Total sham, all those Senators and Representatives paid off and Nixon a liar and a crook, and you can't count on the Supreme Court for hardly anything. All fixed. The corporations moving in, our shadow government.

Second time I hear that song, same station, it's still funny and it made me hate the cops and the military. One time me and Sarah and Frankie and a bunch of our friends sang this other Arlo song, "Coming Into Los Angeles," sitting around a campfire out at South Beach, north of Point Reyes. Anyway, one day I bought a used copy of the album, it's called *Alice's Restaurant*, at Village Music. I owed it to myself to own that album. Being against the war and all.

That one song took up the whole first side. The only other song I knew about took up a whole side was "Sad-Eyed Lady of the Lowlands." There was a scratch through about half of it, the Arlo song, not the Dylan song, but it would play all the way through without skipping. There was about nine minutes worth where you'd hear a little scratchy sound every time the album spun around. Bugged the hell out of me. That's the problem with buying used records, when I was buying them they seemed like such a deal, but later when there's a skip or a scratch sound or a bunch of pops I'd be so mad at myself. I mean why didn't I just spring for a new copy, pay the extra buck or two.

"I'm twitching, old sport!" Jim says. "Twitching!"

I do the lighting quick schizo deal where my left eye stays trained on the road ahead, but my right eye, I flash it on Jim for a fraction of a second, get it back looking ahead along with the left one. Consider the data. What that right eye took in was Jim holding both his hands out, palms up, his head tilted, jaw angling toward his throat, staring at those hands. And those hands were shaking a little, and I know that's 'cause he's so freaked about the whole twitching deal, afraid it's gonna blow his whole "normal" routine.

You hear a song too many times, you burn out. Then when you hear it again, you feel kinda sick. Don't want to hear the fucking thing. That's why Top 40 radio has people on staff who do call-out research. I read a magazine article about it, I think in *Esquire*. All day long they call up suckers who have nothing better to do than talk to a radio market-research drone, and play them 10 seconds of a bunch of songs over the phone to figure out the ones everyone's burned out on.

Burn out.

That's where I was at with that Alice's Restaurant song. I didn't want to hear any more of Arlo's story about the garbage and Officer Obie and the Group W bench and all kinds of mean nasty ugly looking people sitting on that bench. I really didn't want to hear about mother-rapers and father-stabbers and father-rapers, any of that shit. But with Jim total freak-ass tripped-out about the twitch deal, there's no way he's gonna look for another station.

I'm wrong about the nearly three doobies.

The Orange Sunshine kicks in at two doobies, right after I turn onto San Andreas Road, Simone's earthquake exit, the one that parallels the freeway, parallels all those fields of corn and artichokes and spinach and strawberries and whatever else they're growin' out there.

I was driving great, but those fields are talking shit about me, and they could start blazing or dissolving or turning into quicksand.

I feel it. I *know.*

10. FREAKING OUR OWN DESTINY

OH MAN, WHEN WE arrive Simone's got the crazy party scene in gear. Strings of tiki lights hang above the front door and under the eaves over the front porch and the Sugar Mountain couch. More tiki lights out back around the garden, candles in all the rooms. The top of the partition between the kitchen and the living room crowded with food: Simone's homemade tortilla chips and guacamole, cut carrots and celery and zucchini and mushrooms and cherry tomatoes and a fruit salad, whole wheat crackers and black bean dip and plenty more. Gallon jugs of white and red Almaden on the counter, ice chest full of Coronas. Blur of people everywhere, the music loud, and I don't know where all these people came from. I guess everyone in Simone's class brought boyfriends and girlfriends and friends of friends and more friends. Fifty, 60 people, probably more.

Simone is crazy-wild beautiful. Her hair flowing off her head, her face emerging otherworldly within the rough ellipses of lush auburn curly kinky, freckles everywhere. Intense Great Whites, long narrow nose, and those not-quite-Jagger-oversize lips. She's wearing her favorite worn-to-hell jeans, and her tight lavender "women belong on top" t-shirt and of course no bra so her nipples are *right there.*

I never can figure her out.

All that shit about how chicks aren't sex objects, and there she is showing it off to any guy or chick looks her way.

Simone the hostess is a lot same as Simone the teacher, only instead of lecturing, she's here, there and everywhere, making sure the whole lot of 'em feel good, everyone with a drink and food and someone to talk to or share a number. Somehow she's got her homegrown spread around without making a big deal of it.

Yeah, Simone's got the knack.

She's playing the non-sexist rock 'n' roll party tape. The tape me and her made last week. Well I made it, but me and Simone picked the songs. Well mostly I picked the songs and she approved 'em. Figuring what to put on that tape, a motherfucker.

You try and find a non-sexist rock 'n' roll song.

Rock 'n' roll is about wanting the chick, getting the chick, fucking the chick, or losing the chick. The Stones songs are about getting the chick, or hating the chick, wanting the chick, being disgusted by the chick, and The Beatles, same kinda deal, and some of *Highway 61 Revisited* and most all of *Blonde on Blonde*, and nearly every Zeppelin and Doors song.

Anyway, some of the songs on *our* tape:

Martha and the Vandellas, "Dancing in the Street": Mostly what the title says, which would seem safe enough. Problem lyric: "So come on, every guy, grab a girl."

The Beatles, "Paperback Writer": About a guy who wants to be a "paperback writer." Problem lyric: none.

Janis Joplin/ Big Brother and the Holding Company, "Down on Me": Nope, ain't about cunnilingus. Whole song is Janis complaining about how everyone gives her a hard time. Problem lyric: "Believe in your brother, have faith in man."

Booker T. & the MG's, "Time Is Tight": Instrumental. Problem lyric: none.

David Bowie, "John, I'm Only Dancing": A guy tells his boyfriend that "she turns me on," but reassures him that "I'm only dancing." Problem lyric: "Well Annie's pretty neat she always eats her meat" and "She turns me on." Mitigating factor: Sung by a bisexual man to his gay lover.

Mott the Hoople, "All the Way From Memphis": Smart song about the price of the rock 'n' roll life. Problem lyric: none.

Bonnie Raitt, "Love Me Like a Man": Chick complaining about the loser guys she ends up with, and her desire for a man who understands her. Problem lyric: none.

Joni Mitchell, "You Turn Me On I'm a Radio": Chick desperate for her guy who is ambivalent. Problem lyric: "But you know I come when you whistle, when you're loving and kind." Probably shouldn't have been on the list, but it's Joni Mitchell, another of those exceptions to feminist dogma that Simone made all the time.

Yeah, *she* made the rules.

No matter how crazy-wild that party, would have been no big deal, and no need to say more, no need to say even this much if something important didn't happen, and the authentic real truth of it, two major important things happen. Soon as me and Jim get there, the first one unreels.

"Bloody massacre," she says.

Right front of me in Simone's living room, Elise holds a glass of what gotta be wine, white wine, and she's brand new. Yeah, she's changed all over again. Cut her hair, cut it shorter than how it was the first time I saw her, shorter than that Audrey Hepburn deal. Fuck, she looks same as the chick in *"À bout de soufflé,"* you know, Jean Seberg. She's even wearing one of those white and black striped shirts with the crewneck.

Oh man oh man, that severe *"À bout de soufflé"* Jean Seberg short short hair and the revelation of her jaw, the line of it. Hard-edged. And more. Black eyeliner circumscribing her blue million miles eyes and the tight black and white striped crewneck sailor shirt and no bra, *shit*, Elise without a bra, and black pedal pushers. And more. She's lost 20 pounds, and she was thin to start with. Yeah, it hasn't let her skate, the troubles between me and her. I don't know which question this new Elise answers. Is this who she really is? Or change your hair, become someone new? And will she change again come the fall? Or is this the Elise she's growing into?

And will she knife me or kiss me?

She leans in, and I expect the smell of weed and wine, but all I smell is cigarettes. Her voice is sweet how Elise been the afternoon she let me leave my hand on her thigh, no cold eye, no Leopard-Skin Pill Box Hat laugh.

"I'm really sorry, Michael, " she says, and she sips at what's in her plastic wine glass, which is ginger ale, and in her eyes a clarity I never seen before.

"You don't owe me an apology," I say.

"Yeah I do," she says. "I lost it that night."

It was beautiful, the caring in her voice. Still, I mean even if I didn't have something goin' with Simone, this Elise is different the way Jim is different, and you can't roll it back to how it once been. What happens happens and it's there and even in the forgiveness she feels what she felt, the baggage of our time together, good and bad, still there.

"I'm going to AA, Michael," she says. "I've stopped with the doobies too."

"I wondered about the ginger ale."

"You made me realize I'm worth something," she says. "If a boy could love me strong as you did."

And her thin artist fingers on my arm, touching me how a chick touches a former lover. "Some things aren't meant to be, Michael," she says. "I love you, but not how you want," and a quick kiss on my cheek, and that was the final time she said "love" regards me and her.

"No other guy," she says. "Would have put up with me."

My insides, man, an overwhelming love for Elise there in Simone's living room amidst the party ruckus. Not the desperate for sex I felt all those months, no this is a true caring, a generosity of spirit, the four *Brahmaviharas* flowing from my soul to hers.

"So I hear you and our host are great friends."

Goddamn goddamn bitch Sappho.

"More than great friends," she says, "Kama-deva disguised as a little Abyssinian lovebird whispered in my ear."

I busy myself finding my Pall Malls, getting out The Dylan, getting a cigarette lit. Yeah, there are times when smoking has its uses.

"Flew all the way from Ethiopia to tell me," she says.

"Well then it must be true," I say.

Elise has a way of making her face dead-ass serious. Standing close there in front of me, cigarette in her hand, wanting me to light it. Kills me to light that mentholated deal but still 1 do it.

"Hope it's what you wanted," she says. "Or at least what you need," and she can't help herself. "Least I hope you're finally getting some."

Yeah, she's changed.

"Me and my esteemed freakster bro, you know, our mutual friend Jim," I say. "Front porch couch. Care to join us?"

It wasn't so much a surprise her looking same as Jean Seberg, and when she quotes from the film no surprise either.

"Tout comme un homme!" she says.

"What do you mean by that?"

"Oh, nothing."

"You coming?"

"Maybe," she says. "Sure your girlfriend won't mind?" And she knocks the ash off her cigarette, and it falls on the toe of my snakeskin boot.

"Damn it, Elise," I say.

"You need a new pair," she says. "Those are all used up."

Elise swayed, Michelangelo perfect hips Slim Harpo sings about, *and do the hip shake, baby,* swayed front of me, *the hip shake, baby,* pushed the screen door, *shake yo' hips, baby,* dancing through the doorway, screen door *bang* hard against the house, *bang* of that door *bang* of John Lee Hooker. *Bang bang bang bang, you shot me right down.* Elise bopping 'cross the porch, *I love to see my baby walk,* hip shake walk, *walk her walk,* 'cross the porch, *talk her talk,* so cool so fine I wish she were mine, *she wiggle when she walk.*

Yeah, man, John Lee Hooker he loves the white girls.

Jim sitting at far left, if one were also sitting on the couch, gives Elise a stoner nod, me too, tries to seem normal but worried he's twitching. Yeah I can tell. Worried he's twitching bad as a jonesing meth freak.

"Homegrown, old sport," Jim says. "Flight time."

Sure he's got the beard and 'stache making a comeback, but he still wears the straight-man clothes. Light blue cotton collar shirt and the gray slacks and the brown-shoes-don't-make-it brown penny loafers. Yeah, you can never go back.

Elise, glass of ginger ale in her left, burning Kool in her right, plops her ass on that lumpy beater couch this side of Jim, and ginger ale slops on his brown penny loafers. Those shoes they deserve it.

Toss Jim the baggie, Zig-Zags in there too. He gotta be bugged regards his shoes, but damn, doesn't care, lost in a Lucy-in-the-Sky reverie.

Maybe, maybe not.

I swear Jim's quietly singing *and now I* wanna *be your dog, well c'mon!* That song. I didn't understand when the critics made noise in '69, but this day I understand. All the chicks might as well be wearin' "women belong on top" t-shirts, and Jim humming, *well c'mon!* Elise puts her plastic glass down on the porch, bounces herself up and down on the couch, Jim spilling wine, but he doesn't care, *well c'mon!*

"Sit," she says, pats the seat cushion left of where she's happening, and the spell of that couch, beater cracked brown leather couch, *you can't be 20,* none of us 20 yet, *on Sugar Mountain,* the *groovy* groovy trip, *though you're thinking,* cracked beater couch, *that you're leaving there,* soon as I'm on it, *too soon.* Oh man oh man, Elise smells of honeysuckle, same as Faulkner's Caddy, smells of the leaves, no that's not right, Elise smells of menthol and wild strawberries, and in the moment of that moment, me and Elise and Jim, we're Sugar Mountain safe. Jim with my Zig-Zags, and Elise reaches over so sweet runs her fingers through the bird's nest.

"Look like yourself again, Jimbo."

He blinks his left eye quick-like, a dotted-lines eyes kinda wink, the blink and the wink says *see old sport, no one can tell, right as rain, normal as the day I was born, not twitching in the least.*

"And you looking like a movie star, my dear," he says. *"Huit secondes ou huit jours. C'est la meme chose."*

"How's that joint coming, *Michel?*" I say.

Her hand off Jim's head, the leaves and the honeysuckle and the wild strawberries, leans back, her head against my head, and her hair cut so *À bout de soufflé* short.

"*You* remind me of *Michel*, Michael," she says.

I try for that Belmondo tough-guy sound.

"On couche ensemble ce soir?" I say.

"Yeah *that*," she says. "And he's dangerous."

"My secret," I say. "You found me out."

"Oh come on," Elise says. *"Je connais tous tes secrets."*

The three of us sitting there, me on the right closest to Simone's front door, Jim roosting far left, Elise between us, and us all looking past the yard and the fence and the field of weeds and wild flowers, deep dark mystic Forever Infinite Pacific stretching out past infinity. Three fatalists, smoking our cigarettes, two of us working our way through our first glasses of Almaden red. Away from all the death machines, the TV lie machines, the atom bomb machines, the pollute-the-oceans-and-the-air machines, and right then we can feel safe, goin' back to the country, a country we made up, freakster bro country created in our minds, our acid freak minds. Yippie-yi-yo-ki-yay. Freaking our own destiny.

It's cool hanging with Jim and Elise, the three of us teasing each other, this unspoken game where every once in awhile one of us puts the other on, and often as not the one who's the butt of the put-on doesn't get it, not right away, that's the fun of it, figuring out when what Jim is saying, what Elise is saying, jokin' me or the authentic real, or both, before his face, her face, reforms into a freakster grin.

Elise isn't a women's libber, but you know that already. She doesn't try to push a guy around the way Sappho does, the way Simone does. Elise is the kinda chick a guy wants a chick to be. Those pretty flowered skirts she wore, so feminine she was when I was her boyfriend, wanting me to protect her even when there wasn't any protecting to do. And me hating nostalgia, but if that's not nostalgia, don't know what is.

Yeah, she woulda been perfect, if only.

And maybe nothing's ever perfect.

Jim's got a number rolled, a fat one, and we were ready to smoke that fine fat number, and it's the groovy trip for sure, a moment I wish coulda stretched out to eternity. Thinking back on that afternoon. Oh how fine that would be, and forever was. All the wild flowers out in the yard and across the road in that big field, glittering and changing color, little pinwheels spinning, luminous violets and fuchsias and scarlets and yellow-gold, *Thee Freakster Bro* on the funkiest old couch with me, Elise so groovelicious, the black and white stripes of her shirt a flashing strobe light. And she's there, leaning against me and her body warm and sweaty, same as I'm her brother or something, the way we joke on each other, that easy thing you want with a chick. Nobody, and not even the Forever Infinite Pacific, has such singular and slenderest hands, such delicate artist chick long thin fingers. The whole scene an e.e. cummings poem I can't remember the name of, but that's it exactly. Something about the wind blowing the rain away and the dance of death, or maybe it's something else, something only e.e. cummings, or Dylan wishing he was e. e. cummings, could dream.

Jim leans across Elise and asks for The Dylan, and what if The Dylan were rigged so every time I use it, as it sparks to flame it would sing a line from one of his songs, and what would be even better would be if the line were total dead-on to the scene at hand, so right then it would sing, *we sit here stranded, though we're all doin' our best to deny it*, and thinking all that I spark it, but it's not rigged, so the only sound is flame in the breeze, and the ocean, and the non-sexist rock 'n' roll party tape from inside, and all the blather of talking and yelling and carrying on that everyone inside is doing, and everyone in the back garden, and down front of the house too.

Jim tripping so acid freaky he doesn't think to offer the number to Elise first, takes a hog of a toke, passes it to me. I hold it out to her only she gives me an I-don't-want-none headshake, and I remember she's gone clean.

So me and Jim take turns with that fat number, Elise hanging with us, yeah we're so high and groovin' and free and to this day I wish there'd been someone with a camera. That's a photograph I still want. If I coulda been two people, one of me woulda gotten up right then, aimed the Pentax with the 28mm lens, got the whole couch with us three on it. We look groovy, man, each in our own peculiar scene. Elise doing her *À bout de souffle* Jean Seberg trip, Jim all scruffy freakster bro clashing with his straight-man clothes, and me, stoned, and my clothes wrinkled from sleeping in them.

Elise leaning on me with that short short haircut short enough so it makes her look almost teenage, I mean 14-year-old girl teenage, and she's so thin, almost a tomboy deal with the striped crewneck and the black pedal pushers and leather sandals. Me and her, we would've looked a crazy couple in that photograph that never got took, with our weird Uncle Jim, glass of red in his left hand, the number in his other, freakfest bird's nest sticking out every direction.

I sure as hell didn't know, but that was it, that was the best fucking moment of those years, the years at The University, and the summer and fall and beginning of winter out at Morning Glory Way. It was everything I imagined in those moments I dug so much. Sal and Dean and Marylou driving cross-country too fast. Jules and Jim and Catherine early on before it goes bad. Michel and Patricia when Patricia still thinks she loves him. Those moments, when they happen, if they happen, you'd give anything for them to last. Nothing lasts. Nothing fucking lasts. Too bad there was no one with a camera to take that photograph. And it fades more each day.

"So you're living here?" Elise says. "What's that like?"

I look out over that infinity ocean.

"Is that why we never see you?"

"Yeah, I live here," I say. "I guess. For now. Maybe for longer. Probably. But that's not why you don't see me."

Some dark breeze kicking in off the ocean. Jim humming. *And now I* wanna *be your dog.*

"She boss you around?"

Now I wanna be your dog.

She laughs a silly Jean Seberg laugh, the glam boogie-woogie of Mott's "All the Way From Memphis," the sax rattling the window behind us.

Well c'mon!

"Boss bitch type?" she says.

"No, man," I say. "It's good."

She looks up at me again, those eyes.

"Bloody massacre, Michael," she says. "That why you're out here with me?"

And the sun burns hot on the cold steel rails. The dark blue ocean moving, a deer floating across the meadow, across the water, moving, the undulation of the miles and miles, honeysuckle and those damp leaves, the hard fast metal squeals of a hard plastic pick against metal strings, tremolo twang seaweed, moving, rippling and hypnotic and the sunlight glitter ocean.

"We don't have to hang all over each other," I say.

"Funny," she says. "I forgot all about that aspect of you, Writerman."

"What aspect?"

She kicks off her sandals, and her toenails are a dark purple, same purple I once had on my fingernails, turns her body away so her back's against my side, pulls her knees toward her chest so her toes are flat on the couch, the tips of them shy of touching Jim. She's all compact and folded up, fragile origami chick.

"Yeah, old sport," Jim says. "I forgot that part too."

Elise lifts up both arms, got her fingers in her short hair. "What I remember," and she reaches back, fingers on my head, in my hair, and lights are flashing across the dark blue infinity ocean, tremolo twang seaweed, damp leaves and honeysuckle intoxication. "You were practically *living* in my dorm room. We could have been married, how much time you spent there. Staring at me. No matter how much you looked it was never enough."

Her fingers aren't in my hair any more.

"Wasn't he always in my room, Jim?" she says.

Before I can stop myself, "Unconsummated."

I feel her body stiffen, but she keeps leaning against me, and she doesn't say anything, yeah, she has changed, cleaning up her act has changed her. She's got it together in ways she never did before. The three of us sit there and smoke, quiet for awhile, mesmerized by the flux of the ocean.

"So it's excellent, you and her?" she finally says.

"She's my old lady, Elise."

She's looking down, really she's talking to herself, and I barely hear the words.

"A beautiful thing," she says.

Jim heard 'cause he's laughing his I-can't-believe-you're-fucking-that-teacher-chick laugh.

"What?" I say.

"I said it's a beautiful thing," she says.

Her and Jim think that's hilarious.

"What are you talking about?" I say.

"Come clean," he says. "You told me she wouldn't let you say 'chick.'"

"What of it?"

There was one of those pauses in the talk talk talk, the sound of the ocean filling the void, and the next time Jim speaks he's talking to Elise.

"Sounds to me like you miss Writerman," he says. "Jealous Elise?"

Her back against me, and her breath the beautiful sadness.

"Maybe," she says. "Boring not having some guy hanging around."

"Some guy?" I say.

"Why don't you tell him about Jack, Elise?"

"Shut up Jim. He was nothing."

Jim gets another number—just in time.

"Two things matter in life," Jim says. "For men, it's women, and for women, money."

And how high can we fly?

"Who's more the cynic," I say. "Godard or Truffaut?"

"That's not it at all," she says. "They both hate women."

"They love women," Jim says.

"No Jimbo," she says. "They hate women."

Jim passes me the doobie. My head drifts away, and I don't need another hit. We all drink the air, and the air is righteous, unpolluted air filling our lungs. Yeah, the true high, and if we all could eat fruits and vegetables right off the trees and out of the ground. *Jesus was a vegetarian,* Sappho told me. Breathe in the cool pure air and drink of the righteous pure water, and it will be different.

As we groove mellow on that cracked beater couch, a long shadow across me, and it falls across Elise.

"How sweet," Simone says.

Oh man, if Simone walked in on a class of 14-year-olds throwing spitballs, and one of those spitballs hit her face, that's how she looks at me and Elise.

"What do they call it, rekindling an old flame?"

I don't know how she got out here without me noticing, and she stands in front of the couch, unlit Kool in her hand. Well we all defrost, and Elise and Jim laugh harder than before and they know Simone is playing me and I can't see it, not that day and not all summer long. Both of them look at her, look at each other, and the stoned laughter, the you're-such-a-square laugh, and I join in.

"What's so funny?" Simone says.

I shouldn't be laughing, but the Orange Sunshine, man, the bummerosity emanating from Simone, so the fuck funny, and the stoned laughter, we can't stop, and Simone is pissed, and we know she's pissed which makes it funnier, and you know when people get old they slip away from the center and we were in the center, we *were* the center. Soon enough we'd slip away too, but that day we're the center and Simone slipped away years ago. Oh yeah, and we're laughing at Simone, laughing at her whole trip. Orange Sunshine high, homegrown stoned, Almaden red drunk, and I don't care.

Simone could never touch the grooviness of our Sugar

Mountain high.

It was one of those days. The sky a cracked mirror of white cloud wisps and faded blue, what you'd see if you had a football field of broken mirror and you could get up above the clouds and the sky and be the invisible man as you looked down at the reflection, only what you'd see looking down, that's what I saw looking up, that and the glowing ball of bright bright sun, right overhead, white light white heat coming down hard, burning up everything.

There was no football field, no broken mirror. Me and Jim and the dusty road leading from Simone's to Saul's. We were always going somewhere, never settled, never content, never able to accept that this was the way it was, the way things were and would always be. Not us, no, never. Nothing could ever be enough in those days. Could never be, would never be, and never was. We were the fuck-you in the face of complacency. It was a beautiful and righteous and glorious thing.

And we knew it.

Walking along that dirt road, me and Jim. Simone sent us to get Saul, bring him back to the party, not knowing we're tripped out on Orange Sunshine. Simone shanghaied Elise, had her in the kitchen making more guacamole or salsa or some such. We need suntan lotion or long sleeve shirts or we'll be crispy critters, man, no lie. Me, I've got the black fedora pulled down tight, freak-frizz hair shooting out of it. Kick up dust with my Keith Richards snakeskins, start Jim coughing.

Jim wears the-revolution-is-now cap he borrowed from Simone pulled low. Soldier cap, green canvas boxy deal covers his head, olive brim sticking out in front, only Jim isn't a soldier, total anti-war freak, student deferment draft deal. With the hat and the chaos of his beard and mustache, and the bird's nest coming out from under the hat he looks same as some freakster bro who hung with Che or the SDS or the Weather Underground. If you squint. If the Orange Sunshine burns bright. No, man, not the Weather Underground. They're laying low, not drawing attention to themselves. Jim looks too much the freak to pull off that violent revolution trip. *You can count me out,* Lennon sang. *You can count me in.*

"I thought we were going to see a cat fight, old sport," Jim says, and he's singing loud, his voice so loud in that wide open air, that air that stretches infinite forever out over the Pacific and beyond to Russia and Mongolia, North and South Vietnam and Cambodia, China and India, Iraq and Iran and Turkey and stretches in the other direction across the whole country and keeps going across the Atlantic to England and France and Spain and Norway and Sweden and Greece and keeps on going. All of us breathing the same air, walking the same earth, feeling the same sun, so why can't we get along, live in peace, reach out a hand to help a bro get up when he falls.

Oo-ee, oo-ee baby.

Jim sings that Frankie Ford number, "Sea Cruise." Huey "Piano" Smith's boogie-woogie piano holds down the rhythm, those second-line horns kicking in, sour New Orleans horns, sour the way Coke tastes if you pour it into a glass and squeeze enough lemons so the juice gives it the bitter taste of tears, the tears of the slaves working the plantations all those years, and even after emancipation, trying to make it as sharecroppers, not sure who they are any more, living in one-room shacks, and I hear it in Jim's sad-sack ragged-ass voice.

That song's a party, a party so happening and noisy and drunk, all the crazy-wild shit going on in the bedroom, you can miss that scary-ass line:

I gotta boogie-woogie like a knife's in my back.

You could have a go at unraveling that one, but good luck. Dylan could have written that mixed-up confusion. I mean what sense does it make? Knife in your back, you'd be dead, or lying on the floor bleeding. Last thing you'd do, knife in your back, the boogie-woogie. Most of that song's about rockin' out, and how the singer can't help himself, gotta move to the sound, but then he asks his chick to go on a sea cruise. Tells her she's got nothin' to lose. So it's way more than rockin' out. That sea cruise her ticket out of some nowhere deal. You could think he was ready to take her right out of whatever boring bummerosity of a mundane life she been living to a groovy new scene. So the pure state of rockin' out is the freedom of escape. Which doesn't explain the knife in the back. Or maybe it does. Maybe that song is saying wake the fuck up. You got a knife in your back. The hard cold lemon sour life, well there's more to life than that, you gotta take yourself to a higher ground, to a better place, if even for one night. Yeah, got a goddamn knife in your back but still.

Live motherfucker.

"Simone didn't like you sitting so close to Elise, old sport."

Damn Simone. Always talks how she can't stand a guy being jealous but all I gotta do is glance at a chick.

"Ancient history, man," I say. "Yesterday's papers."

"Didn't look that way."

"Fucking *chicks*," I say.

"*Fucking* chicks," Jim says.

And we're high-fiving there in the road, in the dry mustard-brown dirt dust, two freakster bros playing hooky, high flyin' and flyin' high, free of the burden. Fucking *chicks*. Not so hard to understand Henry Miller, where he came from, not wanting the burden, just after a free fuck. Such a goddamn goddamn burden a guy shoulders having a chick.

Jim walking along that dry dirt road, the field on one side of him and on the other, past another field, the ocean. I'd only once seen him in a sorta nature situation outside campus where he had to walk through the trees to get to class, although Jim took the shuttle when he could. Indoors, his world lit by electric light bulbs and the glow of the KLH, and his Sherman's, poet of the night. Inside, indoors, in. Where Jim lived. Only other time, Jim in nature, me and him walked that road to King Editor's Halloween party. Jim dressed up as Lola stumbling through nature in those high heels 'til he took 'em off in frustration. That was mankind for sure. Apes dressed up same as something we're not, pretending we're gods, make a mess of everything we touch same as Midas, only instead of gold, everything turns to shit.

"The smoke," Jim says, "coming out of her ears."

"You're tripping man," I say. "And everyone knows it. You're acting too normal. Aside from the twitching."

He looks at his palms again, tries to figure if he has any twitch action underway.

"Jim, man," I say. "Don't you know anything?"

The dust of the road shimmering, the dust is a million ants on their slow march only it's not ants, it's dust critters, small as small little ants, smaller even, and us two walking on their backs.

"If you look, the twitching stops. It's the invisible twitch deal. You got it *bad*."

Wild flowers in the empty field on our left, between the road and the cliff. Yellow beach dandelions and white American water plantains and pink wild onions and red vibrating bush aloes and scarlet pimpernels and gold fiddlenecks and lavender coastal dunes milk-vetches and blue common borages and the rest. Living with Simone I've learned about the local plants. And the California poppies. Never seen 'em glow how these glow, shimmering in the sunlight. And on our right the corn is growing, two inches in the time we walk by on the dust dirt road, dust critters coming up with each step, us walking down the road on their backs, me in the Keith Richards snakeskin boots, Jim in his ridiculous brown penny loafers.

He gotta deep-six those things.

"I'm going to ruin my shoes, old sport," Jim says. "Tromping around out here in the sticks."

"Should have worn those sandals you used to wear all the time, man."

"Jade made me throw those out," and from the way he says it he's still wishing she hadn't dumped him.

"You need some hipster boots, man," I say. "Change your life."

That's the dream. Change your shoes, change your life. That's what almost no one understands. When Dylan started dressing same as a hobo, talking same as a hillbilly, pretending he's some Jack Kerouac meets Woody Guthrie freakster bro hopping freight trains, bard of the common folk, that wasn't changing your shoes. That's becoming who you really are, not always easy to get there. All kinds of obfuscations. They have no real use for the Bob Dylans and Pablo Picassos and J. D. Salingers. They want uniformed drones who look and talk and act the same. They being the Masters of War, the industrialists, the corporate machine that's gonna kill everything.

It's not a conspiracy, at least not always. Paul Krassner and Mae Brussell and the rest of them conspiracy theorists have it wrong. It's the nature of a corporation to kill. Pretty much no one at a corporation knows that. They understand the agenda to be the bottom line. Maximize profits. Only to maximize profits, when left on its own with no regulation, well everything goes by the wayside. You cut the rainforests if you need the wood or the land. You kill the air and the water with the foulest of toxins if you save a nickel making whatever you make. Produce food that's unhealthy. Clothes with toxins in the fabric. And plastic. Make everything you can from plastic, plastic that'll be here when all the animals and fish and humans are long gone.

A corporation is one of those H.G. Wells "War of the Worlds" Martian fighting machines, the Golden Dragon come to life with a 180 IQ and a huge-ass ray gun.

Only you can't kill it with a deadly strain of bacteria.

"Do yourself up right with a pair of Tony Lama's," I say. "Maybe the Teju lizard skin deals. Those boots'll take you on a fucking sea cruise."

And that's all *Thee* high flyin' Freakster Bro needs, raises his left hand, snaps his fingers, his off-key crazy-ass voice, and only he knows what strange vision of the world unfolds there before him. *Old man rhythm is-a in my shoes.* And he's jiving The Frug, twists his right hand out front of him, then his left, then behind him, one hand, the other. And I'm there in the dirt dust too, my version of The Swim, and I join in singing, the two of us, middle of nowhere, cornfield on one side, wildflowers on the other, and out past the cliff, the Forever Infinite Pacific. Big stoner grin on his face, snaps his fingers. *Won't you let me take you on a—sea cruise.*

We walk down the road, us on the backs of those dust critters, and isn't that how it is, capitalist industrialist pig patriarchs on the backs of the workers, on the backs of the Blacks and the Chicanos and the poor white trash and when it gets right down to it, on the backs of the middle class working stiffs, everyone who gets paid an hourly rate or a set salary to do their job while the Masters of War, they don't work, they let their money do the work. Such a rigged deal, money begets money, power begets power. And I don't want in to that rigged system.

Yeah, it was easy for me to think that back then, when I lived off my parents, some of my dad's salary arriving each month. Free money. It seemed as if I was free of all that, a freakster bro in search of the truth, in search of the ecstatic release a Visions of Johanna chick can provide, in search of *Dharmakaya*.

If a human wants something to happen, don't ask two freakster bros flying high on acid and weed and wine to do it. The two of us out there on the dust dirt road, might as well be the middle of nowhere, and what the fuck are we doing? Yeah we can't remember, so we walk back to the party.

"Where's Saul?" Simone says.

"Hellfuck if I know," I say. "I'm not his keeper."

Yeah I was pissed about her jealousy deal.

"Michael, I asked you and Jim to get Saul," she says. "He gets so lost in his work he forgets about everything else."

Far as I could tell, the only thing Saul got lost in was that chick Lizzie's pussy. Simone has too much going on, guests to attend to, she'll save it for later. Blame me for Saul missing the party. She gets Jim cleaning some homegrown using her *Exile on Main Street* cover, which is all that damn sexist album is good for she tells us. Tells anyone who'll listen her rap about the Stones' sexism and how she's finally gonna toss *all* her Stones albums, she really is, 'cause it's so hypocritical for her to dig the Stones.

Soon as Jim hears that shit about the Stones he gets *Exile* rocking the house and everyone is dancing, some in the living room, some out on the front porch, some out in the garden. I'm talking to Jim there in the kitchen, and Simone standing there too, the three of us grooving to "Hip Shake."

"Simone wants *me* to take all her Stones and Zeppelin albums and sell them at Odyssey," I say. "Cleanse the place of sexist rock."

Man, that freaks Jim and he spills wine on his shirt, but it doesn't matter, that shirt has plenty of stains.

"That's a very bad idea," he says.

"I don't believe in God and I don't believe in the Devil," Simone says. "I'm a spiritual person but I don't experience spirituality as a good-evil-creator-destroyer trip, but the way the Stones seduce me makes me think the Devil's in their music."

"Oh but he is my sweet Susikins," Jim says.

Horror and anger and what-the-fuck across Simone's face in the moment of that moment.

"Just kidding, Ms. Braveheart," Jim says.

The second important thing happens after the party's over. Simone's still pissed at me, so I go for a walk on the beach. There's this thing gnawing at my insides. I stop and look out into the darkness where the ocean is, look toward the huge sounds of waves crashing. Something troubling me, as if it's pressing into my consciousness. It didn't have to do with Simone, and it wasn't the lonesome. This is different. It's something I have to do, and more than that, a truth so powerful inside me. I've been pushing it aside, a denial fueled by weed and booze. Well it won't be denied. It's so simple, so basic to who I am, and right then, the acid still doing its thing, I get it.

I am a writer.

Big bad blues riff explodes my mind.

I spell w-r-i-t-e-r. Writer.

Big neon letters, bigger than clouds, bigger than the moon and the sun and the stars:

A WRITER GOT TO WRITE!

I take in those big yellow-gold neon letters, absorb the

heavy traffic trip of what those words mean. Time to stop with the mind games, put up or shut up.

A WRITER GOT TO WRITE, MAN!

And I *am* a writer, I can feel it in every pot soaked cell of my body. Doesn't mean shit though if I don't write. I feel a change, as if all my past obsessions have regrouped into this one passion. I have a story to tell, I don't know the details of what it is yet, but it's there. A story to tell, a book to write, and tomorrow, I swear, I'll start to write it.

The ocean loud, but it's surface noise and I'm listening at a deeper level, where there's fewer sounds, the sound of my heart and the sound of my soul and the sound of the universe. And the faint sound of my story. Tomorrow, man, *tomorrow*, and soon I'll hear it better.

TWO

1. BIG SUR

THERE WERE TWO THINGS about Big Sur I never told Simone. The first, that Kerouac deal. You know, him calling his novel "Big Sur." Right there, made the place fucking luminous. The second, I'd been to Big Sur before. Me and Sarah. Actually, me and Sarah and a bunch of our friends from the meditation center, you know, where I first met her.

We camped in Julia Pfeiffer Burns State Park. On the cliff, the Forever Infinite Pacific so loud and blue and wild below us. Me and Sarah were still 16, still virgins, still pure. Before I got her pregnant. Before everything went south.

Ghost of 'lectricity. May of 1970. Me and Sarah in the back of that Ford pickup with all the camping gear. Heading for Big Sur. A bunch of us in four vehicles, maybe five.

That day Sarah was hyper-alive, shimmering, as if she'd been dusted with sunlight. Most of the time there was a sadness underlying whatever emotion was pooled on her surface, but this day she was pure joy. Maybe it was the wind making chaos of her long brown hair, or the danger of sitting in the back of the pickup as it wound down Highway 1, the Forever Infinite Pacific crashing below onto the rocks.

There was so much certainty in the firm line of Sarah's jaw, and her unwavering gaze, like the gaze of Victorine Meurent in Monet's "Olympia," whether she was taking in wild nature as we sped past it, or looking into my eyes to find, well, I'm still not sure. When I first met her more than a year earlier, she was a teenage beauty, so pure, so innocent, so, well, scrubbed. On this day her hair was longer, her face sunburned and she wore her typical dust-bowl clothes—the worn denim overalls, the soft white peasant blouse, the faded-brown leather hiking boots— and yet there was something about her that day that made me think anything could happen, and I better hold on for dear life.

We make a couple of stops along the way. The last one is to get gas and 'cause some of us need to use the can. It isn't a town, isn't a full block same as you find in a town or a city. It's some beater houses and a motel and the Texaco. What it is, is a no-name, you remember, one of those places you drive through to get from here to there.

Only reason I even get out of that pickup is 'cause of the Coke machine. It's one of those ancient curved-corners all-red Vendo Coke machines from the Fifties. The V-81a. Filled with cool-ass bottles of Coke. Warhol's "Green Coca-Cola Bottles" kinda cool-ass bottles.

Ever seen that Warhol deal? Homage to Duchamp, Warhol's bottles. Warhol was heavy into Coke. Said Coke symbolized the egalitarian nature of American consumerism. Said it didn't matter if you were Liz Taylor or a bum, a Coke was a Coke and no amount of money could get you a better one than the one the bum on the corner was drinking. 'Course what Warhol didn't say was Liz Taylor could afford to get her cavities filled. The bum gonna end up with a mouth full of rotten.

I guess that's what America's all about. The phony-ass everyone's equal trip. Authentic real, there's a hierarchy. Fortune or fame, enough of either can put you up on your high horse, up on the steeple with all the pretty people. Warhol was wrong, Coke tastes a whole lot different if you're drinking it out on the veranda of some place in Beverly Hills, than in the fucking gutter.

After I check out the V-81a I call to her, "Sarah, a time machine."

She climbs out of that pickup and runs over. We were both into old stuff—rusted signs, dusty felt hats, second-hand clothes. For sure she digs that Coke machine, and the bottles we can see through the glass in the door, and I don't have to say anything more, me and Sarah tuned to the same station. She turns and leans back against the V-81a, her blue eyes filled with me.

I know she wants one. Fifteen cents. That's what a Coke cost back then. I buy two bottles, one for me, one for her. Before we split outta there, her still leaning against the V-81a, I get my arms around her, give her a kiss, her mouth so sweet, sweeter than any Coke.

I could waste time filling you in on us getting to Julia Pfeiffer and setting up tents and all of it, but the reason I'm telling you about me and Sarah going to Big Sur is 'cause of one thing, so that's what I'm gonna tell.

Everyone had crashed out in their tents, and we were in ours too, lying next to each other, me hoping she'd let me touch her, and we'd make out, only that's not what happened.

"Want to get naked?" she says. "Under the stars?"

Oh man, total Sarah trip, pop out with some crazy-ass deal I'd never think of in a million years.

"Well I'm doing it," she says. "You coming?"

We're barefoot, carry our sleeping bags away from the tents, using the moonlight to make our way right to the edge of the cliff. Man, I could hear that huge-ass ocean, dark and wild, far below us. I turn on the flashlight and we find a flat spot where there aren't too many rocks. Nothing worse then lying on a fucking rock. We get the bags down, one next to the other, and that's when Sarah starts to strip.

It's a quarter moon, but the sky clear and the air pure and the smell of the salt water. We're at the edge of the planet, and I'm *so* alive.

There in the moonlight she undoes a strap of her overalls. She gets the other strap over her left shoulder, doesn't even undo that one, pulls her overalls down and steps out of 'em. Her legs pale, and I wanna touch 'em, I want to rub my face against her thighs, but instead I undo my belt. She's unbuttoning her blouse, gets it off, folds it careful and puts it inside her sleeping bag and her overalls too and I get my jeans off, and I stop. Oh man, nothing in the known world could stop my eyes from looking and looking and looking some more. First time I see her naked. Her tits smooth and firm. She pulls her hair out of her face, her nipples aimed right at me.

"God, Sarah."

Back then I'm on the fence about God. Don't know yet there isn't any God. It wasn't until everything's a ruin I figure it out.

She's looking up at the sky. "What is it?" she says. "The stars?"

"Yeah," I say. "The stars. Both of them."

"Which stars?" she says.

"Don't be silly," I say. "Never seen anything—person or flower, tree or animal, mountain or ocean—crazy-wild beautiful as you, Sarah."

Hearing me she doesn't try not to smile 'cause she knows I believe every word of it and she believes those words too, she believes I love her, and will love her forever. It's in the way those bigger blue eyes look at me. That's the deal when you have nothing for comparison. You can think something's gonna go on and on forever. It's only later I know how much I had, and how much I lost.

She gets her panties off, sticks 'em inside the sleeping bag too, and stands there smiling 'cause she knows she's pushing it being naked with me at the edge of the world, and she's laughing too, the laugh of hers that's innocent as a baby finch splashing in a backyard fountain, a pure I'm-so-happy laugh, the both of us under the moon and the stars, yeah she's happy and wild and free as any chick ever been.

I get the rest of my clothes off and oh fuck, major icy chill coming off the ocean. My cock's been hard from me looking at her, but it shrivels how a dick does when a freakster bro is cold.

"Look how little," she says.

"You're making me feel bad."

She comes to me, pushes her body against mine and our

arms holding each other and her mouth right there, lips against lips, tongues tasting each others mouth, her chest against mine, her pussy hair against my cock, and it's not little any more.

She steps away, "Feel better?"

She doesn't know the frustration, 'course not, and I'm not gonna explain. The ocean behind her, the thousand murmurs, but my ears couldn't hear them back then, the warnings in those murmurs, blinded by the luminous glow of Sarah before me and how can I be so lucky? What have I, Writerman, done to deserve Sarah, and every cliché spooling through my mind. This angel, this beauty, this love of my life. This enchantress, this Siren, this dream of a girl. My true love, my one and only, my heart's desire. And we're gonna be one forever, yeah we're different, we're better, we're so special, we're not same as all the others. Yeah, man, this is forever.

I didn't tell Simone about any of that either.

If I'd been driving instead of Simone, wouldn't have paid even a second of attention to that no-name. Not stopped. Not noticed the Coke machine. It was the end of August, 1973, less than a week before Simone would take off for Boston. Yeah, the summer almost over, all my big plans to write my novel lost in the smoke curling up from all the numbers we smoked since the party.

Our *special* weekend in Big Sur, this was it, man. We'd been driving at least an hour and a half since splitting Morning Glory Way, Simone at the wheel 'cause she never let anyone else drive her van. Simone has on her straw cowboy hat, the brim curling up at the sides, and the first number of the trip between her lips.

The van been vibrating since she floored it onto Route 1. I've got the distinct impression whenever Simone pushes it past 60, her fucked-up left front door and rear bumper say their last rites. Lucky's settled in her dog bed behind the driver's seat, and I hear her dog-ass snore, the Eric Dolphy Memorial Barbecue Snore, you know, me joking on that Zappa song, and Lucky is moving her legs, dreaming the chase of a rabbit. One of those times when the simple of a dog's life, it has appeal.

That no-name place probably has a name but there's no sign, as if they removed anything that could hip you to where you are, same as that Bolinas deal up the coast past Stinson where they don't want outsiders. We're maybe 10 miles south of Carmel, almost lost the sun by the time we get there, the sun heading for the horizon, looking to me less than the time it would take to smoke four doobies before it'll drop below the edge of the Pacific, ready to light up Australia and New Zealand and I guess Japan.

That no-name, there's a million of 'em between here and there. In America. I don't wanna have zip to do with a single one. Not the no-name towns, and not the never-left losers who live in 'em. Those losers are contagious, get too near 'em, might catch some of their disease. That loser way of seeing the world, thinking the cards so stacked against them what's the point of trying, to where they don't even imagine something good 'cause they know it's not gonna happen and they'll be disappointed all over again.

That no-name where we stop, right up there with the suburbs, right up there with all the shithole hodunks, right up there with Lowland Drive. Took me 18 years, but I split that scene. That's the deal about a loser place. It's simple. All you gotta do is walk away, get in the car, get the fuck out.

The no-name on the way to Big Sur, all it has is a Texaco station with the American flag at half mast, and a ma-and-pa grocery, flag at half mast too, and a one-story motel with a dark-ass bar attached and some cheap two-story farmhouse kinda houses. And yeah, they have flags flying half-mast, sure they do.

The worst is the cars. Not the handful of sorry cars that belong to the sad sacks who live here. The cars driving by. All day long and into the night.

Driving by, driving by, driving by.

The godawful sound of Dodge vans and VW bugs,

Corvette Stingrays and Cadillac Coupe DeVilles, Volvo 544s and Ford Fairlanes. And all the others.

Driving by, driving by, driving by.

Driving through that no-name blink-of-an-eye fast. It's not that there's so many of those cars at any one time, it's how relentless. Soon as one drives by, gunning the engine, and finally the losers living in that no-name have silence save for the soothing peace of the waves and the gulls, another car comes around the bend, engine roaring, so they can never relax 'cause any moment the peace gonna be shattered. Eats away at their souls. Every time another car drives by, a reminder they're living in a no-name humans pass by on their way from here to there.

Driving by, driving by, driving by.

Reminder to the never-left losers they didn't walk away, didn't get in the car, didn't get the fuck out.

If it been my choice, I wouldn't stop, woulda made the bet there's enough gas to get us to where we're going, but Simone said the tank's low and she needs to pee. And anyway, she's driving.

And anyway, she makes the rules.

Simone been dressed for 95-degree sunburn deal of Morning Glory Way, sleeveless yellow t-shirt, denim cut-offs, sandals and that straw cowboy hat I told you about. But the weather's changed and before she's off to the chicks' room, she's in the back of the van, digs a pair of jeans and a sweater out of her suitcase, that tired olive green suitcase with the burnt-orange and gold and yellow floral pattern on the outside.

I split the passenger side, got my leather bomber jacket to deal with the cold-ass fog blowing off the Pacific. That jacket was Dad's. I didn't ask, just took it. Well he's an old fucker, didn't need a cool-ass bomber jacket. I go looking for the sad-sack Texaco guy stuck running the joint so I can buy us gas. Past the two gas pumps, up to the office door, look through the dirt-streaked window. No one.

I go looking for him in the garage, which is big and dark.

Take off my shades, but still dark as fuck, my eyes try to regroup, and some machine whirring, maybe a large-ass fan, tools everywhere, and one of those grey metal cabinet deals on wheels, top drawer open full of socket wrenches and screwdrivers and pliers and all that. Toward the back an old maroon-red Volvo, one of the curved ones, disintegration paint deal in full effect, up on the hydraulic. Pieces of old car on the cement floor, big rusty oil drums, and the random old-as-fuck tire. Along the right wall, up high, shelves piled with dust-covered tires. The new tires. Although new can be a pretty relative term. So much dust.

That machine whirring away could be one of those Brian Eno discreet music records, only a noisy version. There's a couple windows on the left wall, but it's been so long since they been cleaned, more layers of crud stuck to the glass than on the office window. And something else. Up on the back wall, couple feet higher than the top of my head, a row of deer heads, and a moose head. Fuck, man. Once they were live deer free to dig life, crazy-wild in the wild. Those deer deserved to live same as me. That's how I feel about it. Still. And each deer killed, that was a little of our souls, and our humanity, and the wild spirit of our crazy-wild free selves, dying.

They were sacred, those deer.

The whirring of the machine, the air heavy with an old grease smell, and those deer heads. I walk back to get a close look. Oh fuck! And I've got the creepy-crawlies. I'm freaking, man. Someone's taped paper labels under those heads. Those labels curling, the tape yellow, the paper dirty white, and the words hand written in shaky-ass script.

Under one head it said "John F. Kennedy, November 22, 1963."

Under another, "Robert F. Kennedy, June 6, 1968."

And "Franklin D. Roosevelt, April 12, 1945," and "Abraham Lincoln, April 15, 1865."

Under the moose head, "Martin Luther King Jr., April 4, 1968."

Sick. Gives me the total creeps. I'm sweating, air hot and thick, oil stink, machine whirring and is it louder? Oh I gotta get outta there, and I get myself back to the front, about to split that garage when I hear something else, metal against metal. The maroon-red Volvo up on the hydraulic, a guy with his back to me workin' on it.

Don't know if I wanna talk to Texaco, you know, the guy under there, but we need gas, and no way I could explain it to Simone. If I tell her I'm creeped-out, she won't have any patience. Be same as the time she had to get those Chicano muscle guys to put up the fence around the acre behind her house 'cause I couldn't do it. Anyway, I can handle whoever's under that Volvo. Some no-name loser. Pull myself together, make my voice sound deep and confident, imagine the guy under the Volvo works for me.

"Excuse me, man."

He turns, but from where I stand, can't see his face, only black boots and some kinda blue pants. Voice that answers me, it's the voice a dog left out in extreme weather without any food or water for too long would have if it could talk. Thin-ass, parched, old man Ozark voice, weirdly high and thinly strange.

"*Sir,*" Texaco says, and he turns off the machine making the whirring noise, and takes a step forward, still can't see his face, but he's wearing one of those blue one-piece jumpsuits mechanics wear, the kind that usually has the guy's name written in script over his heart. More of a creak then a voice. Voice of an old fart.

"It's *sir,* kid."

Old fart. Beefheart. Trout Mask Replica. House in Woodland Hills where Beefheart and His Magic Band recorded Trout Mask Replica. Beefheart wearing the fish head mask. Yeah, that poem Beefheart recites, "Old Fart at Play."

Voice of an old fart.

"'Excuse me, *sir,*'" he says.

"Oh, yeah, *right,*" I say.

The way I say "right," I made it sound the way that chick Rhonda—who was coming outta the chicks' bathroom the night Jaded did the glam number on me and Jim, how her smirk woulda sounded if a smirk was a way a voice could sound. He comes out from under that car. Yeah he's an old fart for sure, needs a shave. I don't know how old exactly, but older than Dad. White hair coming out of one of those caps that have panels of netting alternating with panels of cotton in the part that goes around your head. On the front part, above the bill, it says "Gone." Back when it was new it probably said "Gone Fishin'," but the "Fishin'" part's worn off. Think of Harry Dean Stanton, who sings "Just a Closer Walk With Thee" in "Cool Hand Luke," if he were an old fucker with his face longer and narrower, skin same as old dry leather.

Looking closer, I reassess, 'cause he doesn't look much same as that actor. Doesn't look at all like him. Nothing but an old fart standing there in a blue garage-monkey one-piece that doesn't have anything written in script over where his heart is, and a shit-green cap that says "Gone."

What still freaks me are his eyes. They're sunk deep into his head. I think they're black, but right then I don't know 'cause it's dark in that garage. Don't matter anyway, that's not what freaks me. What freaks me is that looking over his shoulder deal I saw in those eyes. Anyone coming into the garage looking for him, guilty 'til proven innocent.

"I'm not selling those deer heads," he says. "Not selling the moose either."

He looks at me and he likes me about as much as I like him. "Wanna buy gas, man," I say.

Those motherfucker hard eyes, yeah I seen those eyes before. Same eyes Dr. Ellingsworth had, you know, Sarah's doctor. Same eyes as King Editor too. Son-of-a-bitch. Doesn't like my hair. Doesn't like my Alice Cooper "I'm Eighteen I Don't Know What I Want" t-shirt. Doesn't like my leather bomber jacket. Doesn't like my bellbottom jeans. Really doesn't like my Keith Richards snakeskin boots. Doesn't like any of it. But most of all, doesn't like my *hey, man* attitude. He knows I think this no-name sucks, and he knows I got my nose stuck up in the air regards him too. We stand there look at each other, and he turns as if he's gonna get back to work on the Volvo.

"*Wanna buy some gas,*" I say.

Pause, and when I finally say "*sir*" might as well be saying "*fucker.*"

"*Sir.*"

"See my brother," he says. "In the office."

"Your brother's not in the office," I say.

Big fucking pause. "*Sir.*"

"Then he's out by the pumps," he says. "Looks like me. Twin brother."

"There's no one," I say. "No one who looks same as you and no one who doesn't."

Another big fucking pause. "*Sir.*"

"Son of a bitch," he says. "Damn fool brother."

"So what about the gas," I say.

"Sir," he says.

One, two, three.

"*Sir.*"

"Fill it up what you need," he says. "Then you pay me."

I walk away from Texaco humming *he not busy being born, is busy dying.* Yeah, I'm so full of myself back then. So much worse. It's grey outside, total overcast deal. No sign of the sun, no sign of any human, not Texaco's twin brother, not anyone. I hinge open the gas cap cover plate, and unscrew the cap. The pump's one of those antiques from the Stone Age, curves where today they put angles. The nozzle is on the right side with a black hose attached, and the crank coming out of the left side. Stand there, nozzle in the fuel hole, cranking that thing, pumping into Simone's tank, and I hear it.

Caw caw caw. One of the black-billed magpies done alighted on the roof of the garage, letting the world know to beware the bad luck that follows it around. Fuck that bird. Drop my eyes, and there it is.

The time machine.

The cool-as-fuck red Vendo. Right where it was all those years ago. Fuck, 'cause that's when I realize this is the station where me and Sarah got Cokes on the way to Big Sur. Only it's not the same 'cause I'm not unconscious how I used to be. I know about the brainwashing, how we've all been hoodwinked by the corporate ad-machine into thinking Coke is cool. Still. I crave one of those bottles. The craving, man. Dope addict shit. From where I stand pumping the gas, can't tell if it's still working, can't see if there's any bottles of Coke in it. Even if it is in operation, they could have changed it over to cans.

I mean it's been a while.

Simone comes around the corner of the Texaco, and she's got on that wool sweater and her jeans.

"Simone, check it out," I say. "It's a V-81a. From the Fifties."

"That old thing?" she says. "Who cares? That's how the corporate patriarchal masters rip us off and rot our teeth at the same time."

She's getting her door open. "And it causes osteoporosis in women."

"Well I'm getting one."

She's stepping up into the van, and even with those jeans, the curve of her ass. Oh man, can't wait 'til we get to the honeymoon suite at that Big Sur Inn place. She's in the driver's seat, leaning out the window and I finish filling her tank.

"Train's leaving the station," she says.

I walk past the pumps over to the V-81a. Bottles, not cans. Cold-ass bottles. And the beautiful sadness. *Sarah, in the back of the pickup right next to me. Naked, edge of the cliff, her arms around me.* Stand front of the V-81a, Simone impatient in the van, and I'm jonesing.

Put a dime, then a nickel, into the slot. Nothing. Normally there's a mechanical sound, the money going somewhere and releasing something and I'd know I could open that narrow door with the glass window and take a bottle. I try the narrow door but it won't open. Press the coin release and my 15 cents falls into the change return and I fish it out. Try again, but still it doesn't work.

"Hey Michael," Simone calls out.

All I want, a bottle of Coke. Turn so I see her, her arms crossed, top of the window ledge, and she's leaning out the window, that straw cowboy hat tipped back on her head, still has her shades on, hair all crazy-wild. See her framed beautiful in the window, and why am I fucking with this Coke machine?

"Don't keep me waiting," Simone says.

"I still gotta pay the guy for gas," I say. "Keep your pants on."

Oh man oh man oh man have I blown it. Far away as I am from her, still I can tell, especially when she turns away. Fucking *chicks*. Well I'm getting me a Coke. One more chance I'll give it, three's the charm and all that, though I never had any personal experience with three being any kind of fucking charm, or any different than two or five or even 11. If three's the charm, then this chick Lauren, you remember, I was into her before things came together with Sarah, yeah she woulda been my Visions of Johanna chick. Sarah was the *fourth* chick. So that three's the charm deal, another of those lame things people say that amount to nothing. I mean I could almost make the case four's the charm. Then again, Sarah being the fourth, not the third, maybe that's why it all went to hell.

I'm gonna put the dime and nickel in again when I look at the label below the coin slot. Fuck, "30¢." That was rich. Same bottle of Coke, only it's costing me 30 cents. Hundred percent increase. What kinda world is it where that can happen? Gone to shit world, but then that's old news. So I put in my 30 cents, get a bottle, have a drink of that Coke and it tastes so good I decide it's worth the extra dough. I know Simone, and soon as we get out of that no-name, us smoking a number, she'll want a drink. So I get her one. That Boy Scout motto, "Be Prepared," you could do worse.

Up on the roof, another magpie has joined the first, Doom and Gloom up there, gotta be, showing up when trouble's on the way, crying their *caw caw caw*. Don't wanna go back into that dark garage, but I gotta pay Texaco. First the walk over to the van, Simone pissed smoking a Kool not looking at me.

"Got you a cold one, Susan."

Freeze-out, her looking out the windshield as if there's anything to look at, which there isn't. Nothing but the side of the grocery and the road, the *caw caw caw* getting louder, and why is everything so hard with these chicks?

"Keep my pants on?" she says. *"Keep my pants on!* Typical sexist crap. When you men look at a woman, do you see anything but a cunt to park your damn dick? I should tell *you* keep your damn pants on."

"Simone, don't mean nothing," I say. "Figure of speech. Come on, our final weekend."

She softens, reels herself back in. "Do you understand how sexist that is, Michael?" she says. "Why would you say that to a woman? You know why? Because you think if you didn't, she'd take them off. And the reason you think she'd take them off is because she wants your dick so bad."

Fuck, everything I say or do isn't symbolic, some deep psychological deal.

"Listen to me, Michael. That's the subtext. Here's some advice for you. Your next old lady, don't tell her 'keep your pants on.' *If* you want to keep her as your old lady."

I reach out with the Coke I got for Simone, "Things go better with Coke," and I laugh, and I'm sure she'll laugh and it'll diffuse the whole deal, but I'm wrong.

"Don't give me that poison," she says.

Oh well, walk around to my side, lay that bottle I got for Simone on my seat. That bottle looks sad, laying on its side. Alone on my seat. It deserves better.

Texaco's futzing with the tools in that metal cabinet on wheels deal.

"Owe you $6, man," I say.

Silence. One beat, and another.

"I mean *sir.*"

"You sure do, kid."

Those spooked eyes on me, scanning to make sure I'm not the one gonna turn him in. Still got on the cap. "Gone." Yeah he'll be dead and gone soon enough. I take a drink of Coke. Sooner though I'll be the one gone, on the road, going somewhere. He'll spend his last day in the damn garage with those deer heads, getting grease on himself, keel over of a heart attack and they'll find his cold stiff body on one of those dead tires.

"Where you headed?" he says.

"What's it to you?"

He steps forward, got a lube gun in his hand. "Don't give me lip, kid."

Fuckers same as him think 'cause they're old they're owed respect. Think 'cause they been around on the planet a while that all the platitudes and homilies and world-is-flat kinda nonsense they've filled their brains with is wisdom. And this motherfucker, simply 'cause he's got a foot in the grave, pretty much his whole sad-sack life already behind him, and I'm young and alive and I've got a whole life full of possibility ahead of me, he thinks he can treat me the way he been treating me. Well I don't need to take crap from this grease monkey. Get a five and a one out of my pocket, drop those bills on top of the socket wrenches.

"See ya around," I say, and spit on the floor of that garage. "*Sir.*"

I'm walking away from him toward the dead sunlight.

"Well wherever you're going," he says. "You chose a hell of a day."

Don't give a fuck what he thinks about this day or that day or any day. Still, it stops me, him sayin' what he said, and all the flags at half-mast. Usually takes some fascist screwball deal to get flags at half-mast, or mourning Lee's surrender at Appomattox, or Custer's death at the Battle of the Greasy Grass, or some such.

"What's with the flags?" I say. "Someone die?"

"Oughta keep your cards closer to your vest, son. Hundredth anniversary of the fire."

Takes off that "Gone" hat, rubs the top of his head through what's left of his stringy white hair. "People 'round here don't like outsiders. Especially if they got attitude. Get my drift?"

"That's their trip," I say.

Goddamn magpies, sounds as if there's a choir of them on the roof above us, *caw caw caw,* mocking me.

"Whole coast," he says. "From here to north of Cambria burned."

That was another thing I don't tell Simone. Why the flag's at half-mast. Don't tell her about the magpies either. She's superstitious about shit same as that. Back then I didn't know I was superstitious too, but I was and that's another funny deal, the way you trick yourself into thinking you're something you're not. Or not something you are. I try to forget about that anniversary of the fire deal, but it's heavy in my stomach, the thing itself, the omen of it, *and* not telling Simone.

I fire up a number soon as we split that no-name. Won't be gas stations or racist motherfucker auto mechanics or nothing 'til we get up to where we're going. Suck in the harsh, "Purple Haze" alive inside me, Hendrix in all his finery at Monterey, the frilly white blouse, the orange velvet pants, the guitar in flames, and I wanna be fucked-up bad, don't wanna think about the curse of that fire or my bad scene with Sarah, my bad scene with Elise, or all the bummerosity inside my skull. But worst of all, 'cause it's about to happen, Simone splitting in a week. Closer it gets, the more strung out I am for her. If we fucked all week, from when we woke 'til when we crashed, wouldn't be enough. Nothing was ever enough. Never. Suck in another mouthful, pass it to Simone, and what's *she* trying to deaden?

On the passenger side, reefer swirling up my mind, and in the moment of that moment I'm trying to remember how all of us, all my friends back home, high school days, how it could be we had such contempt for drinking and drugging. Back then.

When we were 15, 16. Thought we were better than all the boozers and druggies. Back then. Sitting in the van with Simone I have a memory of a feeling, how I felt when we thought booze and drugs were stupid. That feeling I remember, it meant *why would you want to anesthetize yourself?* It meant, *why wouldn't you want to feel everything to the max?* And how could I have once felt that way, and got so far away from it? Yeah that's what I'm trying to remember sitting in that passenger seat, and then I do remember.

Me and Sarah, our love was its own drug, a cloud we were on, and two wasn't a crowd on our cloud. Of course I didn't need reefer or the red stuff or peach brandy or tequila or Jack Daniel's or merlot, there was nothing I had to forget, until the wind changed, got cold and bitter, until I found out God was a lie, until there was no love and I fell through the cloud, came back down to earth. I suck hard on that number. Forget about today until tomorrow?

Fuck, forget about today until forever.

Simone has on that thick wool lavender sweater and the denims, her brown hair all crazy-wild tumbling down over that sweater, the wind coming in her open window, blowing some hair across her face. She's singing Joni's "California," and I figure she's less certain about the Boston deal than she lets on. Seeing her crazy-beautiful the way she is, the smoke rings of my mind, her I-don't-give-a-fuck vibe, her singing that song so loud, yeah it's groovy us together on the road to Big Sur. The bad acid of it was yet to come.

Bo Diddley had his 47 miles of barbed wire. Chuck Berry got his kicks on Route 66, all the way, Chicago to L.A. Dylan, Highway 51, running from up Wisconsin way, down to no man's land, and Highway 61, yeah, those bleachers out in the sun. Me and Simone have 20 miles of corkscrew madness. Worse, the sun near to gone, the darkness beginning. Simone's side, left of the van, that white line and a narrow lane going back to where we came from, and further left, no shoulder, Santa Lucia Range rising straight up.

Before we got to that no-name, the road had certainly had
its moments, winding the way it did, the van vibrating the way *it*
did, the red-headed turkey vultures gliding way above us and out
above the ocean, but soon after we split the Texaco, the road
steepened, so in addition to increasingly frequent twists and
turns, there's a severe grade for the Chevy to ascend, and from
the sounds of struggle—the engine out of breath, the pistons
sweating and groaning under the strain, the tires fighting to
maintain their grip—this battle between man-machine and the
natural earth has already been won.

Once in a while we pass a sign, *watch out for falling rocks*. That
was rich. What are we supposed to do, watch those granite
boulders come rolling down off the mountain, closer and
closer, the van in their sights, and, well, then what? As if there's
a clever way to avoid them smashing the van. If me and
Simone, our names on those rocks, goners. Watching or no
watching. How much California dough been wasted getting
those signs manufactured, figuring exactly where to put 'em,
getting a crew out there with post-hole diggers to dig the hole,
put in the post, pour the cement. So me and Simone can drive
by, see one of those signs, and start to worry. *Watch out for falling
rocks*. Good fucking luck with that one.

And then fog. Simone turns her headlights on, but with the
mountain there, and the beams bouncing off the thick mist that
showed up moments ago, might as well be driving through a fog
tunnel. My side of the road, sometimes a low guardrail there, as
if that can stop anything from careening over the edge, but
mostly nothing but black sky above, infinite dense black mist
stretching out over the water, and the sheer drop. Dead-man
drop. Drive too fast, turn too slow, and your car, you in it,
straight down, maybe bang against the side of the cliff 'til it
crashes into rocks and water, or if you're lucky, the straight fall
'til you hit ocean. That's when the vultures swoop in. If I could
roll the dice between falling rocks and that dead-man drop, I'd
take the rocks. No one survives driving over the edge on that
snake of a road.

No one survives the dead-man drop.

Simone all lit up from the number we smoked earlier, takes the fresh joint from me, gets herself a good long hit, and she wants that Coke I bought her, wants it right now.

"I'm thirsty, Michael," she says. "High and dry. Can you get the cap off?"

"Got a bottle opener?" I say.

"Use your teeth, Tarzan."

That was rich. 'Course she has to tell me about an old boyfriend who could get the cap off a beer bottle with his teeth. I tell her a guy same as that probably used his head for a hammer.

"Kind of deal a jerk livin' in a doublewide does," I say.

"Oh, and what do you snoot-in-the-air trust fund boys from Marin do?" she says. "Ask your maid to get it off with *her* teeth while she gets you off with her free hand."

Makes me feel so goddamn goddamn bad, her bitchy shit. This being our special weekend. If I'd had Jung there, or Freud or the jive-ass from the nut house where I spent those weeks after things went south with Sarah, he woulda told me she can't help it. Her subconscious is getting her some emotional distance to go with the physical distance. Me at Morning Glory Way, far West as a human can get, and her 3,000 miles away at some old house in Boston, nearly as East of Eden as you can get and still be in the U.S. of fucking A.

"No maid. Just a cleaning girl. Came once a week."

"Ooh," she says. "*Just* a cleaning girl."

"Someone had to clean the house," I say. "My mom working. Anyway, nothing sexist. No crime in paying good money to have someone clean your house. Same as you paying the Chicano guys to do the fence."

"And how old was your 'cleaning girl'?" she says. "Forty-five, 50? I'd bet you $50 she wasn't a 'girl.'"

Along my side of the road, near the edge, the dark outlines of the Monterey pines, those saddest of trees, their branches beaten by the wind, reaching out over the ocean. Those trees always make me think of photos I've seen, World War II military wives and girlfriends, their arms raised, their hands waving, watching the trains leave the station, taking their men away to go beat back the Germans and the Japanese, to stop the fascist disease from spreading. That was tragic, that World War II misery.

Not same as Vietnam. Vietnam was tragic, but in a whole other way. The Masters of War sending guys over there for no fucking reason. All those guys dying for nothing. But those motherfuckers who thought they were doing their patriotic duty, who signed themselves up for a tour of duty in those killing fields, or the draftees who chose to go fight instead of splitting for Canada or going the conscientious objector route or playing crazy like in Arlo's "Alice's Restaurant Massacree," hard not to think of them as fools. Tragic fools. No glory, no valor, nothing heroic about going off to fight that Vietnam war.

"Hey Simone," I say. "That bottle-opener mouth boyfriend of yours?"

Dig in my jeans pocket for my keys. You know how bottle caps are sort of corrugated right below the lip of the bottle? Well you get the end of a key under one of those corrugated notches and pry, and after you pry four or five of 'em, the cap pops off.

"What about him?"

I use my key to Simone's house, get the cap off, pass the bottle.

"He go to 'Nam?"

"How'd you know?" and she takes a drink. "This is nice."

She has that Coke bottle in one hand, the number in the other, and how's she steering the Chevy? With the fog cutting down on visibility, she oughta slow down. Hate to admit it but there are times when smoking weed is actually a bad idea. This is one of those times.

We're snaking along that winding road, the van doing its vibrating trip, the turns getting more extreme until it's one total hairpin deal after another. Forty-seven miles of barbed wire or this corkscrew madness? I'll go for the barbed wire. Take the kicks on Route 66 too. Have to pass on those bleachers in the sun, but we don't get to choose. Between her driving too fast, having to jam the brakes, crossing into the other lane to keep from getting too close to the edge, and God-who-don't-exist only knows how far down, the dark sea churning, and in my stomach I have a sick-ass quease.

"You're driving same as a crazy chick," I say. "Even the Incredible Hulk would be sick. Paul Bunyan would be turning green in the face. Charles Atlas, he'd be hanging his head out the window."

She laughs her stoned laugh, everything's so absurd, *an' he just smoked my eyelids an' punched my cigarette,* and I get the number, suck up more of the harsh, and I see the big picture, that in the totality of the cosmos, life or death is a speck on a speck on a speck of a small-ass small grain of sand. Meaningless. If the fates mean for the speck—me and Simone and Lucky—to go down tonight, so be it. The magpies back on the Texaco roof, *caw caw caw,* and what was their warning?

Simone's singing, singsongy kid's voice.

"I made Michael ma-ad, I made Michael ma-ad."

"And *you're* supposed to be the grown-up?"

The both of us, speck of a speck of a speck, more of that gone, baby, gone stoned laughter. Close my eyes, try that Zen White Wall Meditation trip, silence the *caw caw caw,* and maybe it'll cool me out. Super slow inhale, exhale, *white wall, white wall, white wall. One.*

Open my eyes, and it's really night, and the sun gone.
Two.

Simone tries the brights but they make it harder to see. And still she won't slow down.
Three.

Teasing me with her too-fast driving, flashes her silly stoned grin my way.

"I made Michael ma-ad, I made Michael ma-ad."

Fuck it.

"I don't remember a suicide pact," I say.

And the laughing. Both of us. It's the idiot laughter of too-goddamn-goddamn-stoned. Through the windshield, can't see more than a couple car lengths, the white line lit up fading into darkness, the looming shadow mountain, the sea an unseen presence, a vast black hole down below. The light from the moon filtering through the fog, angling through the windshield onto Simone's face, and we hit one of those hairpin deals, her face all shadows. When I see it again, crazy-wild smile, crazy-ass crazy as it is wild, daring me to say something, ask her to slow down one more time.

No way I'll say shit. If we drive over the edge, so be it. Honor in death or death in valor or better dead than alive. Or was it better dead then red?

Or some honky-white jive.

Dig for Pall Malls in the snap-flap cargo pocket of my dad's bomber jacket. *Forty-seven miles of barbed wire.* And right then. *Chicago to L.A.* Hand on the pack. *The bleachers out in the sun.* That was the moment. *Caw caw caw.* Some loud-ass sound. The Chevy jerking. Simone drops the bottle, Coke fizzing out on the floor and the bottle rolling toward the gas and brake pedals. My hand on the dash, *shit,* the van lurching to the right, and for sure we hit a pothole. Simone crazy-flipped-out screaming, *What the hell!* I should freak too, crazy-ass flipped-out screaming my head off as Simone, but I'm not. Instead, and it gotta be how fucked-up stoned I am, it's as if I'm not in the van, as if I'm looking inside it from somewhere outside, me as the Existential Freakster Bro, a version of me without the guilt, the me that doesn't give a fuck about right or wrong, the me that can lie and steal and betray, only this is different. Total detachment trip, and Simone shouting, *Oh my God.*

Oh my God? And all along she's been telling me it's the Goddess who made heaven and the earth. "Oh, oh, oh," she says. "It's an earthquake," and she jams her foot on the brake, both hands gripping the steering wheel the way you'd grip the bottom of a window frame if you were hanging from the 10th floor of some building. Her voice that high-pitched chick trip out-of-control flipped-out.

"Please, God, please."

It's not the time to tell her how God, whatever its sex, is a most likely and almost for certain sham. She's working to turn that steering wheel to the left, to keep us from going over the edge but her strength isn't enough to fight the force of the van, the momentum taking it to the right, toward the dead-man drop, and she screams, "I'm losing it."

Yeah she's a chick, all that feminist baloney, but when Death come knocking, what do I expect? All the talk, chicks doing everything a freakster bro can do, but when it comes down to the wire, helpless. I look through the windshield, if she doesn't hard left those wheels we're goners.

And that's when I'm not outside the van any more. That's when I'm right there in the passenger seat. Dead-man drop dead ahead. Vultures up there somewhere, gliding, waiting. That's when *I* get scared.

A lot of times, when the fear strikes, and I gotta deal with something new, something I haven't come up against before, well I'm frozen, stopped in my tracks.

Total mixed-up confusion scene.

Well lucky for me and Simone and Lucky, for some reason I never get to the bottom of, this isn't one of those times. Instead, I'M THE MAN. Last freakster bro standing, guns a-blaze.

What I do is fucking slick. Total calm trip. I lean over, get both hands on the wheel too, and turn that sucker hard-ass left. She's screaming how chicks do when they lose it. Doing the fucking flip-your-wig freak-out, *You'll kill us! Michael!* There's some kinda supersonic sound in my ears, try to get my life to flash in front of my eyes. I only want the good parts, I mean if I'm gonna die at 20, I oughta get to see a montage of the good shit, but all I can think about is how fucked it is that we didn't have our special weekend, and me and Simone didn't get to fuck some more, and we'll never get to fuck again 'cause we'll be dead and I don't think there's any fucking going on in Hell. And if there is, the only one who gets to do it is the Devil. But if there's no God, there's no Devil, and no way can there be a heaven or a hell. So if this is it, there isn't any more fucking in my future. And that's a sad-ass bummerosity.

It's chilly in the van but I'm sweating all over.

I've got the wheel hard left and the van jerks away from the edge, swerves towards the white line and we're crossing it, headed into that sheer mountain wall, but I guess though I'm feeling calm, my brain knows better, sends me some adrenaline and I grip the wheel tight, put the muscle into it and turn it to the right, get us back in our lane, and yell, "Fucking relax, Simone. Fucking cool it down."

Blown tire, front right, I feel it, the way the van's leaning in my direction, that weird sound coming from the wheel. She has her foot on the brake, and through the fog, has to be a goddamn goddamn mirage or a God-given miracle. Well it's the real deal, a pullout. Ahead on the right. God-who-I-don't-think-exists giving me proof I'm wrong.

"We're stopping," I say, "in that pullout deal," and I turn the wheel hard right again, Simone helping and the van rolls off the pavement and into that dirt area. I turn the ignition off, she jams the brakes, and the van stops.

Dead-ass stops.

Her brights lighting up the dirt and the weeds, and a car length further, the edge, and beyond, nothing. Nothing but that dead-man drop, the silent glide of the vultures and the faint *caw caw caw* echo of the magpies.

2. WORKING AT THE ARTISTS' GARAGE

SIMONE SOMEHOW MANAGED TO hang onto the number, and she's sucking away at it same as a jonesing fiend, staring straight through the windshield, her body shaking as if that shaking has nothing to do with her. I undo my seatbelt, and I'm shaking too, get my door open, step out of the van and fuck, man, my legs don't have any muscles, fall into some weeds. Lay in the foxtails and scrub brush, a rock digging into my ankle, hurts same as shit. *You're OK, calm it down, man, calm it down.* The guy with the hammer pounding the inside of my chest, the throbbing of my ears, mouth dry. *You're alive!* Wanting to forget fast as possible that death trip so close, but my body wants me to remember, and my body is winning.

I sit up and the front right tire, the one that blew, it's right there. The rim digging hard into a pool of spent rubber. Simone wakes from her trance, calls out in a shaky tremolo, "Michael!" An owl off somewhere making those deep strange *hoo hoo hoo* sounds. "Where are you?"

I tell my legs to get it together, get myself up, door on my side still open, "You OK, Susan?" and she's still staring into the dark, insane smokin' that spliff. Walk 'round to her side, yank her door, get her outside, and off the road and both of us in the weeds. I take the roach and there's one good hit left to help me forget. Inhale everything I can get, and when it's gonna burn my fingers, toss it onto the road.

Oh man, 'cause in the moment of that moment I remember those flags at half mast, the bad omen, and something else, 'cause it's summer, all the brush dry as kindling, and me flicking a burning roach. What kinda idiot? Snakeskin boot grinding that sucker. Out.

Smell of weed and cold air and pine, smells alive out here, and that's the deal with being in nature on a cold night, which might seem weird-ass to say since we're on a paved two-lane, but it doesn't matter. It's nature. The two-lane is man's feeble effort to tame nature, put his mark on it.

"Ever check your tires, Simone?" I say. "Bald as an old fart's head."

Old fart at the Texaco, his Gone cap and the deer heads. Beefheart at that Woodland Hills house and Trout Mask Replica, and his fish head mask.

"Old fart at play," I say.

"What nonsense," she says.

"The one that blew," I say. "And all the rest."

"The rest of what?"

"Tires," I say. "Bald as an old fart's head."

"Where's Lucky?" she says.

The both of us climb back in, look behind Simone's seat. That mutt's eyes on Simone and me, grinning, I swear, mouth open dog pant deal. Simone clips the brown leather leash onto Lucky's collar, all of us out of there and we get over on the dead-man drop side of that Chevy.

Damn I gotta take a piss.

"Well you're the man," she says.

Yeah that explains everything.

"Well you're the feminist."

"Men know about changing tires."

"I gotta piss," I say. Fucking *chicks*. "Got a spare?"

"I don't know," she says. "You're the man."

"I really gotta fucking piss," and I don't care if anyone drives by and sees my dick sticking out, and I walk toward the back of the van. I get so I'm about three feet south of it and Simone gets the back door open, the big feminist on an expedition to find the spare.

I really really gotta piss right the fuck now.

My problem, that wind blowing in from the ocean. If I'm not careful it could blow my piss back on me or Simone or Simone and the van. Three good reasons to be careful. That Pacific wind, it's blowing to the northwest so I gotta get my dick facing northwest too and hope the wind doesn't do a sudden directional shift. Unzip, get it out and it's stiff from needing to piss so bad. Simone sees me with my woody in my hands.

"Always at the ready," she says. "Don't you start jacking-off now, Michael."

"I always jack-off after a blowout," I say. "Wanna help?"

"Nope," she says. "I'm not your little cleaning girl."

A thick stream of yellow and the wind catches it, helps it out onto the road, and maybe Simone doesn't wanna take a chance, gets herself and Lucky around to the cliff's edge side of the van. Just in time, man. The wind shifts, and piss hits the back of the van.

"Don't you try to piss on *me*," she says, but where she stands, no chance of piss gettin' on her. I finish without getting pee on myself, but more gets on the back of the van. Bad omen, pissing on the van. Bad feng shui. Jung, Freud, even that shrink at the nut house, they'd all have plenty to say about pissing on your chick's van, although I don't need anyone to tell me what it means. Fuck, we're doomed.

Get my dick back inside my pants and zip up.

"You can change a tire, right?" Simone says.

Yeah, sure. Same as I'm such an expert at putting up a fence. I don't know shit about cars other than put the gas in, turn the key, get gone, baby, gone.

I get out The Dylan, spark it. "Let there be light," and it's weird how when it's real dark, how lighted up a lighter flame makes the scene. There *is* a spare in the rear compartment and a deal for jacking the car. And a red flare.

One sad-ass red flare.

First thing, pick up the flare and try to figure out how to get it lit without burning my nuts off. A flare's a loaded gun if you don't know what you're doing.

If you're me.

Simone stands there, pulls at her sweater cuffs, trying to cover her hands and keep hold of that leash. Lucky's found herself a spot in the dirt and pine needles and she's lying on it. It's cold out there, getting colder. I don't say anything, but my hands are cold too.

"Well," she says. "What you waiting for?"

"Susan," I say. "I know every song Bob Dylan ever recorded. But changing a tire is not part of the repertoire."

"I'm with a guy who can't change a tire?"

Yeah well first things first. "You take The Dylan," I say, and hold it out, the silver casing warm, the orange-blue flame rising, her face warm in the mellow light. Her fingers are cold, touching my fingers, but even amidst this crazy scene, just to touch her.

Oh man, *to touch her,* and in the moment of that moment I don't care about the flat or the cold or the piss on the back of the van. I look at Simone, expect her to be all lit up from us touching, and that's when I realize how out-of-sync we are 'cause here I'm all turned on to feel Simone's fingers but it doesn't mean anything to her.

"It's really Bob Dylan's lighter?" she says.

"For sure," I say. "He used it to light his Marlboros when he recorded 'Just Like a Woman.'"

I pick up the flare, it's dusty, maybe it's too old, maybe it won't work.

"He's such a sexist pig," she says.

Still, she can't deny the pull of it. The Dylan, and she holds it so I can see what I'm doing. Red paper tab at one end, and when you pull it, this sandpaper-like deal sparks. You gotta make sure you pull the tab fast and get your hand away from the end, 'cause once lit that flare shoots fire.

"I thought feminists fixed their own cars."

Stepping out into the road I pull that tab, pull it hard and fast, but what happens, the end of it rips off.

"How long you had this thing?" I say.

I peel off more red paper real careful so I can get another grip and try again. Second time, it sparks, flare comes alive, bright orange gold flaming out the end.

"Some hand-job," she says.

I shoulda been more aware, you know, 'cause of the fire danger, but after all this back and forth with Simone I'm not thinking so clear. I set the flare on the road couple car lengths back of the van. Yeah well I showed her. I can handle this scene. Lucky sniffing in the weeds lowers her haunch, and a stream of pee pooling in the dirt.

"That was the one good thing about my ex-husband."

"What?" I say. "He could pee without getting any on himself?"

Fuck, first the hammerhead bottle-opener mouth boyfriend did time in 'Nam, now her *unconscious* sexist pig ad-exec hubby. Next she'll have something good to say about that freshman she was bangin', night I first saw her at the Halloween party.

"He could change a tire," she says.

Fucking feminists. Want the guy to do everything a macho guy normally does—bring home a decent paycheck, keep the house all maintenanced, take care of the yard and the car—and everything else too. Be all sensitive and understanding and vacuum and cook dinner and do sex their way.

Where's Henry Miller when you need him?

Boy do the feminists hate Henry Miller. They consider him the unconscious sexist pig of all unconscious sexist pigs. King Patriarch. Even Anaïs Nin, his lover *and* his patron, she called him "a sex and a stomach." For a while he lived in Big Sur. I'd read about Henry Miller's sexist trip. Read it in "Sexual Politics." *That* book. Simone kept a copy next to her bed she loved it so much, and sometimes after we fucked she'd lie there naked and read sections to me. Kate Millett wrote it, and she doesn't know the first thing about Henry Miller. Or men either. Probably frigid or a lesbian, that chick.

Henry Miller, he knows it's a war, the power trip between freakster bros and chicks, and who's got the upper hand. And when it comes to fucking, who can say what's right and what's wrong. What's sexist and what's not. Kate Millet makes a big deal about "Sexus." *That* book. Miller's narrator, Val, has his way with that Ida chick, pulls her into the bathtub with him, and she's his, *like a bitch in heat,* he wrote, sucking his dick, bending over so he can give it to her like she was a dog, and when he's finished, gives her a bite on the ass. His mark, his brand.

Well maybe, Ms. Fucking Millett, that's what Ida wanted. Maybe that's how she likes to seduce a man. I mean she did come walking into the bathroom when the guy was naked bathing in that tub. Some chicks are into that, almost an S&M trip. Same as some guys. That naked guy kissing the dominatrix chick's boot in the Diane Arbus photo. How come Kate Millett didn't write about those two? I'll you tell why, 'cause Kate Millett doesn't have any problem with a chick having her way with a guy, especially a macho chick with a whip. Kate Millett doesn't care what goes on long as the chick's in charge. When it's the other way, that's when the feminists go crazy, beating the world up regards how this is sexist and that's sexist and every damn thing a guy does is sexist 'til everyone rolls over and screams *enough, enough, uncle, we give up.*

Simone stands there in the dark, goddamn goddamn ex-husband. Doesn't she know, last thing a freakster bro wants to be reminded of is the other guys their chick fucked.

"He could change the spark plugs," she says.

Lighting her Kool with The Dylan, wanting for me to fix everything.

"He could use a post hole digger."

"I don't get it," I say. "Why am I the one has to change a tire?"

Smoke curling up from her mouth, *like a bitch in heat.*

"Set the posts," she says.

Damn, chicks don't know what it is to be a guy. Moonlight across her chest, curve of her tits pushing against her sweater.

"You're all so gung-ho," I say.

"Build a fence."

"On doing everything *else* a guy can do."

She slips The Dylan into her jeans pocket. "Shut up,

Michael."

"No," I say. "It's a double standard," and there's something about chicks and The Dylan, hell of a time getting it out of their hands.

"If the guy is supposed to change the tire," I say. "Then the chick should suck dick. What's the difference?"

"'Chick'?!"

"OK, *woman.*"

Smoke between her fingers, lit end aimed at me, and I'll have to wait 'til later to get The Dylan back.

"The *'chick'* should lay eggs," she says. "In the henhouse."

My face hot, damn I said it wrong. "One's a macho male stereotype," I say. "The other's a sexist *female* stereotype," and if me and Simone were in one of Henry Miller's novels, I'd take her, right there behind the van, in the dirt and weeds.

"The *chick* should suck dick?" Simone says, and inside me, *She screamed till her face got so red then she fell on the floor.*

"You're hopeless," she says.

Lucky finds a spot of earth away from where she peed, sits on her haunches, then lays down, starts licking between her legs the way dogs do. But this isn't a Henry Miller novel, it's me and Simone and Lucky out in the dark, miles from any other humans.

"You don't understand," I say, and I reach out and she passes me the Kool. I hate that menthol shit, but her mouth on it and I want mine on it too. So much fucking tension, and she's beautiful, on the road, *like a bitch in heat.*

"Oh I understand," she says. "Sometimes I think sexism is embedded in the Y chromosome."

Henry, help me!

The tire jack has three parts, so the first problem is figuring how it fits together. It's not that I don't have an aptitude for things mechanical. I deal with cameras and enlargers and developing film, turntables and amplifiers and guitars, typewriters and movie projectors and cigarette lighters. It's philosophical, the position I've taken. My response to a teacher I had in third grade. She gave us a list of spelling words each week. Colossal waste of time memorizing the spelling of those words. Why did she think they published dictionaries? Even in third grade, I knew. Memorizing, for saps. I had better things to do. Read "Crime and Punishment."

Manual labor, same deal. Only instead of the dictionary, there's guys you hire, practically Ph.D.s in the art of oil changing and house painting and hedge clipping. Did Dostoevsky fix his own car? Henry James? Langston Hughes? How about Picasso? Dali? Pollock? They all worked down at the Artists' Garage, right? Dylan under the hood replacing spark plugs. Lennon installing a new starter. Beefheart changing out the oil.

I ain't gonna work at the Artists' Garage no more, ma.

Well I'm not Dostoevsky, not Pollock, not Beefheart. And anyway, what about Hemingway, he could fix a jeep, clean a gun, and Kesey, he could cut down a tree, and Bukowski, all those years at the post office. Even a great artist is more than a brain in a bottle. And anyway, nothing philosophical about right now. Here on the side of the road there's no Ph.D. in the art of tire changing to hire, no one but me, fucking carjack in pieces on the van floor, and dig it or not, I gotta work at the Artists' Garage tonight.

First thing involved in changing a tire, gotta unscrew the lug nuts while the tire is still held in place by the weight of the car pressing it into the dirt. That's when you use the lug wrench to unscrew the nuts holding the rim to the axle. I get Simone's lug wrench, go around to where I'm standing next to the bum tire.

"Simone, got a flashlight?"

Of course she doesn't.

"Come on Lucky," Simone says, and goes to where the flare is flaming away on the road. Picks it up, fire shooting away from her.

"Let there be light," she says, and walks back to where I am.

"Be careful with that thing, Susan," I say. "It's high fire danger out here. Old fucker at the Texaco told me," and I get down on my knees there in the weeds next to the bum tire. Try to get the hubcap off, but there's nowhere to grip.

"You have to pry it," Simone says. "My ex-husband would take a screwdriver and—"

Break a thumbnail, nowhere to grip.

"Fuck your ex-husband."

Oh man that pisses her so bad. Figure she's gonna split, take the flare with her and I'll be in the dark even more than normal. I try the lug wrench to pry the hubcap off, but I don't have any leverage, and Simone didn't bring her goddamn husband's screwdriver, or any screwdriver, and my Swiss Army knife is at Morning Glory Way, which is the truth of why I'm mad. My hands hurt from the cold and I hit the damn hubcap hard with the lug wrench, beat-the-shit hard. Drop the lug wrench in the dirt and I'm gonna call it quits when miracle of fucking miracles, another sign from that pretend God, hubcap falls into the dirt, clangs against the lug wrench.

"Groovy," I say.

Simone lowers her hand, flame shooting out of that flare, and I feel the heat.

"Careful," I say. "You'll burn me."

"Don't tell me to fuck my sexist pig husband," and she raises the flame away from me. "Still makes me ill."

The lug wrench is in the shape of a cross, I guess so a human can pray for guidance while removing lug nuts. I get one end fitted over one of 'em, you know, a lug nut, get both my hands on that heavy metal cross.

"It was you," I say. "Saying he was such a genius with a screwdriver."

I put my strength into it. Nothing. Lug nut doesn't move and I hate for Simone to watch me fail. Change my position, really grip the wrench. *Help me here, help me.* Still nothing, and I bet I look weak. Third time, *come on, baby,* but no go. That lug nut might as well be fused to the stud.

"Didn't know the first thing about keeping a woman happy," she says. "But he could keep a car running."

Man versus machine, machine winning yet again, and

between dealing with that lug nut, and Simone looking at me same as I have the smallest dick any guy ever had, I could work myself up into feeling same as shit, but I remember something. I'm a writer, not a grease monkey. Fitzgerald wouldn't have been able to get that tire off, not Dali either. For sure not scrawny-ass Dylan.

I'm right. My philosophical position. We need one of those Ph.D.s in tire fixing. We're gonna have to get Texaco or his evil twin to use some kind of high-powered lug wrench to get those nuts off of there, and that means walking back to the no-name. I don't know why, but in the moment of that moment I get this urge to check Simone's spare. Maybe 'cause of what happened the day me and my folks were gonna see "Goldfinger."

Ghost of 'lectricity. It was a Sunday and I was 11. Me and Mom and Dad in the white Rambler heading for the theater in Sausalito, Dad driving of course, and it was somewhere on Bridgeway the tire blew. Dad swearing and his brow in a stranglehold of a clench and the deal that happens when he's furious, the end of his tongue folds back on top of itself and his teeth dig down into the top of that doubled-over tongue, and it makes his face look total horror show, wanting to blame me, wanting to blame Mom, I mean if Sandy the dog still been alive he'd be blaming her. Gets out of the car, gets the trunk open and that's when the swearing really amps up, and guess what? The spare in the trunk was flat, and you know what, I was glad, even with not getting to the movies that day. I felt an exultation. The Big Man, Mr. Always Knows Best, Mr. Genius Handyman, blowing it. He'd forgotten to get the spare fixed and there we were, a tire on the car flat, and a spare tire with a nail in it. He starts yelling at Mom, God-who-for-sure-don't-exist knows why, tries to blame Mom but we all knew the spare was flat 'cause *he* drove over the nail. Year or so earlier he'd changed out that tire for the spare, and put the tire with the nail into the trunk and forgot all about it. That tire with the nail lay in the darkness of the trunk, a time bomb waiting for the day when another tire went flat. And finally that day arrived.

Simone's spare is in the back of the van, under a piece of grody carpet, under a floor panel. Where the tire is, it stinks of old rubber. The orange-blue flame, Simone's face luminous, her hair alive in the wind. She's trying to hold the flare so I can see what I'm doing, but it's tricky 'cause of the flame. I get the bolt undone that's holding the spare in place, get the spare out.

"Your tire's flaccid, Simone."

"Don't get me started," she says.

I set the spare down, lean it against the bumper.

"We'll crash in the van," I say. "We can walk to the garage in the morning."

"You're what's flaccid."

"It's late, we're tired, it's dark," I say. "Come on Simone, get in the van."

She throws the flare at the road and it spins 'round and Lucky fucking freaks, jumps up from where she been lying near Simone's feet, pulls at the leash, barking so loud it hurts my ears.

"Goddamn it, Susan," I say. "Whole fucking coast could go up in flames."

"It's alright, Lucky," she says, and crouching she rubs Lucky's chest, and oh fuck, despite my anger, I wanna feel her hands on me so bad, on my chest, on my back, on my thighs. The love that dog's getting, I want it.

"Poor baby," she says. "He made me scare you."

Simone picks up the end of Lucky's leash and stands. Lucky stands too, turns her head one way, then another, as if the flare hitting the road reminds her of all the spooky critters in the darkness.

Simone puts her free hand on her hip, elbow sticking out, and the way she stands, I think of Lucy or Ethel, one of them, when they're letting Ralph or Ed have it.

"Get in the van, Susan," she says. "Get in the van. Come on, Susan, get in the van."

The flare's too near the rear tire, shooting flame towards it.

"I'm not your pet, and I'm not your little cleaning girl either."

The ugly-ass smell of burnt rubber. "If you wanna jerk-off in the van that's your business. Me and Lucky are walking to that gas station."

I get the flare, set it down a couple car lengths behind the van, out in the road where it can't 'cause trouble, maybe do some good. Fuckers drive too fast and Simone's side of the van is damn close to the road.

"Listen to me, Susan," I say. "The gas station and the garage are all closed up. We're gonna need a guy with a tow truck up here to get the tire off. Nothing gonna happen 'til morning."

Oh man does she hate conceding I'm right. But I am right and so we get in the van, me and Simone and Lucky. Me and her sitting up front, and Lucky in back. I pick up her Coke bottle, and there's about two inches of fizzed-out Coke still in it. It's the only sustenance we got.

"Susan, you drink the last of this," I say.

She takes the bottle, doesn't say a goddamn thing. Light from the moon comes through a break in the black clouds, lights her up, her lips around the end of the Coke bottle, and oh man.

"It's not my fault you blew a tire," I say.

"Don't talk to me."

"I didn't put old fart tires on the van."

"Not a fucking word."

"Oh, getting turned on?" I say. "Should I take off my shirt?"

"Shut up, Michael."

We sit in silence, awkward how-do-I-make-this-right silence, sometimes it's so dark I can't see her at all. She remembers she has the homegrown in her purse, and soon enough she has a number rolled.

"Susan," I say, and I've got my hand out. "Give me The Dylan."

"Why would I have it?"

"It's in your jeans pocket?"

She sticks her hand into that pocket, and I want it to be my hand in her pants.

She's feeling the smooth silver case, holding The Dylan close to her face, moonlight glinting off it. "Let me keep it," she says. "Every time I use it I'll think of you."

"No, you'll think of Dylan."

"Come on, Michael."

"I'll buy you one just like it," I say.

"But this was *Dylan's*," she says, and she slaps the lighter on my palm.

"You don't love me," she says.

"I gotta give you The Dylan to prove my love?"

"I give you my body."

"That's not the same."

"You're an asshole."

I spark The Dylan, light the number, and right quick-like we're smoking away.

"You don't think there's mountain lions out here?" I say.

"The problem's the cougars," she says. "They stalk men. Especially men who can't change a tire," and the glow coming off the number lighting her crazy-beautiful smile. "You were scared a big bad mountain lion was gonna eat you up. That's why you didn't want to walk into town."

"Look Ms. Feminist. *You* coulda walked to town and tried to buy a tire at midnight."

"It's dangerous," she says. "For a woman *alone*."

Trumped. There's nothing I can say. Try to tell a feminist not to do something and you're a sexist pig. But tell them *to* do something and you're an ass for putting them in danger.

"Come morning," I say. "The dark will lift and everything will be different."

How right I am, and how wrong.

Back in that no-name, Texaco probably getting drunk at the bar with his brother, and up on the roof of the gas station, Doom and Gloom, *caw caw caw,* and the vultures somewhere in the black sky, waiting.

The domino effect, one bad move leads to another. I was wrong, we shoulda walked to the no-name, got us a room at that motel, whatever it's called, with the bar attached. I would have made Simone in that motel room for sure after a couple glasses of merlot in the bar, took her naked on the motel room floor or in the shower or up against the wall, you know, pulled a Henry Miller.

One thing for sure, no fucking on the floor of the van gonna happen. If Dante rose up from the eighth circle, a sabbatical to update his "Divina Commedia," he could do worse than include that longest of dark nights, or darkest of long nights, or was it our night of the long knives, *Nacht der langen Messer*, or, oh fuck it, the night me and Simone sleep in the back of her beached van.

> Longest night, with no reprieve, no rest,
> Cold is the van, and hard the steel floor,
> The stink of dog, *eau de Lucky*, in their midst.

> Sleepless, sleep deprived and without end,
> Side by side, the cold steel in their bones,
> The howling of some ravenous beast afar.

> Wind, it shakes the windows, unending,
> Fully dressed they lie, apart, eyes ever open,
> And no love through a sleepless night eternal.

If only the tire hadn't blown we'd already be in Big Sur. Kerouac country! And Henry Miller! And what about Salinger? That Zen Buddhist deal in "Seymour: An Introduction." How could Salinger not have tripped the mystic coast? Traveled incognito. *Einstein, disguised as Robin Hood.* Rendezvoused with Ginsberg and Watts at Esalen. The three of them hot tubbing, the Pacific stretching out below. In deep Zen mind-meld. Finally, to grok zazen. If only the tire hadn't blown.

I'd waited for this night. Big Sur Mountain Inn. Fancy-ass honeymoon suite. Early 19th century room, dark wood walls and high ceilings, the large windows looking out on virgin forest. Maybe even a private lake. A fire burning hot in the hundred-year-old stone fireplace. *Unsere Nacht der sexed-heraus Nächte.* The two of us high from weed and wine, and our wanting. Our I'm-gonna-fuck-you-all-night-long night of all sexed-out nights. Simone, stretched out on the four-poster bed, legs spread. Calling me to her. Our squeeze-me-baby-'til-the-juice-runs-down-my-leg night of all sexed-out nights.

If only the tire hadn't blown. But the tire had blown.

3. CRASHED

WHEN THE NIGHT FINALLY ends, 6 a.m. or whenever it is, the sun blinding bright through the side windows and front windshield, my eyes open to see Simone lying there smoking a Kool. The stink of menthol and dog and us two, sweaty and unbathed. King Snore, she calls me. Hour after hour after fucking hour. Me and Lucky. The Sam Rivers and Eric Dolphy of snores. A cacophony. Snoring two or three notes, over and over, in different keys, out of rhythm, out of tune. A competition, she said, between man and dog. Man won. Me, crowned King Snore.

"I should tape a sign up," she says. "'Abandon all hope, ye who enter here to sleep.'"

Simone's decided her and Lucky will wait with the van while I get a tow truck. Two things before I start walking. First, gotta copy the tire size numbers off the side of that dead tire. Second, pray Texaco has the right equipment on his tow truck to put a new tire on a rim without having to bring it back to his creeped-out garage. Before I split, I write down the tire numbers and consider doing some praying, which is ridiculous, I mean how can a freakster bro pray if he doesn't believe in God?

Me, walking along man's feeble attempt to tame the wild coastline, as if carving an asphalt groove into the side of a mountain laid claim. Our posted speed limits and the other government mandates, *reduce speed, animal crossing, watch out for falling rocks*. And those pathetic guard rails. Artemis and Jupiter and Poseidon high on Mt. Olympus laughing their asses off at man's hubris, and me, speck of a speck of a speck, I'm laughing with 'em. Buzzed from no sleep, buzzed exhaustion. Holding my stomach, my mouth hurting from the grin I can't relax. Oh the absurdity of our self-importance.

The world luminous in the morning light. It's one of those Pacific Coast days, and every step my eyes see another Ansel Adams photo, only I see the authentic real of it, and in color, and for once no way black and white could do it justice. A light wind coming off the ocean, not a car on the road at this early hour, wrens and jays and sparrows in the trees sharing their good cheer, *walk me out in the morning dew my honey*, singing their morning songs. And all at once, the enormity of the Santa Lucia rising, of the ocean stretching into the distance, of the beauty of this very moment, oh the glory of it. I'm overwhelmed, and if I could plunge into an ice cold lake I wouldn't feel more attuned to nature than right in the moment of this moment.

As I look out to the Forever Infinite Pacific, oh man, 'cause I'm far West as a freakster bro can be without being in the ocean, and yet it's not enough, same as the love I want never gonna be enough. Yeah I yearn for something more, an authentic real sense of myself. I mean sure I'm goddamn crazy-wild alive in this moment, but this moment gonna pass. Goddamn goddamn 'cause I wanna hold on to it, I wanna become this moment.

Wild nature, here at the edge of civilization, yeah this is the poetry that brought Robinson Jeffers to Big Sur in 1913, and Henry Miller in the Forties, and a beaten-down Kerouac in 1960, and the others.

And a flash of clarity. A cabin in the woods, a path down to the beach, and *mes visions de Johanna*. And one of those Royal manual typewriters. Simple and pure and perfect.

If only it would be enough.

When I get to that no-name it's not quite 7—over an hour before the station's gonna open. I don't care. Well the grocery's open and I get coffee and too much food—a chocolate donut and a banana muffin and a cranberry muffin and an apple and an orange and some salty peanuts. So hungry I coulda bought out the place. I have a meal of it sitting on a bench front of the store watching the occasional car drive by.

Driving by, driving by, driving by.

Funny how different when you're sitting here in the no-name looking at the road, and past it, out across the ocean to the horizon, fade to infinity. Damn cars.

Driving by, driving by, driving by.

Killing machines, big metal anteaters only instead of ants they're eating up the air, eating up the planet. Noise and speed and carbon dioxide.

Driving by, driving by, driving by.

How can anyone keep on living in the horror of man's creations?

Texaco shows up stinking of last night's booze and cigars, and I tell him what's up. I'm still so high from my walk that even those drive-by cars and his I-told-you-so's—I don't *care*. Still, I need Texaco, don't wanna blow it.

"*Sir,*" I say.

"Got one of them Pall Malls for me?" Texaco says, and I pass him one.

"So anyway," I say. "*Sir.* I'm hoping you can sell me a new tire, got the number right here. And drive up to where the van is to put on the new one."

He burps this gross burp of whiskey and cigar.

"Yeah, maybe," he says. "Gotta wake up my brother to watch the shop. You wait here."

Twin brother. As if one of them motherfuckers with the deer heads isn't one too many. There's gotta be a trickster God, Coyote or Fox or Raven, pulling shit same as that to confound us humans. Humble us. Scare us. Instead of waiting for Texaco and the brother I go back into that grocery, buy a large coffee for Simone, and some fruit—a peach and a nectarine—and three muffins—one blueberry, one banana and one cranberry. With the paper bag of food in one hand, the Styrofoam in the other, I walk over to the gas station, look through the office window. It looks same as it did the other day, doesn't look as if anyone been in there in years. Lean back against that window, look toward the garage, and there it is. Curve of the V-81a, the morning light gleaming off the red enamel. At first I'm tripped-out on it, but the darkness blows in, and I'm seeing the stars, *Sarah, her whole body luminous, naked at the edge of the cliff, and she's over the edge, gone forever.*

All 'cause of me.

Texaco's '47 Ford tow truck is parked between the station and the grocery. Bright red back when, but not any more. Full-dull-faded to reddish and rust, gonna come a time when it's nothing but dust.

"Find your brother?" I say.

"I am my brother," he says.

You stay in a place too long, you start to look same as the place, and he looks a lot same as the garage—pieces of metal, car parts, dead tires.

"Got money for a tire, kid?"

Hadn't noticed the grey pallor of his skin.

"What do you think?" I say, and I hand him the piece of paper with the tire numbers. He lets my hand hang in the air, the breeze making the sound a breeze coming up against paper makes.

"Who taught you manners?" he says. "*Respect,* son."

"Yeah I got money," I say. Fucking pause. "*Sir.*"

He doesn't know a single thing about me.

"Anarchy and chaos," he says, and what I know about him, he's comfortable working each day in a garage with those deer heads and that shit he or his brother or somebody taped under them. "Slippery slope."

Do I really need to know any more than that? Why would I wanna understand a racist motherfucker who's got symbolic deer heads on his wall?

"I really need a tire," I say.

"Tire's the least of our troubles," he says.

Funny thing is, I agreed with him.

"How 'bout we start with the tire," I say.

He goes into his garage, stays in there long enough for me to smoke another Pall Mall. He comes out with one of those dusty tires from up high, makes me pay him, and he tosses it on the bed, behind the cab, next to the towing gear.

"I'll see you up there," he says. "You say the van's two miles up the road?"

Such a motherfucker. "Joking me, right?"

He climbs in, I knock on the window, he guns the engine. Adjusts his "Gone" hat, fucks with his radio 'til it's bleeding Hank Williams' "Alone and Forsaken," pours himself coffee from a thermos. Done with all that, and finally, fucking window going down.

"Whadaya want?"

"A ride."

Fucking window going back up.

"Appreciate a ride, *sir.*"

Fucking window going down all over again.

"Good exercise for a kid like you."

"Come on, man," I say. "I mean *sir.*"

"Damn right you do, punk!"

Back then, when some old fucker called a human *punk,* he meant the human was a juvenile delinquent, or worse. Only the hipster critics, Bangs and Lenny Kaye and Rocket Reducer, when they wrote *punk,* meant The Stooges and MC5 and New York Dolls kinda sound. The punk music sound. The sound I feel more and more. The sound of the future.

"Yeah, alright," he says. "Get in the cab."

Thought about asking if I can ride on the bed with the tire and the towing gear and the air compressor and the generator and his other shit so I wouldn't have to listen to Mr. Know-It-All, but that would be pushing it. He takes it slow driving that old clunker, delivers a cryptic homily that he implies relates to the fire, or rather, to the signs of bad luck me and Simone refuse to see, and the fate of those who ignore them, and his mouth keeps working, him droning on with me offering a *yes sir* when it's appropriate. Listening to him the fine black dust of downerosity seeps into the cab, our final weekend a bust, and bad-luck-and-trouble symbolism everywhere if I only look.

I stop listening to his hickster babble, obsessing on Simone and the bummerosity of her leaving in less than a week and how it'll be. Her gone. Harper taking the bedroom with the queen mattress, and how's that gonna work? Harper nearly the same age as me, she's 19, really cute, well more than cute, but she's a dyke, right? Simone picked her up at the Lavender Club, and what chick goes home from a dyke bar with another chick if she's not a dyke? So I mean Harper for sure into fucking women, or whatever you call what two women do in bed. Is fucking even the right word? I've never thought about whether fucking was a specific term for when a guy's cock is jamming a chick's pussy, or if it's more general, relating to the whole sex deal. Henry Miller knows. Anaïs Nin probably knows. And Pauline Réage, she'd know for sure.

Course Harper also fucks guys. I oughta know. Can a lesbo get off fucking a guy? Or does a chick who gets off with chicks and guys gotta be bi? Can't a lesbo close her eyes and fantasize a chick is doing her with a dildo when it's really a guy fucking her? Maybe there's a book explains it all.

Man, what the fuck? Gotta stay true to Simone. And that's when I feel his fist hit into my left shoulder, not that hard, but hard enough.

"Don't disrespect me, kid."

"Fuck!"

"Listen up when I'm jawing," he says.

"Nodded out," I say. "Didn't get any sleep last night," and that's a lie, but I'd tell that motherfucker anything. I don't give a fuck about him. I need him to fix the tire, and once that's finished he can go back to his dirty garage, his wreck of a rust red Volvo and his deer heads, and I'll be forever done with him.

"That's the problem with you hippies," he says. "Wanna pass me that thermos?"

I get his thermos up off the floor of the cab. He gets it between his thighs, gets the lid off, and it's not coffee in there. It's Irish coffee.

"Best cure in the world for a hangover, kid."

"I'm not a hippie," I say. "That's over."

"You don't respect your elders."

"Respect is earned."

"I'm warning you, kid," he says. "You wanna get out?"

"*Sir.*"

Wasn't quite enough room on that pullout for Texaco to pull up behind the van, so the '47 Ford is sticking out into the road. Boy Texaco doesn't like that. He gets maybe a half-dozen flares from his tow truck, and he's super careful, totally knows what he's doing, gets each one flaming and sets them on the asphalt so the flame is aimed toward the white line, starts laying 'em down back around the bend before you get to where the tow truck and the van are parked. Said he's charging for those flares, no question about that one.

"I warned you," he says.

"Yeah you warned me," I say. "*Sir.*"

"Damn right I did."

Simone has that funky sheet we slept on folded so it's big enough to sit on, and it covers the weeds and dirt. It's between the van and that dead-man drop and she's sitting on it, has her carpetbagger purse close at hand, smoking a Kool. Lucky lies in the dirt near her stainless steel water bowl. Simone doesn't let Lucky or any of the cats eat or drink out of plastic. She's sure chemicals causing cancer leach from the plastic into the food and water. She's probably right. I have my own theory that plastic is destroying the world. There's only one thing made out of plastic worth a shit and that's record albums. Singles too. And I guess cassette tapes.

When I get closer to Simone, I get this strange-ass flash that one of the Manson chicks is sitting there in her place. Three reasons why. First, Simone has a piece of leather, I guess it's for a chick to tie her hair back in a ponytail but Simone is using it as a headband, has it wrapped across her forehead, maybe an inch above her eyes, going around her head tied in the back. Somehow wearing that headband makes her look same as Leslie Van Houten cross-legged on that sheet. Second thing is her looking so bedraggled, her face sweaty and there's dirt on it and the slept-in-your-clothes wasted deal, but more than that, she has a crazed exhaustion vibrating off her. Third is the knife. Sun glinting off that bowie knife I told you about. It's on the sheet next to her.

"Mind putting the knife away, ma'am?" Texaco says.

Man, he doesn't wanna get too close. In my own paranoid state I worry Simone gonna give him some feminist lip, start talking about how the patriarchal sexist motherfuckers need to get their dicks cut off, some shit that'll send him back to that no-name. But she'd never do that. She only says that stuff to me. She's actually sweet, almost deferential to men the first time she meets them. I present Simone with the bag of food and the Styrofoam, and she smiles, a quick love-you smile, and goes for the banana muffin for starters, and of course the coffee.

Texaco gets to work, mumbling all the while about the fire and the blown tire and the turkey vultures gliding through the air high above us. He has a litany of bad news and trouble streaming from between his dried out lips. Has a lug wrench pretty much same as the one I used only his is more heavy duty, heavy-duty lug wrench in the shape of a cross. He walks over to that tire, that kind of arrogant walk, holy war, so sure it's nothing to beat down those lugs.

Yeah well he can't do it either.

"See what I told you," I say, and I want Simone to understand it's not 'cause *I'm* weak. Texaco has to use an impact air wrench, and to get that going he fires up the generator he has in the bed of his truck. Fucking riot act of noise the combo of generator and impact air wrench make. Lucky doesn't dig it, jumps up, joins in barking. Noisy as fuck but that impact air wrench does the job.

I'm pacing, walking back and forth, forth and back, along the road, driver side of the van. I hear Texaco working away.

Jacking up the van, getting the tire off, taking it back to his truck, mounting the new tire onto the wheel, back to the van.

"You'll be lucky if the other three don't blow," he says.

I walk back around so me and Texaco are standing by the side of the van, Simone still sitting on that folded bed sheet. I guess she's put the knife back in her purse.

"That's what I told her," I say.

Texaco doesn't understand that it's Simone's van. I don't know what he thinks about me and her. Probably doesn't think anything about us.

"Instead of telling her, you oughta do something about it," he says. "Drive back to my garage, I can replace 'em."

"We gotta get up to Big Sur today."

"What's the big rush?"

"Yeah Michael," Simone says. "What's the big rush?" and she's trying to keep her mouth straight, that deadpan deal. Between her and Texaco they could teach a class on deadpan humor. What am I supposed to say? Yeah, well, Mr. Texaco motherfucker, we need to get to the Mountain Inn post haste so me and my chick can get really loaded and fuck all night.

I lower my head, hunch my back some, imagine being sad beyond all sadness. "I've got a very sick aunt," I say. "We're going to visit her."

Simone gets a coughing jag going.

"Sorry to hear that," he says. "I know people in Big Sur. What's her name?"

"You don't know her," I say. "A real recluse. She doesn't even use her normal name. I don't know what name she uses there. I call her 'auntie.'"

"Don't know your own aunt's name?"

"She's got Alzheimer's or Parkinson's or Huntington's, one of those," I say. "It's very sad and we really need to get up there. She might only have a few days left. She was expecting us last night."

Yeah, and I'm saying too much too fast. "The only bright spot," I say. "Since she can't remember anything, she won't have missed us 'cause she won't have remembered we were supposed to show up."

He finishes whatever else he's doing to the tire, and wants his dough.

"Forty smackeroos, kid."

I brought $30 so I could take Simone out for dinner at the Inn, but now I hand it over. "Don't fuck with me kid."

"Don't sweat it, man," I say. "I'll get the rest from her."

His hand on my arm, got a metal grip. "What'd I tell you?"

"*Sir.*"

He's loosening his fingers, and I shake him off, walk toward Simone. I want him to wait by the van, but he's tailing me. If I were to stop he'd bump right into me, that close. I get to where I'm standing over her, and Texaco, well he's maybe two feet away. Too close, but at least he's not touching me.

"Got a 10, Simone?" I say. "I just gave him my last $30, and it's $40 for what he done."

"Shit," she says. "This dick of a trip is costing me a fortune, Michael. I'm sick of paying for everything."

Yeah well it was only a matter of time before one of the tires blew, better now than halfway to Boston, and she's not paying for everything. I give her dough each month I get from my dad. But I don't say anything. I sneak a quick look at Texaco, yeah that weathered face of his, he might as well written an essay regards how appalled he is.

"If we pay him, we can hit the road," I say, and the look she gives me, it's a look that says all I want is her pussy, and it pisses her off. Digs in her carpetbagger purse, and throws a couple fives down on the dirt between my boots.

"Not my fault the tire blew," I say.

I pick up the bills, walk all the way around the back of the van, Texaco following me. We're standing there, I'm facing him, he's facing me, maybe three feet between us, Simone still on the sheet, can't see us, and I hope she can't hear us either.

"How old was your mom when she had you?" he says. "Thirteen?"

"She's not my mom," I say. "She's my old lady, you know, my chick."

"That woman's your girlfriend, kid?"

And for once he doesn't pull that sir shit on me. "Give you some advice from someone who knows something about women," he says. "A woman doesn't need to cut your balls off to ruin you. Women think they can do anything nowadays. Slippery slope. Anarchy and chaos."

Yeah well he can get the fuck in his truck and go back to that no-name. Goddamn goddamn Simone.

"One more thing kid. If it were me, I'd take the knife away from her. Pronto."

I don't know if it's the spooky moments, the anniversary of the fire, the magpies or some black cat I don't see cross my path. Or just the culmination of blown tire, miserable night and a coming awareness that whatever might have been has already passed us by. Feels different in the van as we drive the remaining miles to the Inn. A Grand Canyon lies between us.

I roll us a number and we're smoking it and she starts laughing her hysterical stoned laugh.

"You don't know her," Simone says. "She's a recluse. Don't know her name. I call her auntie," the two of us laughing that stoned laugh, and for a while there isn't any Grand Canyon.

The Honeymoon Suite, gone baby gone to some other couple when 10 p.m. came and went. There's no arguing with the innkeeper, an overweight fuck whose grandfather built the place in the 1800s. We can spend Saturday night in the Gaspar de Portolà, a modest room with two twin beds named after the first European to set foot in Big Sur, or try our luck elsewhere. Elsewhere is two shit-ass overpriced motels down the road.

"I hear they both got bed bugs," the innkeeper says.

We take the Gaspar de Portolà. It's a sad deal, that room. On the second floor, right over the entry, so every time someone arrives at the Inn or splits, you hear it almost as good as if you were downstairs near the front door. I push the twin beds together, but it's not gonna be same as sleeping on a double or a queen, let alone that king they've got in the

Honeymoon Suite. There's a window, but it looks out on the parking area, the big neon sign with "Big Sur Mountain Inn" blinking on/off, the road, and the trees on the other side of the road that hide the ocean. The lake that in my fantasy was gonna be on view from our bed, well there isn't one.

I'm to blame for the lousy too-small room, and the twin beds and the lame view and the crap shower. If only we'd gotten the tire fixed Friday night, Simone says, we'd have scored the Honeymoon Suite. I remind her the garage was closed by the time we'd have gotten to it, and if by some miracle the tire had fixed itself that night, there's no way we'd have reached the Inn before 10. Our fate, I say, regarding the Honeymoon Suite, was sealed when that bald-as-an-old-fart's-head tire blew.

Simone is deaf to her own illogic, and it's a futile battle, the more I explain it, the more impatient she gets. She's mad and she's staying mad. Doesn't matter anyway 'cause there's a kind of inevitability to how our luck has turned since leaving that no-name. All the omens, and possible omens, 'round and 'round, and that red Coke machine, red is Satan's color, and Coke's the Devil's juice, and that row of Gorgon deer heads in the creeped-out garage, to gaze on them must mean certain trouble, and it being the anniversary of the fire, and what could be more obvious than *watch out for falling rocks*.

Oh man, the minute we saw those foreboding words we should have turned the van around and drove back to Morning Glory Way.

Caw caw caw.

There are times when circumstances conspire to fuck up whatever plans been made. This is one of those times. Simone planned weeks ago that on Saturday afternoon, which is today, we'd go for a hike. It's a bear of a hike, one of those hikes where if you start off at 11 a.m., by the time you hike to the perfect spot, have yourself a picnic, maybe fall asleep in a meadow for an hour, and hike some more, you're lucky if you get back before sunset. We'll be starting out around 3 in the afternoon—at the earliest.

In the Gaspar de Portolà I'm lying on one of the beds, Simone standing in the doorway to the bathroom just outta the shower, the bright bright bathroom light highlighting her still damp body. She's drying herself off, oblivious to what seeing her naked does to me. Or maybe not.

"Let's do the hike in the morning," I say. "We'll be all refreshed, perfect."

All those freckles on her tits, no way I can think about a hike.

"Lazy fuck."

She has one foot through a leg hole in her panties, then the other, pulls them up, covering the brown curls of her snatch.

"No Simone," I say. "It's not that."

Pulls a blue t-shirt over her head, and down, over her tits and stomach.

"It's been a day and a half since we slept," I say.

It's nearly 3:30 and we've eaten nothing but the crap I bought this morning. She steps into those blue jean cutoffs she made from an old pair of Levi's. Sits on the other bed, gets her socks on.

"All you want to do is fuck me," she says.

When a chick says something same as that, the freakster bro it's said to is fucked. No matter what he says, it's the wrong thing, and for sure no fucking is gonna take place until after the freakster bro does whatever it is the chick wants.

Lucky for me Simone left her hiking boots back on her front porch. Of course she blames me for not loading them into the van. A number takes the edge off and we have the munchies so bad. Ever since she came up with the plan for our special Big Sur weekend, she's been telling me how great the food is at the Inn and how I'll love the dining room with all the antique furniture and big stone fireplace. I was gonna take her out to eat, and brought that $30 I told you about so I'd have enough for food and wine, but of course that money is history.

"Maybe we should get a burger at that place we passed down the road," I say. "I feel so bad Susan, but I spent all my dough on the tire."

Well that's not gonna fly, no way. We're eating in the Inn's dining room, she's got money and that's how it is. We start in the bar, and I don't know what's with her but she's drinking same as an alcoholic. After maybe an hour and two bottles of merlot drained I get her into the dining room. We eat a bunch of overpriced food, and we're starting on our third bottle when she starts in.

"This is hard," she says, and after all the sarcasm and talking about her old boyfriend and her ex-husband the past day or so, she gets down to what's really going on. Yeah, finally the authentic real.

"This goodbye weekend," she says. "I want it all to be over so I don't have to feel anything."

"It's hard for me too," I say, but what she says next, it hurts the worst 'cause I heard it before. I heard it from Elise, and am I doomed, doomed to keep repeating my mistakes?

Her face, man, it stiffens same as she's girding herself to say something she'd rather not.

"You want too much," she says. "I see it in your eyes and hear it in your voice and it makes me glad I'm leaving."

With it out in the open how difficult the whole scene is for the both of us, it's hard to talk about anything. When your chick lays the heavy negative vibe on you same as Simone did, everything's pointless. So instead of talking about anything that means anything, you know, anything regards me and her and how we could make it better again, Simone talks about everything else. All the details regards taking care of the house. And the cats. And Lucky. On and on she talks about nothing that matters, but all I hear, *it makes me glad I'm leaving.*

If it hadn't been bad enough knowing she'll be gone in a week, now I hurt worse than worse. *Please don't mean what you said, Simone. Please don't.*

Even if we'd gotten that Honeymoon Suite, it doesn't matter. The two of us exhausted, total blitzed from too much wine. Still, walking back to the room, all I can think about is fucking.

Finally we're at the Big Sur Inn, we have a room, even if it's the shit-ass Gaspar de Portolà, and once we get on that bed I'll lose myself in her, and in that moment, a moment that will extend out into eternity, all will be right again.

We get back into the room, and it's past 10. Paid much too much for a fourth bottle, but before we finish one glass, before we smoke the number she rolls and get naked, the two of us nod off.

Fully clothed. On top of the bed. Crashed.

THREE

1. HARPER REDUX

AND I'LL HOLD OUT for Simone, I'm so sure. The day she leaves I make my pledge as I stand outside the gate, my eyes on the empty road. I'm so certain she's my Visions of Johanna. She can be a pain in the ass but every chick is a pain in the ass. I can wait. Yeah, Simone said a lot of shit. Not committing, and no jealousy, and needing to feel free. What Simone said, and what Simone did. Swear to God-who-for-sure-don't-exist I'll hold out for her.

If I'd been awake and looked up into the sky, I'd have seen the two turkey vultures, Doom and Gloom. When it's time to eat the carrion, they change shape, no more black magpies haunting me, instead two winged scavengers circle above, ready to dive down to earth with the first smell of death.

The honking wakes me. Bright bright morning sunlight streams in the living room windows, my head a mess. Damn honking. The enemy forces inside my head pushing hundreds of pins out through my skull. Too much wine, too much weed. To make sure I'd forget, but I can't forget. Alone it's different. First you float away and that's groovy same as always, but then it's "The Bottle Let Me Down" and "Just One More" and "Don't Do This to Me."

There's more honking, and Lucky the dog starts in and I push one of the cats, it's the Siamese, Gertrude Stein, off my stomach. Another one, the black longhair mix, Virginia Woolf, is sleeping on the cushion just past my feet. I get myself up, the room tipping sideways, and I gotta pee. I get my black cowboy shirt on, stumble my way to the can and empty my bladder.

How fuck-to-hell I feel, I look worse. My hair coming down, gotta be more than a foot, kinked out mess, all what comes out of my scalp for maybe six inches is brown, and another five or six inches henna black, you know, what's left of Jaded's dye job. My face booze bloated and brown stubble, and the white piping of my cowboy shirt—some of it stained red.

Outside the gate a white Ford pickup, looks to be a late Sixties model, idling. I pull on my Keith Richards snakeskin boots, go down the front steps, hand on the rail, steady man. Down the path past the molten orange-yellow bright of the poppies, past the back-end of my faded blue TR4, burnt-straw weeds everywhere, push the gate open and damn that hulk of a dog.

"Get used to it," I say. "Your owner's gone, left *you* behind too."

As Harper drives past me, her pale white face through the side window. In the yard the pickup slams to a stop right where the white Chevy van used to park, same as it's her spot. Harper's spot. If I was superstitious, I'd think that meant something.

"Cool it dog," I say. "It's Harper, your new best friend."

Harper still in the cab, and I need a number to get my head on straight. The door open, she throws down the end of a roach, steps onto the dirt of Simone's yard, grinds the roach with the toe of her black engineer boot, grinds it out same as this yard is her yard. Harper's yard.

Harper's voice Nico cool, no affect, a low monotone, and dead bluebirds everywhere.

"Always wanted to be a country girl," she says. "Got any farm animals I can play with?"

Another of those talk first, think later deals.

"Just me."

Harper was the girls who live at the Chelsea Hotel. Her blond Anita Pallenberg hair gone baby gonesville. Cut too short and dyed black, dyed so weird-ass black, fake shiny dyed-black of a

Halloween wig. Only a chick beautiful as Harper can look groovy with her hair dyed that fake black color.

Her skin bone white against her shiny black hair. Black Ray-Bans, coulda stole 'em from Jim, and I see her jaw bones and she's way the fuck too skinny. Her thin pale-pink lips dead cold in the sunlight. Baggy black sweatshirt, straight-leg black Levi's, and the boots. Doesn't matter what the chick wears.

"Your roots are showing, Writerman," she says. "And you're splattering heartbreak all over the yard," and she's got her arms around me, and how she felt before, in my dorm room and later on Simone's mattress, yeah I remember, and my arms around her only it's different. I feel her bones, and so close her shiny black hair so short. She smells of dried leaves and damp basements.

And she still wears the skull necklace.

"Been freaky out here alone," I say. "Glad you're here."

"Don't be so certain," she says.

Still have my arms around her, still the shock of her when I get the real shock. There's a crude blue-black swastika on the left side of her neck as if she took a nail to her skin. I should have known right then Harper brought the sickness, and it's a wispy gray fog and it's a heaviness, a heavy heavy bummerosity. Soon it would be worse, a creeping despair, and Faulkner's damn honeysuckle, the sickly odor, and blue passion flower winding its vines around the legs of the orange plastic chaise lounge in Simone's back garden, and growing up over it until all I would see from the kitchen window was the blue passion flower. But that day I don't know about the sickness. That day I don't know Harper's ready to deliver me to the end of the line.

Scary, man, her swastika. The horror of humans who hate me 'cause I'm a Jew. Freaks me. Does she know I'm a Jew? Simple as a child's drawing, mostly concealed by the sweatshirt. Freaks me and scares me, but still it turns me on. A swastika. The last taboo. I still don't get it. All I know is seeing that evil mark on her, and I felt the wanting. Felt it bad.

I want to say *Harper, it's the symbol of death, death to the Jewish people, tattooed into your flesh. The death showers and the torture experiments, the tyranny of fascism, and the virus, the depths of evil and the mark of the Devil.*

I don't say anything. It makes Harper even more sexy, that mark, fucked-up sexy in the wan languid way a junked-out chick is sexy to a lost boy seeking salvation in *Exile on Main Street* and *The Velvet Underground & Nico* and *Raw Power*, who mistakes dissipation for sophistication. Harper's Helter Skelter tattoos, and I want to see all of them. Harper was the girls who live at the Chelsea Hotel. The soul dead girls, the walking zombie girls, the drugging fucked-up lost-their-way girls.

Harper doesn't have much. A black guitar case and a big faded brown suitcase and a black baseball mitt and a melon crate of records and one of those one-piece stereos with the fake wood-grain finish and the detachable speakers same as the Zenith I had as a kid, same as what Elise had. Harper has plants in small red ceramic pots. The blue iris is wilting.

"You're a guitar player?"

"Isn't that kinda obvious?"

"I mean, you serious?"

"Dead serious," she says. "Gonna be a star."

"Me too," I say. "I'm writing the Great American Novel."

"I wouldn't tell that to everyone, Writerman."

"Why not?"

"Makes you sound like an idiot."

Harper grooves on the garden when she looks out the kitchen window and sees it that first morning. The orange chaise lounge where Simone sunbathed. Blue passion flower vines cover the tired redwood fence that wraps around the garden, and the vines creeping away from the fence towards the lounge. Smell of honeysuckle.

I help her bring her stuff into the far bedroom, the one with the orange shag carpet and the queen mattress. The mattress where she's gonna sleep from now on. Harper sets her guitar case down on the rug and I look at the mattress and I look at Harper and Harper looks at me. *Harper on the mattress, finger paint all over her and the sheet, and Simone's fingers in her.* Harper sees my embarrassment. I hardly know Harper. I'm not Michel in *À bout de souffle*. Don't know how to act around a chick I've fucked, but who isn't my chick, isn't even a friend. Despite the sex we're strangers.

"Tu n'as jamais vu de fille?" Harper says, and she laughs, the laugh where she knows something she's not telling. It meant nothing to her what we'd done. Fucking her, or lighting her cigarette, same difference. *Harper on the mattress, paint smeared across her body.*

"Oh, fuck," I say, 'cause it's the first time I put it all together, really get it, you know, me and Harper sharing this house.

Simone's fingers, my face burning. "It's just—well Harper, you think this can work, us both living here?"

"Depends," and yeah, I'm clueless, man. "You'll figure it out."

The awkward of it, and I stand there for too long. A third cat, a black and white, Gloria Steinem, pads in and lies in a pool of sun beneath the windows. I want to say something smart and hip, but all I see is Harper on the mattress. And I don't want to see her on the mattress. 'Cause of Simone. 'Cause of my promise.

"Maybe you could leave me alone now," she says. "This *is* my bedroom."

"Oh yeah, right, for sure," I say. "Your personal space."

"My personal space," she says. "That's really funny, Writerman."

I go out onto the front porch, sit on the cracked leather couch where Jim sat and wish it could be that day. Me and Elise and Jim on the Sugar Mountain couch. And Harper in the bedroom, on the mattress, only she has her too fake black hair so short and her body too thin and a swastika on her neck. Screaming so loud in me: fuck that shit, fuck that shit, *fuck* that shit. Harper so beautiful, and *fuck that shit*. I'm not gonna fuck Harper. She's not my Visions of Johanna, not for a minute, never was. Just a fuck. A free fuck. Fucking her, or lighting her cigarette, same difference.

When I get the first letter from Simone I can't even wait to get back to the house to read it. I stand on Poppy Lane in front of the rusty mail boxes and the Monterey pines. The first time I read the letter, everything about it, how long it is, eight double-sided pages, legal-size, it excites me. All the time she took to write it. And I hear her voice, as if she's whispering in my ear. She wrote about her drive across the country, and arriving at this hundred-year-old house in Boston where she's renting a room. I want to know everything. The color of the walls and if she has a double bed or a queen and what she sees from her windows and if it has a hardwood floor or wall-to-wall carpet. The more I know, the more I'll feel a part of her new life. Only I'm not a part of her new life. As I read the letter I start to wake up to the authentic real of it. She's already got a new life in Boston. It's not only going across the country and teaching for nine months. She'll have new friends and go out to dinner and guys coming on to her and she didn't make a promise, not to herself, or to me.

My favorite part of the letter is the part about her missing me. "I put on *Court and Spark* and it was beautiful to hear Joni's voice, and reassuring," she wrote. "And I started to cry, thinking of Lucky and all the cats and my garden. Don't pout. I was missing you too."

She misses me, oh thank-you-God-who-don't-exist.

I read the letter again, and a third time. I don't like that "too," and the fact that I come after Lucky and the eight fucking cats and the garden. Does she miss me a lot, or only a little? Is it the way you miss a friend you're used to having coffee with once a week, or the pain of the wanting, and the lonesome? I need so bad for her to want me, to need me, to love me. I so want her words to mean all that.

My panic is her writing about this professor, Simon, and how lame is that? Simon? Same as "Simon Says"? Simon's the name you give a nerdy kid who wears glasses with lenses thick as Coke bottle glass. Simon and Simone? What the fuck! He rents a room in the same house where she lives. She went on about him. How he helped her bring all her stuff up to her room. How he teaches a class on Faulkner. The worst, he's a self-proclaimed "Bergman expert." They'd been up half the night talking about "Persona." She's not supposed to talk about "Persona" with some lame-ass named Simon.

That's *our* film.

She ended the letter with "PS: Think of me when you jerk off."

That makes me feel good. It means she's thinking about me and sex. Right? Could mean she thinks of me when *she* masturbates. Right? A chick would only write that to a freakster bro if she feels super close and comfortable with him. Right?

It's not only what's in the letter that disturbs me, it's what's missing. She didn't say she *really* missed me, or that she loved me, or was hellfuck horny for me. None of that in the first letter. I thought her letters would cheer me up. I thought they'd be a lifeline stretched from here to her Christmas visit. Those letters wore me down. The excitement of her bright new life.

Later I put off opening her letters. I wanted to never open them. I'd get the mail at 11, but force myself to hold off. A battle I always lost. The only way to win was burn the letter, and not read it. I never won. All the letters hurt.

The letters came in those cheap plain white envelopes and she wrote them on lined yellow paper ripped from a legal pad. It made them seem not important, written on that lined yellow paper, mailed in those cheap-ass envelopes. As if Simone used whatever was at hand, didn't take the trouble to get nice paper and a nice envelope. Goddamn goddamn Simone. I'll hold out for Simone. The pledge I made. I'm so sure.

2. JESUS

I STAND IN THE kitchen, the garden luminous out through the window, make coffee how Simone taught me. Simone has this plastic coffee dripper, kind of same as a funnel. You set it on top of a coffee cup, put in a paper filter and some ground coffee and pour in hell-hot boiling water.

Harper's in her room playing guitar and singing. I wanna hear the words, but I can't. She has a low monotone mostly, but there's also her bright falsetto. And the beautiful dying, it's in her voice. And sex, and sometimes the hard sharp edge. If a switchblade is a voice, that's her voice. Sometimes. Other times if the smell of dried leaves were a sound or the shaky blue-black lines.

The white Caloric stove with the stainless tea kettle in front of me to my left, white enamel sink to the right, my eyes on the plastic dripper, watch the waterline creep down, hell-hot water slowly filters through the ground coffee, dark brown coffee dripping into my favorite cup, a glazed Egyptian blue ceramic deal Simone always used. From the first morning after I came home with her, after I slept with her. Goddamn nostalgia.

And fuck it! Fuck it! *Fuck it!*

So slow, how long it takes to make a cup of coffee. Not bad as watching a car rust, but still. My whole life, waiting. Waiting for chicks. Four months I'll wait for Simone to fly out at Christmas. I don't know it that day I watch the waterline creep down, but Simone's not coming home for Christmas. I look out the kitchen window and see the raised beds and over near the side fence the orange plastic lounge. I want Simone lying on it sunbathing, but it's empty.

"Make me a cup?"

Harper wears a white cotton dress, and she's barefoot. Death black polish on her toenails. Oh fuck me God-who-don't-exist. Crude tattooed blue-black snakes wind up her skinny legs disappearing under her dress, and I must have seen them, the snake marks, the night Simone brought Harper home. Or were they concealed by the finger paint, and how stoner fucked-up I was, and the darkness. There in the kitchen, Harper's arms scarred too. A tarantula on the outside of her upper right arm. Yeah, she sees me look, and I hold out Simone's Egyptian blue ceramic cup, and Harper's fingers on mine, an electric charge as she takes it.

Yeah, she sees me look. And that afternoon more than a year ago in my dorm room. Harper on my bed, and we're so stoned. She's taken her blouse off, the skull hangs above her tits, and she wants me to fuck her, but first she makes me beg for it. She says the female tarantula bites the head off her mate when they're in the throes of fucking. That day in my dorm room I can't not look at her tits, and there's no black scarred marks. Her fingers around my neck. And she says, *if we fuck, I'll kill you.* And she says, *that's the price.* And what do you call *that* yearning? Is *that* nostalgia?

Oh fuck it! Fuck it! Goddamn goddamn fuck it!

Harper's fingers on mine as she takes Simone's Egyptian blue ceramic cup. That cup means nothing to Harper. I want that cup but it's too late.

"What's Susan's is mine," Harper says.

Her fingers are cold, Harper's fingers, thin bony fingers, to feel them on mine, to be touched. To stand so close. If Charles Addams had drawn a hand with thin bony fingers. A tarantula tattooed on the outside of her right arm about the size of a silver dollar, below her shoulder, and the ink is blue-black, the crude lines, drawn with a nail. The snakes crawling up Harper's legs drawn with a nail too. If someone took mud and splattered it all over a white silk blouse, that's the Helter Skelter markings on Harper.

"There's cream in the fridge," I say. "I got some for you."

Harper has her shades on. She always has her shades on now, even at night, and does she leave them on when she fucks?

"I drink it black," Harper says.

"Since when?"

"Since Frida," Harper says. "Frida thinks it's a crime putting anything white in coffee."

Harper's skin wrapped tight around her bones.

"Frida your girlfriend?"

Black lipstick, and her lips a ghost.

"I don't know," she says.

I'd never seen a chick with black lipstick. Cold hard Nico singing "All Tomorrow's Parties." Harper looks down at her dress, pulls at the hem. "I had a dress like this when I was a little girl," she says. "My mother made it for me. I was the *cutest* little girl."

"She paint your toenails black?" I say. "Tattoo a scorpion on your little ass? Would have been real cute when you were 5 or 6."

The burn of Harper's hand against my face. First time a chick hits me. No that's not true. Elise pounding my chest. This is different. Elise didn't get off on it.

"Don't talk like that about my mother, Writerman."

I rub my cheek. I'll get a bruise and why don't I do something, but that's the sickness, and I can't stop Harper. No one but Harper can stop Harper, and even Harper can't.

"I'm sorry, Harper," I say.

She laughs. You know, her knowing laugh. "You don't get it," she says. "When I tell you not to do something you need to do it again. When I hurt you, you need to hurt me."

Harper's got Simone's cup against her black ghost lips, sipping the black coffee and what if it isn't coffee, what if it's a poison that'll damn those who drink it to feel the wanting unfulfilled, feel it and feel it and never not feel it.

"Makes me sick," she says. "A man being weak."

I get another cup set up on the counter with the plastic dripper. My left hand around the cup. The tea kettle screams, and Harper reaches for it.

"No," I say. "I'll do it."

I pick up the kettle, the water steaming. Pour the boiling water, look at Harper, pour the boiling water, white cotton dress and she's too thin, and the boiling water hits the filter, and I wish I wasn't sarcastic about her mom. Why do I say these things? I look at Harper, and all the mistakes I've made, and how do I dig out of the hole I'm in? Swastika on her neck, and I'd never hurt Harper. Pour the boiling water, and the plastic dripper falls off the cup, scalding water on my hand, the kettle falling, falling.

"Fuck to shit!"

The kettle hits the linoleum. Throw my hand away from me as if I can throw the burn off it. Harper steps back, barefoot, death black nails, eludes the scalding water. She doesn't know about my hand, and then she does. Hand red and shaking.

"You need cold water on it," she says. "Now!"

Hand fucking throbs, and I don't move, red, shaking, and the room spinning.

Harper got the water running, the water hitting the bottom of the sink, and the roar so loud, Niagara Falls roar, echoing inside me.

"Come *on*, Michael."

Harper so close, the smell of dried leaves, and a burnt chemical smell, and that's new. She didn't have that smell before. She has my forearm, my hand in the cold water. A burnt chemical smell. Close my eyes, the cold soothing, the cold of her hand holding my arm, cold hard water against my hand, cold hard water, cold hard Harper.

Harper says we need to go in her bedroom where she's got her first-aid kit. And has she got weed in it, and hash, same as Jim? *First thing you do, Jim said, if you need aid to get high, get hold of the kit.*

Her fingers hard, got my hand, pulling me, *come on, Michael,* and we're in the bedroom and she tells me to sit on the mattress, and I sit on the mattress. The bamboo blinds are up, the morning light bright bright through the windows, and the room glows how it did that first morning when I woke next to Simone. A black comforter covers the mattress. Harper doesn't sit her ass on the mattress, she's on her knees, some of the dress caught under them, lower legs straight out behind her.

"Let's see the burn."

Stick out my hand, fucking hurts, triangle of skin between the wrist, thumb and index burned red, that burnt flesh color. Her first-aid kit is an olive green metal box, same as something some soldier in 'Nam would have, on the bookshelf to the side of the mattress, near her stereo.

"Hey Sister Morphine," I say. "Gonna give me a shot? Turn my nightmares into dreams?"

She pulls her white cotton dress, gets it so it's not under her knees. She gets the first-aid kit on the comforter between us, opens it and it's not a first-aid kit. I don't know what you call what that olive green metal box is. It's got needles in there and bottles of ink, a hash pipe and nail polish, one of those beige plastic birth control dispensers and a baggie of something. A roll of white gauze and a roll of white medical tape and a tube of some kinda ointment.

She squeezes some on the burnt of me, the ointment thick and cold and semi-clear same as Vaseline, and rubs it in.

"Maybe you'll end up with a fab scar," she says.

Great," I say. "So then I'll have three scars."

My three scars. The true love scar on my palm. X marks the spot, the spot that was supposed to symbolize me and Sarah's love 'til the end of time. And the suicide scar from the night I cut my wrist with a razor. And now a scar from this burn, the cost of getting too close to Harper. And I would pay and pay.

Harper reaches into her olive green metal box, brings out what looks to be the handle of a knife. It's black ivory and silver.

"What you got there, Harper?"

She pushes something and the forged steel blade snaps out. It's maybe four inches, that silvery blade, and she catches the light, the flat part reflective as a mirror. Harper turns her hand so the sharp edge faces up, looks into it, her body frozen, and time slows, for Harper there is no time, she's Narcissus and she could stare forever.

"Harper," I say. "Harper!"

Harper's cold zombie stare, and the burnt chemical smell, the fear in me same as the fear seeing her swastika.

"Carve my initials on your ass," she says.

She cuts a piece of gauze with the knife, bandages my hand with the gauze and some tape and puts the knife away.

She goes out to the kitchen, and gets two glasses and the half-gallon of Almaden red I bought after Simone split. Fuck the merlot. She sits crossed-legged on the mattress near me, her white cotton dress up above her knees, and I see she's wearing black panties. She doesn't care what I see, and we drink wine. It's not yet 10 a.m. I never drank so early. The snake marks go 'round and 'round her skinny legs.

We stay in Harper's room and she lowers all the bamboo blinds, and the darkness closing in. She gets her hands on Gloria Steinem, scoops her up, drops her out into the short hallway and closes the door, and even as my eyes adjust, it's still murky, grainy shades of grey. In the darkness the room is smaller, and she steps on the black comforter and her small bare feet so close, her toes so small and the skin smooth.

"When I was a little girl, everything in my bedroom was pink," she says. "Makes me sick to think about it."

Standing on the comforter so close she smells of dried leaves, and basement rooms and honeysuckle. Her bony legs so close, *so close*, her slender ankles, oh man, and the harsh markings crawl up under her dress.

"I bet you were a handful," I say.

She drops down onto the mattress, *Shodō* turn of her head, so graceful. She's on her knees, the way she likes it, facing me, and her skull necklace, well it's not the cheap stainless steel skull necklace she used to wear. This one is silver.

"My grandmother told me I was prettier than my sister,"

Harper says. "'Too pretty,' she'd say. 'Too pretty bring you trouble.'"

Harper thinks that's funny, and she drinks the red wine and I drink the red wine. Morphine would be better, but the wine's working and my bandaged hand doesn't ache so bad. Looking at Harper, this Stooges song plays inside me, and it's overwhelming

And maybe it's the wine, or maybe it's the contact high. I sing, *gimme danger little stranger*, wanna sing it same as Iggy, that low ominous Béla Lugosi deal, *and I feel your disease*.

Harper knows the song, probably has *Raw Power* in her crate of records, and she goes for the disinterest of Nico's low Germanic monotone, and sings the line about dreams being empty, nothing but ugly memories.

Yeah Harper's hip, not only that she's into the Stooges enough to quote those lyrics back at me, but that she starts in and sings. It's something she does, same as me. I bet Harper knows all the death trip songs. The Velvets' "Heroin" and the Stones' "Sister Morphine" and the Groovies' "Slow Death." Van Morrison's "T.B. Sheets" and Bert Jansch's 'The Needle of Death" and the Reverend Gary Davis' "Death Don't Have No Mercy." The Band's "Long Black Veil" and Kaleidoscope's "Oh Death," and the Doors' "The End."

"You'd have intimidated me," I say.

"Who are you fooling?" Harper says.

She has her shades on so I can't see her eyes, but I feel 'em.

"My grandmother was worried so about me," Harper says. "'Too pretty bring you trouble,' and I would think, *Je veux des emmerdes. Tout sauf l'ennui*. When I was older I wrote dirty French words in my diary."

I don't know why, but sitting so close to Harper I flash on her being the first chick I fucked, you know, *after* Sarah and that got me thinking about Sarah and the true love scar right there on my palm, and all that went wrong, and that got me talking about her.

"Sarah was different," I say.

"Sarah?" Harper says. "The chick you told me about? Your

first fuck?"

"Don't talk about her like that, Harper," I say. "She was pure. Whiter than your dress ever was."

Helter Skelter marks, bones of her legs, black death polish.

"Most of us start that way," Harper says.

Snakes crawling, up her legs, toward her pussy.

"Not you Harper," and what would it feel like to rub my fingers on the snakes? Would it feel smooth how her skin felt before, or is it different now? Would I feel the lines, feel them the way I'd feel them if they were ripped into her skin with a rusty nail?

Harper gets the Velvets playing. It's the first album, the one with "Heroin" and "Femme Fatale" and "The Black Angel's Death Song." Harper mostly listens to the Velvets, and John Cale's *The Academy in Peril* and Nico. Death trip music. *The Marble Index* and *Desertshore* and *Chelsea Girl*. Never after that fall and winter at the Morning Glory Way house did any of that music mean anything to me but Harper.

Harper's music.

Lou Reed sings "Sunday Morning," and for so long I didn't hear the words. I remember when I first played that album hearing the beautiful melody and Lou Reed's gentle voice, and I missed the darkness, *it's just the wasted years so close behind,* but there was never mistaking "I'm Waiting for My Man," the pounding street rhythm and New York guitars, wiry lean New York gutter mouth guitars, the waiting waiting waiting rhythm, so tired so jittery so desperate, and that's the music Harper has on. Death trip music.

"The first *mot français* I knew was *baiser,*" Harper says, and is that a Harper story? Well is it? With Harper it was always near impossible to know when she spoke the truth, and when it was a Harper story.

She stretched out on her side, propping her head up with her arm, damn she's skinny and her delicate white skin, her forearm half the width of mine, holds the wine glass in her hand *Shodō* graceful, white dress bunched so I see her knees. The blue-black of the tattoo scratches, up close the lines are shaky. Such crude lines. And she's not only too thin, there's that paleness, and there's more things wrong with Harper. So many things wrong.

Until this day me and Harper haven't talked much. Don't know if it's her patching me up or the wine or a confusion we know each other 'cause in a way we do, maybe more happened in my dorm room than I understood, and the *ménage à trois* with Simone, yeah there's ways we know each other, and we keep drinking and talking. I've got a need to tell her more about Sarah, and all that's happened this past year, and when I'm not talking, Harper's talking. She talks in a way that makes it seem she'll tell me anything, makes it seem I can tell her everything.

It's dark and cool in Harper's room, as we lie side by side on her mattress. The viola drone of "Venus in Furs," Lou Reed's monotone, the nod-out rhythm. Pounding slow. On one wall, the one to the right of the mattress if you were lying on it, head on the pillow, which is how I'm lying, how Harper's lying, our heads touching as we share that pillow, and you looked up, Harper has a framed black and white photograph. She must have cut the photo out of a book. It's a Man Ray photograph of Lee Miller, who was a model and a photographer and Man Ray's lover. Harper's got Lee Miller's nose. Lee Miller is naked and beautiful and perfect in that photograph, naked except for a strange net mask that covers her face. I don't know what it means. Harper trying so hard to erase her own beauty, and that photograph on the wall above where she sleeps.

We'd been listening to the music a while when I start talking about Sarah again.

"You know how much Gatsby loves Daisy?" I say.

"He's a sap, Gatsby," Harper says.

"That's how much I loved Sarah," I say, and I tell Harper how romantic beautiful my trip with Sarah was, high school days, and how me looking at Sarah the first day I saw her, how my look breathed new life into her, and our love same as Lord Byron's poem, "She Walks in Beauty." Oh I'm so caught up in my remembrance, when everything was the first time, and our true love scars, and then I tell Harper how I ruined it.

"Oh, let's light a white candle for poor betrayed Sarah," Harper says.

I should slap Harper, but of course I don't. I would never hit Harper. And maybe it is crap—nostalgia and self-pity. Harper gets up on her knees, her white dress wrinkled, gets off the mattress and puts the album we've been listening to away. Replaces it with the third album, *The Velvet Underground*.

"We should get really fucked-up and listen to this sometime," she says. "You'll see God."

"Whoever I see, it won't be God," I say. "There ain't no God."

"There ain't no God," Harper says.

We listen to the music-box jangle of guitar and Doug Yule's sweet voice. He sings the first song, not Lou Reed—it's the only one Yule sings. On most of the album, with John Cale gone, the music's delicate and pretty.

Candy says I've come to hate my body...

Harper cross-legged on the bed, black toenails, a faint burnt chemical smell and she's got herself a number from the metal box.

...and all that it requires in this world.

I sit up too, get The Dylan out, and Harper leans in, her pale skin, so close, her shiny fake black hair, *so close,* oh man oh man, and somehow I fire up The Dylan, get her joint going.

Her voice Nico cold and so adamant.

"You *don't* want to smoke this," she says.

Smells funny, her joint. Sure there's the pungent weed smell, but there's something else, the chemical burn smell.

"Some kind of exotic weed?"

Harper laughs that laugh.

"Kind of like that," she says. "Angel dust."

I know one thing about angel dust. Creepy chemical burn. Nothing smells same as that smell. Harper takes a deep toke, and her head sways. Her shades and crude Helter Skelter tattoos and the white cotton dress wrinkled. The joint burning in her hand.

And Harper tells me about the Before. Before she got to
The University. Her whiteness. All the things a good girl was
supposed to do. All the things a good girl wasn't supposed to
do. Those were the things Harper wanted to do. Doug Yule
sings about a chick wanting to fuck herself up, and Harper talks
about the Good and the Bad, the Before and the After. Harper
tells me about the After. All the things a bad girl does. The only
things Harper cares about. The Before is over, and there's only
the After.

I tell Harper about Elise, beautiful artist Elise, who
reminded me of Audrey Hepburn, and later Jean Seberg, the
tequila bottle smashed in the dining hall, my hand on her thigh.
Elise pounding fierce on my chest, *the torment of you wanting too
much*, and me sitting in my dark dorm room watching the
Super8 film. Elise's face, her smile that's the Jean Seberg laugh,
blue million miles eyes, and the Beautiful Sadness.

"A toast to darling Elise," Harper says. "Your precious
fucked-up Elise. Anxiety-ridden Elise. Prick teaser Elise who
left you high and dry. Who never let you fuck her. Never even
jerked you off."

Harper lifts her joint up into the air, laughing and dramatic,
before bringing it down to her black lips. The chemical burn
smell, it grows on me. I can't stand it but I want to keep
smelling it. Harper tells me about the boys she fucked after me,
and the drugs, and going to the porn theater and picking up
men and letting them take her to the Star Hotel next door,
upstairs to the rooms that rent by the hour.

She's smiling as she tells me, and is all of that a Harper
story?

She smokes the angel dust and her eyes so spaced. Her face
frozen, and she's far far inside herself. She doesn't offer me a
toke and I don't ask. Same as the fucking. I won't fuck Harper.
There's an unspoken understanding. I was wrong. Both times.
Harper doesn't understand there's any understanding. Not about
the angel dust, and not about the fucking.

Harper told me about the Lavender Club and cocaine and
the first time making a chick, and the excitement of that danger.

Her fingers on the silver skull.

"Frida got me this," Harper says. "She has its twin."

I wanna smoke the angel dust with Harper. The smoke's in my nose, the chemical burn. In my nose, in my mouth, in my throat. So close to Harper, a contact high. Groovy cold detachment from my body, kinda same as when I was the Existential Freakster Bro, only different, and a soft fog between me and everything. It's as if my burnt hand's not part of my body anymore, grokking Harper so intense.

"It's like dying," Harper says.

And that sounds *so* groovy.

"It's like you're dead and you watch yourself do shit," and I would learn how that was true, but that wasn't the whole truth. Harper left out the part about how the you that you watch do stuff, *that* you doesn't know guilt or shame or right or wrong. *That* you will do anything. And the you that's watching can only watch.

I tell Harper about Jaded, how I let myself be seduced by my best freakster bro's chick, the visions of Jaded naked against the white marble, and the glam trip, her painting my nails and dyeing my hair, and fucking me in the gondola. Jaded same as the poet's wife in Baudelaire's "Benediction."

Still the guilt, still the shame.

I want to smoke the angel dust with Harper, but I don't ask.

I tell her about Jim, my best freakster bro, and how despite the betrayal somehow we're still friends, how I comforted him after Jaded plucked his heart right out and threw it "with intense disdain upon the ground." And I tell her how groovy it was, me and Jim dropping acid and sitting on that cracked beater couch with Elise, Sugar Mountain safe.

"Don't give me that bullshit," Harper says. "You don't give a fuck. You'd sell him out again just like he'd sell you. No one cares about anyone. Our nature is narcissism," and she tells me about Frida who fucks guys for money and chicks for pleasure. Frida the whore. Frida the angel dust addict.

Harper says it's scary with Frida.

We're quiet again. The soft fog around us, and Lou Reed

singing "Jesus," and what brought the Velvet Underground from "Heroin" and "Venus in Furs" to a prayer to Jesus? *Jesus, help me find my proper place.* Six lines. *Jesus, help me find my proper place.* Repeated over and over and again. *Help me in my weakness.* Harper smokes the angel dust. *'Cos I'm falling out of grace.* I want the angel dust. *Jesus.* The angel dust. *Jesus.*

Finally I tell Harper about Simone. How special I felt, an older chick wanting me, and that first night, and the sex, and in the morning when Simone stared at me naked the way a guy stares at a naked chick. I tell Harper about Simone's feminist trip, and how I don't know how to defend myself, Simone knows so much, and the craziness of her, and the hypocrisy, what Simone said and what Simone did. I feel bad because I want it to sound groovy, what I said about me and Simone, but none of it sounds groovy. It sounds sad and perverse and I feel used up by Simone. I try to explain to Harper how it isn't the way it sounds, that it's something sweet and loving and beautiful. Harper knows what it is 'cause Harper's been there. Simone picked up Harper at the Lavender Club. Simone did it with me and Harper in this room, right on this mattress, same mattress that's under us as we talk. So Harper knows. Harper knows there's nothing sweet and loving and beautiful about it. Harper knows Simone's an old woman who gets off on doing it with guys and chicks half her age. A free fuck, that's what it was, what Simone took—from me, from Harper.

That day I sorta get it. The anything goes of Harper, and how you can go too far to turn back. That's when I learn about risking it all—about really living and fuck the consequences. Live as if it's the last day of your life, the last fuck of your life. *Sha-la-la-la-la-la, live for today.* When you risk *everything* for a chance at something transcendent.

That is the beautiful dying.

I don't know why I tell Harper everything I tell her, so many things I swore I'd never tell anyone. All of it I tell her.

There's no salvation that winter, not for me and not for Harper.

3. BEAUTIFUL DYING

IT'S LATE MORNING, I'M washing the dishes and I look out through the kitchen window and Harper's in the back garden sunbathing, lying naked where Simone used to lie on the orange plastic lounge, smell of honeysuckle, and the blue passion flower creeping toward where she lies. I look away. I hardly looked, but I saw Helter Skelter tattoos all over her. It's wrong for me to look. Honeysuckle, too-sweet ill smell. I'm not going to fuck Harper. She isn't my old lady. What right have I to look at Harper? It's wrong. I wanna look at her lying on the chaise lounge. I know it's wrong. For a while I keep from looking, but finally I look again and I let myself see Harper's body with the crude hieroglyphics. Are they her sins? Her humanity? Or something else? She lies there, one of the ruined chicks in those E. J. Bellocq photographs, and I make myself look away.

Harper wore her white cotton dress again and she was beautiful. It's funny how innocent the day seems in the late morning, not a cloud in the sky, the calm of the water out to forever. Lucky lying in the dirt in front of my TR4 chewing a bone. If Harper had been eating a vanilla ice cream cone it wouldn't seem any more innocent. Harper wearing her white cotton dress, Helter Skelter snakes crawling up her legs. Laughing at me without laughing.

She sits on the couch, right where Jim sat, and Harper doesn't have a vanilla ice cream cone. Harper smokes the angel dust and chemical fire burning up, it's all over me and in my nose, in my mouth, and I can't get rid of it, and I don't wanna get rid of it.

"I'm already dead," Harper says. That's what she says when she smokes the angel dust, and at first I don't understand.

"Give me a toke."

"Really, Writerman," Harper says.

I sit right where I sat when Jim sat where Harper sits. If Elise been there she could fit between us, but she's not there. Elise is at The University living her bright new sophomore life. Some bright new freakster bro's hand on her thigh.

"I'm not addicted or anything," Harper says.

Harper was the girls who live at the Chelsea Hotel.

"But people get addicted," Harper says.

Died a thousand tiny deaths.

"Frida's an addict," Harper says. "Every time I see her she's smoking it."

Harper doesn't think she's an addict. Of course Harper's an addict. We don't give a fuck anyway, not anymore. I look at Harper the way you look at someone when you think what they're doing is a really bad trip, but you don't say anything 'cause you know they know, and worse still, you know they know you know, and nothing you say gonna change a thing. What Harper said the day I burned my hand. "And I would think, *Je veux des emmerdes.*"

Harper looks so feminine in her white cotton dress. She thought it was funny, her wearing that dress. I couldn't see it, but the sickness was all over Harper's white cotton dress. Harper has small feet and her toenails are painted black. Harper wearing the white cotton dress and her toenails painted black doesn't have anything to do with her being a lesbian. It has to do with her wanting me to fuck her. Only I don't know that yet.

I'll hold out for Simone, I'm so sure.

Harper moves over so she's on the couch right next to me and there isn't room for Elise between us. Harper smells of burnt chemicals and dried leaves, the way leaves that have fallen off trees in the forest smell after they lie there awhile. Harper said it's pathetic how Simone treated me, said Simone might as well taken a shard of broken glass and cut me. I see her tits pressed against the dress.

"What kind of man are you?" she says. "Let chicks treat you that way."

"What could I do?" I say.

Honeysuckle so strong I could gag, and which is more beautiful, Harper's face pale against the shiny black of her hair, or her nipples pressing against her white cotton dress. Or that Helter Skelter swastika on the smooth skin of her neck. Or the crude snakes crawling up her legs. Harper was the ill-fated girls who live at the Chelsea Hotel.

"The obvious," Harper says. "Leave."

That tequila bottle Elise threw broke into shards of glass, and all these chicks, they're the shards of broken glass, and I'm rolling in them, my body nicked and cut and scratched, same as that Frida Kahlo painting, *"Unos Cuantos Piquetitos,"* blood and sores and scabs and every wound is the suffering of desire and humiliation and why aren't I the man these chicks want me to be, why the fuck why?

Un moment decisif. Yeah, that was one of those decisive moments, when you reach a turning point, and your life is gonna go one way, or another, all dependent on what you do. Right then. All dependent on what *I* do. Right in that moment.

Un moment decisif.

Only I don't know it, not then. And I don't think twice, not even once. Reach for the joint. Harper stretches her skin and bones arm out away from me.

"You don't want this," she says.

"Give me a hit, Harper," I say. "Or I'll buy some from Louie."

Louie the dealer who sells Frida and Harper the angel dust.

"*Really*, Writerman," Harper says.

The snake marks disappearing under her white cotton dress, and how far up her legs do they wind, and where are the heads, and the tongues licking at her. The angel dust is Harper, that's why I want it. So me and Harper can smoke it together, get dead together. I won't be lonesome, smoking the angel dust with Harper.

She stares hard and long at me through her shades, and the hard line of her jaw and her cheek bones, her white skin smooth and tight, and the shiny black of her short hair, her face a beautiful death mask. If the Devil were 19, if the Devil were a chick, if the Devil had tits pressed against a white cotton dress. Harper brings the joint to her thin ghost black lips so slow, takes another toke, sucks in the smoke, and the invisible cloud of burnt chemical all around us and my hand on her arm, her skin smooth and cold, and I feel the fragile bones of her forearm, the radius and the ulna.

"I'll go to the Lavender Club. Buy it off Frida. She'll do anything for dough."

"You're hurting me," Harper says.

Fuck, and I don't mean to hurt Harper. Ghost black lips I wanna kiss. And I let go of her arm.

"Damn Writerman, you still don't get it," she says. "How many times do I need to tell you? When I say, 'you're hurting me,' you're supposed to hurt me more."

Harper wants me to smoke angel dust with her. I can tell.

"If a man doesn't draw the line a chick will push and push until she's got everything and you've got nothing," Harper says. "She'll suck every bit of who you are out of you. And she'll be disgusted. You oughta know about that. It's what that Jaded girl did to your best friend," and the sarcasm so strong, *"Thee Freakster Bro."*

I'm supposed to hurt Harper more. Harper's low laugh floating in the air amidst the burnt chemical smell.

"Have a taste," Harper says.

We're gonna die together smoking the angel dust.

Have a taste, have a taste, have a taste.

And the time has come.

Un moment decisif.

Have a taste, have a taste, have a taste.

Had a taste.

At first it's same as weed, and I begin to drift. But it's not the same, the burnt chemical smell, as if my throat is coated, and my nose and my mouth. And that thing going with my head same as a headache coming on, only it never actually becomes a headache. The numbness spreading from inside to outside. And I remember, summer is over, and all my big plans to write my novel lost in the smoke curling up from this joint.

"We're already dead," Harper says.

"Yeah," I say. "Already dead."

Sometimes the wanting is Simone, but more often it's Harper. The wanting never stops, never. Only when I smoke the angel dust it's even stronger. It isn't supposed to be Harper. Between me and Harper there's nothing. That's what I keep having to remind myself. More and more the wanting is Harper.

"A girl wants a *man*," Harper says. "A strong man."

"With you isn't it a girl wants a girl?" I say.

And the remove begins. The too strong smell of chemicals burning and the remove, the way I'm watching myself smoke the angel dust, watching and watching, can't do anything but watch. I watch Harper reach over and take the angel dust from me. I expect Harper to laugh but she doesn't laugh. Harper smokes the angel dust and I watch. I watch her hold the joint to her thin ghost-black lips and I watch and I watch and she fills her mouth with the poison black smoke that does that thing to my head, and I watch and I watch and I watch and her legs so thin and beautiful, the way the crude snake drawings are crawling up her, crawling under her wrinkled white cotton dress.

"But if I split," I say. "I lose her."

My head is wrapped in layers of Styrofoam, layers of burning Styrofoam that smell same as burnt chemicals. Already I'm dying, and Harper's dying. It takes a long time to see the sickness when a chick is only 19 and so beautiful. Harper has the sickness, but I can't see it. Or maybe I do see it, only I don't know what I'm seeing.

"If a man acts like a dog," Harper says. "He gets treated like a dog. Worse than a dog," and she laughs her mean laugh, the laugh that said I let Simone take me for such a fucking ride.

I'd be washing the dishes and look out the kitchen window and she'd be naked on that old plastic lounge. Sickly honeysuckle smell, and the blue passion flower growing and growing, a ravenous cancer, Christ nailed to the cross in every flower. Crude marks on her body and always the burnt. I can't escape the burnt.

Sometimes she lies on her back and I look out the window see her dark shades and her Lee Miller nose and black ghost lips, and her too thin bony arms and there's black Helter Skelter lines on her tits and flat stomach, the snakes crawling up legs slender as my arms, and her small perfect bare feet black death painted nails, so much darkness swallowing her up, but there's one bit of sunlight, the slit of her girly pussy and around her pussy a gentle downy moat of light brown hair, separating her girly young pussy from the rest of her, the rest of her so damaged, but no crude black markings inside her, and I feel the wanting stronger and stronger.

Sometimes she lies on her stomach and I see her shiny fake-black hair on the back of her head and her bony arms, the tarantula mark on her shoulder and more marks on her back curving down to her ass and thighs and the snakes on her legs, her bones and skin. And I look and look and look. When she's lying on her stomach I can't see the black death painted nails but I know they're there. I can't stop looking. I can't stop smoking. I can't stop wanting.

Sometimes Harper splits after dinner and doesn't come home 'til the next afternoon. At first I don't think about it. After a while, when she splits, I think about it. I don't like it. I want Harper home. I like knowing she's in the other bedroom. Safe. Sleeping. Sometimes Harper goes to the Lavender Club. To see Frida. Frida and Louie. I'm scared for Harper when she goes to the Lavender Club. I want Harper to come home.

The letters Simone wrote me. Each one the same only the words all different. Each letter the proof that her life is 3D living color and mine is the dust blowing away. The letters that said how busy she was and her new friends and Simon, fuck-ass

Simon this and fuck-ass Simon that. The letters that said Simone had a bright new life, same as Elise, and probably Jim too, and meanwhile mine is dying.

There's a letter three, maybe four weeks after she left. The day it arrives, that day I'm out waiting at the mail boxes for the mailman. It's late morning when he hands me the mail. I don't try to hold out. Soon as I get back to the house I read it. Makes me sick how excited she sounds.

"The Revolution is alive and well here," she wrote. "It's like everyone is working so hard to change their consciousness. There are feminist slogans and artwork everywhere, posters in the windows of the boarding houses where the students live, stickers on the telephone poles, feminist power symbols spray-painted on the sidewalks around Harvard Square. It's ground zero and I could live here forever!"

I want to be happy for Simone. I want to be one of those freakster bros who wants his old lady to have a great life. I'm not happy for her. What she wrote isn't what I wanna read. *Every waking moment I'm in pain without you, Michael dear,* that's what I wanna read. *My body aches to feel you inside me,* that's what I want. *I'm checking off each day 'til I see you.* If only.

What kills me is her going on about Simon. At the end of the letter she wrote that her and her new friends were going to see this lesbo folky Cris Williamson at The Brown Shoe. "You'll love this," she wrote. "Dylan played there in 1960 before anyone knew who he was."

She ended the letter: "Love, Susan P.S. You're watering the garden, right? All my beautiful cats are healthy? And Lucky? P.P.S. I think Simon's going to the show too."

I get the cork out of the half-gallon of Almaden red and fill a large water glass. I sit on the rug at the wire spool table in the living room next to the blue velveteen couch, and in my most ugly-ass pinched voice, "P.P.S. I think *Simon's* going too."

Another cat, an orange tabby, Alice B. Toklas, springs onto the table and imitates a sphinx. I'd smoke the angel dust but Harper has it and she's not up yet. Harper knows Louie so she buys it and I give her money. Soon as I get good and blitzed off the wine I'm gonna roll a fat number of Simone's homegrown. I get a cig lit and sit drinking 'til I really feel it. Get my voice sneering my best Dylan whine, "P.S. I think *Simon's* going to eat me out after we get back from hearing the *shitty* lesbo folk singer."

"Don't you think it's a little early?" Harper says, and she's coming out of the short hallway that leads to her bedroom, and what's funny about her saying that is she's smoking the angel dust.

"Well since you're drinking, pour me a glass too."

She picks up Alice B. Toklas and tosses her onto the rug and sits next to me close so our knees touch. She's wearing a different dress, a light cotton summer dress. A yellow summer dress with small flowers. Harper wearing that dress is black humor.

"Well it worked out great, didn't it," Harper says. "You babysitting the menagerie while she's off in Boston fucking her new boyfriend."

"She doesn't have a new boyfriend," I say.

She holds out the joint, and I take it. I always take it, and I don't know how long it's been from when it was Harper smoking and me watching. For too long it's the both of us. Harper laughs that laugh of hers, and this is such a joke we have between us.

"We're already dead," she says.

"Oh yeah," I say. "We're already dead."

Me and Harper smoke the angel dust, and what happens when I smoke it happens, the burnt and the remove and me and Harper becoming the same person.

"OK," Harper says. "I'm sure she's just having a cup of tea with Simon."

Harper's knee and my knee the same knee.

"Men are such fools," Harper says. "If only a woman had a dick."

The Buddha said the suffering was wanting things to be other than they are, a craving, and that craving can never be satisfied. Harper wants a girlfriend with a dick, and I want Harper. I mean Simone. I mean Harper.

And we both suffer.

"A good woman," Harper says. "She'll respect you drawing the line."

Always more, and nothing ever or would be enough. She takes a hit, I take a hit, Harper falls back against the blue couch, eyes closed and her head slumps. And her head jerks forward and she gets herself sitting up straight.

"Susan's a fucking cunt and you know it, Michael."

And which is more beautiful, Harper's face pale against her shiny black hair, or her nipples against her light cotton summer dress with the flowers. Or her legs with crude snake marks. And her feet are black crows, and I want to touch them, hold my palms against the thorns.

"You said that 'cause *you* want Susan, Harper."

The Buddha said the end of suffering comes when we accept the moment as it is.

The Buddha never smoked angel dust.

The Buddha never had Harper sitting so close with her hand on his thigh.

"You don't get it," Harper says. "So you'll keep getting hurt."

Harper's thin black lips. "Guys are so clueless," and she looks at me, wants to be sure I listen up. "I think about that night I came home with Susan."

"I *bet* you do," I say.

Her index finger traces my lips, as if she's memorizing the terrain. "You have a pretty mouth," she says, and we both remember that night on the mattress in the room that's become Harper's room.

As if the angel dust uses some of me up each time I smoke it. Every morning I lie in the single bed and swear never again. Another promise I make. Never the fuck again. Maybe it's the day I think about how Dylan lost his way. And how can that be? Dylan? Fucking Dylan? All the same he did, after the motorcycle accident, after the Basement Tapes, after *John Wesley Harding*. Should have known with *Self Portrait*. Never found his way again. You can say all you want about *New Morning* and *Blood on the Tracks*. Fuck, they can't touch the outtakes from *Highway 61 Revisited* or *Blonde on Blonde*.

Well then it can happen to anyone. And how about Kerouac? One, maybe two masterpieces. Yeah he lost it. Fitzgerald, took him eight years to write "Tender Is the Night." And that was it. That was the end. And Salinger still lost in the woods. I guess I'm in good company. As I sink slow toward the bottom, that's when it comes to me. All my heroes, man.

Angel dust. Never the fuck again.

And the day would begin, and Harper would have a joint for us to smoke, and I'd forget all about my second promise. At first me and Harper smoked the angel dust in the afternoon, the late afternoon, but soon we started mid-afternoon 'cause, well, Harper wanted to, and it got to where we started right after lunch and later it got worse. Every day I swore I'd stop. In the morning I felt hollow, as if my insides were missing. As if the angel dust used more of me up each time I smoked it, and more, and more.

One day we're smoking the angel dust and the phone rings, and Harper says, "Dare you not to answer it," and we both laugh, and it rings again. We think it's funny, man, someone on the other end of the line trying to get through and we smoke the angel dust and laugh, and the phone rings a third time, and I yell, "Fuck you, bitch," and a fourth ring and Harper yells, "Fuck you, motherfucker," and the phone doesn't ring again.

After that when the phone rang we'd laugh. We never answered it. Yeah it was hilarious. The phone rang and we didn't give a fuck, man.

4. THE WHITE DRESS

ALL THE LETTERS HURT. But there was one letter. Maybe it has to do with the day I read it. That day I wait until 6 p.m. I'm out on the porch, sitting where Jim sat, and I have a glass of Almaden and the unopened letter. I take a drink and look at the envelope. The wind is coming off the ocean, and even if there wasn't wind, winter's here and the nights are cold and the mornings too and in less than an hour the sun gonna set. My plaid flannel shirt isn't enough.

Harper was sunbathing out in the back garden earlier in the day. Harper was often in the back garden and sometimes, even with the cold, if the sun was out she'd lie there. When Harper was in the back garden the house felt terribly empty, you know, a house where nobody lives. I don't know why I feel more lonesome and hopeless than the days that came before, but I do.

Simone didn't have anything that meant anything to tell me in her letters. I didn't get it, I thought all that stuff about her roommates and her classes and her students and the house and Boston, all that chatter was important. It wasn't important. Still, she wrote the letters and I read each one. She had to write them. I was living in her house. I was caring for her dog. For her cats. Collecting rent money from Harper.

I set the wine glass on the wood railing. I get out The Dylan, spark it, have it in one hand, the envelope in the other. If I burn the envelope I won't have to feel anything. I don't wanna feel the wanting how I feel it when I read Simone's words. I don't want to feel I've lost her, and that's barely hidden beneath her words.

Bring the right edge of the envelope into the flame and it catches fire. But if I read the letter, maybe something's changed, maybe something in *my* last letter made her feel how she felt the first night.

Oh *fuck* and I shove the flaming edge into the wine, extinguish the flame. Smell of burnt. The burnt is different from the burnt of the Angel Dust. Got the burnt edges of the envelope between my fingers and rip it open. The right edges of the letter are burnt, some words missing, but reading that letter I fill them in.

It's all the usual stuff. Her students, her classes, her roommates. Her house, her room, and how she had to buy snow boots. And another victory for the feminists. A teacher friend, Irene, who has a house husband for an old man. "Living here you could think the revolution is over and we won!" she wrote. Yeah, soon enough all us guys gonna be shackled, heavy iron *jougs* around our necks.

And Simon. He's such a fucking nice guy. She keeps bringing him up. Some smart thing he said or thoughtful thing he did or groovy café he took her to. "PS: I told you Simon's got the other attic bedroom, right?" she wrote. "The two teachers on top and the students down below. Funny, huh."

She's fucking Simon. How can it be any other way.

Harper stands there, a fading apparition in her white cotton dress. She has the half-gallon bottle of Almaden, her hand grips the neck, and a glass in her other hand, her fingernails painted black, and the black snake lines crawl up her beautiful dying legs.

Harper wears the white cotton dress, flimsy and wrinkled the wind blows it against her body and she's cold and she doesn't care. The way it blows against her body, she's naked under the dress, I know it and still she doesn't care.

"Burning your latest love letter," Harper says. "How sweet."

I drink the wine, taste the bitter ash, and I don't care.

"She's having a great time," I say.

Harper holds the empty glass.

"A dog who gets kicked once and sticks around gets kicked again."

"What's she supposed to do," I say. "Have a miserable life for my sake?"

"Oh how trying it must be for Susan," Harper says. "Having you out West whimpering while she tries to get on with her life," and she sits on the couch and the wind blows her dress.

"Did she write about how he tongues her? Or is she still being coy?"

"Gimme a break, Harper."

She gets her shades off, sets them on the beater couch and I see her eyes for the first time since she moved here. Harper's eyes are the nail scratching the marks into her skin, the invitation to the last dance, and the tragic spin of the roulette wheel, the one where you, you being me, put it all on double zero and lose everything.

Wipe my lips with the back of my hand, and there's black on it from the ash.

"I'd like a glass of wine," she says, and from inside the house the phone rings and we laugh, and it rings again, and I pour the wine.

"It's sexy when a man pours wine for the girl."

"I wouldn't know," I say.

"What the fuck is with you," Harper says.

She's shaking from the cold so I take off my plaid flannel shirt for her. The plaid material is blue and burgundy and black —my colors, Harper's colors. She's naked under the white cotton dress, I know it, and she wants me to know it.

"Put this on."

The shirt's overwhelming big; her hands lost in the sleeves.

"You don't need a break, Writerman," she says. "You need a fuck."

I dig her wearing my shirt, as if it means something about her and me.

"I made a promise," I say, and the shaking, I can't stop it, the wind coming in.

The wind conspiring with Harper.

"So what does your promise mean?" she says. "You going to fuck her in hell?"

Harper's right, it means nothing 'cause time is running out, we're in the boat rowing our way across the Acheron. The time for promises—making new ones, keeping old ones—has passed.

I follow Harper into her bedroom and sit on the mattress. Harper gets on her knees, lower legs straight back under her, tops of her small feet stretched against the black comforter, black death nails hidden but I know they're there.

It's dark in Harper's bedroom, and warm. I don't care about the heat. I'm there for the angel dust. I'm there to fuck Harper. The angel dust. To fuck Harper.

To fuck Harper.

She hands me the burning joint and takes off my flannel shirt, tosses it on the rug.

Me and Harper smoke the angel dust and time passes, and time passes, the room a cloud of burnt chemicals and the black fog we can't see but know is there, and time passes, and we listen to the first side of *The Velvet Underground* all the way through and Harper puts the needle on track one so we can listen again, Doug Yule singing about Candy hating her body. Beautiful dying blue-black swastika cut skin. White cotton dress hangs against her body, the white cotton almost see-through thin. In front of her knees the dress wrinkled against the black comforter. Harper has her olive green metal box open, and she holds the black ivory handle.

"What's with the knife, Harper?"

"Et que ferais-tu si tu devais mourir pour me baiser?" Harper says.

She pushes the metal release, and the silvery steel snaps out faster than fast. Not there, is there. Fuck, man, the tip of the blade is the length of her hand from my stomach.

"Careful, Harper."

She takes the blade between her fingers.

"Why would I be careful?" she says.

She flips the knife so it spins up in the air, does a half revolution and as it falls, bottom end of the handle first, she catches it, her hand around the black ivory.

"You could hurt yourself bad."

"I want to hurt myself," Harper says, and flips the knife again, and up it goes, flash of silver, but this time she flips it harder and it spins a full revolution, right over Harper's head, and it's falling, the blade first. *Fuck.*

Somehow I push her so she falls back on the mattress, and the knife lands between her knees, cutting through the dress and the black comforter into the mattress. All I see is the black handle.

"You fucker," Harper says, and she sits up.

"I think I saved your life."

"I would have caught it," Harper says. "You ruined my fun, Writerman."

She pulls the blade out.

"Et puis quoi si je dois mourir aussi?" she says.

Harper has the knife in her right hand, and she holds her left hand palm up, blade against her palm, and I feel it, close my eyes, open them, a quick cut, she might as well have cut me, maybe a half-inch cut, and there's blood on Harper's palm.

"Your turn," she says.

"No."

"Come on. We'll be lovers immortal, like you and your little pure-heart."

"You and me, Harper," I say. "Nothing same as what I had with Sarah."

"Oh, and would it defile your true love memories?" she says. "Would it cheapen them? You're a pussy, Michael. You come in here to fuck me but I'm a slut to you."

Harper's right and I'm ashamed, and the wanting, the burnt filling the room, and I'll do anything. How could any man resist Harper.

"Cut me," I say, and hold my palm out.

"Hold still," Harper says. "The blade could slice through your hand."

I feel the cut, a shiver, the knife so sharp it doesn't hurt, and then it hurts and there's blood and her bloody palm hard against my palm, and she drops the knife on the comforter. Her other hand under mine, pressing my hand hard against hers and we're one beautiful dying creature. She pulls her palm away and licks the cut on her hand, licks our blood, and wipes our blood on her dress between her legs.

Lou Reed sings his prayer to Jesus and Harper sings along.
Jesus, Jesus, help me find my proper place.
And I don't care. Already we're beautiful dying, so what does it matter. I don't care. I could die if it's me and Harper. I could die, long as I'm not alone. Harper turns the knife around, and holds the silvery steel blade between her thumb and index finger, the handle in my direction. So quiet she sings, *Help me in my weakness.*
There's blood on my hand, the sting of the cut. Me and Harper on the black comforter, her with the knife. Holding it out. The sting of the cut. The remove, and all I can do is watch. Blood on my hand. All I can do is watch. Watch the wanting. Wanting Harper. The wanting. Harper. Watch me want Harper. Watch me want the fucking.
"Cut it off me," Harper says. "The dress."
And between Harper's legs, blood smeared on the dress—our blood.
"Let's smoke some more," I say.
"Cut it off me, Michael," she says. "Or get out."
Harper holds the blade between her thumb and index. I wrap my hand around the black handle, the silvery blade coming out of my fist, and current flows from Harper to me, and I feel the charge.
Harper lets go, and lies back, back on the blackness, her head back. She's watching me, her legs together, her thin arms stretched out, the white cotton dress against the blackness, and her eyes are the last dance.
Lou Reed sings, and the quietest breath of Harper, *'cos I'm falling out of grace.*

I taste the burnt. And the remove. I watch myself hold the knife. I take hold of Harper's white cotton dress at the collar, the material so thin, pull it away from her skin. Beautiful dying blue-black marked skin. The crude swastika there at her neck. Maybe she did it to herself, safety pin and India ink. Maybe Frida did the crudeness.

"Why the swastika, Harper?" I say. "You know I'm a Jew."

I slip the shiny steel blade beneath her collar.

"It's a Hindu symbol you know," she says.

I hold the cotton dress away from her, the blade against the collar.

"You're so full of shit," I say.

Harper laughs that laugh, and I wanna slap her.

"It means 'well-being,'" Harper says. "A good luck charm."

Harper lies there, her body a cross, and I'm holding the blade against the collar, and neither of us, not me and not Harper, think there's anything lucky about the crude swastika scratched into her body.

"Six million, Harper," I say. "My grandfather, my dad's dad, was one of 'em."

I watch me and Harper on the bed, she lies there and I pull the top of the dress away from her skin, cut into the flimsy cotton and the material tears, and her skin, tanned from all the days on the orange plastic lounge taunting me, and I smell the sickly honeysuckle and the room full of blue passion flower.

I can't hear her breath. She could be dead.

The knife is sharp and the cotton thin. My hands shake, her bare skin so close, hold the dress a few inches above her body, and as I cut the cotton, pulling it back, and there's more markings, as if someone took a knife and stabbed her again and again, only no blood, only crude black lines. I cut the dress past her tits, flesh and blood dirty tits, and I can't not look, her dark brown nipples, as if they've been inflated. She lies there and I cut past her stomach and stop at the waist where the dress is tight against her body.

"Don't stop," she says.

I can't pull the dress away from her. Real careful I get the knife under the waist band, the back of the knife pressed into Harper's skin. I cut through the waist band, Harper's legs together, her legs touching under the white cotton dress, the knife glides through the soft cotton, above her pussy, and I've cut through nearly the whole dress, and I stop.

I turn to the windows at the far end of the room and throw the switchblade through the air, and the knife penetrates the wall—and hangs there.

"Why did you stop?"

"I didn't stop," I say.

And I take some of the dress in each hand and rip it so fucking hard, tear the final bit apart. All those times in Elise's room, lighting her Kool, lighting a number. My hand on her thigh, and it's Saturday night and there's a party in Elise's room or even the whole floor is partying. Jim must have a new girlfriend by now. Even the bitch Sappho isn't mooning for an old lover. You've got to keep moving. Keep on truckin', what R. Crumb said.

Harper sits up and the dress falls away from her, falls limp, the cut torn white dress against the black comforter and Harper naked except for her skull necklace. Harper's body is so thin, and though her skin is tanned from being out in the sun, there's a sickly pallor. It's as if the skin barely covers her bones. Intense overwhelmed rush of Harper naked, so close, and the swastika, crude shaky-line swastika.

It excites me, the swastika.

Crude black lines on the side of a tit, on her stomach, snakes crawling up her legs. Naked and the crude marks. In the midst of her deathly beauty, the way a human might gasp in wonder at seeing a rose growing from the rubble of a bombed city, the glow of Harper's blond pussy hair so pure, and the slit of her snatch so innocent and fresh and I know she's not innocent, I mean I've fucked her, and how many others, does she even remember? She doesn't care, and none of it matters. She reaches into her metal box and gets another joint. A fuck or a cigarette, no difference.

"Just a taste," Harper says.

And she has another joint and I have The Dylan and me and Harper smoke the angel dust. Harper's beautiful dying body scarred, the swastika, the tarantula, someone took a nail, crude shaky lines on the curves of her tits, black blood, her beautiful body scratched and scarred and cursed, and we smoke the angel dust and we smoke the angel dust, and we smoke the angel dust.

"You're a chump," she says. "But I like hanging with you."

"What about Frida?"

"Here," she says. "Have another taste."

I got the joint and Harper undid the clasp, reached over and dropped the skull necklace into her metal box, and she was naked.

Harper's ghost black lips, kiss of death lips wet, and her body wan and languid and too thin, hard brown nipples and the Helter Skelter marks, the brand of death, slave to the sickness, slit of her snatch, and I take the angel dust from Harper, and we smoke it and we smoke it and we smoke it. And I fuck Harper and I fuck Harper and I fuck Harper.

5. ALL USED UP

I WATCH HARPER SUNBATHE in the garden through the kitchen window. Naked except for the silver skull. Harper brought the sickness. I smoke the angel dust. Sometimes Frida would be there too. Frida the chick Harper picked up at the Lavender Club. Frida brought the sickness. Sometimes Frida whored for drugs, and anyway she fucked Louie for the angel dust. I know 'cause he bragged about it. I know, 'cause Harper told me.

Frida has the Helter Skelter marks all over her body. I saw them. Louie for sure brought the sickness. And brought it again, and more. The more you give in to temptation, until you can't not be bad and wrong and dirty, and the guilt never as much before as now, and more and more. Until bad and wrong and dirty is what happens each day. Until smoking the angel dust is what you are, is who I am.

Sometimes the two of them, Harper and Frida. There in the sunlight. In the garden. Harper wanted me to watch. Frida's fingers in Harper. It was hard to watch them fuck, or whatever you call what they did. After a while it wasn't hard to watch. The suffering even through the dark glass and the fog, the wanting, it was worse then before, worse because of the fucking. I couldn't not watch.

Angel dust made the wanting to fuck Harper my obsession. Angel dust made me not able to say no, never. And I watch. And I watch. And the wanting so strong. To see Harper. Stoned always, laugh at something, laugh her knowing laugh. When you're young it takes so long for it to show. The corrosion, and the dying. It showed now. Naked, and my eyes wouldn't look away. How could any man look away from Harper?

You're the man. I'm the man. I should be in charge. Why am I never in charge? The sickness made me forget who I was, worse ever and more than before, made me forget. Until I was nothing but the guy who smokes angel dust and watches Harper lie on the chaise lounge. I forgot to eat. Harper forgot to eat. Sometimes only the cats ate. And Lucky. Dogs are always hungry and they won't let you forget.

I didn't like Frida. She had her hands on Harper. She wore a tarnished silver skull necklace same as Harper's. She was friends with Louie, if anyone could be friends with a dealer. Louie, the scumbag who brought the angel dust and fucked Frida on the yellow plastic lounge while Harper watched. And I watched. Why did I watch? I hated Louie the dealer, hated that whore Frida. And I watch Louie fuck Frida on the yellow plastic chaise lounge. Fuck Frida while I stand in the kitchen and watch through the window, watch Harper lie naked on the orange plastic lounge watching, her fingers rubbing herself, watching. Louie's jeans pulled down to his knees, his pale ass moving rhythmic in the sun, Frida clutching his ass, digging her nails in. I see Frida's shiny dyed-black hair against the yellow plastic, and Frida's naked thighs and bare legs and her fingers let go of Louie's ass, and I hear her cry out.

"Tie me up," she says. "So I can be free," and she was Simone, and she was Harper, and I was on the floor and I was naked and I was ashamed. The angel dust deadens you. You're watching yourself through a tinted window, the glass dark as dark dark sunglasses, only the tinted window is darker, too dark. Your body becomes someone else's body. Feel nothing. Smash your fingers with a hammer, feel nothing. The dying, every time I smoke it, and die some more.

I wanted to fuck Harper. No love or merging of souls, no Visions of Johanna. I wanted to fuck Harper. The purity. No mixed-up confusion. Simple and pure. Everything I wanted to do with Harper was fuck her, smoke the angel dust and fuck her, and the only thing she wanted to do with me was the fucking. Smoking the angel dust and the fucking. Harper was a thing to fuck. A sex thing. The feminists said it was wrong. I knew the feminists were wrong.

Fucking was God-who-don't-exist. Higher than merging of souls, higher than yin-yang unity, higher than love. Physical pleasure, the ecstatic rush, the blinding transcendent moment. Her a sex thing, me a sex thing. The fucking. Nirvana. Salvation. Redemption. The *bodhisattva*. The fucking. What if. And Shakespeare when he wrote "Romeo and Juliet" was a con man. All the poets wrong. Love was a lie, love was the pretense, the story the mind told to get to the fucking. After Eve with the snake and the apple, after God-who-don't exist banished them, Eve and Adam, from the Garden, after they knew the shame. A story. I love you, so now we can fuck. It's not your tits it's your charming personality, so now we can fuck. Love, the shared delusion, so now we can fuck.

And she had the rope around one wrist. I was on the floor and I was naked.

"But you said I was the one," I say, "who made you know you were straight."

The heaviness of the angel dust. It's hard to keep my eyelids open. We lie together on the mattress in Harper's room smoking the angel dust. Our bodies limp and heavy and naked. Sometimes I want to fuck but we just lie there.

"I lied," Harper says.

"Why did you let me fuck you?" I say.

Harper wants me to pay Frida $50, and Harper wants to watch me fuck Frida.

"So I could hurt you," Harper says.

I told Harper I'd give her $50 if I could fuck her, not Frida.

"Because I hate men. I hate their wanting. No matter how much, it's never enough."

Harper let me fuck her for a week. Then she was tired of me, she said. She let me fuck her for a month. Then she brought

Frida home, Frida the junkie whore. Every day Harper lay out
there in the garden. Her pussy hair was golden yellow in the
sunlight. Even when the weather turned bad and the wind came
up and it rained. Droplets pooling on her stomach, black clouds
and the ocean was at war, running down her tits. Her face
soaked. No that's not right. I made that up. By the time it
started raining Harper was gone. The rain fell on the orange
plastic lounge when no one was on it.

Harper knew my madness, watching her naked on the
plastic lounge, still she lay there. One time, right after the month
was over, you know, the month she let me fuck her. Maybe it
was a week. One time I didn't only watch her through the
window. I walked out into the garden, over to where she lay. She
was reading *"Tous les hommes sont mortels,"* by Simone de Beauvoir.
Yeah she thought that was a fucking riot. She didn't try to cover
her pussy or her breasts or anything. She lay naked. Reading.
She didn't care.

She knew why I was there. I had $50. Two 20s and a 10. She
told me if I wanted to look at her and jerk off it was OK. She
didn't care. I had the money in my hand, stood there holding it
out. She looked up from her book, two 20s and a 10, she took
the money, let her arm drop to her side, and the bills fell from
her fingers. She didn't care. My money in the dirt.

"Do whatever you want," she says. "Only you can't touch
me."

Sometimes she said that, I don't know when, over and over
I heard it or I remember it, or I made it up. We both smoked
the angel dust. I looked at her lying naked on the plastic chaise
lounge, beautiful blue-black swastika cut skin, beautiful blonde
downy pussy hair, beautiful slit of her pussy, the snake marks
crawling up her beautiful bony legs. Beautiful dying.

"Only you can't touch me."

I didn't care. I was an animal. She lay on the chaise lounge. I
stood naked in the garden looking at her, and I did it. Right in
front of her. There were voices in my head now. Harper's voice
mostly, but Simone's voice, Elise's voice, Jaded's voice.

Anything is permitted.

But how can I fuck you if I can't touch you?
Anything, she said.

I was ashamed, but still I did it. Ashamed. It didn't turn her on. I did it anyway.

"Don't get any of it on me," she says.

I got nervous and it took a long time.

She got bored watching me. She picked up her book, her French novel.

Harper's voice, or Simone. I smoke the angel dust and I can't tell anymore, it's all the same. The days are the same day, and I'm alone. I think I'm alone. Harper gone. I mean at some point Harper got her stuff into her white pickup and split. No one but me here and I smoke the angel dust and drink the red wine, and I think Harper's with me and I think Simone's with me but I'm all alone, me in that room, Harper's room, Simone's room, dying, and dying some more.

All the letters the same letter. I hate to read Simone's letters. The letters are ivy, and it's covering the wall, her new life growing and growing and covering everything and I'm nowhere to be seen. No, it's the blue passion flower covering it all. I'm dying. The sickness creeps up on me, infiltrates my being slowly, gently, silently. Until one day I don't see the point anymore. No point. One shitty gray nothing day after another. Everything all gone. That was too funny about Harper. No it wasn't. Wasn't funny at all. There was no Harper.

Another heartbreak. That's wrong. If you don't love a chick it's not heartbreak when she leaves. If she's a sex thing, then what is it when you can't use her anymore? When she won't use you anymore? Another chick done let me down. Sleepy John Estes sitting on a rotting front porch in Brownsville singing about his woman done left him. No, that's wrong. Another chick where I've failed. Weak when I needed to be strong. Didn't draw any line when she told me to draw the line. Feminists. Harper wasn't a feminist. Probably. Some days she was. Harper was. Harper was. Harper. There was no Harper.

And I'm fading. I can see the flame right through my hand.

I'd look out the window, hoping I'd see Harper lying there on the orange plastic lounge but no one was there. Blue passion flower growing up and over the lounge. I could barely see it. And the sickly smell of Faulkner's honeysuckle.

Louie would come by with the angel dust. I told him I didn't need to smoke the angel dust. I told him I only smoked it to keep Harper company.

"Well Harper split," Louie says. "So I guess you don't want any."

Every week I'd buy the angel dust from Louie except when Frida came instead of Louie. For $50 I could do anything I wanted to Frida. I didn't want to do anything to Frida. Sometimes I paid Frida $50 and I fucked her. Sometimes I paid Frida $50 and tried to get her to talk about Harper. Harper didn't mean anything to me. I bought the angel dust. I smoked the angel dust. I would look out the kitchen window to see if Harper was out there sunbathing on the orange chaise lounge. The dank smell of rotting honeysuckle and the blue passion flower covering the orange plastic lounge, and sometimes the rain splattering against the plastic, pooling in the dirt. I was the sickness and I was dying. And all that beautiful dying glamour, the sad girls who live at the Chelsea Hotel, that was gone baby gone. I was all used up, I was already dead.

6. THE END

SIMONE'S HOUSE IS A tomb. I float through the mess of
ash and empty Almaden bottles, Oreo cookie wrappers and
empty Coke cans, cat bowls encrusted with dried-out food,
empty cans piled in the sink, the flies and the trails of ants,
smell of cat shit—all the dirt and squalor of who cares.

Oh the goddamn goddamn ringing. Well we don't answer the
phone any more. Oh yeah, there isn't a we. That was what me
and Harper do. Did. Not answer. There is no Harper. Ringing
and ringing. Is that bitch Simone calling to check on Lucky and
the cats or tell me how she played Simon Says last night? Or
Frida, looking for money?
    The mind plays tricks, and the mind fucked by angel dust
plays many many tricks, and you lose your way, you forget, or
you remember what never happened, and what really happened
and what never happened become what happened. I pick up the
receiver of Simone's heavy-ass Pacific Bell black metal phone
with the rotary dial—a phone built same as a tank.
    Through the lost, so lost, lost-my-way gone gray fog,
through the burnt that's everywhere, through the Styrofoam
wrapped around my mind, Dad's voice. Dad's dry dusty voice
sounds same as how I felt that car trip we took, stepping out of
the car into hot dry Death Valley heat—a Death Valley
defeatism.
    "Mike?"
    At first it's a sickly heat, and it's in my stomach, how it
always felt when I got found out. When Dad caught me doing

something I knew I wasn't supposed to do, getting home too late from seeing Sarah, or the time I was smoking weed out by the apple tree, you know, down the hill from the house, and Dad yells at me, thinking I'm smoking a cigarette, which would be bad enough, but when he gets up close, right in my face and smells the weed smell, and he doesn't know what weed smells like, but he's no dummy. The phone cold against my ear, and my stomach convulsing.

"It's me, Dad."

"Where you been?"

I been to Comala, Dad, I been where there's no one but the already dead telling their sad stories over and over. I don't say that, and the heat in me isn't heat any more, it's nausea, only it's a different nausea. My free hand against my stomach, and I'm bent over, my stomach an alien creature on the attack, struggle to get the words out.

"Nowhere," I say.

"I've been calling," he says. "And calling. Your grandpa got sick. I thought you'd want to see him. You never answer the phone."

Yeah, well, we don't answer the phone here. Only my body doesn't care about my sarcasm, my body knows I fucked up, 'cause it was Dad all those times and that means it was important, something I shoulda been present for instead of fucking myself up on angel dust and Harper. The sick ache in my stomach is deeper than the flu or eating bad food, and the shame, man, for what I've done—and what I didn't do.

"I could drive up to see him," I say. "How's he doing? He's OK?"

His voice was a voice I never heard before, yeah this was heavy traffic serious and the sweat, my head and chest wet with it.

"No, Mike," Dad says. "He passed. Pancreatic cancer. We lost your grandpa three weeks ago."

It was as if Dad was crying, only he wasn't crying. Well that's what was in the sound of his voice, and more, 'cause Dad's voice had nothing to do with the Dad I knew. Grandpa passing and what it done to Mom had changed my father, I could tell. Right then I was too fucked up to think it through, but still. Something same as that doesn't go by unnoticed.

I hear Dad's words, hear what he says about Grandpa passing, and I know I should cry, but I don't cry. I'm dead too. But not dead enough. The dry heaves, oh fuck, my empty stomach wanting me to puke it right outta my body. I know it's so fucked up, Grandpa gone, but I've got the Styrofoam wrapped around my mind. The remove. And I watch myself doubled over, watch as I scream from the pain.

Oh fuck, and it was such a joke, me and Harper letting the phone ring. Fuck to shit. He's gone. Grandpa.

Oh man oh man oh man.

I flush the angel dust down the toilet soon as I'm off the phone —no chance to procrastinate. That's easy with drugs. Wake up and lie there and swear you're going clean, but you procrastinate and you're a goner. No chance, man, dump the packet of dirty white into the toilet, watch the water swirl down into the pipes. Dad's hundred bucks of food money swirling gone.

I call Lucy. You remember. Lucy Free, Simone's best friend, who inspired Simone to change her name and all the rest. Well I don't know how Lucy's gonna deal with Lucky and the cats but she said she's gonna.

Time to pull a geographic. That's what they call it in AA when you move to a new place hoping to leave the troubles behind. Never been in AA but I know something about it. Know about a geographic. Wherever you go, there you are. You can get away from everything and everyone but yourself, so the troubles you had there, you're gonna have here, if there's where you've been, and here's where you're going. So moving isn't ever the solution. They have a lot of theories same as that one, AA does, but that one for sure doesn't make any sense. If I stay where I am I'll have Louie and Frida coming 'round every week with the angel dust and things gonna go nowhere but down. It's not pulling a geographic, it's grabbing at a lifeline.

I still think of it as Harper's room. My clothes there on the orange shag carpet—unwashed jeans and inside-out t-shirts and balled-up boxers and sweat-stained socks—where I left 'em for another day. The queen mattress still has the bloodstained sheets, and my palm aches, the blade slitting my skin, her bloody palm against mine. Fuck you Harper. The mattress where me and Simone fucked until she didn't want me to fuck her any more. Well fuck you too Simone. All the ways they sucked my soul outta me, and everywhere I look, there they are.

The ghost of Simone. The ghost of Harper.

I find my car keys and get myself to the front door, take a last look and the place is a goddamn ruin but I'm not gonna clean it, not gonna do anything. There's no way I can stay another moment in the purgatory of this house. I don't take anything—not my books, not my stereo, not my dirty clothes, not my records—it all belongs in this tomb along with the already dead Michael I'm leaving behind.

One last look out the back window, the blue passion flower, and I wanna feel nostalgia for the good old days, only there's no good old days. Not here. Before I split I leave *Sticky Fingers*, with Warhol's crotch shot cover, on Simone's single bed.

I get in the TR4 and out onto Morning Glory Way and stop. Outta the car and close the gate and stand where I stood the day Simone left, over three months ago, the day I watched her white van drive away, the day she left me behind to start her bright new life, and I look back at Simone's house, Lucky jumping up on the gate wanting to come along. I feel that sad feeling, and I want it to mean I've lost my Visions of Johanna but it doesn't mean that—that sad feeling is the hole no chick ever filled, not even Sarah. The hole no chick ever gonna fill. There's never been a Visions of Johanna chick, and for sure there's not gonna be one. That shit is over, man.

Mom's the one answers the door and she's a basket case, torn and frayed from what she gone through with Grandpa. She's wearing a dress she sewed herself made of a pale blue cotton material with the burgundy outlines of birds on it—canaries maybe. Her brown hair in the beehive, and she looks through her ugly pink plastic frame glasses.

She gets a look at me, and she screams, her voice a high-pitched I-just-seen-one-of-George-Romero's-zombies.

"Leonard!"

For sure Mom's gonna faint, hand to her chest. She doesn't faint. In the front doorway I stand, nothing outrageous clothes deal, no purple lipstick, no nail polish, not smoking a Pall Mall. Just me. Jeans and the black cowboy shirt and dusty snakeskin boots. There's a bad bad feeling creeping quietly inside me. The cheap brown linoleum tiles with phony marble-like streaks beneath my feet falling away.

"Len, Len," she says. "Something's wrong."

"Don't freak, Mom."

The cold hard bad of all the fucked-up months at Simone's. The gray fog of the angel dust, how it was with me and Harper, the already dead of our neglect, and I'm scared dying. Haven't smoked any all day, and the craving, clawing at me, thousands of sharp needles pushed from inside my body toward the outside.

She's doing her best to squash her fear but her best isn't so good. I wish those birds on her dress could fly off and perch on the fireplace mantel, sing their pretty bird songs. Cheer Mom up.

"I'll freak if I want to freak," Mom says, "Maybe I'll even do a freak *out*."

Dad comes from the kitchen wiping his hands on his plaid pants, and he looks older. He's changed some way I don't know him. What Dad says, well it's not what he says, it's how he says it. If he said it the way he used to say everything it would be an attack and no big deal. Only that's not how he says it. He says it how a human would.

"Mike, what have you done to yourself?"

Dad comes forward, his hand out, right up to me, and his right arm around my back, pulling me against him. A goddamn goddamn hug. My fucking dad. "Glad you're home, Mike," and this can't be my dad. Has to be a shape-shifter, same as that guy in "Whom Gods Destroy" who impersonates Captain Kirk.

They want me to eat. No problem there. Walk past 'em toward the kitchen, get to where the Versailles mirror hangs, and holy fucking shit. The corrosion of the sickness over the months, from day to day I didn't see it, but the craving, and the angel dust, the burned-out basement of my insides. I see what Mom and Dad see.

Frizzed two-tone hair, thin greasy unbrushed split ends and the hair chunks Rasta-matted hang past my chest. Probably weigh 110, maybe 115. Black cowboy shirt wrinkled and stained and one of the pearl snaps chipped. But that doesn't let you in on it. Same sickly death skin as Harper, and worse, black shadow no sleep skin to the left and right of my nose under my watery red eyes. I'm a pale fucked-up junkie ghost floating inside that mock Louis the Fourteenth frame, and that's when I know how close I came to dying. I could've been a body gets found, or the bones—eight cats and Lucky making a meal of my rotting flesh. The beautiful dying a sham, nothing beautiful in my dying.

Hadn't known the hunger, but once I start eating Mom's good food my body remembers what it hasn't got in months and I'm scarfing salad with Italian dressing and a third of a meatloaf, and a big-ass plate of spaghetti with meat sauce. I been the total vegetarian trip all year, but fuck it. Scarf whatever there is to scarf. Sorry animals, but I'll make it up to you. I promise.

Well there was a moment of *bodhi*. I'll explain it best I can, only whatever I tell you, amp it up a bunch. All three of us in that shit-ass kitchen. Ugly-as-fuck Formica counter and the Stone Age white stove, and the stupid flowered wallpaper. I mean it's the same shit-ass kitchen it's always been, and Mom standing at the stove boiling water in that stainless kettle to make a pot of tea, and she has on that apron says *Bon appetite!* Dad sitting where he always sits, his right hand on the counter, nervous horse gallop taps.

Same as it's always been in the kitchen, only I swear it's all different. I'm sitting at the counter eating Mom's good food, and I look over at her and sure she's bummered, but there's love, and Dad watching me eat, authentic real concern vibes off him. How he looks at me, it's a look I've been wanting to see but never seen. For the first time in years I feel their love, and it's not contingent on nothing. I'm fucked-up already dead, and still they love me. Sounds corny, but it's not corny.

Don't get me wrong. All the shit I hate I still hate, and the craving, and I'm ice cold shivers, but then I'm sweating so the water runs down my face, only in the moment of that moment I don't mind any of it. The relief of sitting in that shit-ass kitchen with Mom and Dad, and not having to prove a thing. Can you fucking believe it? Me? I look up at the stupid flowered wallpaper, I've seen that wallpaper my whole life, and if there's a God, which there probably isn't, but if there is, well she's the best. *Thank you Ms. God, thank you for letting that stupid flowered wallpaper be there.* The stupid flowered wallpaper, the Stone Age stove, the ugly-ass Formica, it all feels same as home. Only instead of wanting to get the fuck gone, I'm glad to be there.

Home.

Oh man, lying in the bed of my kidhood, the darkness all around, all my ghosts there in the closet ready to invade my dreams, my waking dreams and my sleeping nightmares, and the needles being pushed out through every muscle of my arms and legs. Oh my stomach, all that food going nowhere. Spaghetti sauce and garlic and Italian dressing, and I don't know how long I lie there before the cramps, a convulsion that starts in and every wave of pain is a cleated boot kicking me, *Mom, Dad, I'm dying, come here, please,* and another kick, and the sick puke oozing up into my mouth, and I'm banging on the wall behind my pillow, the wall separating my room from their room, *please, please,* and Dad's helping me to the bathroom, step by step, fucking shit-ass marble streaked tiles, he's in his boxers and a sleeveless t-shirt, has his arm around my back and his other hand grips my arm, my own dad helping *me* and it's gotta be 2 a.m. or some shit, and I get down on my knees, head over the cold white porcelain, and Dad's hands under my armpits holding me, another kick of the cleated boot, and another, and I'm puking, spaghetti and meatballs and lettuce and carrots and tomatoes and onions and meatloaf, and the stink, the God-who-can't-possibly-exist awful stink, and I'm puking all over again, puke on my t-shirt and legs and feet, and my hands, hands holding onto the toilet bowl, and all the piss and shit that's been pissed and shit into this toilet, and I'm holding it. Oh fuck, man, oh fuck-to-hell, fucking kill me already.

Burroughs talks about the nod, you know, *the nod*, after you've got the junk in your vein, the warm drift into the warm cocoon. Don't have to see the horror everywhere, total adrift in the nod. The nod's different than the remove, and it's the same. The nod's the ultimate escape to nowhere, short of dying. The nod's a different kind of beautiful dying. Maybe some of us feel too much, and maybe we need the nod. There are other drugs than junk. Angel dust can fog the mind, hocus-pocus a spell you fall under and never come back. It was touching death what I'd been through, and death didn't wanna let go. I'd wake in the middle of the night and if I didn't have to run to the bathroom for another round of puking, I'd lie there, the creepy-crawlies under my skin. I'd crave the nod, or the remove or a goddamn goddamn drink. Anything to escape the hellfuck of me.

Everyone says it's tough to kick an addiction, and they're right. Every minute doesn't ever end. No one who says you've gotta live in the moment says it when they're kicking angel dust. Probably no one says it who's kicking anything. Dad, man, I don't know who the fuck he is. I don't think he slept that whole first week. I'd feel it coming on, and get up, be trying to hustle myself to the bathroom again, and he'd be there, his arm around my back, or a hand on my arm, *you'll get through this Mike, the worst is over*. Yeah well the worst wasn't over, but that's what he said, and it helped. You got your dad rooting for you—*my dad* rooting for *me*.

I don't wanna talk about this, but I guess I gotta. As I get clear of the drugs, I begin to feel shit again, and everything crashing in on me. Grandpa and Simone and Jim and Elise and how fucked up I left Simone's house and Lucky and the cats. Oh man, endless the guilt and shame, and a scummy depression settles in me same as I see life through a film of downerosity. And something else. Creeping up on me, flashes of an image, huge black crevices, and a dread shivering under my skin. Death Valley defeatism. I'm doomed, and life is never gonna get good for me, and I know the who-I-am of who I am.

I'm a never-left.

I'm back with all the losers too scared to go out into the world. Swore I'd never be one. Yeah I was gonna get out of there, do big-ass big things, only the biggest thing I've done was me being already dead. And I know I've reached The End. You know The End, same as when the cops chase the bad guy and get him cornered in the dead-end back alley. Everyone eventually gets to The End, when the noise stops, when the craziness is over, when the mad rush from here to there and there to here, same as the mad scene of "On the Road" comes to an end, and Mexico isn't nirvana, endless chasing of booze and chicks and drugs and kicks gets old, and finally you're alone with your lonesome sorry-ass self. Dean broken and tired and lost, Dick Diver an alcoholic and broken too, and Holden trying to cool out in that psych ward or wherever it is his brother D. B. visits him. Yeah, there comes a time when it all slows to a stop. Take a look at myself there in the cocoon house of my kidhood, all of me burning up, and all I see is a goddamn goddamn never-left.

Fuck, man, I was at The End.

It wouldn't let go. Huge jagged shards of black cutting into white. Sometimes when I woke from a bad dream I saw those black shards, and sometimes when the anxiety freaked me I'd see them too. One night I woke up, my t-shirt soaked, and I knew this image of black cutting into white was a *fucking painting*. Yeah, I'd seen it somewhere. It haunted me same as the angel dust nightmares, same as the creepy-crawlies. The next day I went to one of Mom's history of modern art books and I found a photo of a painting that I knew was the same artist. Clyfford Still. That's when I knew where I'd seen it. It was at the art museum. It was one of the paintings he called "Untitled." Clyfford Still has a lot of paintings he called "Untitled." Fucking horror show, that painting. It was as if someone took a switchblade to the sky, and through the cuts, cuts through the surface of the surface, I saw a little of what's beneath the façade. I saw The End. It was scary, that painting. It came and I couldn't get it outta my head, and the dread shivering under my skin. When the darkness descended worse than usual, "Untitled" was there and I knew there was no salvation. The hopeless of nothing gonna change, of this is your life, and your life is fucked. The hopeless of The End.

Sometimes I dream about my final days. It's the cracked lunacy of my old final days, not the new final days at Morning Glory Way. The old final days in the nut house. After I lost it and two-timed Sarah. After I took that 14-year-old chick Mercedes to L.A., and tried to fuck her. After the cops busted me for the bad checks. Yeah, after all that went down. On a mental ward all the crazies float in their own reality, and the nurses and orderlies and therapists and psychiatrists, they all know the crazies are crazy so they pay them no mind. Everyone's on drugs. Some drugs or more drugs or even more drugs. The drugs make all the crazies into zombies. A glassy-eyed detachment. A different kinda remove. If you're sane on the mental ward, the only one who knows it is you. In this case, you was me—well, back in the summer of 1971. When the drugs and the craziness were too much. Yeah, I was the sane one on that nut house ward. All the rest of them, crazy fucking loons.

I wanna sleep, but I can't sleep. I'm scared to sleep. All my ghosts waiting. When I sleep in my kidhood bed I have nightmares. Nightmares worse than Simone, worse than Harper, worse than Louie and Frida and the burnt chemical smell.

Nightmares worse than anything at Morning Glory Way. I wanna sleep but I can't sleep in that bedroom.

I'd been home a while. A month for sure but it coulda been six weeks, maybe longer, the gray rain of winter made every day seem the same. One day Dad sat me down in the den for a serious man-to-man. Yeah, him and Mom loved me and they'd always love me, but I needed to get a job, and my own place. He could see I was major bummered out, maybe it was a depression, and maybe one reason I used the drugs was 'cause I was depressed. He didn't know, but that's what he said. Dad didn't know if a job would make me feel better, but he thought it might. If it doesn't, he said, well everyone doesn't go through life as if they've been chewing happy pills. It was too much, man, the scummy depression, the jagged black shards of "Untitled." A job? A *job?* Who was gonna hire a fucking never-left? Put on the baby blue clown suit, and sell Big Macs and fries at McDonald's again? Only Dad wasn't done talking, and he jerked me out of my woe-is-me. Dad knew this reporter who owed him one, who could set me up with a copyboy job at the *San Francisco Chronicle.* Well, now they call them copy*persons,* Dad said, 'cause all this women's lib stuff. He wanted to know if I'd cut my hair and put on the money suit. 'Cause until I was ready to take those steps, wouldn't be any job.

You shoulda seen me the day I went for the job interview. I looked same as Woody Allen in "Sleeper," if you can imagine Woody Allen when he was 20. Hair parted on the left, combed back mostly off my forehead, trimmed so it ended well above my shirt collar. You combine that hair with the money suit, oh man. Mom took me to Macy's to get the money suit and some other clothes. It was pathetic, me trying on that straight-man shit. She picked out a pale blue button-down and we settled on gray wool slacks and black dress socks and black penny loafers. *Black, not* brown, and a dark blue blazer. I mean that was an outfit.

Dad told me keep your mouth shut. He said let the man interviewing you do the talking. The more he talks, the more you listen, the more it'll go your way. The day of the interview it's so fucking corny, Mom makes sure my collar's right and I've got the shirt tucked in all around and she uses this lint-remover on the blazer. She walks out to the driveway with me, all the way out telling me *Mike, you look great, you look like a million dollars, I haven't seen you look so good since your bar mitzvah,* and as I start up the TR4 to drive into The City, a smile on her face same as I haven't seen *since* my bar mitzvah.

For the interview I figured me and the boss-man would be in a private office or conference room and he'd grill me about my qualifications, but no, we meet in the newsroom, all the havoc going on, him barking out orders same as a drill sergeant to the copy*persons,* while talking to me about the job. I think it's pretty much fait accompli, and the only reason he meets with me is to make sure I'm not psycho or a total idiot. Turns out you don't need qualifications to be a copy*person* 'cause any schmo can do it. Fuck, they owe my dad one; getting the job has nothing to do with me. Yeah. Me. A never-left. Me. A schmo. And the authentic real of who I am falling right into place.

It's after 2 a.m.—this is when I was still living at home, a day or two after the call saying I had the job—my folks dead to the world, Dad snoring through the wall our bedrooms share. Dad sawing away so loud I figure he's going for the crown. King Snore. Got my socks on, holding my Keith Richards snakeskin boots, walk down the hall, through the kitchen, exit via the back door. Up the stairs leading to the garage, and I stop. I'm not superstitious, but for so long I thought those boots were good luck. Got as much good luck outta them as I did from The Dylan. "Thanks for nothing," I say, and drop them into the garbage can. Next I get out The Dylan. Now as good as any to rid myself of it too. Hold The Dylan up, but there's no moonlight to shine off it. Bob Dylan's lighter. Yeah *sure.* How did I ever believe such bullshit. Rub my fingers on it, and there's where Jaded scratched the check mark—and it stops me. I don't drop it into the garbage. The Dylan goes back in my pocket, a reminder for all eternity.

Somehow I'd get myself to the *Chronicle* building at Fifth and Mission a few minutes before 8 a.m. every weekday morning, try to calm myself, take the elevator to the third floor, struggle to give a credible smile to Anna the receptionist, get buzzed into Editorial, walk past the massive doors of millionaire publisher Dick Theriot's office, and down the hall past Executive Editor Bill German's office with the glass walls so you could see him holding forth during news meetings, his editors sitting in a half circle in front of his desk. And stretching out before me, bigger than an Olympic-size swimming pool, the newsroom, the modern faceless newsroom with the rows and rows of utilitarian metal desks, fluorescent lighting and the shit-boring gray carpet—a vortex of ringing phones, clicking typewriters and reporters chatting up sources.

I was a cog, man, doing the duties of a cog—getting coffee for the reporters on deadline, running proofs from the back shop to the news desk, making the City Hall run to pick up copy from the political writers, and when I worked the occasional late shift, doing a dinner run to three or four restaurants to pick up to-go orders. And all the other mindless shit-ass tasks. A cog. Anyone could do what I did.

Weird how you can work among dozens and dozens of humans and never have to say more than *hi* or *nice day*. Me and all the other copy*persons* were interchangeable, and every one of us was there as a favor to someone—sons and daughters of editors and reporters and friends of the publisher or the publisher's wife. When a reporter or editor needed something they called *copy*—they never called your name. For the other copy*persons* the job was temporary—they all had grand ambitions. They were doing the duties of a cog, but they didn't see themselves as cogs. I'm the only one figured this was it. You know, The End. I was a ghost, a dead man, and goddamn goddamn lucky to have the job.

The copy*person* table was in the middle of the newsroom. During the day shift there were four of us working, and during the afternoon and early evening—the busiest time at the paper —the day and evening shifts overlapped and there were eight of us. The other four copy*person* guys were stoners—some of them and some of the three copy*person* chicks would slip away during dead time and smoke weed up on the roof. The copy*person* chicks were absolute positive for certain they were the next Martha Gellhorn—tough, cynical and unsentimental.

I liked it when I was sent on a run. Well *like* is too strong a word. When I was sent on a run, you know, to drop some legal documents at a downtown high-rise office for instance, I could float total anonymous through The City. No one knew me. No one looked at me. No one said a word to me and I said nothing to no one. There's such a relief in being a nobody. There's none of the anxiety of when someone would single me out and want me, Michael Stein, to do something for them I hadn't done before. Hellfuck scary if anyone expected something new outta me. The best thing about the job was the routine—there's such relief in a routine. Didn't have to reinvent my day every day. Didn't have to think about what I was doing. Didn't have to think. I did the duties of a cog—one foot front of the other.

Another good thing about the job. Turns out you don't gotta wear the money suit once you get hired. Don't gotta keep cutting your hair either. It's not the worst, looking in the mirror and seeing Woody Allen wearing the money suit, but it's a drag. I started growing my hair out once I saw how the other copy*person* guys looked, and after I earned a few weeks' pay I bought new jeans and new cowboy shirts, and eventual a pair of black Tony Lama boots. The darkness didn't go away, but it was a relief to see someone familiar when I looked in a mirror.

There are long stretches when nothing happens in the newsroom, and we sit at the table total boredom scene. That's OK as long as no one says anything to me. One day when the others are busy doing the duties of a cog and I'm sitting alone

reading "Notes from the Underground," this copy*person* chick
Louise sits down. She starts talking about one of the editors
who works on the city desk, Johnny Baker. She sits right next to
me and she's too close. The chick is a sophomore at S.F. State,
has wavy auburn hair to slight past her shoulders, hair same as
some movie star whose name I can't remember right now. She's
one of those modern post-Freak Scene Dream city chicks,
wears her skirts too short and too tight so they show off her ass
when she walks around the newsroom.

She's too *fucking* close.

"Did you know Baker teaches feature writing out at State?"
she says.

I'm looking at my book, move my head to indicate the
negative. Too goddamn close. I don't wanna have nothing to do
with chicks. It's already too much doing my job. I mean just
living is too much.

She's got freckles all over her face. Yeah, fucking freckles.

"It's crazy," she says.

Chick gets a pack of Kools from her purse. Fucking Kools!
Lays it on the table.

"He shows up with a gallon of Gallo and tells war stories
for two hours," she says. "Brags about the great reporting he did
when he was young, *like a thousand years ago.*"

Well it freaks me, this chick too close, talking at me, and I'm
seeing "Untitled," dread shivering under my skin.

"Baker's a lech," she says. "He's always grabbing for my ass
when I have to walk near his desk. Hassling me to go have a
drink with him."

Still I don't look up from that book, only I sure can't read it
anymore.

"Report him to the Guild," I say. "They'll get his ass fired."

"The Guild's a joke," she says. "And anyway I don't think
that would improve my chances for landing a reporter's job."

Too goddamn goddamn close.

"I don't drink anymore," I say.

"You're kidding?" she says. She gets out a lipstick and
compact and gives her lips a refresher. "How old are you?"

"Why?"

"How can you work at a newspaper and not drink? It's in our blood. How you ever going to get a source to spill the beans?"

She's wearing a low cut blouse, and I can't help it, look over and see the white skin, top of her tits, and yeah, more freckles, and the wanting man, even a burned-out basement ghost feels it, and I feel it, and it's more than too much. I don't wanna feel it. Chicks are trouble, that's one thing I learned. Living is too much of a burden already without having to deal with one of them. Another chick.

"I'm not going to be a reporter," I say.

"Not enough status?"

"Well no, I don't have any plans. Just doing this job."

Oh man she can't believe my trip. She shakes a Kool out, and crosses her legs, and her skirt bunching, showing too much thigh. That's when she touches my arm, *the torment of you wanting so much,* and she asks if I got a light, and no goddamn it, *no.*

She's seen me light up a Pall Mall a million times using The Dylan. I don't know what to do. I don't wanna light her smoke. Her hand on my arm, *don't fuck me like a gentleman, Michael.* Oh man oh man oh man. Too goddamn fucking close. Gotta get out of there.

I jerk my arm away, can't get enough air inside me, and I'm standing.

"I just remembered," I say. "I gotta go out to the back shop right away, there's a proof I gotta get for, uh, Baker."

"Baker's off today," she says.

"I mean Gavin."

Before she can say anything more I'm walkin' away same as I'm in some Olympic competition, that fast, got the cold sweats, my whole body a twitch, I know it, and everyone can see. Oh man oh man oh man. Split to the men's room and I'm in there at least a half hour, and when I come out I hang near the city desk away from the copy*person* table and that Louise chick 'til my shift's up and I can get outta there.

Once in a while I got a buzz working at the paper. When a big story broke I'd get lost in the moment, forget I was a never-left loser, feel part of something bigger. Yeah, all of us—reporters and editors and typesetters and printers and copy*persons*—working together to get a breaking story out into the world. The Patty Hearst deal, for instance. Paul Avery at his desk, an open can of beer in a brown paper bag, a cigarette burning up in his ashtray, typing his front-page story on deadline. Each time he finished a page he'd wind it outta the typewriter, yell *copy,* raise his hand and wave the newsprint page and keep waving it 'til one of us would jump up, run over, grab the page and hustle it up to the city desk for editing before another of us ran it out to the back shop.

They still used the big linotype machines, and you could smell the hot lead and proofing ink. Man was that the smell of a newspaper. When the first edition finally came off the press downstairs with one of those breaking stories, it was goddamn exciting.

But goddamn exciting didn't happen much. Mostly it was boring at the *Chronicle,* and I sat at the copy*person* table reading to kill time and ignore that chick Louise. Yeah, each of us only has so much time on the planet, and every day I was killing mine.

You're not supposed to be 20 and still living in the room of your kidhood, only that's not why I had to get out. I couldn't sleep in that room, and when I did sleep the nightmares came. I'd be going from here to there, some easy journey, only the more I tried to get to *there,* the further from *there* I got. It creeped me. I can't explain why but it did. I'd wake with the cold sweats, lie there and try to forget. One day I got a call from my old freakster bro Rock 'n' Roll Frankie. Him and this guy Sam were sorta making a living playing folk-rock at fern bars and steak-and-lobster joints while they waited for a record company to show up and sign them. Those two had lined up an apartment in the city, on Frederick Street, couple blocks up from Haight, and they wanted me to go in on it with them.

There's nothing easy about the move. Everything new is huge-ass scary since I stopped using. My folks drive me to the apartment. It's what they call "semi-furnished," which means there's a shitty bed and a chest of drawers in each bedroom, a small table and chairs in the kitchen and a ratty couch in the living room. My room's small, but it's got a desk where I can write. Well, sit there for two hours every night staring at a blank page. The faded beige walls have brown water stains, supposedly whatever caused it been fixed, but Frankie said the landlord's shifty-eyed. In my room there's one small window. It's a sad thing that window. I wish my room had no window 'cause no window would be better than that window. A window is a promise.

When I move in I have one suitcase full of the clothes my folks got me. I go into my room with the water-stained walls and close the door, sit on the saggy mattress and look over at the small window, and through it see the gray paint peeling off the building next door, and I see "Untitled," and the dread shivers under my skin and I get the cold sweats. I'm unsteady how it is during an earthquake, and there's nothing here for me. I'm fucked as guilt ravaged Raskolnikov lying on the couch in his small room, a room *more like a cupboard than a place to live,* and impotent Arturo Bandini in his small room on Bunker Hill trying in vain to win the love of Camilla, and Juan Páramo trying to sleep in the room where they *hanged Toribio Aldrete and locked the door and left him to turn to leather.* This small room I live in is Death Valley Defeatism. Ugly water-stained walls and a window. I'm on Desolation Row. Every day I wake up in that room I die. And every day I die some more.

We weren't the chosen ones. Not Sarah, not Jim, not Elise. Not Jaded, not Simone, not Harper. And not me. For so long whoever was in my circle, well it was the magic circle. We were the ones destined for greatness—the cool ones, the hipsters, the freakster bros and freakster chicks. The world turned all around us, only that was wrong. There were no chosen ones. *Special,* but *not special. Special* only in the way every creature on this planet is special. *Not special* 'cause no creature is better than any other. Bob Dylan's not better than me. He's accomplished more, Bob Dylan has, but he's not better. We all have our sins and our imperfections inked into us.

Even Bob Dylan. Yeah, imagine that. Even Bob Dylan.

FOUR

1. "UNTITLED"

ALL THE DAYS ARE the same day, and according to the
calendar I have tacked on the water-stained wall, gonna be a
year and a half in July. Every day the same day, a kind of hell I
live over and over. Since I started the cog job. Same regards
living at the Frederick Street apartment. Over and over. The
same day. I'll be 60 and sit at the table, some reporter half my
age yelling *copy*, and I'll get him coffee or run a page of his story
up to the city desk. Day I die I'll still live in the room with the
water stains and the window. I hoped the job and moving to
Frederick Street, the darkness would lift, but it hasn't, and that
Clyfford Still painting won't let go. The jagged cuts revealing the
void—the beautiful dying of the universe, the dread shivers
under my skin.

Every day the same day. Get up. Breakfast. Take the streetcar to
work. Do the duties of a cog from morning 'til evening. Take
the streetcar home. Get pizza on Haight Street, or cook
something simple—brown rice noodles with a bunch of veggies
and tofu. Sometimes I listen to records with Rock 'n' Roll
Frankie and Sam. I turned them on to *The Wild, the Innocent and
the E Street Shuffle*, and they started including "Rosalita" in their
sets. A song about a freedom I'll never again know.
    The hardest is those guys back from a gig blitzed with a
couple sleazed-out smalltime groupies. I'd pass one of those
chicks in the hall goin' to the can or something, so fucking
awkward. How can they fuck chicks they don't even know? Hole
up in my room and watch an old movie on the black and white

and try to ignore the fucking in rooms either side of mine. Sit at my typewriter but I can't write. Every night I fail. Go to sleep. Get up, do it again. Weekends are the worst. Two whole days to kill. Sleep late. Take my dirty clothes to the laundromat on Cole. Buy groceries. Take the bus to the Parkside Theater on Taraval and watch whatever is playing—kill a couple hours. Wait for Monday. The apartment. The *Chronicle*. The pizza joint. The apartment. How I get through each day, I don't know.

There comes a Saturday I'm deep in my darkness, the black crevices of "Untitled." That day I get it into me that if I see the actual painting it'll let go of me. All I have to do is go to the museum. That's impossible. The apartment. The *Chronicle*. The pizza joint. The apartment. It's same as I'm agoraphobic. I haven't been to the museum since me and Jim and Jaded went, the day Jaded leaned back against the white marble. But I *did* go there. So many times. Before. I need to go to the museum. Well that's impossible. To think of going freaks me. When I was a kid Mom took me. I was with her the first time I saw "Untitled." I *can't* go to the museum.

The depression same as an elephant on my back. Getting up is impossible. Getting dressed is impossible. The museum is near City Hall, a block from where all of us copy*persons* go for the City Hall run. All the why-I-can't-go beating up on me. I don't go to the museum any more. I might run into that Louise chick. Sweat runs down my face, the dread shivers under my skin, and the earthquake tremors.

Finally I said fuck it. I was sick of my goddamn goddamn life and I wanted to see "Untitled," and I was going to see it. It takes me forever to get ready. Dragging everything out. My shower and shaving. Such an ordeal picking out what to wear. It's past 1 p.m. by the time I'm ready and if I stall much longer it isn't gonna be worth the trip. I can put it off 'til Sunday, but that's bullshit. In procrastination lies defeat. One of my mottos —one of my *old* mottos. Well some things are true, even for a never-left loser.

There was no one in the gallery where "Untitled" hangs other than the guard. I keep my eyes on the floor, get myself in there and my whole body twitching, twitching worse than Jim ever imagined. Sit on a polished wood bench in the middle of the gallery facing the painting. If I'd run the two and a half miles from the apartment to the museum no way I'd be more exhausted. Pounding blood loud. Don't know how long I sit there, *not looking,* staring down at the polished wood. A riot going on inside me. Well not looking isn't doing any good, the creepy-crawlies bad as they ever been. So I look. It's a huge rectangular painting—about 13 feet wide by 9 feet tall. Staggering, the horror—so much worse than I remember.

And the pounding blood loud, fuck, and I look away, I look down, the room spinning. And if I let it continue I'm gonna pass out—I know it.

Oh fuck this. Fuck it fuck it fuck it.

I won't let it. Gotta keep it together. Make myself face the painting, and I do. Look up, take it all in.

These jagged black crevices cutting into the beige-yellow surface, cutting into the façade. Looking at those crevices makes a lie of everything around us—the surface of the surface. It's Guy Debord's "The Society of the Spectacle," if his book were a painting. Maybe what's so unsettling is knowing how my own life is a façade. Me going through the motions day after day, letting the authentic real slip away. Once I'd been brave. Once I tried to live every day as a Days of the Crazy-Wild day. But that was so long ago. My life such an utter failure. I mean even to get myself to this museum, to see this painting—well I'm barely here. I'm so fucked, and looking at "Untitled" I know it, and worse, this is how it's always gonna be. The painting, coming to me in my worst despair, refusing to leave, a constant reminder of all that I've lost, and what I've become.

I had to get out of the gallery. I couldn't stand it another moment. I needed a cup of coffee. I hadn't drunk coffee in a long time. It makes me anxious, well, more anxious. Gets my mind racing everywhere I don't want it racing. Fuck it. I was there in the museum and I was gonna have a cup. Coffee. Black coffee. Black.

The museum café is luminescent with high ceilings and white walls and retro-modern furniture—white Eames chairs and tables. I'm shaking when I get in there. The jagged black crevices, the dread shivers under my skin, and a nausea coming on. No. Gotta get it together, can't fall to pieces. I get in line to buy a cup of black coffee behind a couple skinny-ass art chicks —one has black hair, the other's a blonde—and if I focus on them, get outside of myself, maybe it'll help.

"The heaviest," blonde chick says, and her hair is cropped short, but she has shiny hair gook on it so it spikes off her head, a helmet of short porcupine needles, and she wears a black leather biker's jacket over a black dress with a pleated skirt comes out around her legs same as a big inverted cloth funnel. Her friend's hair is short too, but it's too too fake shiny dyed-black.

"You saw her?" blonde chick says.

Black-haired chick wears a dark gray sweatshirt, and black straight-legged jeans, and polished black engineer boots. There was a time I would have tried to get something going with the black-haired chick, but that was so long ago. There's something familiar about her, but I'm still trying to get my sea legs, and it's not coming into focus.

"Close as me to you," black-haired chick says.

These two, man, they're different. There's something compelling about them, as if they're a new strain of hipster cool college chick. That's it, they're something new. They're not Freak Scene Dream chicks. They're not chicks too young to be Freak Scene Dream chicks who wanna be Freak Scene Dream chicks. The next New Trip, they're *it*.

"Between sets at the bar," black-haired chick says. "C.B.G.B.'s."

I didn't get it right away.

"The heaviest," blonde chick says.

"Coulda got her autograph," black-haired chick says.

Oh man, these chicks look young, 18, 19. And the way they stand, they both have this natural hipster stance, it's how their bodies are, more weight on one foot than the other, how their heads are angled, the way their arms hang at their sides, or move through the air. The way they stand, probably practiced standing so cool when they were kids, but now it's second nature.

"I couldn't ask," black-haired chick says. "It's, you know."

"Fan girl!" blonde chick says.

"Zip it, Liz."

Blonde chick giggles the way young chicks giggle when they share a secret about some boy, and she puts her arm around her friend and leans into her, casual, nothing heavy or sexed out, their own conspiracy of two, and black-haired chick giggles that same shared-secret giggle, and blonde chick lets go of her.

"Her legs," black-haired chick says.

I knew so much when I was young as them. Younger than yesterday.

"Perfect, right?" blonde chick says.

The black-haired chick leans toward her friend, whispers something but all I can hear is "tattoos."

"Jesus Christ," blonde chick says.

That blonde chick has a camera around her neck, one of those Rollei 35 deals, really small, touches her friend on her shoulder, asks her to hold still, and the blonde chick takes a picture. Oh man, when she did that, I want to hug her, I want to hug them both, I want to tell them, yes. Yes! Take pictures, dye your hair strange, make art, love the obscure, question authority, burn down the institutions, kill the old farts, invent the future. I love their supreme confidence. The certainty in their voices.

"What's she like?" blonde chick says.

And I felt that way once, the certainty that I was right.

"Iggy," black-haired chick says. "Iggy if Iggy was a girl."

Took a long time before I figured out that the more I thought I knew, the more certain I was right, the more ignorant I was. A part of me would always yearn for the certainty I'd known when I was young, the certainty in their voices.

"Oh God!" blonde chick says. *"Iggy if Iggy was a girl."*

I can't talk to these chicks but I'm gonna talk to them. I gotta talk to them. I touch black-haired chick's shoulder, do my best to make it a firm nothing-sexual touch. I mean it's to get her attention but it's awkward and she jerks away, turns and sees the fuck-up of me, and gives me the drop-dead vibe. Something black silk-screened on her sweatshirt.

"Whadaya want?"

Hard to see black on dark gray. I see it, an open switchblade, and there's a panic along with the dread under my skin.

"That singer you were talking about," I say. "Who is she?"

Black-haired chick takes in my scene. "You wouldn't know her," she says, and looks to her friend, "It's not the *Doobie Brothers*," and they do their shared-secret giggle and the jagged black crevices of "Untitled," I'm being sent back to my sad-ass room, and a cleated boot kick to my stomach.

"It wouldn't be a chick who calls herself Harper?" I say.

Black-haired chick looks at me through Keane eyes, and yeah, her eyes were same as Harper's eyes that first day I met her. "You know about *Harper*, man?" she says. "No one outside the Village knows about her."

Harper. It is Harper. Harper in New York. Harper fronting a band. Harper playing C.B.G.B.'s. Harper with *fans*. Fuck, nothing turns out how you figure it.

"Old girlfriend," I say. "She wear a white dress?"

"Harper was your *girlfriend?*" and how she says it, she's not seeing a burned-out basement never-left, and my stomach doesn't hurt any more and I'm not in my room.

"Before she moved to New York," I say.

That makes it hipper, that I dug Harper *before*.

"Wow," blonde chick says. "The heaviest. What's your *name?*"

"Yeah, she did," black-haired chick says. "A white cotton dress."

Harper in New York. *I hate you. You're the man.*

"During the last song she takes a knife and cuts down the front," black-haired chick says. "Tattoos *everywhere*."

Harper a rock star. *When I say, "you hurt me," you're supposed to hurt me more.*

"It was *so* heavy," black-haired chick says. "The white dress was her mask of innocence, you know, hiding the darkness. When she got to the hem she drops the knife and she rips it off."

"Wow," blonde chick says.

"Harper's the dark secrets of our souls laid bare," black-haired chick says.

Man, it sounded so melodramatic, still it was true. Funny how clear things are, later, after.

"She sang a Velvets song," black-haired chick says. "For an encore. Beautiful redemption."

"'Sweet Jane'?" blonde chick says. "'Rock 'n' Roll'?"

"It was 'Jesus,'" I say. "That was her favorite."

Yeah, and nothing stays the same. Nothing can you count on. Nothing.

"She has a 45 out," black-haired chick says. "'Jesus,' and one she wrote. It's called 'We're Already Dead.'"

Of course it is. That's the deal with art, you take your skin and bones and blood and hair and spit and sperm, and make something. Yeah, I guess me and Harper had to live those months we lived for her to tell that truth. I was part of that, maybe she wouldn't have written it if me and her hadn't done what we done.

The two of them get their coffee and walk away. Harper in New York. Harper, a rock star. *Iggy if Iggy was a girl,* that's a good one. Is Frida with her? Or did Harper split her whole West Coast scene? Pull her own geographic. Always I was gonna be the last freakster bro standing, guns a-blaze. Well I was wrong, dead wrong. Wrote Harper off for already dead, and she's a star.

I'm still in the café line, Harper singing "Jesus," Harper naked on the orange chaise lounge, and what does it sound same as, "We're Already Dead"? Does it sound how the angel dust would sound? How the blade cutting into my palm would sound? Or the snake tattoos carved into her legs? *Do whatever you want. Only you can't touch me.* Is that how it sounds?

I ask the guy behind the counter for a black coffee. Man, I'm sure not who I used to be. Those chicks seem so young and innocent and alive, but what do I know? Surface of the surface. Who knows what dark shit they gotta live. I pay the guy and he puts my coffee on the counter. Fuck, this is a bad idea. I don't need to amp up my anxiety. Well I don't care. Today I'm doing shit I wanna do and fuck consequences. I take a sip and it's good strong coffee, worth a buck, none of that bitter taste, a jolt of caffeine. I'm buzzing, and that's when I hear his voice.

"Well look what the mangy hound dragged into this most glorious and phantasmagorical museum."

Fuck, and if I were 64 and losing my hair and my hearing shot to hell, that voice I'd know it. There he stands, *Thee* Freakster Bro, goddamn goddamn Jim Costello. If me and him been sitting on the Sugar Mountain couch, Elise between us stretched out so she's leaning back against my shoulder, her toes touching Jim, that's how close he is to me.

"Writerman," he says. "What a thing. You *here*. Excellent. *Michael Stein at the art museum.* More than excellent," and the clap of his hands echoes in the airy café.

He's forcing his I-got-the-world-by-the-short-hairs too wide smile.

"Cut your hair, old sport," he says. "Lost some weight. Lost the snakeskins. Sorry to see them go."

How he says it, yeah he sees I'm a burned-out basement, he gotta see it. He starts in singing, straining hard to be the old Jim. The Jim I met fall of '72, walking across the quad same as he was a god. *Ch-ch-changes, don't want to be a richer man, ch-ch-ch-ch-changes, just gonna have to be a different man.* Yeah, well I'm not the only one who's changed, and singing an old Bowie song won't turn back time. He's not his crazy-wild self no more, at least not so crazy-wild as our days at The University. Somehow he's different. Sure the bird's nest grown some since I seen him. Not so out-of-control, almost shaped, a calculated chaos hair theory. His beard well under control too. The vibe, this is crazy, I mean it's *Jim*, but he's, well, mature.

He's really goin' for a college professor vibe. He's worked

on his straight-man scene. Wide-wale corduroy sport coat with leather elbow patches, that golden corduroy color, over a V-neck herringbone sweater, button-down collar shirt, golden cords to match the coat, and of course he has the brown penny loafers. *Brown.* Still, what's different doesn't really have much to do with his outfit. I don't know what to tell you except this. He's not *Thee* Freakster Bro any more, not the Jim who walked across the quad with such arrogance, not larger than life.

The guy standing in front of me is plain old Jim Costello.

Yeah, we change. There was a time when there were things me and Jim agreed on same as one mind, as if each of us were a helix, sections overlapping. But other sections were always eons apart, and after all this time, do any of the sections overlap?

"Jim, this is so unexpected," I say.

Oh man, it really is Jim Costello. He knew me before my flameout. Him there smiling, fuck, how long's it been since anyone was genuine glad to see me? It's as if a switch been flipped, and the darkness fades to white. Reach out my free hand, and what the fuck, this is my bro, my *freakster bro,* two years since we hung out tripping Orange Sunshine homegrown stoned Sugar Mountain couch, and I'm gonna *shake* his hand? Fuck it, set my white cup down on the counter, and both arms around him, hug his pudge of a body, the curls of his bird's nest against my ear. We hug the appropriate amount of time for two friends, two male friends, but I don't wanna let go, and I don't let go, and fighting it back, the sadness overwhelming, and the window. What I wanted from life, how high I used to fly, I mean I was gonna be the last freakster bro standing, guns a-blaze, and the sad-ass of what I've got. Day by day.

Been so long since I touched another human, I mean other than Mom and Dad and that's different anyway. His trimmed beard against the side of my face, and there's a strong smell of aftershave, that stuff the barber splashes after he's done cutting your hair. If I can keep on holding Jim, maybe the dark film won't come between me and the world any more. Only I can tell Jim wants it to end, any guy who's not a fag, or fucked up how I am, would want it over. Oh fuck, the awkward deal, he gotta wonder what happened, and does he know me anymore. We were once freakster bros, but maybe I'm not who I used to be, maybe I'm a stranger, and he doesn't want a stranger hugging him.

I let go and he steps back, and he's a pudgy college professor and it was too intimate. What's Jim gotta be thinking? He can feel my desperation, I know it. How I'm barely holding on. I look at Jim, look into his eyes and fuck, all those months during sophomore year, and the dotted-lines eyes, and yet I never really looked at his eyes. Well Jim has soft brown eyes the color of a song sparrow's feathers, and I look deep into those song sparrow brown eyes and see a kindness, and the kindness reminds me of something—only I can't remember what it is. What I knew right then, our dotted-lines eyes deal meant something to Jim too.

"Still tooling around in the TR4?" he says. "What a car, old sport. Riding in it with you in the good old days, so excellent."

"No, man," I say. "I don't have a use for it here in The City. My dad unloaded it."

"Oh well," he says. "No use hanging on to what you don't need," and in a rush of words Jim, and yeah, he really is *Jim* now, not *Thee* Freakster Bro, *Jim* tells me he just graduated, B.A. in Literature with a minor in teaching. He's on the professorial track wearing the money suit, college professor-style, getting poems published in a long list of literary journals. He doesn't have the cane, that's gone, and what else is changed, 'cause there's something else. A certainty in the way he stands, not the certainty of youth, no this is the certainty of experience, hard fought and hard won.

"How long has it been, old sport?"

"The party," I say.

"The party," he says.

Simone's end of class, end of school party. For me it was the end of the world party—everything crashed and burned after the party. And is it the shadow of Doom and Gloom across his face? Maybe what Jim remembers is me and Jaded in the Ferris wheel, and the hellfuck end of him and her. The past always waiting for an opportunity to sabotage the present. Yeah, that's all in the shadows staining his face, and it passed, the past is the past.

2. TWO OLD FRIENDS

WE TAKE OUR COFFEES and find ourselves a table, sit across from each other, same as back in the day, you know, when we'd hang at The Owl, listen to jazz and talk about the heavy shit. It's a beautiful perfect modern white table, whiter than Sarah's virgin body, and Jaded's pale white skin against the white marble, and Harper's face against the black comforter as I cut away her white dress. And they're all there, all my ghosts, crowding the space between me and him.

"You really must meet Ellen, old sport," he says. "She's my princess, my lover, my soul mate."

"Sounds serious," I say.

He blasts me, another rush of words. Ellen's a freshman, a lit major he met in the fall while TAing a modern American lit class. She's been his chick for nearly nine months, and this is the one, he's so sure.

"She's elsewhere at the moment," he says. "She's looking at art, she's in the chick's room, she's at the museum gift shop. Hell, I don't know where she is, she's that kinda chick, that's what I love about her. She'll be here. *Wow,* Writerman at the art museum. If I was going to run into you anywhere, this would be the place."

His smile so big his lips gonna crack. "Big news," Jim says. "A chap book of my poems," and slaps his palm down hard, and dark brown coffee overflows from both our cups pooling on the white table. "Can you believe it?"

I blot up the coffee with a couple napkins, and I can't stand those coffee-soaked napkins defacing the white table. "I'd buy you a drink," I say. "But I don't think they sell booze here. Anyway, I'm not drinking these days."

"You? Writerman?" Jim says. "A teetotaler? I'm stunned."

He's not stunned, he gotta see I'm changed.

"Well, a beer once in a while," I say.

I pick up the wad of soggy napkins and go throw it away and as I walk back he's looking at me, his soft song sparrow brown eyes, and I remember. It was after Sappho listened in on our conversation. I wanted to hit her but Jim grabbed my arm, kept me from doing something I'd regret. He calmed me down, and let me sit in the orange Eames. Let me sit in *his* chair for the first time.

Back at the table he laughs his so-great-to-be-hanging-with-you laugh.

"I'm a poet, I know it, hope I don't blow it."

"You will," I say. "We humans always blow it."

Jim is older, I'm older, and coming up behind us there's 18- and 19-year-olds same as the black-haired chick and the blonde and they have a whole new scene, and yeah, for sure, the *next* New Trip. Oh man, what's funny was me thinking I was *ever* relevant—another joke at my expense.

"Which philosopher, pray tell," Jim says, "lent you those words of wisdom?"

"Not Dylan," I say. "Been too long since he had anything to say."

Jim goes into too much detail about his book and who's publishing it and how this particular professor who was Poet Laureate back in '64 or '66—somewhere back in the Sixties—got the manuscript in front of the right editor.

"I'm calling it 'The Invisible Twitch Deal,'" he says. "Remember the day we dropped the Orange Sunshine?"

Of course I remember, I'll always remember, and I've got both hands around my coffee cup, look into the deep dark of the coffee, and wish I didn't remember.

"I don't use *any* of that shit any more," I say.

He's looking at me how he did after we hugged. Not the awkward part, but after, and again, his song sparrow brown eyes. So weird how all that time at The University I never noticed the kindness in Jim's eyes.

"You doing alright?" he says.

For the first time since I cleaned up my act I feel the pull of the beautiful dying. And Harper, lying on the black comforter in her white cotton dress, *Cut it off me, Michael, she said. Or get out.* Jim would never know, he could never understand. I mean I'm not sure I understand. But the wanting for Harper, I feel it so strong. Sitting across from him, staring into the abyss of my coffee, I would plunge Harper's knife into my heart to be back with her again, to feel the everything of it as if it hadn't already happened, as if it were brand new. To be already dead with Harper. To smoke the angel dust. To feel the beautiful dying. One more time.

OK, well that's when I try to tell him. I wanna lay it all out, how Simone beat me up with her feminist dogma 'til I couldn't fight no more, and led me on while she fucked Simon Says, and how Harper used me up and left me for already dead, alone with the angel dust so it could finish off the job. Only I can't. I can't begin to tell it. How would Jim understand how wrong it's all gone for me? The futility of my life, my small sad-ass room and the saggy bed *and the window.* I might as well been watching that scene in "Breakfast at Tiffany's" with Holly and Cat, when she leaves Cat in the alley, and I can't look at Jim and I can't help it, I'm bawling.

Jim's hand on my arm, "Hey man, it's OK. Cry if you need to cry. I feel for you, bro. Really Writerman, whatever you been through, you're right by me. Freakster bros for life, old sport."

Try to fucking pull myself together.

"Fuck, Jim," I say. "I'm not as messed up as it gotta seem."

"I understand," Jim says. "I had my own version of slipping into darkness. Wasn't pretty how things went down between Jade and I. You know some of it, but that wasn't the worst. Let's just say you weren't her only sidetrack."

We're quiet, and I never been so close to him. He works so hard to keep his feelings hidden. All the bluster and bravado of *Thee Freakster Bro*. But I haven't forgot that afternoon at The University, the first time we met, his insecurity in the quad, weight on his left leg, then his right, back forth, back forth. Yeah Jim knows about the lonesome, and heartache, and how life can break you.

"How's Elise, man?" I finally say, just to say *something*. "She still living on Middle Earth?"

"I guess you didn't hear," Jim says. "She's back in L.A. She got a scholarship for the Otis Art Institute."

He gets out a Pall Mall, and I get out The Dylan, only it's different, it doesn't make me cool, it means nothing it was Dylan's lighter—*if* it was Dylan's lighter. Finally I understand. *Nothing*. Only a lighter. The Dylan only meant what I wanted it to mean.

"She wasn't the same," Jim says. "After you split on her."

And he sees it, really sees it, The Dylan, you know, my lighter that he found in Jaded's purse. After me and her fucked in the gondola atop the Ferris wheel down at the Boardwalk. *My* lighter in *his* chick's purse with the scratch she made, a notch-on-a-gun-barrel kinda check mark, and I guess the whole scene of me and him reunited has got him more emotional than I ever would have figured, 'cause he loses it, falls apart here so he's got his head face down, cushioned by his arms, bird's nest curling onto the table, and he's the one bawling, and the hellfuck of what Jim been through is there in the low moan he can't hold back.

"Fuck it," he says.

You never know what's gonna make you feel what you felt all over again. Never know when the past gonna rear up and sabotage the present, and I place a hand on *his* shoulder, same as the first time I comforted him. The day he was walking so dejected across the quad singing "Evil." It was Jim who was a mess that day. I held him and I was the strong one, and I feel my strength again. I'm better than who I've become.

"Sorry, man," and I pocket The Dylan. "I wish it coulda gone down different."

Sitting up he wipes his eyes. "I'm ridiculous, old sport," he says. "I got a girl I love. I don't know what's wrong with me. All this memory lane."

We're two old friends in the art museum café. We talk more, but there's long stretches when we sit quiet, and it's funny, how comfortable it is to sit there quiet, the two of us vibing on how groovy it is to hang out again. Fuck yeah. Talking's overrated. It's not always so important.

I don't know how long we sit before Jim says, "Whatever happened between you and Elise, Writerman, you gave up too easy," and he gets out his Cricket, flames it, the smell of tobacco burning, the past burning behind me, ashes, of what has been, no, what might have been, ashes, ashes.

"You're rewriting history," I say, and he tips his head back, yeah trying hard to be *Thee* Freakster Bro, pinches his lips to an oval and the smoke rings rise above him. "Elise told me it was you who gave her the guts to really pursue her art, made her believe in herself."

"You don't understand."

"What's there to understand?" Jim says. "She's a *fucking* chick. They're all the same. No different than Jade."

Well that's the least of what he doesn't get. Jim doesn't know anything about Elise. He hasn't lived with Simone, hasn't read "Sexual Politics," hasn't dug deep into the New Trip of men and women, and the changes. He doesn't know. He hasn't lived with Harper, hasn't sat at the table with assertive feminist chick copy*persons* who are so dead certain they're gonna be star reporters.

"Come on, man," I say. "Would you say that about one of our black brothers? You can't generalize about chicks."

"Lighten up," he says. "Can't you tell when a freakster bro is joking you? I was in that 'Women in Film' class. I've read Ellen's copies of *Ms.* I know it's a different world."

Yeah, and maybe he's changed in more ways than I could anticipate. "I remember one time," Jim says. "You came to my dorm room. 'Jim, man, chicks are the road to ruin.'"

"Chicks say that about us," I say. "History of the world."

"Guys fucking chicks?" Jim says.

"No man, guys fucking *over* chicks."

Jim laughing at our past. "Road to ruin," he says, and yeah, perhaps there are new sections of the helix overlapping.

I'd driven the gotaway car. Gotaway from home, gotaway from Mom and Dad, gotaway from Sarah. Gotaway from Elise, gotaway from Jim, gotaway from The University. Gotaway from Simone, gotaway from Harper, gotaway from the angel dust and the already dead. Gotaway, gotaway, gotaway.

"You're better off without her," Jim says. "She's one of those chicks who's impossible."

"It wasn't Elise," I say. "A lot of times shit doesn't work out."

"I guess no one knows that better than you," Jim says, and soon as he said it he wishes he could take it back, but he's right, almost nothing's worked out. Well that's not quite true. I've got my job, and here's Jim taking me serious.

"Was she still into that Jean Seberg look?" I say.

"She'd grown her hair out," he says. "Dyed it black. You'd hardly recognize her."

"I'd recognize her."

"Hey, old sport," Jim says. "I got a funny story for you. Have you heard about Ms. Braveheart?"

"Simone, I mean Susan? She still with that jerk professor? Is he teaching at The University now?"

Jim gave me the dotted-lines eyes, and this time the understanding we have is I-don't-got-a-clue. "I guess you haven't talked to Kate either."

"Kate? Dead to me, man."

"Kate moved in with Susan," Jim says, "and it's *not* platonic."

Fuck, Simone trading me and Simon Says in on that bitch of a chick Kate. Guess I was prescient calling her Sappho 'cause she's Sappho for sure now.

"Kate was so appalled," I say. "Seeing Susan kiss that freshman."

"I believe the phrase was 'cradle robber,'" Jim says.

"That *is* funny, man," I say. "Those two, it's not gonna end pretty."

Ellen's different than Jaded, but in some ways she's the same, and I hope the differences are the kind that matter—that the chick really loves him. I hope Jim can stand up to her when it's required, and there's always a time when it's required. She has bleached-blonde shag hair, ecru skin from too much time in the sun, and those glasses with the thick stylized black rectangular frames. What makes me think of Jaded is how sophisticated Ellen seems, and her clothes. Ellen's style is a total different trip than Jaded, but I can tell her clothes cost dough. She has on this crazy-ass retro dress, this vinyl deal with large black and white squares—as if the dress was cut from a huge vinyl chessboard.

"Looked serious," she says. "Whatever you two were talking about."

"Jim was passing along the bad news," I say. "An old girlfriend of mine swallowed up by the abyss they call L.A."

"Let's change the subject to something *fun*, shall we?" she says. "Have you seen the de Kooning exhibit? It's absolutely fab."

Jim does a drum roll, hands moving fast on the tabletop. "Ellen," he says. "This is Writerman. I've spoken to you about him. Remember? Back in our sophomore folly he was my esteemed associate, partner-in-crime, and one and only freakster bro. Meet the once and forever Michael Stein."

Ellen's olive green eyes go luminous, and she's checking me out serious, trying to adjust whatever idea of me she had to the me sitting there, and that's when I realize how much I've meant to Jim—maybe more than he meant to me.

"You're Writerman?" she says. "You wrote for *The Paper* too.

Took those fab photos. Jim said you two did a lot of drugs together."

"Yeah," I say, and it's funny how meaningless her litany sounds, and I understand how the experiences me and Jim shared were embedded with meaning in a way no one but me and him could ever grok.

"That's me," and I give Jim the dotted-lines eyes. "Although I don't remember the part about the drugs."

"No idea you were even *in* Frisco," Jim says.

"I moved here last year," I say. "I'm working at the *Chronicle.*"

Another drum roll, this one faster, the beats louder. "A job?" Jim says. "My freakster bro has a job? Is that allowable in the freakster code of ethics?"

Oh fuck-to-hell, 'cause that's it. Hearing it from Jim, oh man. Sure he's joking, but still. Right the fuck then that's when I know I hate my job. Hate being a fucking cog. Before I know what I'm saying I tell them I'll be quitting before winter.

"I'll starve to get my novel written," I say.

Jim brings his palms and fingers together, fingers aimed to the heavens. "And let us now have a moment of silence," and he drops his hands to the table and delivers a third drum roll, the beats faster still, louder, louder, and he stops drumming, has a go at scatting a few bars of "Taps."

"Writerman, willing to sacrifice it all. His best freakster bro, his girlfriends, his addictions—sacrifice *everything* for his art."

The three of us kept talking, and after a while there was a turn in the conversation. Things got serious heavy. I don't know how we got there but somehow we did and I was talking about my Grandpa dying.

"It was tough," I say. "Pancreatic cancer. Such a bummer— that whole scene."

Well then Ellen tells me about her Aunt Judy who died from breast cancer end of March, and how her sister spent three months caring for their aunt, and was in the room when she passed.

"Back when we were kids, Eve and I lived with her for a while when Mom suffered her depression," Ellen says. "Eve was 8 and I was 3. Eve always had a special relationship with Aunt Judy."

"You know," Jim says. "You ought to meet Eve. She's really your type, old sport."

"What's that mean?" I say. "She's a frigid artist, a feminist man-eater or a self-mutilating sadomasochistic lesbian dope fiend?"

"She's a *creative*," he says. "Almost as lovely as my own dear Ellen of the spring meadows and crystal clear rivers, of the untouched ice caps and virginal rain forests."

I look at Jim's lovely Ellen, and see Ellen of the *voitures rapides* and *nouvelle cuisine* and *haute couture*.

"My sister's *unpredictable*," Ellen says.

"All chicks are unpredictable, my dear," Jim says.

"You're saying *I'm* unpredictable?" Ellen says. "*I* have a telephone, Jim. *I* get eight hours sleep each night. *I* don't take off for parts unknown without telling a soul."

"She's a great chick, Writerman," Jim says. "Has a B.A. in English Lit, and she's working toward an M.F.A. at S.F. State. Seriously, Writerman, this chick could do you good. There's something about her—she reminds me of you. I've got a hunch she'll bring out the best in you, old sport, and vice-versa. You must meet her."

Eve wrote her sister's address in large black print on a white café napkin and handed it to me. "You forgot her phone number," I say.

Jim laughs again. "Eve doesn't have a phone."

"She doesn't believe in them," Ellen says. "She hates phones."

"I said she was a *creative*," Jim says.

"Doesn't have a phone?" I say, and that was funny, I mean I guess it wasn't only me and Harper had a problem with phones.

"I said she was *unpredictable*," Ellen says.

"What do I do?" I say. "Send her a telegram?"

"With Eve everything's got to be spontaneous," Ellen says.

"She's *that* kind of girl," Jim says.

"You have to stop by," Ellen says. "If you two are fated to meet, she'll be there."

"The moon and the stars and the planets, old sport, they must all align."

Well Jim and Ellen have things to do and it's getting late. We stand up and Jim has his arm around Ellen, and she gives him a fast kiss, the kinda kiss a chick sometimes gives a guy in public when she doesn't wanna get into it. Jim has a satisfied smile, doing his best to rein in how thrilled he is to have a chick again, and he's fussing with his corduroy coat, getting the collar right, trying to smooth out some wrinkles, the future professor getting ready to leave the museum. He looks to Ellen quick-like, and I guess those two have their own version of the dotted-lines eyes.

"Hey, you know we're having dinner with Eve tomorrow night," he says. "This restaurant in Chinatown. It's out of a Raymond Chandler novel. Down these stairs and they have private booths and marble-topped tables. You want to join us?"

I get the name of the restaurant from Jim, but as I tell him I'll be there I know there's no way. Back in my room, after the bright bright big heart of my hours with Jim, the lonesome comes crashing down on me, and it's as if the café scene—the two art chicks and Jim and Ellen, all that transpired—is a dream that's faded.

There in my small sad-ass room I see other rooms. Meursault's room with a brass bed and a wardrobe whose mirror has gone yellow, and the room in Memphis where Popeye forced Temple to turn tricks, where she rose from the bed and saw herself in the dim oblong mirror, a thin ghost, a pale shadow, and the Florida hotel room where Seymour blew his brains out.

The horror of "Untitled," the horror that shows through the cuts into the surface of the surface to the void, and once you know the authentic real, that everything is fucked and it's never gonna be different, you can't go back to the innocence. Well it's the same with me. Don't matter how much kindness in Jim's soft song sparrow brown eyes. Sunday night I call and leave a message I've come down with the flu—can't make it.

Me. A schmo.

Me. A never-left.

Me. A burned-out basement.

Me.

3. THE MOON AND THE STARS

YOU SURE CAN'T ANTICIPATE the future. I was going along doing the duties of a cog, slogging through my life, when the day came I forced myself to go to the museum. *Harper was your girlfriend?* In a flash of a moment, from never-left loser to *someone* in the eyes of that black-haired chick and her friend. *The heaviest. What's your name?* And Jim, man, and Ellen too—to them I wasn't a burned-out basement.

It was heavy getting the low-down from Jim. What he'd done, and Elise going to a serious art school, and Sappho moving in with Simone. What I'd been through, it didn't have be The End. Look at Harper—who woulda figured? And I understood something else. *Bodhi.* Maybe I was a sad-ass loser, but I wasn't a sad-ass loser *never-left.* No, man. Never a *never-left.* 'Cause I *did* leave. Split from my folks, split from my friends, split the no-name. Sure The University isn't "The Odyssey," isn't Kerouac on the road, isn't Siddhartha's journey or the reach for transcendence in "Steppenwolf." Then again, maybe it is.

You don't have to voyage on the rough seas or stick your thumb out along the roadside or enter The Magic Theater to learn about life. I learned plenty, maybe same as Odysseus and Kerouac and the others, and maybe I learned more. Certainly I learned different. They don't know the authentic real mixed-up confusion of feminism, or the already dead of angel dust. Or Harper. You think Circe or Mardou or Hermine got anything on Harper? Yeah it's different if you leave, go head-to-head with the darkness, and come back home. You're a different human than if you never left. Authentic real of it, you do what I did, can't never be a never-left.

I wasn't the same after seeing Jim. Nothing on the outside, but inside something was happening. I began to have purpose. Beginning of the beginning. Of the New Trip. Fuck, man, got a start on my novel. And the sound, *my sound*. What Elise heard, well I found it. Each night from 11 to 1 I didn't sit front of the Smith-Corona and fail anymore. I wrote. The words came, and they were the right words. *My sound*. Finally it was for real, my novel. Hundred pages for real.

Coulda been a month after I ran into Jim and Ellen. Another Saturday and same as the day I went to the museum I was antsy for *something*. I was looking for my Pall Malls. Going through the pockets of my coat, and that's when I found the white café napkin, the one that girlfriend of Jim's wrote her sister's address on. I unfolded it and there it was, in big black print. *Eve 1603 C 16th Street*. Fuck, from my sad-ass apartment it was maybe a 10-minute streetcar ride and a two- or three-block walk.

Me finding the napkin, in the old days I'd think it's a sign. Yeah well look where signs got me—the purgatory of that sad-ass apartment. I sat on my bed and I looked at that name. Eve. I looked at it for a long time. Well then I thought about the museum. Goin' to the museum got me somewhere. Maybe this would get me somewhere. Maybe.
  Un moment decisif.
  There was nothing easy about it. To take a chance. To go see a chick. The horror rising, "Untitled" seared into me, the dread slithering beneath my skin. Only I couldn't accept the purgatory any more. Seeing how Jim cared, how I was his best freakster bro no matter the ups and downs of my life, and my writing finally happening, yeah I *knew*. I was gonna have to change some shit or I'd end up slitting my wrists. I wasn't gonna settle for being a burned-out basement. Gotta take a risk, Harper said, and she was right, and I had to take a shot at the transcendent. Fuck yeah, I was *in*.

Regards Ellen's sister, I had a problem. I'd stood the chick up. I was Mr. Flake. No one believes a dog-ate-my-homework story, and no way sister chick bought my so-sorry-but-I-got-the-flu. There's ways to handle an awkward situation. I could fess up to how beaten-down I was, go the tea and sympathy route—but that's risky in the worst way. Most chicks don't wanna hear that kinda loser story. Or I could make something up. But I didn't wanna lie. Nothing good starts with a lie.

When I got to her building I stood on the sidewalk, the creepy-crawlies under my skin. There were two one-car garages flanking a stairwell with no security gate. Only one reason I didn't turn around and split for home. I'd already made my decision, and if you make a decision you gotta stick by it. That was my new rule. My post-getting-a-job-and-a place-to-live new rule. Back in my sad-ass room, sitting on the saggy bed, I decided I was gonna see this chick today no matter what, and now I was coming up against the *no matter what* part of the deal. And when all the *you can't*s start in, you've got to ignore them.

Well fuck the goddamn anxiety. On the first level were two apartments, 1603 A and B. "Please Come to Boston" cranked too too loud from 1603 A, the one on the left. Goddamn Boston. I bet that's where Simone had her awakening. Some college chick's tongue between her legs. At the mid-way landing I stop to look out the window, down on 16th Street and past it to the old Mission. Built in 1918, long before I was born, and it's gonna be standing long after I'm gone.

In procrastination lies defeat. So up the stairs I go.

The wood landing is painted with glossy grey deck paint, pretty recent, looks super clean and shiny, as if someone swept and mopped this morning, and next to her door a brick-red ceramic planter with a dark green fern rising from the center, and all around it, the soft beauty, white and pink impatiens. Eve's door is painted that same brick-red. Feng shui trip, that red door gotta be. Red, the color of prosperity.

I do the twice over once deal. Run my hands through my

hair, get it kinda fluffed out, pick a piece of lint off my black cowboy shirt and check my zipper. Last thing a freakster bro wants to do is show up at a chick's door with his fly unzipped.

OK, this is it. Step up to the door, and there's a peep hole so the person inside can get a look at who's ringing their bell. Well it's me ringing the bell.

I stood there awhile, rang the door a bunch. Nothing.

I might as well been wearing the bad luck snakeskin boots 'cause she wasn't there. To hell with it. I didn't need it, man. I fucking didn't. Come on. A chick doesn't have to love the Pac Bell system to use it.

That was it for me trying to meet Ellen's sister, what I figured. Only a week later I end up at this café on 16th Street four blocks south of the chick's apartment. This huge drafty café probably left over from when the Beats were happening, where arty types, the ones with highfalutin ideas and worn notebooks and empty pockets hold forth from stained oak tables all day for the price of a coffee. The café was down the block, and across 16th from the Roxy, where they show a lot of films about the revolution: "The Battle of Algiers" and "State of Siege" and "Le Petit Soldat," and coming out after a couple hours of that kinda film a human can almost believe we're still gonna change the world.

Since I was so close, what the hell. I walked the four blocks to Eve's place. That day booming relentless from the bottom floor apartment, Bachman-Turner Overdrive's "You Ain't Seen Nothing Yet," with that ripped-off Roger Daltrey stutter. Fake-ass phony Bachman-Turner Overdrive belong with Grand Funk and Black Oak Arkansas in the Bermuda Triangle of shit bands.

I got up to Eve's landing, and it's the same scene as last time. It was all spic and span up there, shiny grey landing, and the brick-red pot with the fern and the white and pink impatiens, and the beautiful feng shui door. 1603 C. Even with the pounding music, it was an oasis on that landing. That building been built some time after the 1906 earthquake, maybe in the Thirties, I don't know, it felt old-timey. They used those thick, wide planks for the landing and her door was an antique, beautifully painted with cool trim and it was solid wood, not a cheap-ass hollow-core door.

Another thing, the windows above the mid-way landings had old glass in them. The quality of light coming through that old glass is different, it really is, better than northern light, and northern light is supposed to be the best, and up at the next mid-way that different light came through the window and down the stairs. I was covered in that different light and it made me super positive the chick would be home.

I adjusted my glasses so they sat on the bridge of my nose how I like it, made sure my cowboy shirt was buttoned right and reached down inside my jeans. I don't know if other guys care which side their dick's on but I've always had a thing about my dick being on my left. It never felt good if it got itself on the right. So I moved it over.

Fuck, Captain & Tennille singing "Love Will Keep Us Together" right as I was gonna ring the bell. The Devil had to be laughing his ass off, or maybe it was God-who-probably-don't-exist-but-maybe, making me pay.

I rang it anyway. And I waited. And I waited. And I waited.

Ridiculous. Same as picking a lottery ticket, trying to meet up with the chick.

Rang it again, and again, and again.

Well it didn't make any difference how many times I rang it, or what kinda light I was standing in, she wasn't home. I guess I coulda left her a note, but how lame is that? *You don't know me but I met your sister, who's my best freakster bro's old lady, and I was gonna have dinner with you and them at the Chinese restaurant only I was sick and couldn't make it, remember?, yeah I'm that guy, but anyway, they both said I really needed to look you up, so I stopped by but —.*

No point in leaving a note for someone you've never met. Someone you've stood up. No point. None.

Well a couple more weeks gone by, and it was another Saturday and I couldn't stand it hanging around that sad-ass of an apartment. Saggy bed, and the window. Rock 'n' Roll Frankie and Sam were gonna be out at some steak and lobster doing four sets of background music all night, and they were talking about a couple chicks who wanted to party with them afterwards. It was so depressing, man.

I mean I couldn't stand it. Another dinner of ramen noodles in that house by my lonesome, and then the night would be worse. Sitting in front of the TV 'til it got to 11 when I'd get myself into my room in front of the Smith Corona. And when Frankie and Sam and the chicks rolled in, already well lubricated, sometime after 2 a.m., and me the fifth wheel under solitary confinement having to endure the sounds of them partying.

Oh kill me right now God, if you exist, just do the deed.

Yeah, I had to get out of there.

I took the N Judah through the tunnel, down past Castro, yanked the let-me-off wire strung above the streetcar windows, and got off at the intersection of Market and Church. I was glad Eve lived in the Mission 'cause if there's one place in San Francisco you've got a 50-50 shot at some sun, that was it, and not only could I see the bright bright sun in the crisp pale turquoise sky—I felt it. The warmth of the sun. Yeah, and I heard Brian Wilson's fragile heartbreak, the sun warming my arms through the black cotton of my cowboy shirt, the sadness of love lost—it still amazes me how a song can show up, unannounced, and make me feel something so intense.

Right where I got off on Market was Rainbow Records, big multi-colored neon sign announcing the store above the entrance, but I wasn't going in, wasn't letting it distract me. Up at the corner of Market and Church was Frank's Liquor. Yeah, I needed a smoke. In the liquor store there was a short stubby Italian guy behind the counter, balding, short sleeve white shirt discolored around the armpits. One good thing, wasn't an Iron Cross on his shirt. And another, didn't have his nose in Kierkegaard or Heidegger or Kant. Well, he looked at me same as I was casing the place.

"You buying something, kid?" he says. "This isn't a bus stop."

Walked along Church Street past a Chinese restaurant buzzing off my smoke, and from an open second story window came that voice. *She doesn't have to say she's faithful, yet she's true like ice like fire.* I took it as a good sign, especially after that liquor store jerk. In the moment of right then all was right with the world—buzz of nicotine and Dylan floating out above me.

I avoided the dog shit on the sidewalk and kept my third eye open 'cause I was in the Mission. Humans get killed in the Mission. 'Course people get killed all over San Francisco. Have to never leave your apartment, have a guard dog patrolling, a gun at the ready, and still you could get killed. On the other side of Church was that place with the groovy pastries. Just Desserts. That was the name of it. Would I get my just deserts? But that implied fate, or maybe a yin-yang balance to life. Karma. Only that was a lie. Life isn't fair. That's what I learned from Grandpa dying, and from Elise, and Harper. The good get shit on easy as the bad—except when they don't. If there's a yin-yang to life, the pattern is not apparent.

I turn onto 16th, shouts of kids playing at Dolores Park a few blocks away, constant stream of cars up and down the street, people walking in both directions. A half block south and I reach Eve's apartment building and that's when the worry of being Mr. Flake is alive and well, and I'm freaking. How's a chick who's been stood up on the first date gonna ever get over it? Indecision had shown up, and this dark-skinned guy with a neatly trimmed moustache and a pit bull coming up 16th toward me, heading for Church. I hate those fucking dogs, and I got the cold sweats, *and* the creepy-crawlies. I'm glad he had that fucking dog on a leash. I mean I'm not only glad, he had to have it on a leash. Those dogs can kill a human. What if this Eve chick is home this time? How's a burned-out basement loser gonna deal with her? You see a lot of guys with those dogs in San Francisco. I don't know why, ugly as sin those dogs. I should catch a streetcar home. Actually, ugly as the ugliest thing you ever seen. Those dogs.

Yeah well I made my decision. Gotta live by it, and let all the *can't*s be damned.

Outside Eve's apartment building I drop what's left of my cigarette and grind it into the sidewalk. Third time I been there. This day. This third-time-not-the-charm day. Third time. I mean even if she is there, still won't believe in third-time's-the-charm. I'm not gonna be superstitious, no fucking way.

On the first level "Kung Fu Fighting" shake-the-windows loud coming from 1603 A. I stop on the mid-way landing, and maybe this is a mistake. Take a look out the window at the old Mission. Probably have a statue of Jesus nailed to the cross in the church. I mean of course they do. It's a Catholic church. *Help me in my weakness.*

Eve's landing.

And as I come up the stairs, I see the landing, and the apartment.

Eve's apartment.

That oasis is beautiful, exactly same as the last time. Glossy grey landing looks super clean and shiny, and there's the brick-red ceramic planter with the fern and those beautiful white and pink impatiens. And her fantastic beautiful feng shui door. All of it, same as before. Exactly. Is that a good thing, or a bad omen?

Well I stood there for a while, let the light come down through that midway landing window onto me, Yeah, I was covered in that different light, and it reminded me I wasn't a never-left, I'm a responsible freakster bro with a job. Not a burned-out basement. I'm a for real writer, and I'm worth a chick's time.

I do the twice over once, you know, fuck with my hair, adjust my glasses, make sure the snap buttons on my black cowboy shirt are snapped right, my fly zipped, my dick over on the left.

OK. Step up to the door with the peephole. What if she was there both those other times, looked through the peephole and didn't wanna have nothing to do with a burned out basement loser? Fuck it, fuck it, *fuck it!*

Well I ring the bell. Shiny red feng shui door. Ring it again. Stand there and look at the fern, look at the door, look at the peephole. Check my fly. Ring it again. The dread slithering under my skin. Ring it. Ring it. Ring it. All around me the void. If she isn't here no one gonna know if I ring it a million times. The *you can't*s so goddamn loud. And I ring it and I ring it and I ring it.

What if she's not there? I said.
    Then it's not meant to be, Ellen said.
    The moon and the stars and the planets, old sport, they must all align, Jim said.

Why can't she be a chick who's got a phone? Only there's a reach for utopia in her not having one. She's banished the telephone from her world as if it doesn't exist. Who else ever done that? Well me and Harper sorta did, only we didn't. It's different. We had a phone but didn't answer it. This chick doesn't have a phone, so a human can't ever get an expectation they can call her.
    Ring the bell again, and "Get Down Tonight" booming up from below. Ring again and again, and knock in case she has a thing about doorbells too. Or maybe the bell's not working. That's it. Knock a couple more times—just in case.
    I contort my mouth into a goofy smile, *do a little dance, make a little love,* raise my hands to the left and right of my chest, palms facing away from me as if I'm a mime feeling an invisible plate glass wall, fingers aimed toward the heavens, although I'm quite sure there aren't any heavens, and there on the landing I do an inane retard's jig, raise each knee ridiculous inane high, mouth the inane idiot words. If this chick saw me she'd call the cops for sure, and the paranoia strikes deep. I stop my ironic dance, look to the door and the peep hole, *oh come on man,* shake a Pall Mall free, and reach for my lighter, you know, the one I used to call The Dylan.
    That team of carpenters, the ones who usually get to work inside my head, they've moved into my chest, and they're taking

sledgehammers to me. The pounding blood loud. What if it's my last cigarette? The final cigarette.

Michael Stein, known to his friends as Writerman, was found dead on the second floor landing of an apartment building in the Mission District Saturday evening. He was apparently waiting for the arrival of a young woman, whom the police believe lives in the building. The butt of a Pall Mall he may have been smoking at the time of death was found near the body.

I sit on one of the stairs that leads up to the next two apartments, my boots on the landing and I wanna be same as the Buddha, appreciate the duality of all things. Brick-red ceramic planter with red and white impatiens. Impatience. *A lesson in patience.* OK, it's not meant to be today. I'll have to come back. No such thing as luck. No such thing as third-time's-the-charm or three-strikes-you're-out. There's only what you make of this life. The dread slithering, and what if this is a sign, what if Doom and Gloom are still around, perched on the roof laughing at me.

The syrupy schmaltz of Paul Anka and Odia Coates singing "(You're) Having My Baby" echoes up the stairwell. It's sick that song, sexist and patronizing and licentious. I mean the National Organization of Women, and they're not exactly the radical arm of the libber brigade, gave it their "Keep Her in Her Place" award. If feminism didn't exist, that song would've caused the libber movement to spontaneously erupt into being.

I sit smoking my Pall Mall, and what the fuck, there's a smudge on one of my boots. Goddamn dirt mark bugs the hell out of me, get some saliva on my index and go at it, and that's when I hear something.

Someone is looking through the peephole, somehow I know it. Well the door opens, only it's chained—opens less than the width of my hand—and from inside the apartment, her voice floating out over that sick song.

"Hey," she says. "Why were you ringing my doorbell like a crazy person?"

She's standing back from the narrow opening, the hall light has her silhouetted, and all I know is long hair, and a dress with bits of color.

"Sorry, I didn't think your doorbell worked," and I get up, take a step on the shiny gray landing toward the door. Her voice is louder, and kinda girly.

"You looked awfully funny dancing to that gross song."

The chain rattles, the door opens wider and I see enough to know she has a Laura Nyro vibe. She has raven hair parted in the middle falling past her shoulders, hint of a wave same as the cover of *Gonna Take a Miracle*. Her face has a scared fragility, as if she's seen her own version of "Untitled."

"I don't know you," she says.

"Well you almost know me," my hand hitting against my thigh, cigarette ash falling onto her shiny gray landing. "I know *you*. Well, I know of you. Your sister. I'm her boyfriend's freakster, uh, Jim's friend. Writerman, well, Michael Stein. I'm the guy was supposed to have dinner with you and them in Chinatown last month."

She watches from inside, wavering at the near end of the shotgun hallway running through the apartment.

"Oh that jerk," she says. "I'm in the middle of something important. I have to go."

"Look, there were extenuating circumstances," I say and I'm closer, but not too close, I mean if somehow there were a sheep up here, it could stand tail to head between me and her.

"I was really wanting to meet you," I say. "It was just—I mean don't dwell on the past, you gotta be in the moment. Think regards today—right now in fact. Let me make it up to you for my faux pas."

The salacious come-on of Barry White's "Can't Get Enough of Your Love" forcing itself on us, and she wrinkles her nose and that's when I see Eve has a Dora Maar nose, a slight bigger than a chick's nose oughta be for her size face. Not perfect but actually it's her imperfect Dora Maar nose that makes her pretty face something special.

Yeah, she hates that steamy pseudo soul crap too, Barry White going on and on about how he can't get enough, he don't know why, can't get enough.

"Eve," I say, and is it too familiar? As if saying her name is same as seeing something I don't have permission to see, and I'm sleazed by all the Barry White slime. She angles her head so the right side is higher than the left, *what-do-you-want-from-me, man, what-do-you-want.*

"I hate that pop crap," I say.

"Gives me headaches," she says. "I've tried to talk to him. The boy downstairs. I've left a million notes," and she's closer to the doorway, her side of the oak threshold. "When he gets home from school he turns on the radio, or puts on one of those Top 40 hits collections. One time I was so furious I lifted up one side of my coffee table and let it drop to the floor, made it skip. He turned it up louder."

"Don't go," I say. "I'll fix it. I'll get him to stop."

"Yeah *sure*," she says. Her dress comes down past her knees to somewhere between her knees and ankles.

"How are you gonna do that? You can't even show up for a dinner date."

With a calm certainty I draw on from I don't know where, "If I get him to stop, you'll let me buy you a drink. Right?"

"Oh will I?" she says. "Who told you? My half-sister? Don't believe everything someone tells you. Especially Ellen. My crazy *younger* half-sister."

That's when I realize we're talking the real deal, talking same as a freakster bro and chick who know each other, closer to the bone than it oughta be given we're strangers. No artifice. Kinda how me and Sarah would talk, only me and Eve aren't teenagers, and there's more of my confidence freeing itself from where it's been hiding for too long.

"I was so hoping you'd be here," I say.

Her left foot on the threshold and she's barefoot in huarache sandals, you know, with the thick strips of wine-brown leather. She's got small feet, no polish on her toenails, and is she gonna come outside?

"Maybe you hope for too much," she says.

"You gotta have hope," I say, and I'm closer, standing

maybe a yard back from the doorway, and I remember Jim in the quad, back and forth, left, right, left, right and that's not gonna be me, man, and I concentrate, make sure I don't do that insecure trip. "I mean what else is there?"

"Despair, angst, futility."

We laugh 'cause it's funny and tragic and true—her girly laugh that's got the sarcastic in it, and my trying-to-get-along laugh.

"Maybe I don't hope enough," she says.

"Hope sustains us," I say. "Through the troubles," and is that true? Sure wasn't any hope to sustain me.

She's in the doorway, sunlight coming down the stairs through the old glass, and it's that different light on her face, lighting her eyes, and Eve's eyes are the dark green of the forests up the North American coast, Inverness green, Siuslaw National Forest green, and that Olympic National Park Kalaloch green, that dark misty pine needle green. Catch-your-breath green.

Such a beautiful green, and there's specks of gold, and as I see her troubled eyes for the first time, right outta nowhere this children's rhyme running inside me. *Cross my heart and hope to die.* I look into her gold-specked forest green eyes. *Stick a needle in my eye.* Somehow I know she saw a lot those months with her aunt. *Wait a moment; I spoke a lie.* Sickness, and dying, and death. *I never really wanted to die.* The ache knowing her aunt was fading, but maybe the soul leaving the body. *But if I may and if I might.* For something better. *My heart is open for tonight.* And right in the moment of that moment I promise myself whatever happens I'm gonna be authentic real with Eve. *Though my lips are sealed and a promise is true.* No lies, no bullshit, no betrayal—that's my promise and I better keep it 'cause if I fuck up I'll suffer Ondine's curse. *I won't break my word, my word to you.*

Eve's at least half a foot shorter than me, and her face in the light, I flash on Bettie Page, only she doesn't look same as Bettie Page, not at all. It's more she's got some of that Bettie Page trouble girl danger beneath her skin ready to surface. She looks, and listens, and waits, and what a drag how chicks gotta wait for the guy to make the first move. I guess it's changing with feminism, maybe, but I don't know. Not so much. Maybe it's gonna change, but that day, despite what I been through with Harper and Jaded and Simone, I don't think it has.

"I was—," she says, and a heartbeat pause, "studying," and during that pause, between "I was" and "studying," her voice changes. She starts out ready to blow me off, a hard edge same as something she's used before, but in the moment of that pause she changes her mind, lets herself feel *this* moment. Yeah, that pause is everything. She's floating above the threshold, a blue iris in a thin antique-blue curved-glass vase.

"Look, Michael," her voice softer, but still the edge, one wrong move and she'll retreat back into the apartment, gone baby gone. "What do you want?"

Un moment decisif.

The earthquake tremors gotta be a 6 on the Richter scale, the dread shivering through me, and in the moment of that moment I'm so past pretense, the phony surface of the surface long gone, and the surface of *my* surface is as authentic real as the water-stained wall, and the window.

If I can say one true sentence to Eve, *one true sentence.*

"You don't have a clue what a miracle it is I'm standing here talking to you," I say, and I'm looking direct into her eyes—her gold-specked forest green eyes. "I'm here, Eve, 'cause I don't wanna be afraid any more. My freakster bro Jim told me to come see you, so here I am. A human gotta be willing to risk it all. I mean if they wanna live. Really live. Well I'm willing."

Our eyes, man, and she's looking deep into mine, and whatever about her brought Bettie Page to mind softens. An echo of the first time I talked the authentic real to Sarah. A kind of wonderment—Eve's amazed a freakster bro would flat-out level with her so soon, and she sees the dread shiver of my hands.

"Hey," she says. "I didn't mean to put you on the spot," and she laughs an explosions-in-the-sky laugh, and I'm sure she's laughing at me, and I guess she sees I don't understand.

"It's refreshing to hear you talk this way," she says. "I'm

used to guys trying to impress me," and that's when the vibe changed again, and my dread fell away and I laughed too. I laughed the laugh of she-gets-it, the laugh of thank-you-Jesus, I mean if there ever was a Jesus, and oh man oh man, maybe things were starting to go right for me.

4. TO STEAL THE FUR-LINED TEACUP

"COME ON," I SAY. "You need some air, and a break from your *very* important studying."

"Well it *is* important," she says.

"I'm certain of it," I say.

"Well I don't know," she says. "It didn't feel good to get stood up, Michael."

I was gonna bribe Mr. Hit Parade, give him a Hamilton, get him to cool it for the day and see if I could make him understand, you know, the pain he's inflicting. Only right then Blue Suede wrapped up "Hooked on a Feeling," and there's silence. *Silence.* Can you believe it? Eve in the doorway, beautiful light coming through the old glass falling on her, falling on me. The awful music had stopped. It's same as we're both holding our breath, waiting for the next shit song to fuck it all up, only there's no next shit song.

"Well there you have it," I say. "Yeah."

"Yeah," she says, and her explosions-in-the-sky laugh. "*Yeah!*"

And she can't help it, for the first time since she opened her door she's smiling, and in her smile there was hope and joy and relief, yeah in the moment of that moment, and it didn't last long, her troubles lifted.

"Rum and coke," she says. "You buying?"

"Of course I'm buying."

"Give me a minute," she says, closes her door so it's barely open, and I hear her walk off down the hall.

When she came back it looked as if she took a brush to her hair, and she's got some kinda cloth purse, maybe from Mexico, hanging at her side, and her keys. She steps out onto the landing, and this is when I get it. I mean it was a pail of water in my face kinda wakeup. This chick Eve is going out with me, and *it means something to me.* All the nights I sat on the saggy bed, across from the damn window, nothing to look forward to, day after day, every day the same day, so long nothing mattered, so long I couldn't imagine wanting anything. Forcing myself to come here three times despite my inertia, and finally this is authentic real happening, and I got a stake in it.

Oh man oh man oh man.

She locks up, and she turns around, and when she turns I see all of her in that different light. She has on some faint hieroglyphic perfume, and a pale lavender dress with off-white and pale yellow and light blue flowers, and green flowers too. Oh man was she beautiful.

Eve's so at ease in that dress, but it's weird 'cause what chick hanging around her apartment studying wears such a beautiful dress? And hieroglyphic perfume? And thin stainless steel Calder earrings? And a thin silver chain around her neck? Maybe it's 'cause she's a creative, or maybe it makes her feel better to look so pretty, helps her fight off her fear, 'cause of her aunt dying, or the lonesome of living alone, or something I don't have a clue.

Her hair parted in the middle curves down falling past her shoulders, and it's so groovy, her hair. Authentic real black hair, not fake shiny dyed-black. And her Dora Maar nose. And is there a cool bar nearby? Yeah, she says, there's one on Market.

I see something different regards her mouth, 'cause when it's closed and she's not smiling there's a toughness, and I know this sounds weird but it makes me think she's the kinda chick could plant a bomb in an Army recruiting office—Bernardine Dohrn vibe. Eve has those same tough and sexy hard edges as Dohrn, or maybe that Gudrun Ensslin chick. Beautiful blue iris in a thin antique-blue curved-glass vase—and she'll blow you to pieces.

We make our way down, down, down toward the sidewalk, and it's near dusk, the sun getting ready to drop out of sight. Eve's ahead of me, floating, the thin flowered fabric of her dress catch the wind, billowing out, floating, floating toward the sidewalk, and when she steps onto the pavement she lets go of the hand rail and spins around. A moment of certainty.

"Michael, I," only she doesn't say it, or maybe can't, and right quick we're walking, side-by-side, back the way I came, toward Church Street.

"What is it, Eve?" I say. "What's going on? What were you going to tell me?"

I hear the metallic scream, and see a black-and-white, red light flashing, speed by toward Valencia Street. Heading to the scene of the crime.

It scared me, what happened next. Well Eve stops walking, so I stop too. It's same as she's gonna crawl inside herself, and I thought she was gonna cry. I mean her face does a number. Oh man, she closed her eyes and shook her head as if she were shaking the shadows off her, or something worse. Somehow she manages to reel herself back in, and she didn't cry. Her eyes were different, as if a gloom filter been placed between them and the world, and her voice heavy with some of the angst, or maybe futility. Could even been despair.

"You know you saved my life," she says.

I don't know why but I turn and look up at Eve's building and there's a couple black-billed magpies taking off from the roof. I could tell you it's Doom and Gloom, and how that's the last I seen of 'em, and that would wrap that part of the story up same as a birthday present got a big-ass bow, but I don't know if it's those birds. I don't know if any birds were Doom and Gloom. Fuck, man, probably never were any Doom and Gloom.

We walk slow towards Church Street, not in a rush, and she's close, right next to me close, and I wanna take her hand but I can't. So long since I touched a chick, I mean other than that Louise chick and that doesn't count. There's a cool breeze, and she looks over, and how she's looking, she's still thinking about what I told her. I know it. How sometimes you gotta risk it all. Right then it's as if her face been coated in chalk dust, and her voice a thin black line.

"I got up this morning and I knew this was it," she says.

Her eyes are wide, and her face tight. "I put on my best dress and my favorite jewelry and I lay on the couch, it's in the front room, and knew I couldn't go on."

She's looking right at my face, her gold-specked forest green eyes into my brown eyes, and it was her version of my *cross my heart and hope to die* look, you know, when I stood outside Eve's door and spoke my truth to her.

"I was gonna slit my wrists, Michael. There's a carving knife in the kitchen. I lay there thinking about that knife. How I could do it fast. I thought, if something doesn't happen by sundown, something different, something wonderful, something brand new, something to save me. I'm going to do it."

Oh fuck, and I stop, the creepy-crawlies under my skin. *Lying in my kidhood bed, the ghosts circling, needles pushing from inside to outside, puking my guts out.* There we are on the16th Street sidewalk, corner of 16th and Church up ahead, this is the heavy shit, man, and here comes this hipster in a porkpie hat and a bright orange Hawaiian shirt, stinky cigar in one hand, singing the blues, *How long do I have to wait, can I get you now, or must I hesitate,* and we gotta wait to talk 'til this clown walks past.

There's all kinda ways a chick can be intimate with a guy, and vice-versa, all kinda ways she can get too close before there's an understanding, before it's a conspiracy of two. Meet a chick at a bar by the end of the night you're fucking her. Yeah that could turn into one kinda intimacy. Collaborate on a school project same as me and Elise, that's another. What's odd is how quick me and Eve have our own kinda intimacy. Freaks me how fast. Too fast.

"That's a joke, right?" I say.

The closest I can get to what she does next is to tell you she got physically smaller and far away, almost as if she'd gotten in a fetal position, only that's not it. She hasn't moved. It scared her same as it scared me.

"Yeah, *sure,*" she says. "I got a peculiar sense of humor, Michael."

We're walking again, almost at the corner, and it's no joke. Eve's backed away from her truth, only far as I know she didn't make a promise, *cross my heart and hope to die*, didn't commit to being straight with me. So she can say anything. Lie all she wants. She doesn't have to worry about Ondine's curse.

"I was scheming as to whether I should get out my pearl handle revolver," she says. "And take care of the asshole kid downstairs first. Or start with the asshole who keeps ringing my doorbell."

"Next time answer the door," I say. "Might solve the problem without getting you on a most-wanted poster."

"Maybe I want to be on a most-wanted poster. Wanted, alive or dead."

The sun's shining the last of the light we'll see direct from it today, ready to bow out, and the Mission is so beautiful, an orange-red tint everywhere I look, and I want her to laugh her explosions-in-the-sky laugh, but she doesn't laugh, and it's as if the sun's been blotted out from the sky.

The fear's back, I know it.

"Eve," I say. "Are you fucking with me?"

It's as if me and her been lovers, and this is the morning after, I mean we're talking the authentic real, and same as it's freaking me, it's freaking her. Well we can't help it, what we're saying, and fuck it, I gotta know the truth.

"Your life's no joke, Eve."

She's afraid, her lips trembling, her green and gold eyes checking me out, weighing it 'cause she doesn't want to scare me off, but maybe this is too much for her, I mean there gotta be a reason she doesn't have a phone.

"When I said you saved my life, that was true," she says. "But that stuff about the knife—well I've thought about it, but I don't have the nerve. It's felt so hopeless, the day by day. My life."

Oh man, the gold is gone from her eyes.

"Eve, if any of us get out alive, it's a miracle," I say. "I'm not going anywhere. Life can be scary as shit. But right now, you're OK. Right?"

She doesn't know who I am.

"I been through hopeless," I say. "You don't even know."

"It's unbearable," she says.

Some guy who knows her sister's boyfriend.

"Already one good thing happened," I say. "The shit music stopped. We'll sit in a bar and have a drink. No hasty exits. OK?"

"Yeah," she says. "No hasty exits."

We turn onto Church Street, and that guy with the pit bull is coming toward us. If they gave out an award for ugliest dog, that pit bull would get it. I don't know if the dog scares her, but Eve holds onto my arm as we walk, and it's good her hand touching me. More than good, and yeah we don't know each other, but it's same as we're best friends, as if we been goin' out for a late afternoon walk for years.

I'm glad I'm between her and that dog.

"You know what Michael, let's not go to a bar," she says, and what's haunting her is gone. Her face tough and sexy—that Bernardine Dohrn vibe. Then again, maybe it's more Ulrike Meinhof.

"Let's get a bottle and go back to my apartment."

On the next block, when we reach the Chinese restaurant, you know, where the upstairs window's open, they're still playing Dylan. "She Belongs to Me." That's the song. Me and Eve below that window and the serendipity of what Dylan's singing. We've moved past her darkness, at least for now. We're in another world, me and her. A fantastic alternative world of symbols and codes.

She's got everything she needs she's an artist she don't look back.

"I wish I was that girl," Eve says, and there's gold in her eyes again.

"If I were her, everything would be perfect. Will you buy me an Egyptian red ring, Michael? Will you?"

Yeah, Eve knows the secret alphabets. Gotta be serious into Dylan, well serious enough. He only sang about an Egyptian red ring on the bootleg live versions. The versions you gotta be hardcore to know about.

She's not wearing any lipstick, her lips pale lovely, and the faint smell of hieroglyphic perfume.

"Will you steal me everything I see?" she says. "That's how I'll know."

"I don't think the guy in that song fared too well," I say. "Will you crawl out your window and run away with me?"

"Maybe," she says. "If you peel back the moon and expose it."

It's important, Eve says, she gotta tell me her dream. Right there, right now. Dylan up above us, and he's still young when he recorded that song. Me and Eve, still young too though we don't know it. There's wisdom and bitterness in Dylan's voice, and sometimes in Eve's too. And more. Eve's voice is explosions-in-the-sky and gunning the getaway car and wanted, alive or dead.

She says that in her dream she was an artist and a thief.

"I stole everything," she says. "I didn't look back. Stole lines from books, and ideas, the really big ideas, and taste, I stole taste from the very best. Oppenheim and Varda and Woolf."

"In your dream?" I say.

"Well, yeah," Eve says. "Of course. In my dream," and how she's looking at me, she's not letting the world get away with nothing.

"This dress I'm wearing tonight, I stole it from a debutante," Eve says. "Stole my hair style from a nightclub singer. Stole my fortune from a gypsy woman who read my palm when I was a child."

"This was all in your dream?"

"In my dreams," she says. "But yeah. In my dream."

Dylan starts into the next one, about his love who speaks softly and knows there's no success same as failure, and failure's no success at all.

"Snuck into people's heads and stole their thoughts," Eve says. "Robbed 'em blind. Left old and discarded thoughts in place of what I took. I didn't look back. You can't worry about morality, not when you're an artist. Especially when you're an artist."

"In your dream," I say.

"In my dreams," Eve says.

And that was when I realized I was sorta myself again. I'm not gonna say all the fear lifted. I'd been beat up and it would take more time to heal, but being with Eve I understood the who-I-am of who I am. I was unique—not special—but unique, and I was more than a cog, more than a loser living in a room with a water-stained wall and a window.

It didn't make sense what I was thinking right then. Eve was cool, and she'd been through some hellfuck shit too. I didn't know what to think. I was just glad we were gonna have a drink together.

At Frank's Liquor that stubby guy is checking the curved mirrors below the ceiling that let him see in the aisles where he can't see from behind the counter. Watching every customer he hasn't known for years. Watching. Still, at least he doesn't have a smirk going. This time when he sees me it's different. I'm a customer now.

"Hey kid," he says. "Take your time."

I get a large bottle of Coke from the refrigerator and bring it up to the counter and Eve puts a bag of Fritos down. It's an old wood counter, stained the way wood looks that's had dirt and grease and tobacco ground into it for too many years.

"Pint of Bacardi Gold," I say.

"Got a driver's license, kid?"

Pull out my wallet and lay my own driver's license on that stain-ass counter. I'm two weeks into being 21 and no fucker can stop me from buying whatever booze I wanna buy. Which is ironic 'cause the only booze I been buying since I'm of age is beers for me and Frankie and Sam. The old guy picks up my license. He looks at the date, looks at the photo, looks at me, and hands it back.

"I remember when I turned 21," he says.

I didn't think he was gonna talk so much, but what the hell can you do once a guy same as him starts jawing your ear off?

"1940. The war full steam but I had a medical deferment," he says. "My best buddy and I drove to this liquor store near the park on Judah in his dad's Oldsmobile. We waited until it was 12:01 a.m. We didn't have a cake or candles so he lit a cigarette and handed it to me. 'Happy birthday Phil,' he says. 'Let's get drunk.'"

Well then he tells us about getting a six-pack of Lucky Lager X Stubby beer that him and his buddy Gunther drank, and they split a bottle of Thunderbird too and he got so fucking sick he puked all over himself and ruined a pair of new shoes his mom got him for his birthday. Eve steps closer to me, and it's hard to keep listening, only it's not me alone listening to the guy—it's the two of us listening.

"Next day I bought three more of those Stubbys and drank them," he says. "I did that every day for a week. When that week was over, I went and bought the Stubbys and another bottle of Thunderbird. That night I drank the beers and the wine. You know what? I didn't throw up."

He looks across the counter at me, and Eve takes my hand, and the warmth of her hand is the warmth of the sun, and it warms all of me—yeah, me and Eve, a conspiracy of two. And in that moment, and for that moment, I got it. I understood it was good with me and her. I mean right then. The future, that I didn't know about and I wasn't thinking about it. No future tripping. Wasn't thinking about Visions of Johanna chicks or any of that. Moment by moment was how I was living. And right in *that* moment, me and Eve, it was OK.

"So here I am," he says. "Thirty-seven years later, an alcoholic working in a liquor store."

He rang me up and bags the Coke and the chips and the rum.

"Happy birthday kid, try not to puke on your shoes."

Me and Eve are walking back to her place, the sidewalk lit by streetlamps, but no, there's something I gotta do. She has her serious face again, and you know how chicks are, always going over everything again and again. Yeah she's probably wishing she hadn't laid her Bell Jar trip on me.

"You heard *The Wild, the Innocent and the E Street Shuffle?*" I say.

Something strikes her funny 'cause her serious deal dissolves, and her lips open into the big smile, you know, the smile I told you about before, after the music stopped.

"I *am* the wild, the not-so-innocent and the Church Street shuffle," and she claps her hands together, and it's as if Eve's the first chick I ever been with, and she's *so* beautiful in her flowered lavender dress, and her long black Laura Nyro hair catch the wind.

"Well, come on," I say. "I'll buy you a present. It's better than an Egyptian red ring."

And is that true? When a guy gives a chick a ring, it's a symbol of his love. But what about me giving Eve that Springsteen record? The poetry of the songs, the fire in the music, and the romance of the stories he sings. Our songs, our music, our romance—and each time she hears it, she thinks of me.

We walk to Rainbow Records on Market, and I'm excited 'cause I'll be with Eve the first time she hears Springsteen sing those songs. Wanna see her feel the rush. Inside they're playing a new Elton John album. Wow, "Someone Saved My Life Tonight." Crazy, man. Eve waits up at the front while I get the Springsteen record, and she's impatient, maybe the Elton John song bugs her. Or maybe it's 'cause she doesn't know Springsteen—he's still an East Coast phenomenon. It'll be another couple months 'til *Born to Run* gets released and all hell breaks loose.

When we get outside the sky is dark and the light from the neon puts an electric dust on Eve, and it makes her hair and dress shimmer, and it's another of those moments where she's so close. "They have these conferences," she says. "Where people who've been struck by lightning get together."

"You're kidding?" I say.

She looks at me same as *come on, man,* and her hand on my arm again.

"What's stranger than fiction," she says. "Turns out there's a lot of people who've been struck by lightning *twice,"* and she dances out in front of me, twirls around, twirls this grand twirl, and when she stops her gold-specked green eyes are larger, as if she's seeing things she hasn't seen before. "That's how I feel tonight. Like I've been struck by lightning twice."

Oh man, and has there ever been so beautiful a sight? Eve in her lavender flowered dress, arms out, hair wild in the wind that's replaced the afternoon breeze, spinning on that Church Street sidewalk.

"Hey," she says, and oh man oh man, 'cause the sound of her voice, her saying "hey," but it's more than her voice, it's everything about her.

And right then I *knew.*

We were gonna steal the fucking heavens blind, gonna walk on water, gonna drink a magic elixir from a fur-lined teacup. Maybe it wouldn't be the beautiful dying. Maybe we'd never take it that far. Or maybe we would.

THE FREAK SCENE DREAM TRILOGY

That was how it ended. Well, how that part of Michael Stein's life ended. There was more, much more, and maybe he'll tell you about it sometime. Later. Way later.

But until then, if you haven't read the first two books of the Freak Scene Dream Trilogy, which are titled "True Love Scars" and "The Flowers Lied," what are you waiting for?

You'll find out how Michael Stein first met Harper, back when she was still sorta innocent, and what went down during the Sarah years. And Elise, troubled Elise, and what Stein's months with her were all about. And more, so much more.

Michael Stein is obsessed with sex. Only the sex is more than sex. Sex is the door to intimacy, and transcendence.

For Michael Stein, the Sixties ended in the nut house. Where they put the crazies. His parents blamed his erratic behavior on drugs. Michael Stein just blames himself.

Aware. Michael Stein is aware he has lived through one of the biggest social changes America has experienced. The trouble is, Michael Stein's not aware that the biggest social change has already changed, moved on down the line.

The Freak Scene Dream Trilogy is one long deep breath. The exhale is obsessive, transgressive. How macho meets feminism. How second chakra rises up to third. Through all the women: Sarah, Elise, Jaded, Simone, Harper, Eve. A puff, a party, a tragedy—from marijuana to angel dust, teenage heartbreak to addiction, from "All You Need Is Love" to the junkie garage rock of the New York Dolls.
How the dream died and what there is left after.

If you enjoyed, "Untitled," why not check out how it all

began, as Writerman struggles to escape his past and invent a brave new life.

"True Love Scars"
by Michael Goldberg

For more information about the Freak Scene Dream Trilogy, and "True Love Scars":

www.truelovescars.com

If you want to keep up with what Michael Goldberg is up to as a writer and blogger, please sign up for the Days of the Crazy-Wild Communique at:

www.daysofthecrazy-wild.com/novel/email

ACKNOWLEDGEMENTS

If you checked out the Acknowledgements pages of my first two novels, "True Love Scars" and "The Flowers Lied," most of this will be familiar. Some is new.

Just sayin'.

I want to thank my wonderful family: Leslie, Joe, Anne, Norah and Sam. You're the best!

And my good friends Pearl the dog and Barky the cat and Donut the dog.

This book could not have been written without the help of the 2008-2009 version of Dangerous Writers in Portland, OR. And a hats off to Tom Spanbauer, the most dangerous of the Dangerous Writers. Thanks for listening, Tom, and for six years of support.

Thanks to the Writer's Cafe, September 2010 – November 2013, for your comments, support and advice. I learned at least as much from you, as you may have learned from me.

My best buddy, singer/songwriter David Monterey, is one of a kind for sure. They don't make friends like you anymore, Dave.

Thanks to Jolie Holland, Emme Stone, Brittany Flynn, James Cushing and Mark Mordue — in addition to Tom Spanbauer, the five of you were the very first to read the Freak Scene Dream Trilogy, and your enthusiasm was and is appreciated.

Thanks to the following, in no particular order, for media coverage, reviews and/or other support: Jann Wenner, Nathan Brackett, Simon Vozick-Levinson and Colin Fleming at Rolling Stone, Larry Beckett, Holly George-Warren, Maria Bustillos, Dennis McNally, Fred Mills at Blurt, Simon Warner, Roy Trakin at Trakin Care of Business, Paul Krassner, David Browne, Greg M. Schwartz at Pop Matters, Tyler Wilcox at Doom & Gloom From The Tomb, the folks at Book Passage, Denise Sullivan,

Jack Boulware and the folks at LitQuake, JC and everyone at Down Home Music, Burtis Downs and R.E.M., Barney Hoskins at Rock's Back Pages, Brian Wise and Des Cowley at Addicted To Noise, Mike Foldes at Ragazine, Wallace Blaine at the Santa Cruz Sentinel, David Wright at Sterling & Stone, Sarah Burke at the East Bay Express, Paul Liberatore at the Marin Independent Journal, Holly Hooch at Cheap Hooch Radio, Andy Phillips at Wax Atlas, Norm Honbo, Jeanne Lavin, everyone at the Marin Vegan Meetup and everyone at the Matin Vegan Book Group, Bill Lamb, Chris Scofield, Brendan Halpin, Adam Strong at Kronski Confidential, Michelle Swide, Alan Zoldan, Silas Valentino, Nicole Cohen, Jen Lemons, Frank C. Tortorici, Aria Mencken, Linda Watson, Melanie Hoist, Mark Cunningham, Darcee Kraus, Bradley Hanebrink, Jason Gross at Perfect Sound Forever, Karl Erik Anderson at Expecting Rain and Gigi Little at ut omnia bene. And I want to acknowledge the late Barbara Shelley, who said she dug "True Love Scars," and told me repeatedly she couldn't wait to read this book. I reget not having it completed sooner.

Thanks to Rebecca Grove, Mike Linn and everyone at the very excellent Octopus Literary Salon in Oakland, CA.

Thanks to my wife Leslie Goldberg for the amazing cover drawing, Emme Stone for the cover design and Mary Eisenhart for copyediting.

Thanks to Jeff Rosen for being so gracious regarding the use of song lyrics.

Thanks to Direct Action Everywhere (DxE) for all that you are doing for the animals, and for changing my life. Until every animal is free!

And to Bob Dylan, the Rolling Stones, Captain Beefheart, Neil Young, Frank Zappa, Jack Kerouac, Bruce Conner, Sam Rivers, Skippy James, J.D. Salinger, Greil Marcus, Richard Meltzer, Lester Bangs, Albert Ayler, Daniel Kramer, F. Scott Fitzgerald, Jean-Luc Godard, D.A. Pennebaker, François Truffaut, Robert Frank, Diane Arbus, Andy Warhol, Picasso,

Salvador Dali, and all the other musicians, visual artists, film directors and writers who have been so much more than an inspiration.
— Michael Goldberg, March 2017

ABOUT THE AUTHOR

So what do you wanna know?

When I was a kid, rock 'n' roll and literature made life worth living.

Or rather, it was literature that rocked my world—"Treasure Island," "Crime and Punishment," the Hardy Boys books, the Oz books, all those sexy 007 novels—until I turned 12, and then rock 'n' roll—The Beatles, the Stones, Dylan, The Yardbirds, John Mayall's Blues Breakers—blew my mind, with literature a strong second.

Well girls trumped both, but that's another story.

I started writing my own stories in sixth grade and by high school I was certain that writing was my vocation.

So while my friends and I promoted dance-concerts at the high school (mostly so we could project psychedelic lights behind the bands), I was also writing for the school paper. And I did have one of those "Almost Famous" moments, writing *Creem* editor Lester Bangs and getting an encouraging letter back asking me to send him some record reviews (which he didn't end up using).

Fast-forward to 1975, the eve of the punk rock revolution, and I was in the thick of it, interviewing Patti Smith and The Ramones and the Talking Heads and Crime and so many more for stories that ran in the *Berkeley Barb* and the *San Francisco Bay Guardian*. I also interviewed many non-punk artists including Townes Van Zandt, Ramblin' Jack Elliott, Jesse Winchester, Muddy Waters, Professor Longhair, Captain Beefheart and the Flamin' Groovies.

I had some close calls. The Clash nearly threw me out of the San Francisco recording studio where they were recording their second album, the Sex Pistols tried to break my tape recorder and Frank Zappa said if I was one of his fans he was in big trouble.

The life of a rock journalist.

Things did work out, and I spent 10 crazy years talking to everyone from George Harrison and George Clinton to Brian Wilson and Stevie Wonder for *Rolling Stone* where I was an Associate Editor and a Senior Writer. My writing has also appeared in *Wired, Esquire, Vibe, Details, Downbeat, NME* and many more.

In 1993 I got hip to the Internet and by 1994 I'd founded *Addicted To Noise (ATN)*, the highly influential music website. *ATN* was the very first Web music magazine. People said I was a distinguished pioneer in the online music space; *Newsweek* magazine called me an "Internet visionary." Those were heady days, and inventing what an online music magazine could be was one of the high points, thus far, of what has been an exciting and meaningful life.

I joined forces with SonicNet in 1997. I was a senior vice-president and editor in chief at *SonicNet* from March 1997 through May 2000.

While running SonicNet editorial I interviewed Neil Young, William Gibson, Patti Smith, Lou Reed, R.E.M., Ani DiFranco, Prince, Courtney Love, Tom Waits, Metallica, the Smashing Pumpkins, Sonic Youth, Pavement, Sleater-Kinney and, and, and…

In 1997, *Addicted To Noise* won a Webby award for best music site, and a Yahoo Internet Life! award. While I was at *SonicNet* the site won Webby awards for best music site in 1998 and 1999, and also won Yahoo Internet Life! awards for three years running as best music site in 1998, 1999 and 2000.

I started writing the books that became the Freak Scene Dream Trilogy in the mid-2000s. The first book, "True Love Scars," was published in 2014, and the second, "The Flowers Lied," in 2016.

You can expect a collection of my music writing in 2018 or 2019. I currently write an occasional column, The Drama You've Been Craving, for the Australian version of *Addicted To*

Noise.

And I occasionally post at and maintain the video-and-audio-intense culture blog, *Days of the Crazy-Wild* at www.daysofthecrazy-wild.com.

Any other questions?

PERMISSIONS

Lyrics for the following songs are by Bob Dylan:

www.ingramcontent.com/pod-product-compliance
Lightning Source LLC
Chambersburg PA
CBHW020839020726
47497CB00005B/1169

9780990398363